For My dear dear friends Karen & James

LUCIFER'S CHILDREN

A NOVEL

TOM LEWIS

[signature] May 31 '09

Tease Publishing LLC
Swansboro, North Carolina

Lucifer's Children

This is a work of fiction. Names, characters, places, and incidents are products of the author's imagination or are used fictitiously and are not to be construed as real. Any resemblance to actual events, locales, organizations, or persons, living or dead, is entirely coincidental.

Lucifer's Children

A Tease Publishing Book

Copyright© 2008 Tom Lewis

ISBN: 978-1-60767-0-036-0
Cover Artist: Ash Arsenaux
Interior text design: Tonya Nagle
Editor: Lori Hufty

All rights reserved. No part of this book may be used or reproduced electronically or in print without written permission, except in the case of brief quotations embodied in reviews.

Tease Publishing LLC
www.teasepublishingllc.com
PO BOX 234
Swansboro, North Carolina 28584-0234

Tease and the T logo is © Tease Publishing LLC. All rights reserved.

Tom Lewis

Acknowledgements

I am very grateful for encouragement and assistance from so many people, as usual. But a few are deserving of special thanks. Tonya Nagle, for her patience--and everything else she did in this book, even when under the weather and swamped with other important tasks. Thanks as well to Lori, Ash, and all the staff at TEASE. You are all terrific, and much appreciated. I know I will owe you even more in the near future!
  Also, for all my family, friends, and colleagues who are always there for me. (You know who you are) I love you all!

Tom Lewis

February, 2009

Lucifer's Children

OTHER BOOKS BY TOM LEWIS

MY KING THE PRESIDENT

THE PEA ISLAND GOLD TRILOGY:

    SUNDAY'S CHILD

    HITLER'S JUDAS

    SONS OF THEIR FATHERS

Tom Lewis

For

KAA BYINGTON

Gratefully

Lucifer's Children

PROLOGUE

Christmas Day was unusually cold in 1950, even for Pella, Iowa. No one felt like going outside to brave the bitter blasts of the continuous northwesterly which had whistled unimpeded across the snow-covered cornfields for a week, dropping the already sub-zero temperatures to a wind-chill factor of twenty-eight below.

But Dr. Henry Villem had to. He thanked his Lutheran God the Chevy Suburban had an electric heater plug and a Die Hard battery, and that his small clinic was less than a mile from the warm womb of his well-insulated house. He and Wilhemina ate a quick brunch and were on their way by noon. By two-fifteen, having decided the baby would have to be born by C-section, he looked across the undraped, bloated mound of Lena DeVries' distended belly at his wife. Willi had been his faithful— and only— nurse for going on twenty-two years. He could tell the wrinkle appearing in her mask was caused by a smile. This was a task they had done together countless times, but he couldn't remember ever delivering one on Christmas Day.

He thought he knew what Willi was thinking. Of all the people in the county they wouldn't have minded caring for on a holiday, it had to be Lena DeVries, the spoiled and pampered wife of their young Pastor, Joseph. Petite, and quite attractive, Lena's sharp, opinionated tongue and galling vanity had made her just as unpopular in their ultra-conservative Dutch community as her hard-working husband was admired. It was ironic, perhaps even just, that this would be a difficult birth. Lena DeVries was a difficult woman. Had been all her life, from the moment Villem had brought her, squalling, into the world— on this very same table. Villem knew Lena didn't like him, and trusted him even less. Small-town doctor and all that. Barely one notch above a veterinarian. If she'd had her way, this baby would have been born at Des Moines, or maybe even Minneapolis, where they had 'good' doctors. Oh, well. He sighed behind his own mask, picked up his scalpel, and bent over.

By four o'clock it was all over, and Dr. Henry Villem had performed a masterful piece of surgery, committed a terrible sin, and for the only time in his life, broken his own strict code of ethics— all in part of the same Christmas afternoon. The baby was a healthy six-and-a half pound girl, and Willi was already cleaning it up, when he had noticed something else.

The baby's twin, or rather, what was left of him.

From Lena's abdominal cavity, he extracted the pathetic, cord-wrapped, strangulated fetus that had never had a chance to grow, not since maybe the second or third month. A hideous, six-months-dead miniature monster that had almost been a boy. "My God, Willi, look at this!"

In the time it took for his wife to turn around, Henry Villem made a quick, irrevocable decision: With the tacit agreement of his wife-nurse, he would never tell either parent about the dead twin, and bending over again to make sure of it, he would have to inform Lena DeVries she could never have any more children.

This sad fact would not be sad news to Lena herself, since she'd never really liked children anyway. She'd had a very difficult pregnancy from beginning to end, and wanted no more of such wearisome work that had already destroyed her figure and would leave a ghastly scar she'd never be able to look at. Plus, there was her husband's certain reaction to consider. Like most first-time Dutch fathers, Joseph had wanted a boy. Too bad. He'd have to take what he got.

Thus, Lena was not particularly pleased when that clumsy fool Villem deposited a "Beautiful baby girl" in her arms. Still, the child was pretty enough, Lena thought, and would be named Margaret, after her grandmother, who'd been a real beauty. She hoped people wouldn't call the child Maggie when she grew up. The infant had her own black hair. A lot of it, too. Maybe she'd be pretty enough someday to be a cheerleader. Maybe Homecoming Queen. Marry a rich man and get out of this miserably drab town. This miserably drab existence. Do something exciting in her life.

Little did Lena DeVries know...

At the exact same moment Margaret DeVries took her first breath of germ-free, climate-controlled air, another Christmas baby was born— thousands of miles south, in a sweltering, fly-infested plywood shack on the squalid western edge of Guatemala City. There was no doctor present, nor was there a real need for one. Having given birth to eleven girls in thirteen years, Rosita Barillas simply grunted two or three times and popped out a boy-child with no more effort than dropping a peeled potato into a pot. Her oldest daughter washed and wrapped the baby, as she had done with three of her sisters, and handed it back to Rosita, who clucked and silenced its crying instantly with a brown nipple that was nearly too large for his tiny mouth.

"He is beautiful, Mama," the oldest daughter said. "Papa is going to be so happy."

"Yes. This time he will be. God has finally answered our prayers. But wait, *Cara*. I feel— is there another one?" Without disturbing the new one at her breast, Rosita grunted again. What the daughter held up for her to see was horrible. Rosita blinked, crossed herself over the boy-baby's head, and whispered, "Wrap her in an old towel and drop her in the toilet out there. Listen to me, now. You must never say anything of this to your father or your sisters. Anyone. Do you understand? Never! Swear it."

Rosita Barillas' oldest daughter swore. And did as she was told.

Rosita's husband would not see his new son until long after dark. Knowing there was to be yet another mouth to feed, he was driving his taxi extra hours, hoping for generous tips from the American businessmen to be ferried between the grand hotels and the airport or from the high-priced whores who trusted him to take them to their rich clients, then safely back to their ugly pimps. Besides, he had taken part of the day off to go to Christmas Mass. He had never missed weekly Mass. Not once in his entire life. Carlos Barillas was a devout man.

He was also a very good taxi driver. One of the most respected in all of *Cuidad de Guatemala*. He had been a good bus driver before that, too. Good because he was careful, and because he was also a fine mechanic. Carlos Barillas could fix things. Keep his vehicle rolling when others could not. He was proud of that. He was also proud that he was a Ladino. A poor one, to be sure, but little, if any, Indian blood ran through the veins of his wiry body.

During the early morning hours of the following day, he would gaze at his son, kiss his wife tenderly, wipe tears of joy from his own eyes, and tell her that this time, she had brought him supreme happiness. "*Perfecto*," he would say. "Look at him. He is perfect. In every way."

And Rosita would smile. "Will you teach him to be a good mechanic? A good driver like his Papa?"

"Him? Oh, no. He will be no ignorant taxi driver like me. This one will grow up to be an important man. Do important things. He will have a real mission in life."

Little did Carlos Barillas know...

৽

Lucifer's Children

Chapter 1

Maggie Ellis hated the telephone. Though hers was an unlisted number, she had little respite from its obnoxious ringing when she was at home. Nine out of ten calls were usually bad news, par for the course for a conscientious news anchor, and Maggie had never believed in screening callers with her answering machine. But today – New Year's Eve and the last day of what had been a very newsy 1985 at WRDU – was blessedly different. Not one single call had invaded her precious day off, and it was nearly noon. Wonderful! Still, Maggie didn't trust the plastic monster, and had brought it into the bathroom while she enjoyed her first long tub bath in more than two weeks.

With effort, she pushed her thoughts away from the phone, the television station, the world and everyone in it for a while, enjoying the rare liquid luxury as the hot, scented water began loosening the up-tight muscles of her thirty-five year-old body; a body that was still holding up pretty damn well, she thought, all things considered. Her very next thought, and one which caused her to smile and sink lower into the suds, was that Sam thought so, too. She sighed. She'd marry Sam Abrahms in a heartbeat if her son Bo wasn't so—

As if it had a malevolent mind of its own, the jangling plastic monster bit into her thoughts like a chain saw. Maggie reached a soapy arm and hand for it, sitting up. *Knew it was too good to last.* "Hello?"

"Margaret, the turkey's done. What time do you want me to bring it over?"

Since the death of her father, Maggie's mother had bullied her into maintaining two of his sacrosanct family traditions: her own Christmas Day birthday dinner, and New Year's Eve supper, which Maggie and Bo both dreaded, especially since Maggie's divorce. Telling her mother she could come over any time she wanted to, Maggie wondered which of Lena DeVries' pet phrases ("I-told-you-so" or "What-did-I-tell-you" or "You-should-have-listened-to-me") she'd serve up with the turkey. "No, wait," Maggie said on second thought. "Give me an hour or so. I'm trying to take a bath."

"For a whole hour? Why don't you just take a shower?"

"Please, Mama, just one hour, okay?"

"Well, all right. Is Bo going to wear a tie? Your father always wore a tie."

Maggie sighed again. *He probably wore one to bed!* "Don't worry, I'll see to it."

Maggie hung up and leaned back, trying to recapture her dreamy mood. The water had cooled some. She reached for the hot water faucet, but before she could turn it on, the phone rang again. Damn! "Hello?"

"Hi, Mag, it's me. How's it going?"

The sound of her ex-husband's voice never failed to irritate Maggie. If Robert Ellis was sober, he invariably called to spoil Bo with yet another expensive present or outing. If he was drunk, or hung-over, he usually whined about his latest excuse for being late with the alimony check. Robert Ellis was just as easy a man to hate as he had once been to love.

Maggie frowned. "What is it this time?"

"Can I talk to Bo? I've got some terrific news."

"What news?"

"Ted French has invited Bo and me to fly to New Orleans for the Super Bowl game. Four days and nights, all expenses paid. Can you believe it? Bo will be knocked out! You, ah, will let him go, won't you? Might be the only thing that'll drag him away from his computer."

    Maggie didn't answer right away. She could believe it alright. She'd heard things about Robert's wealthy station manager before. Yet that wasn't what bothered her. What stuck in her craw was that she wouldn't be able to say no. Bo's hero-worship of his father amounted to nothing less than pure adoration. In Bo's eyes, Robert Ellis could do no wrong. She knew, from broad hints nearly every week, that Bo couldn't see any real reason why his Mom and Dad couldn't get back together. It was no wonder Bo had such a negative reaction to Sam Abrahms. There was simply no way Sam could compete, at least not until Bo was more mature— or until Robert ran out of money. Maggie wondered which would come first. "I'll think about it. You'll have to call back later. I'm trying to take a bath."

    "Hey, no problem. I'll call back in ten."

    "You'll call back in an hour."

    "You got it. Good to talk to you again, Mag."

    "You, too, Robert. Made my day."

    Maggie hung up before Robert could respond to her sarcasm. She reached for the tub's plug, yanked it, and turned the hot water on full blast. The cooled water was quickly replaced by fresh heat. She pushed the plug back in, but a full five minutes passed before she felt any of the new tension leave her body. Another five passed before the phone rang again. "Hello?"

    "Hi, gorgeous."

    "Sam! Are you still at the office?"

    "Yep. Three more hours to go. Had a break and thought I'd give you a quick call to tell you I love you."

    "M-mm. You don't know how much I needed to hear that, boss man."

    "We still on for tonight?"

    "Nothing could keep me away. I'm soaking in the tub right now, just thinking about it."

"Want me to come over there and join you?"

"We wish. I should be able to get away by eight or so. Bo's trying to teach Mama how to play games on the Apple. So far, she's learned how to boot the thing up and that's about all."

"Great. Maggie?"

"What?"

"Wear the little black thing tonight, okay?"

"Naughty, naughty. We'll see."

"Gotta run. See you later."

"Okay. Sam?"

"Yeah?"

"I love you, too."

"No you don't. If you did, you'd elope with me tonight."

"Sam Abrahms!"

"Okay, okay. Just kidding. See you at eight."

"Or so. Bye, lover."

Maggie hung up, grinned and settled back down in the tub. The tiny vanity clock on the wall read 12:03. After noon, and one nice call out of three, she thought. Pretty good average so far, even for a holiday.

New Year's Eve was the singular day of the calendar year when Monsignor Ramon Barillas' schedule was light. Light enough to allow him time to go to his annual confession. Earlier in his life, he had gone much more often; not that he needed to any more than now, since the sin he needed to confess was considered venial. This was a good thing, because he was now kept so busy with work he scarcely had time to eat or sleep.

He sniffed as he sat down in the dark box. The stale air in the confessional smelled of sweat, old and new, but that was not surprising. The small church he visited for this purpose was one of the oldest in Rome, and one of the poorest. Ramon had often wondered if it was kept so on purpose. It was also quite cold. Why, he asked himself, with all the money Catholicism had, did they allow churches so little heat in winter and so little air in summer, especially in Rome where both seasons were severe?

The thick air budged slightly when the priest on the other side pulled the sliding port part way back. Ramon, knowing the poor man would be hearing confessions well into the night, and not wishing to add more than necessary to his burden, promptly said, in flawless Italian, "Father, I have sinned. It has been a year since my last confession."

"What sins have you committed, my son?"

"I have sinned against myself."

"The sin of masturbation."

"Yes."

Ramon heard the sound of a chuckle penetrate the frigid air. When the familiar voice came back, it was the same as before. It was always the same. "How many times?"

"Twelve."

"The same number as last year. How many years have you been in Rome, Monsignor?"

Ramon was quite aware the old priest knew who he was. Knew that he was also a priest. And, he was reasonably certain the old man knew his name and knew to the day how long he had lived in Rome. "Several years, Father."

There was another pause, which lasted longer than Ramon expected. He turned up his collar and waited. He thought he could hear soft words being exchanged in the adjacent box. There were only two, separated, like Siamese twins, by a thin common wall.

"And every year, always on New Year's Eve, you come here and confess the same sins. Always the same number, too. Twelve times a year. Once a month. Would it surprise you to know I have had young men come here and tell me they have done the same thing that many times a day?"

"But I am a priest, Father. I believe my sin to be offensive to God. It certainly is to me."

"I know who you are, Monsignor. There isn't a priest in all of Rome and the Vatican who doesn't know of your work, right up to the Holy Father himself. However, that's beside the point isn't it? So, this time, in addition to the same prayers I have instructed you to say before, your penance is to perform one wedding, one funeral, and one baptism extra this year."

"Yes, Father, I will."

"One other thing. I want you to seek some outside help. Medical help."

"You mean a psychiatrist?"

"Yes. There has to be a cause for your— your discomfort."

"I know what the cause is."

"Really? What can it be? Perhaps I can help."

"I have dreams. Or rather, just one dream. The same one that comes once a month, regular as sunrise."

"Can you tell me about it?"

Ramon hesitated. He had never told another living soul of his torment. Of the nights he'd awakened beneath soiled sheets, still haunted by the image he could not banish from his consciousness, no matter how hard he tried. And he had tried. For years.

The old priest on the other side of the screen was a good guesser. "You dream of women?"

Ramon jerked his head up. "Only one woman."

"Ah. The same one? Over and over? Who is she?"

"I don't know, Father. It seems as though I know her, but I have never seen her face."

"Strange indeed. Tell me what you feel comfortable enough to reveal. I truly do want to help you if I can."

Ramon believed him. "The first time I remember dreaming of her was when I was just a boy. Before my confirmation. It was as if she was another of my sisters, only about my own age. As if she were growing up with me. Sharing my childhood. The— the actual problem I have with her didn't start until I was at Seminary. I was older then, and so was she. She began appearing in skimpy clothing. Bathing suits. That kind of thing, but her face was always hidden from me. In shadow."

"She was like a tease?"

"Not exactly. No, that came later, after I was ordained. She began showing me glimpses of her body in a provocative way. As if she knew I had sworn myself to celibacy, and she was therefore safe from my clutches. That was when the real teasing started."

"And, I presume, she was neither fat nor ugly."

Ramon laughed in spite of himself. No, the lady of his tortured nights was beautiful. At least her body was. Since he had never seen her face, he had no idea whether she was pretty or homely. Once every month she would invade his sleep. His mind. His innocence. Showing him long legs and round breasts. Baiting him. Tempting. Teasing him with the most carnal of fantasies, replete with variations, and always with lilting, infuriating laughter. "No, Father. She is neither fat nor ugly. In the beginning, I feared I was possessed. Then, for a while, the dreams stopped coming. I don't know why. But they came back, fourteen years ago. She seemed older. More— I don't know, like she had grown up into a mature woman. But she still brought the same torture. Worse, even. She now shows me what she does to herself."

"Remarkable. And you have no idea who this fantasy lady might be?"

"Not without seeing her face. I don't know if she is someone I have met, or a total stranger. As I said, she is a little like my sisters. Her skin coloring and her hair, anyway, but beyond that, I have no idea at all. I have prayed, Father. I have prayed hard to be rid of those dreams. I am usually a very disciplined man and priest, but when those dreams come, I seem not to be able to control either my emotions or my— my actions."

"Are you awake when you do these things to yourself?"

"I don't know. I can't tell if I am or not. I simply cannot help myself."

Tom Lewis

Again there was a period of silence, and then once more Ramon heard subdued laughing coming from the other side of the screen.

"Well," the old priest said, "No real harm has been done. You are not the first priest to be tempted by dreams of women, nor will you be the last. At any rate, you haven't gone blind, and apparently, none of this has affected your work for our Lord and His church. My guess is these dreams will go away someday, just as they did before. Go on your way, my son, and do as I have instructed you. Perhaps you will have even less to confess next year, and in the meantime, do try to see one of those head-doctors."

But Ramon Barillas' dream did not disappear. A little more than two weeks later, on the night of January sixteenth, the woman appeared to him again.

And he reacted in exactly the same way.

And felt just as guilty and ashamed as ever, only with this dream, he realized there had been one big difference. There had been something new. She had been standing outside a church. She had been standing in the shadowed, empty parking lot of a small stone-built church that was set among stately pine trees. And this time, when he awakened, he suffered from a headache painful enough to make him scream out at the top of his voice. A headache that took three whole days to subside.

෴

Chapter 2

On January 17th, Maggie kissed Bo, and pushed him through the gate toward the waiting plane. "Behave yourself, and don't eat too much junk food."

Bo wasn't yet aboard when Lena said, "They're going in that little thing? I've got a bad feeling about this, Margaret. I think it's another big mistake."

Maggie didn't answer her mother. Instead, she raised a gloved hand and waved at her son, who was now grinning at her from the right hand front seat of the single engine plane.

But Lena didn't let up. "Bo's my only grandchild. What if something happens? They have to cross over mountains to get to there, don't they? What if there's a storm, or they can't—"

Like a scrap of paper caught in a gust of wind, the rest of Lena's sentence was lost in the slipstream of the prop when the plane's engine revved, then slowed some as the four-seater jerked forward, began to turn and move away.

Once more Maggie ignored her mother, though she knew Lena was still talking. Still complaining. She watched the plane bounce a little on the uneven surface of the tarmac, headed for the runway. The engine's air pushed back on her face was warm, but that warmth lasted only a second or two before the slight northwest wind chilled her all over again. She was still waving, knowing Bo couldn't see her any longer, and was suddenly conscious of how cold the galvanized steel of the chain link fence was, penetrating right through the wool of her left hand glove. In spite of what the Chamber of Commerce brochures touted, Myrtle Beach could have some raw winter days, especially in mid-January.

Maggie shivered involuntarily, wishing she had worn a heavier coat. At least the sun was shining, and Robert had told her they expected clear weather for each leg of the flight to New Orleans. She wondered if those small planes had adequate heat. *It looks so flimsy. So tiny out there on that runway.*

The pretty green and white plane didn't need much runway for takeoff. It banked almost immediately after and was soon just an intermittent glint in the cobalt sky. Watching it disappear, Maggie wasn't even aware that she had removed the glove from her right hand, and was waving it uselessly.

Lena's comment was more biting than the cold. "Well, there they go. I hope the good Lord Jesus has them in His hand."

With a wry smile, Maggie glanced sideways at the frowning figure shivering beside her. Her mother had left her fur coat in the car, and without it, seemed so little. Fragile enough to break, like a thin icicle. But that was deceiving. Maggie knew her mother's strength came from will power, not physique. The only time in her life Lena DeVries had weighed more than ninety pounds was when she'd been pregnant; a fact she reminded Maggie of often. Nearly a foot taller and considerably more shapely than her mother had ever been, Maggie had nonetheless inherited Lena's two best physical features; large brown eyes and the coal-black hair. Lately, Maggie had increasingly been forced to camouflage a few gray streaks with frosting, while Lena's had remained black as midnight. *She's too stubborn to let her hair grow white.*

"So do I, Mama. Let's go inside the terminal and get some hot coffee. We're both freezing out here." Maggie knew the coffee would be awful and Lena would no doubt complain about it, but she'd drink it anyway – several cups – and then make Maggie stop at least a dozen times on the three-and-a-half-hour drive back to Raleigh for trips to the bathroom, but that was okay. Those pit stops would at least break up the steady stream of Lena's worn-out criticisms, half of which would be why Maggie had married Robert Ellis in the first place. The other half would be why she had stayed married to him as long as she had. And in between, Lena for sure would want to know who the bleach blonde was who had been sitting next to Robert in the plane's back seat.

The flight plan Ted French had filed called for three stops between Myrtle Beach and New Orleans; the first one at the local airport at Hickory, North Carolina. French knew his plane would have made it to Nashville without refueling, but he had the Cessna's tanks topped off at Hickory anyway. French was proud of being an experienced and careful pilot.

Satisfied the refueling process was done properly, he walked into the terminal and sat down next to Beth Oliver, who had thoughtfully ordered coffee for him. He poured sugar into the paper cup full of steaming brew, stirred, and looked around—without thanking her. Robert's son was standing by a photographic display of old barnstorming aircraft, munching a cinnamon bun, totally absorbed with the contents inside the glass case.

"Seems like a bright kid," Ted commented. "Handsome he ain't, but bright he definitely is."

"Robert says his I.Q. is off the charts," Beth agreed. "But you're right, he's not the most attractive boy I've ever seen. Those thick glasses and his braces don't help, either. I think he was so excited about the trip, he forgot to eat some breakfast. That's his second bun."

"Where's the Coach?"

"Men's room, I guess. I think his stomach may be bothering him."

"Well, if he needs to throw up, I hope he does it in there. I hate it when people get sick in my plane."

Beth didn't offer any response, and Ted was immediately sorry he had mentioned it. If Robert tossed his cookies while sitting next to her, she would probably get sick, too.

"Maybe he laid off the booze last night, Ted," Beth said. "Knowing he was going to make this trip, and that his son would be with him..." Her voice, and the thought behind it, trailed off as if she knew it was wishful thinking.

"Yeah, maybe," Ted replied, doubt showing all over his handsome face.

"Have you told him yet? Beth wanted to know.

Ted French scowled. It was just like Beth to pour salt on a de-scabbed sore. To avoid answering her directly, Ted sipped his coffee. He suspected Beth still had a soft spot for Robert Ellis. He knew they had been lovers before he had come on the scene, and probably still would be if the man had ever straightened himself out. Besides, he liked Robert, too. Hell, everyone liked the guy his fans called "Coach" but then, the whole world loves a lovable lush.

Beth persisted. "You haven't, have you?"

Ted's frown deepened. "No. Not yet. Christ, Beth, it's not easy to fire a guy knowing the next job he gets, if he gets one, is most likely going to be in some market behind the fucking moon. Maybe Utah or Montana. Some place like that. You think I don't feel for him? I can just imagine waking up one morning finding myself sportscaster in Cut and Shoot, Wyoming."

"Cut and Shoot's in Texas."

"Whatever."

"You won't give him one more chance?"

"Come on, Beth. He's had chance after chance. You've seen the November book ratings. He's dragging the whole news department down the toilet with him. I like the guy, God knows I do, but we just can't afford to carry him any longer. I wish we could hire his ex-wife. I hear her career is going up faster than Robert's is going down. Have you ever met her?"

"Couple of times a few years ago. Don't change the subject, French."

Ted watched Beth's face. If he didn't know her better he'd have sworn there was a faint hint of a tear forming in her eye. Then she lowered her head. "So, this Super Bowl trip is your way of softening the blow," she said.

"Something like that. I've had the tickets for some time, now, and I thought maybe if he could go, and bring his son along. . . You know."

"You're a shit, French. Most of the time you're a real shit, but I've got to give credit. This trip was a decent thing to do. I take it you plan to drop the hammer when we get back?"

"Yeah, that's the plan. Listen, I'd better go in there and fish him out. We're on a pretty tight schedule. You okay?"

"I'm good. Don't worry, I won't say anything."

"Ted stood and smiled down at her. "That'll be a first."

Robert Ellis chewed on two Rolaids, hoping for once they'd do their job. He was grateful that the flight, so far, had been smooth. He twisted in his seat to glance at Beth, who gave him a warm smile and a pat on the knee. Robert returned her smile, and quickly looked away. There was a time when Beth Oliver would have done a lot more than pat him on the knee. Her hand would have been in his crotch in no time. Robert heaved a sigh. Hell, he couldn't blame her. Ted French had power and money. Lots of money, which he could be very generous with when he felt like it, and Beth loved the nice things money could buy even more than she did sex. Besides, the last time they had been together, he couldn't—

"It's awesome, Dad." Bo's fourteen year-old voice was still changing, and when he was excited, he was unable to control the octave it broadcast in, much to his mortification. Robert looked down at the majesty of the Great Smokies beneath them, and had to agree. "Sure is, Champ. It's a lot more fun flying over mountains in a plane like this. Jets fly too high."

"This your first time up in a small plane, Bo?" Ted French's voice was totally without condescension.

"Yes, sir. First time up in any kind of plane, but when Dad told me I could come, I boned up some on flying, and small aircraft."

"Bo spends most of his spare time in the library, Ted," Robert put in. "He's pretty much a computer whiz kid, too." Robert felt a tad guilty saying this. Outwardly, he was always careful to let his son know how proud his Dad was of his considerable academic accomplishments, and it was true that Bo was practically a computer expert. But deep down, Robert would have wanted his only son to be an athlete. Hell, when he'd been Bo's age, he was playing three sports and already chasing girls, both with some success. Unfortunately, Robert Ellis, Jr. – nicknamed Bo from the day he was born – had come into puberty with plenty of height, but skinny as a fungo bat, with almost no physical coordination, and eyes so bad he couldn't see a basketball coming at him, much less a baseball or tennis ball. The only thing Bo lacked in being the Complete Nerd was a face full of acne. He had inherited his mother's olive complexion and a mop of hair black as sin itself. Robert hoped Bo's looks would improve at least a little more next year when those ugly braces came off.

"Really?" Ted was saying. "What did you find out about the Cessna 172?"

"Well, sir, she probably has a Continental engine, which generates up to 200 horsepower. She can fly at a maximum of nearly 10,000 feet, but you can't fly much higher than that without oxygen. Her ground speed in light wind is about 170, and she comes with standard equipment that includes altimeter, compass, airspeed indicator, oil and fuel gauges, a dual electrical system, VHF radio, tachometer, dual controls, of course, and an autopilot. I noticed you also have radar, and there's—"

"Whoa, man!" Ted said, laughing. Then, on the intercom,

he added, "Jeez, Coach, this kid of yours knows more about this damn plane than I do." To Bo, he said, "I'm impressed, son. Glad you're enjoying yourself. What you said a few minutes ago was right on the money, too. Awesome is a good word for the view from up here. I never get tired of it. Hey, Coach, I doubt if the Bears and Patriots will put on a show to match it. Should be some game, though."

"Yeah," Robert agreed, "Ought to be a close one for a change. Vegas says Bears by two. Ted, I can't tell you how much this trip means to Bo and me. I swear I'll make it up to you."

Robert meant what he'd just said. He was bound and determined to do it, too. He'd show 'em, by God. Not having a single cigarette or one lousy drink last night was maybe the hardest thing he'd ever done, but he had somehow managed, though he'd had no sleep and his gut was giving him hell for it now. He was also glad they'd had to take off from Myrtle Beach so early. He hadn't had much time to fall off his new wagon, plus, he'd vowed to himself he'd be stone cold sober when Maggie and Bo showed up. Damn, Maggie had looked good! Lena had been the same old bitch, but Mag—

"That's funny," Ted was saying.

"What is?" Beth asked.

"The compass is going nuts." Ted reached forward and tapped one of the glass-encased dials on the instrument panel. "We're on a westerly heading and the compass is all of a sudden reading south. I don't know what's—"

Without warning the Cessna went into a hard bank to starboard.

"What the hell's going on?" Ted yelled. "We're on autopilot for Chrissakes."

"Ted?" Beth's voice was close to panic.

"I can't control her," Ted screamed. "We're going down and I— The controls are stuck! Shit! So's the throttle. Oh, God, I'm sorry, you guys. I'm so—"

Instantly terrified, eardrums bursting from Beth's own scream, Robert's field of vision all at once became severely limited. All that registered in his already numb mind was the image of his son's face, chalk white against a bullet-fast changing backdrop of blue, then green, and then — as he reached helplessly for Bo – pitch black.

Robert had no idea when he regained consciousness, nor for how long. Still, in that indeterminate period, he became sharply aware of several things:
Bo— half way through the windshield.
The Cessna's steering column resting on Ted French's shoulders, where his head had been.
Beth's body, flung over the back of Bo's seat.
Two ugly bones— one protruding from his own right sleeve and one rising like a grisly walking stick through the top of his left thigh.
Lots of shattered Plexiglas and bent aluminum, all smeared red, and, through the amazingly unbroken window on Beth's side, a face.
A bearded face.
And then, he lapsed again into the black nothingness...

In the small, over-furnished house where she and Pastor Joseph DeVries had raised Maggie, Lena sat on the edge of her bed and spoke to the tinted eight-by-ten photograph of her dead husband resting on her nightstand; a habit she had formed the day after his funeral and had continued every day and night since. "We did the best we could, Joseph. The best we could. Margaret's a good girl. A good Christian, too, even if she doesn't go to church much anymore, but she's still just as stubborn as you were. We told her not to marry that good-for-nothing Robert Ellis. Would she listen? No. And just look what happened. I've told her time and time again she ought to marry that nice man Sam, even if he is a Jew, but she claims Bo would never stand for it. I'll tell you something else, too. I'm glad you're not here to see how she lets Robert spoil that boy. Bo wants a ten-speed, he gets a ten-speed. He wants a new computer, he gets one. I tell her not to let Bo go on that trip, but does she listen to her Mama? No. All the way to New Orleans in the middle of winter. And for what? To see a stupid ball game he could watch on TV. I swear, Joseph, it's sinful the way that boy worships his drunk of a father. You ought to—"

Lena's monologue was interrupted by the ringing telephone. "Hello?"

"It's me, Mama. I was so bushed when I dropped you off, I didn't feel like going by the station. I came home and took a nap. But I woke up with a whopping headache and the worst chill I've ever had. Scary."

"Are you sick?"

"No, overtired, I guess. Are you going to church tomorrow morning?"

"You know I haven't missed a Sunday service in fifty years. Of course I'm going. Why?"

"Mind if I come with you?"

"You're serious? You haven't darkened the door of the church in years."

"I know. Part of being a P.K."

"A what?"

"P.K. Preacher's kid. Forget it. I don't feel like arguing. I'll pick you up on the way."

"Well, fine, Margaret. I'll be ready."

Lena hung up, pursed her thin lips, and spoke again to the picture in the silver frame. "So, Joseph. What do you think of that?" Never mind, don't answer. Come on, I'll make us a good cup of coffee."

Twenty minutes later, Lena finished her strong Folger's, carefully washed the cup and saucer, and returned to her bedroom. She turned off the light, slipped her nightgown on, and then turned the light back on. She said goodnight to her husband, careful not to glance at herself in the mirror. Lena DeVries had avoided mirrors for a very long time.

༄

Chapter 3

Sleep.
Dreamless sleep.
That delicious, temporary death from which there is always resurrection.
Robert's nose informed him he was awake — and alive — long before his eyes adjusted to his surroundings. He smelled wood smoke. And food. Food. He discovered he could move his head, toward, he thought, the source of his new olfactory awareness, but he couldn't be certain. His eyes were still clouded over. He blinked rapidly. Because the place where he lay was so dark, so wonderfully dark, this took some time.
But gradually, a shape came into focus. A face. Long blond hair. Green eyes. A mouth. Very pretty mouth. I know this face.
"Beth?" Damn. He could talk.
"Shh. Don't try to talk. Yes, it's me. Welcome back, Coach."
It was Beth Oliver's voice, all right. Beth's alive, too. Robert blinked again. Yeah, it was definitely Beth's face. he could see more and more detail after every blink, but her face was, what? Younger? Robert ran his tongue around the inside of his mouth. His teeth were all there. Amazing. The movement of his tongue, combined with the incredible aroma filling his nostrils was causing instant salivation.

"Hungry?"

Robert wanted to laugh at her question, but wasn't sure he remembered how. Yet, like a reliable old engine warming up in cold weather, his brain was beginning to function— generating memory. "Bo. Where's Bo?"

"Bo's here, Robert, in the other room. He's going to be okay. You are, too. Can you move? Don't try to if it hurts."

Robert tried, and it didn't hurt, but there was something...something wrong. "What's the matter with me, Beth?"

"Nothing. At least, not now. It's your muscles. You've been lying in one position for a while. How do you feel?"

"I don't know. Yes, I do. I'm hungry. Something in here smells fantastic."

"It is fantastic. In more ways than one. Come on, let's get you sitting up, and I'll bring you some."

Robert tried to help, but his arms and legs were like Play-Dough. And, as she pulled him from behind, her hands strong under his armpits, he saw that beneath the fur coat covering him, he was naked. Fur coat? No, not a coat. Fur blanket?

Beth stuffed something behind him and moved away. What's that she's wearing? Looks like a leather jumpsuit. His eyes were now focusing just fine, and he could tell the room he was in was lit by flames in an open fireplace, shadowing Beth's body as she ladled something from a huge black pot hanging from a hook over the hearth. But Robert's hunger was by far stronger than his curiosity. His stomach was doing flip-flops, and Beth was taking her own sweet time. Didn't she know he was starving, for Christsakes?

Finally, she was back, kneeling. Dipping into a wooden bowl with a wooden spoon. "Okay, big boy, open up."

Robert needed no prompting. Whatever it was she put in his mouth was the best food he'd ever tasted.

"Eat it slow. A little at the time," Beth was saying. "I know it's hard to do. It was for me, too. Tha-at's it. Good boy."

After a dozen spoons full, he managed to ask, "What is this stuff?"

"Stew."

"What kind of stew?"

"It's just stew, Robert. Come on, don't talk. Eat."

Robert ate.

And slept again.

And awakened again.

Beth fed him again, twice more, and gave him water. Water like none he'd ever tasted. The only thing she said was that Bo was in the other room. Bo was going to be fine. Bo was going to be just fine.

And Robert slept the dreamless sleep again...

Maggie was not sleeping. She was in bed, but not sleeping. Sleep was something she'd had very little of since...since the first phone call that had come on January 24th. The day of the Super Bowl. There had been a lot of calls that day. A lot more since. Too many to count. Maggie looked at the clock on her nightstand. Three in the morning. She'd made her decision before midnight, but having made it, was still unable to go to sleep, and it would be another two or three hours before she dared call and wake Lena up. No matter. She could use the time to rehearse what she'd say to Sam. In addition to being friend and lover, Sam Abrahms was the best news director any anchor could hope to have, but Sam wasn't going to like her decision any more than Lena would. That was just too bad. They'd have to live with it...

It was the cold that woke Robert up.

Something very cold on his body.

He opened his eyes and once more focused on Beth's face. She was washing his body with extremely cold water. Robert was immediately aware of his nakedness. "For God's sake, Beth, what are you— "

"Relax, Coach. It's not like I haven't ever seen you this way before. How're you feeling?"

"Feel? I feel fine." To his astonishment, Robert realized he'd spoken the truth. He did feel fine. He didn't hurt anywhere, discounting the discomfort of the damned ice water Beth was washing him with. He tested his arms and legs. Found he could move them without any pain at all. "I gotta get up. Where's my clothes?"

"Hold your horses." Beth got to her feet and carried the basin of water to a table, which stood in the middle of the small room. Then she walked over to the far wall. Robert pulled himself up to a sitting position, his eyes following her every step. From a peg, she removed Robert's shirt and pants, brought them to him and handed them over, smiling. "Abner patched them pretty good."

"Abner?"

"Abner Highsmith. The man who rescued us, Robert. We owe him our lives."

Robert made a strong mental attempt to digest this news while pulling his pants on. Pants that were much too large. He'd apparently lost a lot of weight. But he was standing, by God! He tightened his belt four notches, then, barefooted, tried a few steps toward the table, moving uncertainly, like a cripple without his crutches. He reached the table and sat down heavily on one of the two wooden chairs, not trusting his legs any further. "Beth, where are we? What is this place?"

"Abner's cabin. Cozy, isn't it?"

Robert didn't answer. His mind was bursting with a million questions, but he was unable to sort them out enough to ask the first one. He looked down at his trouser leg, the left one, where the bone had been sticking out. The hole had been neatly sewed up, and there was no trace of blood anywhere. Then he remembered. Remembered it all. "Bo. Is Bo all right?"

Beth reached over and squeezed his arm. Smiling at him as sweetly as she ever had, she said, "He's going to be. He's still...

he's still asleep."

"Where is he? I want to see him."

Beth pointed to a doorway, which was closed off with a coarse blanket instead of a door. Before he knew what he was doing, Robert was back on his feet. He moved quickly to the opening and pushed the blanket aside. His son was lying on a bunk-type bed similar to the one he himself had been on, and was also covered with some kind of fur skin. Bo's face was flushed, but otherwise unscarred, and he seemed to be sleeping peacefully.

Beth's voice came from behind him. "He's going to be all right, Robert. Trust me. Here, come sit down with me. I'll try to tell you what's happened. You've been out for quite a while."

Robert retraced his steps and took the chair opposite Beth, who was holding something in her hand. His watch. She handed it to him and in a near whisper, said, "Take a look at that. Not the time, the date."

Robert took the watch from her and stared. The digital time showed 3:14 PM, but the date read— May 3rd? Robert looked up at Beth's face. "You mean to tell me I've been unconscious for—"

"Almost four months."

"Four... No way. Somebody's been messing around with this watch. Changing the dates."

"No, Robert. Nobody's touched it. I doubt if Abner would know how to change it, even if he wanted to."

"Fucking Abner again. Beth, this is all some kind of dream, isn't it? Some kind of nightmare?"

"No, it's not a dream, Coach. I was out for over two months myself."

Robert stared down at the watch again. Impossible. The digital seconds were flashing normally. Robert tested them by counting one thousand one, one thousand two, for some twenty-five or thirty seconds. The watch was working perfectly. But his mind was not. At least he didn't think it was, because if it had been, Robert would have — under these circumstances — wanted a drink. He'd have wanted a drink in the worst way. Yet, his mind was telling him he didn't want a drink. He didn't need one. What he wanted, what he desperately needed, were some answers, beginning with, "What about Ted?"

He watched Beth's mouth tighten. "Ted didn't make it, Robert. Abner told me there was nothing he could have done. It's a miracle any of us survived that crash."

Robert squeezed his eyes shut. Once again he saw Ted French's headless neck, blood spurting from where it had been in a pulsing, dark red fountain. With great effort, Robert pushed the gory image from his mind. Taking a deep breath, he looked around. "Telephone."

"What?"

"This guy you keep talking about. Abner. He have a phone in here?"

Beth's laugh was natural. Totally without her usual sarcasm, as if she'd heard the funniest thing in the world. " 'Fraid not, Coach. Sorry, no telephone. No bathroom either. No running water, no stove, no TV set, no—"

Beth was interrupted by the sound of the latch of the only door to the outside, which Robert hadn't noticed until now. Through it came a tall man of maybe thirty, dressed in a leather outfit like the one Beth was wearing. He was carrying a rifle in one hand and a burlap sack in the other. Robert found himself looking into the bluest eyes he'd ever seen; eyes that were the most prominent feature of a tanned, black-bearded face, through which a double row of very white, perfectly formed teeth showed in a wide smile. Then, a broad southern baritone came from between them. "Well, sir. I do believe you are awake at last. I'm powerful pleased to see it. How do, Mr. Ellis. I'm Abner Highsmith. Welcome to my humble home. . ."

To take his mind off his work, Samuel Abrahms liked to make comparisons. People-watching was one of his favorite pastimes— when he had time for meals in restaurants. Especially at breakfast. Some people did crossword puzzles over breakfast. Or read the sports pages. Sam loved to surreptitiously observe them. He amused himself by tacitly comparing one person, a couple, each personality or random situation with another. It was a stimulating mental exercise that got the old brain going, bothered no one else, and it was cheap. This particular morning, waiting for Maggie at a corner table in the non-smoking section of Hardee's, there were no interesting people sitting near him, and he found himself shifting his thought process to Maggie, whose Honda was just now pulling into the parking lot. Her call last night had been something of a surprise. Lately, he'd heard nothing from her, but he'd been patient, honoring her need for space and time for grieving. But he'd been perplexed when she'd finally called and asked him to meet her here, and so early. He stood as she walked to his table, not knowing whether he should come around the table and hug her, or what. Instinct told him to just stand.

"Hi, Sam. Thanks for coming." She sat down across from him, looking better than she had in weeks. Her eyes were clear. Makeup carefully applied. Hair washed and brushed to a high gloss.

"No problem, baby. How do you manage to look so great at six-thirty in the morning?"

Maggie rewarded his gallantry with the faintest of smiles. "You're the world's nicest liar, Sam. I'm a wreck and we both know it."

"Coffee?"

"No, I've already had my breakfast. Thanks anyway. Sam, there isn't much time before you have to go to the station, so I'll get right to the point. I asked you to meet me here to tell you I'm quitting. I wanted to tell you face to—"

"You're what?"

"Quitting. Resigning. I brought a letter with me. I won't be coming in today."

One of the reasons Sam Abrahms was a first class news director was that he'd learned early on to know when to talk and when not to. The shock of what he'd just heard registered with enough force for him to know Maggie was serious. This was a time to listen. He leaned forward, elbows on the table, waiting. It didn't take her long.

"I don't believe Bo is dead, Sam. He's out there somewhere, alive. Robert, too. I know they are, and I'm going to find them. The main reason I asked you to come this morning is because I knew you wouldn't laugh at me. You may be the only person I know who won't tell me I'm crazy. I was up all night thinking up answers to all the questions I knew you'd ask me, like, why now, after all this time? Like, if the police, the rangers, and practically the whole Federal Government couldn't locate them, what makes you think you can? Questions like that. I don't have any answers, Sam, at least not any that make sense. All I know is that deep down inside me, I know they're alive, and I'll find them, even if it takes me the rest of my life."

Sam listened to Maggie's speech — delivered like a truant child getting a memorized confession off the chest — with what he hoped was a poker face. He knew she'd gone through hell since January; first with the news that the plane carrying her former husband and her son was overdue, then, the week-after-week, day-by-day torture she'd endured when no trace of the plane or its four passengers could be found. One of the most exhaustive land-air searches ever conducted in the states of North Carolina and Tennessee had produced not one single clue. Not one shred of wreckage had been found. It was as though that small plane had disappeared off the face of the earth. Vanished into the unknown, like those that had become lost in the Bermuda triangle.

The frustration of just not knowing exactly what had happened, one way or the other, had taken its toll on Maggie. She was showing up for work every day, but was only going through the motions, and he was keenly aware that everyone in their market area— on both sides of the cameras — felt tremendous sympathy and support for her, especially himself.

As if reading right through his poker face, she said, "You've been wonderful, and patient, Sam. I won't forget that, but we both know I'm doing a lousy job right now, and it's time I did something about it. Besides, if you and I are ever going to have a future... Well, I simply have to know." She handed her letter over and added, "Tell me you understand."

"I understand, Maggie."
"You'll wait?"
"I'll wait."
"Maybe I will have that cup of coffee after all."

Sam got up to go for her coffee, and a refill for himself. In the few steps it took for him to reach the counter, he realized again just how much he loved this stubborn woman. He'd already waited. But he'd wait some more. Oh, yeah. He paid for the coffee, and in the few steps back to the table, seeing her little smile, he also realized just how much he hoped she'd find her spoiled rotten son, and how much he hoped, God help him, with all his heart and soul, she'd find her son-of-a-bitch ex-husband, too— deader than a fucking doornail.

His second cup of coffee tasted just as bitter as the first one had.

Chapter 4

Still smiling, Abner Highsmith handed the sack to Beth. "Two squirrels and one fat rabbit. We shall dine well tonight. Save the bullets, please Miss Beth. I will need to remold them."

Robert watched in utter disbelief as Beth took the smelly sack from him, nodded, and walked through the outside door, whistling. "What's she going to do?"

The tall man hung his rifle on pegs over the door jamb, turned, and said, "Why, she's going to skin and dress them."

"You mean gut them and all? Beth?"

"Certainly. She has become mighty good at it. She is also learning to shoot and hunt, although that may take a heap more time."

"I don't believe it."

Highsmith laughed. "Mr. Ellis, you have been — as she would say— out of it for quite a long time. Her injuries were not as serious as yours, or your son's. Miss Beth has been a most willing nurse, and a helpful assistant. She has learned a great deal she didn't know before, and to be frank, I have quite enjoyed the pleasure of her company."

Now that, Robert thought, is one statement I can believe. He caught himself just short of blurting what was on the tip of his tongue, and said, "I guess we all owe you our lives. I'm sorry, my mind is so...so crammed up. I want to thank you for everything, especially for my son. Thank God you were here."

"No thanks are called for, sir. I did no more than the next man would. I truly regret I was unable to help your friend. It was a most terrible wreck."

There was something about the man's manner of speaking that was beginning to bug Robert. It wasn't the accent, it was the way the guy put his words and sentences together. Robert couldn't quite put his finger on it, probably because his skull was so full of questions; an ocean of water pushing against a weak dike. He took a deep breath and tried hard to focus on what to ask first, but before he could, Highsmith, as if reading his mind, clapped him on the shoulder and said, softly, "Do you feel strong enough to take the air?"

Robert puffed his cheeks out and exhaled, nodding gratefully. Maybe he wouldn't have to pump the guy with questions after all. Maybe Highsmith would start filling him in. His mind was warning him to absorb any forthcoming information in small bites, like the way Beth had been feeding him. Patience had never been Robert's long suit, but he was suddenly thinking he'd better start using some. "Outside? Yeah, sure."

Highsmith opened the door. Robert stepped out onto a narrow deck that ran the length of the front of the cabin. He glanced left first, and saw Beth busy at a cutting board at the end of the porch, her fingers and hands bloody from the animal carcasses she was cleaning. She gave Robert a flashing smile and went back to her work, using a bone-handled knife. Robert was once more filled with a sense of amazement. Beth Oliver was a news producer, for Christsakes. The only work, as far as Robert knew, she'd ever done in her adult life was to sit at an IBM console banging out bad scripts or run tape decks in an editing bay. During the whole time they'd been together, Beth had never cooked one single meal. Not even toast. Her domestic talents were limited to the bedroom and the shower.

Robert smiled back at her, shaking his head. Then, holding on to the rough wooden rail, he looked around. The porch was surrounded by trees, mostly pine, and he was instantly struck by two of the log cabin's other features. It seemed to be built right into the side of a mountain! Only a few feet of its facade protruded into open space, and, it was some thirty or forty feet above the ground. A few steps on the extreme right hand side of the deck led to a narrow footpath which apparently wound down to the valley floor. Robert twisted around and looked up. Above the foreshortened roof of the cabin, the jagged rock face of the mountain rose straight up.

From where he and Highsmith stood, it was impossible to see any sky at all. Trees and scrub bushes, poking out of the mountainside at weird angles, created a natural umbrella. Though it was cool, the weather and the obvious vegetation all around the cabin confirmed the time of year. It certainly wasn't January anymore. Songs of a dozen species of birds added further proof that it was spring.

"Come along, but be careful of your step," Highsmith said, starting down the path. Robert followed, surprised that his legs carried him with no problem. It was as if he'd never been injured at all. Within ten minutes, they were standing on the valley floor, by a fast-flowing stream. "This is my water supply, Mr. Ellis," Highsmith said. "Try some."

Robert knelt, scooped up a handful, drank, and commented, "I've never tasted water as good as this in my life." Like the first pang of a headache, the thought speared Robert's mind that he hadn't consciously drunk plain water in years. But this tasted better than any brand of gin, vodka, or any other liquid he could think of, alcoholic or not. He tried another handful while Highsmith stood and said, "You may not believe this, sir, but this water is what saved your life. That's why we call this stream the 'River of Life'. But more of that later. Would you care to see some of the valley?"

"Sure. Why not?" Robert got to his feet and caught up with his host, walking along the left bank of the noisy little river. He noticed they were walking on smooth rock, or pebbles worn down to fine sand by centuries of weather. There seemed to be no grass growing on the valley floor. Curious, he looked back, up, then stopped abruptly. They had walked no more than a few hundred feet, but he couldn't see the cabin at all. Besides, he could see no smoke coming from its chimney. But wait, he suddenly thought, where was the chimney? Nine-tenths of the cabin was inside solid rock. He'd seen no chimney. Where was the smoke going? He automatically looked up again, and caught his breath. For as far up as he could see, there was no apparent opening between the two mountains. It was as though the fabric of green had opened, allowed the plane to crash, then zipped itself closed again. What light that reached the valley floor was filtered through the canopy maybe two thousand feet above their heads. It was as if some primeval force, some gigantic lightning bolt had split one mountain in two, creating a valley which was no more than a large but narrow crevasse. Trees, growing toward the sun, had effectively hidden the cleft. Robert realized at once that it would be impossible to see the valley from the air, which would explain why no one had found them, or spotted the wreck of the plane. And if it was May already, and they'd crashed back in January...Jesus Christ! Maybe after four months, nobody was searching for them anymore. "How long is this valley," he asked.

"Less than two miles, end to end," Highsmith replied.
"Where did the plane come down?"
Highsmith pointed down the valley, and up. "There. It was difficult to bring all of you to my cabin from up yonder. There was a goodly amount of ice."

Robert stared at the man, mouth open. He said ice, not snow. If what he said was true, he'd performed an incredible feat, one that would require tremendous strength and stamina. A full appreciation of Highsmith's actions hit Robert like a sledgehammer blow. Highsmith would have had to carry each of them, one at a time, down an icy mountainside and over impossible terrain to the valley, a distance of over a mile, and all in no more than one day. Otherwise, they'd all have frozen to death. The thought of what the man had accomplished was so

Lucifer's Children

staggering, Robert felt like crying. Unless...Unless he'd had help. Maybe Abner Highsmith is not the only one in this valley.

But Robert held his tongue. They walked another hundred yards or so, then he asked, "How long have you been here?"

Highsmith stopped dead in his tracks. He gestured for Robert to sit down. Robert complied, and Highsmith squatted, looked him in the eye, and in the softest of voices, said, "Mr. Ellis, I am aware you have many questions you need answered. Perhaps I can help you best with a short history lesson, but you may have some difficulty in believing me. However, I assure you I shall be entirely truthful. Please do me the courtesy of hearing what I have to say with an open mind. Do you agree?"

"Sure."

"All right, then. I came to this valley back in '65. I started building my cabin that same year. As you may imagine, it took me several years to finish it. I had few tools—"

"Wait just a minute, Highsmith. This is 1986. You just said you came here in '65. You don't look a day older than thirty to me. Thirty-five tops. You would have to have been a baby back then, maybe not even born yet. Who're you trying to kid?"

Highsmith gave Robert a quizzical look, then burst out laughing. Robert felt his own face turning red. Highsmith wiped tears from his eyes and said, "No, sir, you misunderstand. I am not talking about this century. I came here in late summer of eighteen and sixty-five. I've been here nearly one hundred and twenty-one years."

"Sure you have," Robert said, "And you brought Beth, Bo, and me all the way down that fucking mountain all by yourself, too. Look, buddy, I may have been out for a while, but I'm okay in the head now, and I'm not a gullible kid or a total fool. What kind of cockamamie bullshit is this?"

"Please, sir, I never said I brought the three of you to my cabin without help. I most certainly did have assistance. I share this valley with one other man. Like myself, a former soldier. A Spaniard named Munoz. He helped me with your rescue."

"Yeah, right. And just where is this pal of yours now?"

"He lives at the other end of the valley. Senor Munoz is even more a hermit than I. That is why you have not seen him."

"Has Beth seen him?"

"No, she has not."

"Not in four months?"

"No."

"You and this guy Munoz come here together?"

Again Highsmith laughed. "No, sir. He was here long before me. It was Lieutenant Munoz who first discovered this valley. Like myself, he was a deserter."

"Deserter from what? Look, Highsmith, I don't mean you any disrespect. After all, you saved our lives, but what you're telling me just isn't possible. I mean, nobody lives over a hundred and fifty years, not even those old guys in Europe, or Mongolia, or wherever it is. What are you trying to do, mess up my mind? Some kind of hermit's game?"

The good humor disappeared from Highsmith's eyes. "I am not joking, sir. I understand your doubt. Miss Beth was equally skeptical. And like Beth, you will also soon realize what I am telling you is the truth. I was a soldier in the Army of Cessation. The Confederacy. A Gray-coat rebel with a particularly onerous duty. By the middle of 1864, I had a craw full, and deserted. Perhaps I will tell you my entire story someday, when your mind is more receptive. For the moment, however, I will simply tell you that I came upon this valley quite by accident, found it to be pleasant in all respects, with game and water aplenty, and have been here since."

Robert stared into the blue eyes that had become cold as ice cubes. Either the man was the best actor in the world, or a raving lunatic. Maybe both. He was on the verge of losing his cool and saying so when he heard Beth's voice calling from somewhere behind him.

"Robert?"

He turned at the sound, but then, several echoes of his name — each one slightly more faint but just as clear — assaulted his ears from different directions. He twisted all the way around, peering back down the valley floor, then up toward where he thought the cabin must be, but he couldn't see it— or her.

"Abner?" Beth's multiple voices rang again. "Robert? It's Bo. He's awake."

Instinct told him to run through the echoes back the way they'd come, following the river. And run he did. Flat out. He'd covered maybe a hundred yards before he realized he was running— something he hadn't done in fifteen years! He glanced to his right as Highsmith easily loped past him "This way, Mr. Ellis..."

"It must be dark by now." Robert muttered this statement in an aside to no one, after glancing at his watch, which showed it was after eight. Beth, standing by the hearth stirring the aromatic contents of the big pot, heard him and laughed. "It gets pretty dark around four in the afternoon, Robert. The sun doesn't stay overhead long between the mountains. Otherwise, I'd have had a tan by now."

The irony of Beth's words went right over Robert's head. He hadn't had enough time yet to fully understand how deep and absolutely hidden the valley actually was. He turned in his chair to glance at his son. Bo was sleeping again. Robert watched him for a couple of minutes, then chuckled.

"What?"

"Oh, nothing. I was just remembering one of Yogi Berra's famous sayings."

"Which one?"

" 'Déjà vu all over again'. Watching you nurse Bo the way you did me. You know. It was the same thing. I owe you big time, Beth, and I haven't even thanked you. I swear I completely forgot to. It's just that all this is so... so— "

"Overwhelming."

"Yeah. I mean, the simple fact that we're all three alive blows my mind."

Beth placed the lid on the large pot, swung it back over the fire, and sat down facing him, her voice nearly a whisper. "I know. I felt the same way when I came to. Abner did for me what I did for you and Bo."

Robert shook his head slowly. "How did you —and he— do it, Beth? With no medicines, in this backwoods cabin and all? We should have been skeletons, if not corpses, after so much time unconscious."

"Broth."

"Come again?"

"You remember the stew, don't you?"

"Sure."

"The stuff makes a terrific soup, too. I was able to get quite a lot of it down your throat every day while you were out. Bo, too. Works better than an I.V."

"Telling me. Bo looks great. You think he'll be up and around in a day or so, like me?"

"Of course. Did you notice his smile? Abner took those braces off while Bo was sleeping. Must have been almost a month ago. Don't ask me how he did it."

Robert didn't ask. Frowning, he glanced at the pegs over the door. The rifle wasn't there. "Our Mr. Highsmith is some piece of work, all right. Where is he?"

Beth's answer was a smile and a shrug of her shoulders.

"I think I've got it figured out, Beth," Robert said.

"Yeah? How's that?"

"Okay, he's probably a brilliant doctor, with a penchant for Civil War history. Got fed up with the system, found this valley on some camping trip, decided to escape the rat race and come out here to live off the land, grow a beard, build a cabin and make like he's some kind of latter day Thoreau. Wouldn't be the first time that's happened."

"Hey, that's pretty good, Robert."

Mistaking Beth's sarcasm for encouragement, Robert went on. "Only thing is, after a few years out here in Daniel Boone country decking himself out in buckskin duds, he gets fantasy mixed up with reality. Starts actually believing he's a reb deserter, but Beth, that rifle he carries ain't no Civil War blunderbuss. It's a very up to date hunting rifle. High powered scope and all. The man's a hero where we're concerned for sure, but he's totally bonkers. Certifiable."

"That's what I thought, too, at first. Especially when he told me the little river down there is the River of Life. The actual Fountain of Youth."

"Jesus!"

"I believe him now. How else do you explain our recovery?"

"Oh for God's sake, Beth. Sure, the water tastes fantastic, and it may be that it has some sort of therapeutic qualities. But the Fountain of— You're not buying that bullshit are you? You're almost forty years old, not some star-struck teenager gullible enough to really believe this lunatic. Gimme a break."

Robert searched Beth's face. The tone of her voice had implied she was serious, but he just couldn't believe someone as street-smart as Beth Oliver would ever buy into such a crock. 150 year-old Civil War vet. Fountain of Youth. Jesus fucking Christ.

Her face full of scorn, Beth stood, reached both arms up and unpinned her hair. The rich blond curls — her pride and joy — came cascading down, beautifully highlighted by the flames from the hearth. Robert grinned in spite of himself.

"You're right about one thing," Beth said, "I am a forty year-old broad. I know the light in here is pretty dim, but take a good look at this hair. It's been almost four months since I put any rinse on it. My hair's as natural as it was when I was twelve."

She sat down, pulled her hair back behind her ears and leaned forward, her face only inches from Robert's. "Check out my face. Look closely, Robert. Not a wrinkle. Not one single crow's foot. Is this the no-makeup face of a forty year old woman?"

Robert had to admit what he'd noticed before. Beth did look younger. Years younger. "Maybe it's living up here like this. The altitude and all. Maybe this change in your lifestyle has something to do with it."

"Oh come off it, Robert. You're grabbing straws. You want more proof? I'll show you more proof."

She got up again, walked to the mantle and brought back a small, wood-framed hand mirror which she handed to him. "Take a look at yourself. Then tell me how crazy Abner is."

Robert shifted in his chair so the light was full on his own face. He glanced at his reflection in the antique mirror, blinked twice, looked up at Beth, and then stared back into the mirror, speechless.

Beth spoke for him. "Is that the same guy? Is that the same pushing-fifty-chubby-slob you'd become? Is that the head that was bald as a doorknob four months ago? You look ten years younger. Hell, you are ten years younger. At least."

Robert couldn't deny the incredible sight in the mirror. All the puffiness was gone from his face. Though the light was indeed poor in the cabin, he could nevertheless see that the purple, alcoholic veins that had been so prominent in his nose and cheeks were gone, and instead of a head he'd had to cover with pancake makeup every time he went on the air, there was a good two inches of dark brown hair. Hair. Reflexively, he reached up and touched it. Ran his fingers through it. "My God. It's true."

Beth smiled without smirking. "Mirrors don't lie, Robert. If I hadn't shaved you every other day, you'd have a pretty bushy beard now as well. As for Abner, I... Wait, let me show you something else."

Beth walked across the room to a shelf hung over the bunk Robert had been in. He hadn't noticed until now there were several books neatly stacked on it. Beth reached up, pulled one off, brought it to the table, and said, "Look at this. Aside from losing ten pounds and twenty years, this was the only proof I needed."

Lucifer's Children

The book was leather-bound, maybe fourteen by twenty inches, about an inch thick and obviously very old. Robert opened it to the title page and immediately saw it was a collection of photographs of Confederate soldiers. He'd seen similar volumes by Matthew Brady, but this book was attributed to some man named Adams. Robert began thumbing pages. The faded images were very much like the Brady pictures, but without the gruesome shots of the maimed and the dead. He'd turned only a few pages before Beth, impatient to make her point, reached over and turned to page eighty-six. There, in the upper half of the page, was a group shot of four reb soldiers, posing stiffly in front of a tent. The one on the left, holding a long-barreled rifle, his arm boasting two inverted stripes, was Abner Highsmith. There was no doubt.

There were also two loose photos wedged between that page and the next. Robert picked one up. It showed a handsome — and buxom — young woman, a demure smile on her face, and wearing a rather fancy frock that looked to be typical of women's fashion of the time. The second picture was of Abner again, with the woman, and two small children. From their costumes and long curls, Robert could only guess the children's sex. "Girls?"

"No, they're both boys, three and two. They lived in Atlanta. The way they died isn't a pretty story."

This was all too much for Robert. The camel's straw. He dropped the two old tintypes back in their resting place and slammed the book shut. "Fakes"

"What?"

"I'm saying they're phonies. Anybody can fake pictures today. Books, too. this whole setup smells to high heaven, and this guy Highsmith's got you brainwashed, Beth. I can't understand how somebody as intelligent as you are can fall for— Wait a minute." He looked sharply up at Beth's face. "You're sleeping with him, aren't you?"

Beth stood, tossed her hair and crossed her arms in front of her. "I swear to God, Robert Ellis, you're a bigger asshole than Ted French."

Robert knew he'd gone too far. Beth's eyes were on fire.

"Well what if I am? It's none of your damn business what I do. But since you bring it up, let me tell you something, Coach, Abner's a real class gentleman, especially compared to you or Ted French. And for your information, he understands the difference between lovemaking and raw sex."

"I resent that, Beth."

"Bull. Ted's idea was when he got in the mood, all he'd have to do was snap his fingers. And you! Your idea of lovemaking was two drinks, one kiss, then slam dunk. Look at you. Here you are, your miserable life saved, nursed back to health, practically ten years younger, and calling the man responsible for it a liar and a lunatic. If I was Abner, I'd beat the crap out of you. You can kiss my— "

"Dad? Dad?"

Robert jumped to his son's bedside, not hearing Beth slam the cabin door on her way out. "I'm here, Bo. I'm right here. It's okay. You hungry, son?"

"Yeah, I guess so. Dad, is Mom here?"

"No. No, she isn't, Bo. I'm sorry." Robert slid up onto the bunk and enfolded his son in his arms. Rocking him gently.

"I'm scared, Dad."

"You're gonna be fine, Bo. Don't worry about anything."

When Bo started crying, Robert found tears running down his own face. "I'll take care of you, son, I swear to God I will." He squeezed Bo tighter to his chest and whispered, "We gotta get you up and well, then I'll find a way to get out of this craziness and take you home. I promise."

෴

Chapter 5

Action.
Activity.
Maggie felt better. A lot better, now that she had something to do besides sit and worry, waiting for the one call that wasn't going to come. Like an adrenaline rush, the motivation to find Bo and Robert herself was giving her energy she hadn't had in months, shaking off the heavy cloak of depression she'd wrapped herself in. In almost a happy frame of mind, she'd canceled the newspaper, put the phone on vacation, and gone to her bank where she got some cash and several hundred dollars in traveler's checks, nearly depleting her checking account. Sensibly, she'd also had her old Civic serviced and new tires put on the front.

Packing the last of her casual summer clothes, she paused for a moment, thinking she may have made a mistake allowing her mother to travel with her. Lena had tried her best to talk Maggie out of going at all, and at the last minute had insisted on coming along, claiming she would worry less about Maggie if she did, and might even be helpful. In a weak moment, Maggie had agreed. Well, too late to worry about that now. She zipped up the suitcase, took one last look around her apartment, and walked out to the car. She was about to close the trunk when someone drove up behind her.

"Sam!"

"I tried to call, but the phone... I just came by to see if there's anything I can do."

"Thanks, Sam, but I don't think so. Tammy— my neighbor's going to check my place every day or so. You know, water my plants and all, but you're sweet to come by."

"No problem. I had to let you know I've talked with some of our big shots. I'm pretty sure you can get your job back when you come home — if you want it."

Maggie smiled and squeezed Sam's arm. "Tell them I really appreciate that. I hope you'll have some time off this summer yourself."

"Oh, I will. Play a little golf, catch up on some sleep. Read some. Maggie, I... Listen, I want you to call me when you, I mean, if you need me or anything. Anything at all. Promise me."

"Promise."

Maggie knew Tammy Henderson was probably watching from her living room window, but she slammed the trunk lid down, threw her arms around Sam's neck and kissed him long and hard. She looked into his gray eyes and said, "Take care, Sam. I'll be back...Whenever. Remember what you said."

Sam nodded. "Good luck, and drive carefully, okay?"

"I will. Bye, Sam." She got in the Honda and drove away, watching his tall figure shrink in the rear view mirror. His mouth was forming words, but she couldn't tell what they were.

"Okay. That's it!" Maggie pulled over onto the shoulder and stopped the car. I-95 traffic streaked by as she turned to Lena and said, "Mama, let's get something straight right now. For the rest of this trip, no matter how long it takes, I don't want to hear one more word of your badmouthing. Bo might be dead, for God's sake. Robert, too. But if you keep this up I swear I'll stop at the very next town and put you on the first bus home. You hear me?"

Lena's lips formed a tight thin line. Her eyes flashed momentarily at Maggie, and then she stared forward, through the windshield. "All right, all right. I'm sorry. How much further is it to Myrtle Beach?"

Lucifer's Children

Maggie sighed and shook her head. "I don't know. We're almost to Florence. Maybe another hour. Why? You need to go to the bathroom?"

Lena's answer was a quick shake of her head. Maggie waited another minute to compose herself again, checked the traffic and pulled back onto the highway. Trouble was, practically everything her mother said about Robert was true. From the first time she'd brought Robert home to meet her folks, Robert and Lena had clashed. Her dad, who'd loved sports, had liked Robert instantly, but her mother, who had little enough trust in men generally, and less in those who were in "show business", had taken just as quick a dislike of the glib, overconfident man who was bragging how he was "gonna take Maggie places." "To the top of the world". Lena'd been sure Maggie would be forever happy in the spot on the earth she already occupied, and wasn't in the least impressed that Robert had a winter tan. (Especially when she found out it came from a tanning booth.) Or that the fool had started calling them Papa and Mama right from the get-go.

After their marriage, Lena's opinion of Robert didn't get one whit better, even when his career took off like an Indy car; first the promotion to Charlotte, then to Kansas City, and then Chicago, with only "The Whole Enchilada, the Big Apple, Mama, Baby," left to go. Not even when Bo was born did Lena soften her attitude toward Robert, even though she was truly proud of her new grandson, who 'took after his mother, not his father'.

Then came the first shirt with the lipstick on the collar. The first time Robert's breath had smelled like a distillery. The first time he'd had to call in "sick". Then the weekends covering non-existent sporting events. Out of town games. Late calls from hotels. The "missed" planes. And the parties. Post game parties that Robert had to be brought home from; sometimes by a male friend, occasionally by a nervous woman. (Once by one still in her cheerleader's costume!)

The first time she and Robert had a real knock-down-drag-out. The first time she'd taken Bo and flown back to

Tom Lewis

Raleigh — when Lena got her first earful from Maggie and had promptly spoken her first venomous mouthful. When the inevitable separation came, Lena's mouth had gone into high gear.

"Where are we going first?" Lena was saying.

"What? Oh. The airport. We'll get a motel room and run out to the airport first thing tomorrow morning."

"I thought you'd already talked to that guy."

"Mr. Forrest? Sure, I have. Several times, but I want to see that flight plan with my own eyes."

Lena muttered something under her breath, facing away from her. Maggie couldn't hear what it was. Good thing...

Raymond Yancey hung up the phone and leaned back in his chair. There were days, and then there were days. Being Chief of Police in Myrtle Beach was no easy job, especially on Fridays, but all the same, it was a hell of a lot easier than the ass-bustin' job he'd had in New Orleans. Puttin' up with snooty Yankee tourists and the college snots on spring break was nothin' compared to the shit that went down in Orleans Parish. The salary wasn't great here, but he'd been attracted to the resort area because of its relatively low crime rate, and the perks. Mostly the perks. Like the sport fishing, which he wasn't gonna get to do today because of that one lousy phone call. Durwood Ames, his Assistant Chief, was still in the hospital with gall bladder trouble, and there was nobody else he could dump the lady off on. He'd have to see her himself. One of those days. Damned air conditioning was down too. He'd already sweated through his second uniform shirt of the day, and it wasn't even ten yet.

Yancey pulled out his already soaked handkerchief and mopped his beef-red face. Well, maybe it wouldn't take too long. He shook out a Camel and lit up, frowning. His buddy, Bill Forrest, the head honcho at the Airport Authority, had told him the woman was persistent as hell, but was quite a looker. Classy lady, he'd said. Felt really sorry for her, Bill had said. Yancey frowned again, leaned forward and punched the intercom.

"Yessir?" came the prompt response.

"Smith, go down to records and pull the file on Theodore French."

"Yessir. Be right there."

"You do that, son. And Smith?"

"Sir?"

There's a woman named Ellis comin' in to see me. Oughta be here in a few minutes. She gets here, bring her right on in and hold my calls, okay?"

"Hold the calls. Yessir."

Chief Yancey took two calls before the young officer laid the requested file on his desk and three more before Smith buzzed him. "Chief, Miz Ellis is here."

Yancey wiped sweat again and heaved his two hundred and forty pound bulk out of the chair his shirt was stuck to. Young Smith rapped twice, then ushered two women into his office; a skinny little woman and a very attractive Brunette in her mid- thirties that had to be—

"I'm Margaret Ellis, Chief Yancey. This is my mother, Lena DeVries."

Ray Yancey wiped his hand on his pants before offering it. "Miz Ellis. Ma'am. Bill Forrest told me you were comin'. Ya'll take a seat. Sorry about the air." He walked to the corner and adjusted the large floor fan so the air would blow on his two guests. "Maybe that'll help a little bit."

"Thank you." Maggie said. "Mr. Forrest told us you were good friends, and that you might have some information you'd share."

Yancey moved back behind his desk and sat, leaning forward as much to catch a little of the fan's air as to show polite interest. "Yes, ma'am. Bill and I work together quite a lot, mainly on the drug task force, along with the Coast Guard, the FBI, and other agencies. Drug smugglers bring their junk in all up and down the east coast, any way they can, usually by fast boat or plane. We manage to catch a few, but it's kinda like puttin' a Band-aid on a cut throat. That's how come they pay us the big bucks, I reckon. Anyway, I want you to know I'm real sorry about Mr. Ellis and your boy. I don't think I'll be able to help much, but I'll be glad to share what I found out, and give you my own opinion of what might of happened."

"I'm not sure I understand what you mean," Maggie said.

"Lemme try to explain. Like I said, Bill Forrest and I try to cover all the bases when a plane or a boat goes missing." He tapped the file resting on his desk. "When Mr. French's plane was a week overdue, our office did a thorough investigation into his background and activities. That plane of his was a Cessna. Just the kinda plane drug dealers like to use. It's possible for a real good pilot to fly low to avoid radar, and a plane like that would have enough range to reach Cuba, or Bermuda, or some of the Caribbean islands."

"You think Ted French might be mixed up in dope dealing?" Maggie said.

"Anything's possible, Miz Ellis. French was a good pilot. Had a lotta hours in the air, and we knew he was well off. Single guy, from a well to do Charleston family. We also knew he'd flown a lot down to places like Miami, Shreveport, Palm Beach, Houston, you know, a lotta port cities, and, we knew that he'd also flown over to Bermuda a time or two. Anyway, it was just another blind alley. French checked out to be a solid citizen. Turns out he owned a right smart amount of stock in WMBT, as well as bein' the station manager. Pretty big spender, but only on the ladies. Locally, he was highly thought of. Very active in civic affairs, that kinda stuff, but the out of town trips in his plane was mostly for pleasure. Like I said, he was quite a ladies man, but he was real discreet around Myrtle Beach. Liked to fly his women somewhere else. Good thing, too. A few of those ladies were married."

The tiny woman with the snapping black eyes spoke up for the first time, "What's all that got to do with Bo and Robert?"

Yancey smiled at her. "Well, ma'am, as it turns out, nothin' at all."

Maggie spoke up. "Wait a minute. I think I understand. You also investigated Robert, didn't you? Did you think Robert might have had some kind of connection with drug people?" And may have forced French to—"

"Now hold on, Miz Ellis, don't get yourself all riled up. It's our job to look at all the possibilities, but aside from the problems your husband had with alcohol, we didn't find any evidence whatsoever that he was using any other kinda drugs. Far as we know, Mr. Ellis and your son were just along for the ride."

"I'm sorry," Maggie said, softening her tone. "I realize you have to be suspicious of everyone. What were the conclusions you came to?"

"Law enforcement people deal in facts, Miz Ellis. Hunches are for TV cops, but I do have an idea or two. Look over here a minute, please." Yancey got up and pointed at the dingy green far wall, which sported a large, detailed map of the eastern United States, Cuba, and the Caribbean, which was decorated with dozens of brightly colored pins stuck in various spots. With a fat but well-manicured finger, Yancey touched several of them. "We checked with all the areas Mr. French's plane could have landed, just in case we were wrong, and he really did, for whatever reason, fly out of the US. If he'd landed in any of these places, we'd of known about it five minutes later. No, logic says the plane went down in one of three places."

"Where?" Lena asked.

Yancey pulled a face. "Well, Miz DeVries, in my opinion, it coulda gone down in the Florida everglades, or the ocean, in which case nothin' might ever be found, but I don't think it did. I think French and your folks really were on their way to Nashville when they left Hickory, and musta crashed somewhere in here." His finger traced a circle, and tapped the border between North Carolina and Tennessee.

Tom Lewis

"The Smoky Mountains," Maggie said. "But they searched all through there for weeks. Twice."

"Yes'm. I know. But if I was gonna start searchin', that's where I'd start. A lot of that country up there's pretty wild. Places you can't even get to on foot. A small plane? Painted green? Hard to see from the air. It's just possible they missed it. Not probable, now, but possible."

Maggie and her mother stared at the map for a long moment before Maggie said, "Something tells me you're right, Chief Yancey. I don't believe they're in the everglades or at the bottom of the ocean. They're alive. I know they are, and if they're somewhere in those mountains, I'll find them, even if I have to cut down every tree. I appreciate your taking time to see us. Good luck with your work."

Ray Yancey gave her his best smile. "Thank you, ma'am. Good luck to you, too. I mean that. You're one gutsy lady."

The two women hadn't been gone two minutes before Yancey called Bill Forrest back. "You were right about her, Bill. She's a looker, all right. Those eyes of hers could melt a fuckin' iceberg. Tell you something else, too. If you and I were right about those people goin' down in the Smokies somewhere, I bet that little gal finds 'em. They'll be deader'n hell, and that's a damn shame, but she'll find 'em. Wanna put some money on it?"

Bill Forrest didn't, and Yancey hung up, chuckling. Then his face became serious, and he punched in another long-memorized number — to his twin brother, who was also in law enforcement, Sheriff of Lee County, in western North Carolina. "Hey, Bro, it's me. How ya doin'?"

"Same as always, Ray. What's up?"

"The Ellis woman just left my office. Had her Ma with her. She's on her way."

"About time. Thanks for the call, Ray. We'll be waiting."

On the way back to the Flamingo Motel, Maggie stopped at an Amoco station, gassed up the Honda, and bought road maps of North Carolina, South Carolina, and Tennessee. When they got to their room, Maggie spread the maps out on the twin beds and the floor. "Mama, why don't you get your suit on and take a dip in the pool. I want to figure out our route."

"Are you kidding? I wouldn't put my big toe in that filthy thing. No telling what kind of people have been in there. Colored people and all!"

"Oh, Lord, Mama, they use enough chlorine in those pools to kill AIDS. Maybe some prejudice, too. At least go see if you can find us a place to eat supper tonight."

"Fine. I can take a hint. I'll get out of your hair for a little while. You think that fat policeman was right? I swear, I never thought much about why they call cops pigs, but that Yancey sure looked like one. Bo would call him 'gross'."

"Maybe," Maggie said. "But you know what? Pigs are smart. Very smart."

℘

Tom Lewis

CHaPtER 6

In most respects, they were different as night and day. The host was an enormous, powerfully-built Irishman whose private personality was as outgoing as that of a circus clown. His German guest was short, thin, probably weighed no more than 125 pounds wringing wet, and was usually withdrawn and scholarly, whether in public or *in camera*. One was loudly progressive, the other an arch-conservative. But as different as they were, they had much in common. Both loved the game of chess, good wine, and rare books—all of which they liked to share. Each had the same first name, Peter. Both were Princes of the Church, having been appointed to the College of Cardinals on the same day, and each man loved Ramon Barillas like a son.

"Why is it we never finish this stupid game?" said Cardinal Peter Reilly.

"Because we eat too much and drink too much before we sit down to play, and talk too much when we do," answered his dinner guest, Cardinal Peter Zimmer. "How did you like the Bordeaux I brought?"

Cardinal Reilly frowned. "Too fruity for me, especially with leg of lamb. I prefer something with a real bite to it when I eat red meat."

"You're a hard man to please, Peter."

"Look who's talking. Last time, at your place, I brought three different bottles. I seem to remember you turned your Bavarian nose up at every one of them."

"They all tasted cheap. Like you. It's your move."

Lucifer's Children

"I'm thinking, I'm thinking. We've got all night." Peter Reilly eyed the board. If he took Zimmer's knight, he'd surely lose a bishop. No way. Better re-think this. "Too bad Ramon couldn't make it for dinner. I take it you loaded him up with too much weekend work as usual?"

The small man across the board grinned, showing his new upper plate, which had not yet become comfortable. "Now look who is talking. I don't work the poor man nearly so hard as you did."

"Touché. We both owe him a lot, don't we? I owe him my red cap, and you owe him your lofty position—at least your holding on to it."

"I cannot disagree with you on that," said Zimmer. "Not to mention our own friendship, and this weekly truce."

"Ain't it the truth. Peacemaker. 'Blessed are the peacemakers—' "

" 'For they shall see God.' "

Both men studied the board, mulling over the truth of their statements more than their chess strategy. The two Cardinals were both important members of the Curia, and Zimmer was actually the assistant dean. Seven days and six nights a week, the two were strong—and vocal—adversaries; Reilly being far to the left of Vatican II, while Zimmer was just the opposite. Their heated arguments had at times nearly become violent until Monsignor Ramon Barillas had miraculously brought them together on unseen common ground, having served both men faithfully– first as Reilly's right hand man when he'd been Archbishop of Los Angeles, and now as Zimmer's personal secretary and envoy.

To keep from having to make his next move, or perhaps goad his host into distraction, Cardinal Zimmer craftily jabbed another figurative splinter under Reilly's fingernail, "You would never have gotten to Rome in the first place if it hadn't been for Ramon. You got all the credit for those race riot and gang fight successes in Los Angeles, but we both know Ramon did all the work."

Reilly grunted good-naturedly. "True, Peter, true as hell. I'll never forget the way he simply walked right down the street through burning buildings, rock throwing, and stray bullets into the Latino gang's headquarters. The police wouldn't even come near the place. Before it was all over, he'd managed a truce where we all thought there would be a devastating war, and after Watts, we certainly didn't need that. What the Holy Father noticed was that we—he'd done it five times! He squinted at the small man. "Are you going to move or not?"

"You have such little patience, Peter. Just like your namesake. I will make my move when I have decided on the correct one. The one that will hurt you the most."

Reilly laughed. "You've got the heart of a Nazi and tongue to match! And what about you, you little fox? Ramon is doing ninety percent of your diplomatic work now. The way he brought the two of us together was a minor accomplishment when you consider how his behind-the-scenes patience has kept your camp and mine from embarrassing the whole church. Don't think the Holy Father hasn't noticed that, too. I have a feeling he's going to steal Ramon away from you the way you stole him from me."

Zimmer ignored that and calmly castled; a move that took his host completely by surprise. "Your move. You may be right again. I could lose him as early as next year. You know what he's been up to lately?"

"Who, the Pope or Ramon?"

"Ramon, you fat fool. He's been studying Polish."

"So he can communicate with John Paul in his native tongue! I'm not a bit surprised. The way that lad learns new languages is amazing."

"It's a gift from God. One of the reasons why I use him so effectively."

Reilly nodded. For the past five years, Zimmer had sent the young priest over half the Catholic world, pouring highly effective oil on the troubled waters caused by the slow but turbulent reactions to Vatican II. "You use the boy far more than

Lucifer's Children

I ever did, Peter. But you'd better be careful. You're working him to death. Last time I saw him, he didn't look good at all. Is he sick?"

"No, not physically ill, but something is surely bothering him. I don't think he's getting much sleep. He came to work day before yesterday unshaven. By the way, I took the liberty of asking him to stop by here after he finishes tonight. Will you have your overpaid cook brew some coffee?"

"Of course. Colombian, too. It's his favorite, you know. The poor guy never had time to develop a taste for good liquor. Hardest thing he drinks is communion wine. But if you don't kill him, I predict he'll soon be the youngest Bishop in the Vatican." He pointed down, "I don't understand that last move. Castling ain't going to help you." But Reilly, playing safe, moved his second knight forward so he could castle himself on his next move. Then he poured the both of them another glass of the expensive Port. "Your move."

"*Jawohl, mein Lieber. Ein moment, bitte.* You know, you never actually told me how you found Ramon anyway."

"I didn't find him. Your predecessor did. When I was moved from San Francisco to L.A. I wrote asking for a Spanish-speaking priest who'd been trained in diplomacy. They sent me Ramon. I had no idea how talented he was. Seems he'd been something of a phenomenon all his life, right from the get-go down in Guatemala." Reilly eyed his guest. "I didn't realize you knew so little of his background."

"He rarely speaks of himself. Besides, we have no time for chit-chat."

"Don't I know it. At any rate, he comes from a very large family, mostly unmarried sisters, all poor as dirt. Matter of fact, I think he sends them money every month. When he was a boy, his local priest recognized the boy's intelligence and hunger for learning. Regular sponge, he was. Got him sent to Seminary in Mexico City. That's where they found out about his unique gift for languages."

"And where they obviously discovered he had a photographic memory."

"Right. Perfect candidate for advanced study here in Rome. Far as I know, he broke all records of scholarship while he was here the first time. By the time he graduated, he spoke seven languages and could read and write Greek and Latin better than Homer and the Caesars. Funny thing is, he's no wimp, either. Splendid athlete, he was. From what I hear, he could have been one of Guatemala's greatest soccer stars if he'd decided to go that route. I watched him one day in a kind of pick-up game. I couldn't believe what he could do with that silly little ball. Those good looks didn't hurt him a bit either. I think every Latino girl and woman in L.A were half in love with him. Hell, so were the Anglo women, for that matter."

"Yet he is so unassuming. So without—what is the term, personal ambition? I believe he is the only priest in Rome with no enemies."

"I agree, but if you don't ease off his schedule, he may be the next dead priest in Rome."

"You may have a point, Peter. Do you happen to know how long it has been since he had a vacation?"

"Vacation? Are you serious? To my knowledge, he's never taken a single day off in his life. The church tells him what to do and he goes and does it, with no more whining than Billy Budd. Whose move is it?"

"I don't know. I think it's mine. You moved your knight, then poured the wine so I wouldn't notice. Why didn't you take my knight?"

"I may be a big Irishman, but I'm not a big dumb Irishman, you conniving little Himmler, you. I don't fall so easily into such foolish traps. Would you like some more of this Port?"

"Yes, I would. It's quite good."

"It should be. Cost me enough. There's another bottle of the same in the cellar. Speaking of cellars, why don't you find a place here in town? I'd feel like a convict living like you do inside the walls of Vatican City."

"I like it there. I feel close to the ghosts of the saints."

"Some of them weren't too saintly."

"Let us not get off on that again. Have you read the book I sent you? My dealer in Munich told me it took him two years to find it."

"And it may take me another two to get to it, but I will. Come on, dammit, move."

"Don't try to bully me. I'm not dumb, either. You know, this really is a good port. Where did you find it?"

Ramon Barillas smiled as Cardinal Reilly's housekeeper led him to the study. The door was open and through it, he could see his two mentors, past and present, bent over the chessboard, one looking for all the world like the famous American football player who now gently sold flowers on television, the other like a bird poised on the edge of a birdbath font. Better to make war, he thought, with chess pieces than tear at each other's throats in the Curia council meetings, which they would surely do tomorrow. Both men looked up as he entered.

Reilly spoke first. "Hello, lad. I'm glad you could come by. Please take a seat. Are you hungry?"

"No, your Eminence, thank you, but if you have some of that wonderful coffee, I'd like a cup."

"It's brewing as we speak."

Ramon sat on an ottoman which had obviously been carefully placed to the side of the chess table. "Who's winning?"

"I am," said Zimmer, with a thin-lipped smirk. Peter talks too much and thinks about the game too little. You look exhausted."

Ramon puffed his cheeks out. "Only a little tired. I have had trouble sleeping lately."

"Well," Zimmer continued, "While my fat colleague here has been running at the mouth, I've been thinking. I have decided that my English is now good enough to finally accept the invitation to lecture at Georgetown University."

Tom Lewis

Ramon laughed as he accepted the porcelain cup and saucer handed to him by the housekeeper. He thanked her, then said, "Your English has been good enough for that for many years, Eminence. What made you change your mind about going to the United States? I thought you—"

"I've changed my mind, though the place is a snake pit full of Jesuits. And, I've decided to take you with me."

"Good idea," Cardinal Reilly commented.

"But what about the trip to Peru?" Ramon asked.

"I can send you there any time. Besides, I want you to have some rest. Away from Rome, at least for a few days, and if I don't order you to, you won't do it. They say Washington and Georgetown are lovely when the cherry blossoms come out."

Ramon sipped his coffee in silence, knowing full well the two adversaries had been talking about him before he'd arrived. And he could guess why. He knew his fourteen-hours-per-day work was probably suffering lately, because of his lack of sleep, which, in turn was caused by the terrible headaches, which now accompanied his monthly dreams. Perhaps a week away from Rome would interrupt their regularity. Perhaps he would be able to enjoy cherry blossoms. They would be a good deal more enjoyable than the pine needles, which framed the small church that now crowded into each nightmare. Perhaps he'd even be able to forget the last dream, four nights ago. The worst one yet. **Perverted.** She'd been splashing around naked in a hot tub, **placed**, like a profanity, just below the steps to the front door of **the stone** church.

For an instant, he was tempted to tell his two well-**meaning** mentors of his personal hell, but just as quickly decided **not to.** These two great men of the church, both now in their seventies, had quite enough to think about; far more important things than whose move it was. It would be a sin to bother them with such insignificant drivel, especially on their precious night off. No, better to drink his coffee in silence, eat two of the sugar cookies that had been prepared especially for him, then make his polite excuses and go home. He needed to write letters to his sisters anyway. He hoped he would get an hour or so of sleep before dawn.

Chapter 7

Robert knew he would never underestimate his son again. The mind-boggling physical progress Bo had made during the past three days (Bo's body looked like it was at least fifteen or twenty pounds heavier) had been matched by a growth in mental maturity Robert wouldn't have dreamed possible. Instead of whining that there was no bathroom or hot shower, no TV, or computer — nor the electricity to power them, Bo had listened to his dad's fantastic account of what had happened to them without the sneering, adolescent reaction Robert had expected. Bo's only negative statement had been, "Jeez, Dad, nobody's named Abner anymore!"

Robert had planned to feed Bo information in small bites, the way he'd fed him the equally wondrous stew, but once he'd begun talking, and Bo's reaction had been far more adult than juvenile, Robert had spun out the entire tale. Bo had eaten, slept, and listened. For three days and nights. Abner and Beth had apparently sensed their need for privacy, and had left them alone.

On the morning of the fourth day, after breakfast, and after Beth and Abner had left the cabin, Robert got up from the table and brought the mirror to his son. "Take a look, Bo. You're not a kid any longer. You're a... You're practically a man."

Bo's response was to pull his lips back, as if he couldn't quite believe the braces were gone. He laid the mirror on the table, looked back across at Robert, and said, "It's hard not to believe it all, Dad. I mean, you look...Well, your hair and all."

"I know. But none of it makes any sense. It's like all three of us are going through some kind of triple hallucination. Some kind of drug-induced nightmare."

"Except that all three of us are okay. If this is a nightmare, it's the best one I ever had! That crash should have killed us all. Maybe... Maybe we are dead, and all of this is, you know, hell."

"Unh-uh. No, we're alive all right, but you may be right about the "hell" part. We've gotta get out of here. All of us. If we don't, we're gonna wind up crazy as Highsmith is."

"You really think he's crazy?"

"Mad-hatter nuts. And the world's biggest liar to boot."

Bo's face was blank. Questioning.

Robert got up again. Walked over to the shelf over the fireplace. Pointed. "Look at this, Bo. Coffee. Sugar. Canned food. This is store-bought stuff, son, and it sure as hell isn't left over from Gettysburg. Where'd it all come from? If Highsmith's getting supplies, there's gotta be a way in and out of this valley. You were watching Beth cook last night. She put potatoes, onions, carrots and other things in that stew. Abner have some kind of garden hidden away out there? I haven't seen one. And where's he getting the tobacco for that silly looking pipe he smokes?"

"Yeah, I see what you mean."

"He's lying to us, Bo. This whole thing is all one big lie, and he's got Beth snowed one hundred percent. Another thing. This fireplace. I mean, there's no chimney outside. Where's all the smoke going? And how'd he manage to cut into solid rock to build this cabin in the first place? By himself? With this five hundred year-old Spanish dude he keeps talking about that nobody's seen? No way."

"It's weird, that's for sure. Like some kind of sci-fi movie."

"Right, except in a movie, you can get up and walk out if you don't like it, and no movie lasts four months. Neither do nightmares."

Like a lawyer who'd just finished making a point to a jury, Robert crossed his arms and looked at his son. Bo's head was bent down. He seemed to be studying the grain of the table top. After a minute or two, he lifted his eyes. "But what if it's all true? Beth was out for two months, Dad. You were out almost four months, and I've just woke up, and I feel...I feel real strong. My legs feel like they're twice as big as they were before. Beth told me they were both broken. My neck, too. What's more, I can see fine without my glasses! Maybe that river down there is what he claims it is. Beth looks a whole lot younger than when we got on Mr. French's plane. So do you."

Robert turned and smiled at his son. Bo was scared. Whistling past the graveyard. His young mind trying to deal with their situation by rationalizing. What did shrinks say that was? Denial? He was about to say something about escaping when Beth came through the door, something tucked under her arm. "Hi, guys. Christmas comes early this year. Try these on for size."

What she'd brought in with her were two buckskin outfits. "Shirts, pants, belts, and moccasins. Made 'em myself." She was grinning from ear to ear. Robert could only stare at her, then at the clothing she was holding up. "Yours may be a tad tight, Robert," she said, "But at the rate you're losing weight, they'll fit fine in another day or two." Looking at Bo, she said, "I made yours a size or so too large, Bo-Bo, but my guess is you'll grow into them in a week, the way you're going."

Robert and Bo were both speechless.

Beth looked from one to the other. "Hey, you guys, those things you're wearing are rags. Falling apart, and none of our suitcases survived the crash."

Bo was the first to react. "Wow. These are cool. Thanks a lot, Beth." He snatched his outfit up and went into the back room, pulling the blanket like a curtain over the doorway.

Robert finally found his tongue. "You're something else, Beth. One surprise after the other. When did you find time to do all this?" He held up a sleeve of the leather shirt, surprised at how soft it felt between his fingers.

Beth tossed her hair. "I've had plenty of spare time lately, haven't I? Didn't take long, and Abner helped. He'd already cured the deer hides."

Yet again, Robert had to grudgingly admire the homespun skills Beth had so quickly learned, so assiduously practiced, and was so unselfishly sharing. He felt a tinge of guilt for the way he'd pointed an accusatory finger at her less than a week ago. Nor could he help feeling more than a twinge of jealousy toward Abner Highsmith. Beth was gorgeous. Absolutely radiant. But Robert had more important things on his mind. Lowering his voice, he said, "Listen, Beth, we have to talk. We have to figure out a way to—"

"I'm sorry, Robert, I don't have time right now. Can it keep till tonight? Why don't you take Bo out for a while. You know, get used to the moccasins. I have to start supper and then grind some meat for sausage."

Robert was in the middle of a temper-tamping ten-count when Bo walked back into the main room. "Check it out, Dad, what do you think?"

Robert turned. It struck him that Bo seemed a lot taller. Two inches at least. "You look like a lean and mean Davey Crockett machine, pal. All you need is a coonskin cap." With a smile at the beaming Beth, he picked up his own new clothes and started to the back room. "Give me a minute to change, and we'll go out a-lookin' fer a b'ar."

The following morning, Robert sat down to a plate of eggs and sausage. His appetite was stronger than his curiosity about where the fresh eggs had come from. He certainly hadn't seen any chickens in the valley. Beth was bustling about, humming like a *hausfrau*, and Robert didn't feel like starting another argument over something trivial as eggs. For all he knew, they might have been wild turkey eggs anyway. "Where's Bo?"

"Abner took him hunting. They left an hour ago. More coffee?"

"Sure. Thanks."

"You guys look good in your new outfits. How do they wear?"

"Fine. I can't believe how soft they feel. Like a second skin."

Beth sat down across from him. "How about you? How are you feeling?"

"Great." This was no lie. Yesterday, he and Bo had walked from one end of the valley to the other, following the stream until it disappeared between narrow fissures in the rock that formed the south wall of the boxed canyon. Neither had talked much. Bo had seemed preoccupied with his new body, especially the amazing strength in his legs, breaking into wind sprints every few hundred yards, while Robert had marched along at a steady pace, studying the canyon walls for some path, some trail that might lead up and out. He hadn't spotted one, and when they turned back, Bo had challenged him to a foot race. Robert had covered two hundred yards before he realized Bo was running with the easy stride of a well-conditioned athlete. Athlete? Where was the skinny, 98-pound-weakling type that Bo had been?

"You two looked like a couple of colts down there yesterday," Beth was saying. I have to tell you I was surprised to see you keep up with Bo like that. You've gotten yourself back in good shape, Robert."

Over the rim of his coffee cup, Robert threw a grin across the table at her. What she's said was also true. He'd gone out after supper every night, down to the valley floor, and given himself long workouts, inwardly proud that he was now a flat-belly who could do a hundred push-ups without even breaking a sweat. He was stronger, more muscular, than he'd been in his entire life. I'll soon be capable of climbing. Those rocks at the north end of the canyon don't seem so—

Lucifer's Children

Laughing, Beth broke into his thoughts again, "You've been doing a lot more than just walking every night after supper, haven't you?"

"Yeah, I guess I have."

Beth's face changed into a furrow-browed, mock pout. She waggled her forefinger from side to side. "But you shouldn't have spied on us last night. That wasn't nice."

Instantly, Robert's face turned crimson. "Jesus, I'm sorry. I didn't mean to—"

Beth laughed again. "Hey, don't worry about it. Better for you to be the voyeur than Bo, I guess. Hell, I didn't even see you. Abner told me. He's got eyes like an eagle."

Robert dropped his head in genuine embarrassment. From the beginning, when he'd realized he was sleeping in one bunk and Bo in the only other one, he'd wondered where Beth and Abner were sleeping. Last night, on his way back to the cabin from his workout, he'd passed them, holding hands like a surreal John Smith and Pocahontas. An hour later, not sleepy, he'd walked out onto the porch, stared out at the blackness for a while, trying to think of where the entrance to the valley might be, when he'd noticed the faint glow of an obvious campfire. He'd gone down the steps and followed the river for maybe quarter of a mile. He'd crept closer, thinking he hadn't made a sound, squatted and watched. Abner had pitched some sort of tent on the river bank, spread fur-rugs under it, built a small fire, and he and Beth were splashing noisily and naked in the cold, shallow water. Beth had done a sensual impromptu dance around the campfire, then had dropped to her knees, pushed Abner's white legs apart, and bent over. That was when Robert had turned and gone back to the cabin. Beth was apparently giving Abner Highsmith a few twentieth-century lessons of her own every night.

He decided not to say anything just yet about escaping from the valley. First, he wanted to have more of an idea of how it could be done. There had to be an opening somewhere in the rock-face, on one side of the river or the other. He'd just have to search until he found it. He muttered another weak apology to Beth and went out onto the porch. He stood there by the rail for several minutes, trying to think it all through. Then he remembered asking Highsmith where the plane had come down. It occurred to him that if Abner and Senor— what was his name? Munoz? Yeah, Munoz — had brought all of them down from the mountain, the way both up and down must not have been too steep. Shouldn't be too hard to find, if he searched methodically. Feeling suddenly optimistic, he took the steps down to the valley floor three at a time.

    He had no idea how long he had spent looking before he found a faint path that led up through the pines. Climbing at nearly forty-five degrees, switching back and forth, he made his way up, pausing every few laborious steps to look for some sign of human presence. He saw nothing. Stubbornly, he kept climbing, having no clue as to how much altitude over the valley floor he had gained. He stopped, leaned on a tree, and gazed straight up. There was no gash in the green canopy where the plane might have fallen through, shearing branches and limbs on its downward plunge. There was no evidence that anything other than birds had sifted through it. He must be in the wrong place. Still, he felt encouraged by having made so much headway out of the valley. Maybe if he kept going, he'd find a way—

    The sting on his right earlobe caused him to stop and reach for it. Before his arm and hand had moved an inch, he heard the crack. That was a rifle shot. Amid its echoes, he stopped in his tracks. His fingers came away from his ear bloody. *That bastard Highsmith is shooting at me!* Instinct took over. Robert scrambled behind a tree, cursing. The echoes died away. Robert had no inkling of where Highsmith was, or how the man had managed to spot him in such heavy vegetation. He started to move up again, thinking he was keeping trees between himself and his attacker. He hadn't climbed two more feet before he felt the same bee-sting on his left ear. Again came the crack and echoes. Robert dropped to his belly, not daring to move a muscle. He knew without reaching that his left earlobe had also vanished. The instantaneous pain was not nearly as severe as his anger and humiliation. He kept still, hardly breathing, hoping his body was hidden from view. Then, without a single echo, came Highsmith's voice, sounding as though the man was no more than ten feet away. "Robert, come back down, please. Take care not to fall." It was a command, not a request, and something told Robert to obey.

Reversing his direction, Robert found it was far more difficult descending that it had been climbing. It seemed to take him forever to reach the spot where he's started up. Abner Highsmith was sitting by the riverbank, the rifle lying over his legs. When Robert emerged into the open, Abner stood, a benign smile on his face. "Dip your head in the water, Robert."

"What?"

"Do as I ask, please."

Robert took one look at the cold blue eyes, then at the rifle cradled across the bearded man's chest, and waded into the stream. When he'd gone in enough so that the water was up to his knees, he bent over and plunged his head under its icy surface. He straightened, gradually realizing the reason for Abner's second command. He knew, even before reaching both hands up to confirm, that both his earlobes were restored. The throbbing pain was immediately absent.

Still standing knee-deep in the water that didn't feel cold anymore, Robert asked, "Where's Bo?"

"I sent him back to the cabin two hours ago. Miss Beth will be teaching him how to skin the two rabbits he shot. You should go back as well. We will talk of this later."

Robert had heard no other shots besides the two Highsmith had fired at him. But he held his tongue, waded through the stream, and began walking back, like a rebellious, but defeated member of a chain gang whose punishment had only just begun. His anger and feelings of frustration were not helped when, nearly to the cabin path, he spotted Beth jogging toward him. He stopped, but she didn't, and in passing, gave him a silent look that spoke volumes of fear. What had spooked her? Robert picked up his pace.

He found Bo, not at the cutting board, but inside the cabin, sitting on the floor of the back room, rocking back and forth, his face pale as flour. Before Robert could open his mouth, he sensed something was out of place. Not what it was before. His eyes swept the room. It only took a split second to spot it: A few feet to the right of Bo's bunk, a section of the back wall seemed cracked. Robert moved to it. Pushed. Noiselessly, the false panel opened inward, revealing a small room, carved out of solid rock, with stone steps leading down— to what? Robert was half way down the chiseled staircase before he became aware of two things simultaneously: The stairwell was illuminated by light coming from nowhere, and, the temperature was dropping with each step down. He began counting steps. Forty more landed him in a sort of cave, maybe twenty feet square. It was freezing. His breath was coming out in clouds. He looked around. What he saw at first made him smile, and release a frozen breath of relief. Everywhere he looked were dressed and partially butchered animal carcasses lying on slabs of rock. Aloud, he whispered to himself, "Be damned. It's a fridge. Abner's meat locker!" There was a hardwood table, which sported various cleavers and knives set squarely in the middle. Then his eye caught sight of something else. In the corner. Lying on a low shelf, minus one arm and one leg, was the nude body of a man. Even before he gasped the first time, or noticed the head— placed on a small shelf above the rest of the still white form, he knew it was Ted French. Gagging, he turned and rushed back up the stairs.

Bo was still where Robert had left him, on the floor, rocking in shock. Robert gave him only a glance as he headed for the open door to the porch and leaned over its rail, retching violently. When his shaking subsided enough for him to start thinking again, the nausea returned, because he remembered that French's head wasn't— normal. It had been opened.

Lucifer's Children

Expertly. And empty. Along with two of his limbs, Ted French's brain had been removed.

※

CHaptER 8

For her base of operations, Maggie chose the Day's Inn motel just off I-240 on Patton Avenue. It was within walking distance of a large mall, where she hoped Lena would spend a lot of time, plus, Patton gave Maggie a straight shot into downtown Asheville. The motel was clean and, thank God, their room was large enough to please her mother. The next morning, leaving Lena switching channels between the three network morning shows, Maggie found the Asheville Visitor Center, and picked up tourist brochures of bus-tour excursions to several of the attractions in and around Asheville she thought Lena might enjoy, including one to the famous Biltmore Estate, which Lena had specifically mentioned interest in seeing. Luckily, the Chamber of Commerce office was in the same building. Following impressively clear directions, Maggie had no trouble locating a small printing business, where she left the photos of Bo and Robert she'd brought with her after extracting a solemn promise from the sympathetic printer that her flyers would be ready in twenty-four hours.

Back at the motel, she dumped the brochures on Lena's bed. "Look through these, Mama. If you see something you might like to do, ask the desk clerk about transportation. I'll be back by lunchtime."

"Where are you going now?"

"Into town again. I need to find a bank, and there are a couple of other errands I have to run."

"All right."

Maggie kissed her mother on the cheek and left again. She'd lied about the bank and errands, not wanting Lena to have any inkling where she was actually going, knowing Lena would violently object. She followed I-240 to I-26 south to the airport. Forty-five minutes later, she was seated in the small pine-paneled office of Thompson Aviation, facing the man who was "President, chief pilot, office manager, bookkeeper, and secretary, ma'am. What can I do for you?"

Maggie thought it would be tough to judge B.J. "Bud" Thompson's age. His thin face was as creased and leathery as the old brown flight jacket he wore. In deference to Maggie's sex, (she guessed) he pushed the faded NY Yankees baseball cap to the back of his graying head and chewed gum steadily while he listened to Maggie's story and request.

"Now, let me get this straight," he said. When he leaned forward and unfolded his long arms, the jacket made a creaking sound. Maggie was surprised his voice didn't as well. "You want me to hedge-hop you all over these mountains to look for a plane that may or may not have gone down several months ago, back in January?"

"That's right. The people over in the terminal told me you were the best charter pilot in the area."

"Well, they got that right. I am the best, Miz Ellis. Around here at least. The oldest, too. The reason I'm the oldest and the best is because I don't do stupid things with my airplane, like ducking in and out of ravines, fighting updrafts and windsheers. Besides, it's already late spring. Vegetation's 'bout as thick as it's gonna get. We wouldn't see anything but a green rug. What you need is a helicopter. That's most likely why they didn't spot the crash before. They used planes instead of helicopters. Unfortunately, I don't fly helicopters."

"Who does?"

"Who does? And who flies 'em just about as good as I fly my plane?" Thompson grinned, showing a pronounced gap between his front two teeth, making him look a bit like David Letterman, the rising young comic she and Sam liked so much. "My little brother, that's who. Flew choppers in 'Nam for three and a half years. If there's anybody south of the arctic circle who could spot that wreck — I mean, that plane, it's Connie."

"Connie?"

"Real name's Cornelius. Hates his as much as I do mine."

Maggie tilted her head down and raised her eyebrows.

"Buford. Buford Jeremiah. Our old man had a fun time with names."

Maggie laughed with him. "Do you think Connie might help me?"

"I know he will."

"Really? How can you be so sure?"

"Lady, any man lucky enough to have a woman like you go to all this trouble and expense deserves to be found. Your boy, too. I got a son of my own. Connie's got three of 'em."

"How do I get in touch— "

"Look, you just be here at sun-up tomorrow morning. I'll take care of everything with my brother. Hell, I might even come 'long with you. Extra pair of eyes, no extra charge."

Maggie offered up her best smile. "Speaking of charges..."

It took most of the morning of the first day for Maggie to get used the rhythmic thrump of the rotors. She had never flown in a helicopter before; a fact which (when she thought about it) somehow surprised her, considering all the accident and police chase stories she'd covered when she'd been a news reporter. The gravity-defying, side-slipping motion, so different than that of fixed wing aircraft, might have made her airsick if her concentration on the mission wasn't so acute. Besides, she wasn't exactly warm in the Plexiglas bubble. She hadn't given any thought as to what to wear, and had come to the airport dressed in only slacks and a sweater. Connie Thompson, who neither looked or talked like his older brother, had loaned her one of his nylon jackets, but it wasn't helping much.

Lucifer's Children

Before takeoff, over the strongest cup of coffee she'd ever had, she'd been surprised yet again when the Thompson brothers told her they'd already mapped out a route. "We got to talkin' last night, Miz Ellis," Connie had said. "According to the flight plan you told Bud about, your husband's plane was on a direct line from Hickory to Nashville. "I called the Weather Service first thing this morning. They told me the weather that day was clear, not a cloud in the sky, with a steady northwest wind of about twelve knots."

"I don't understand what you're getting at," Maggie admitted.

"Let me try to explain what Connie's tryin' to say," Bud said. "If it had've been me flying that plane, knowing I had passengers who weren't used to flying in small craft, I wouldn't have flown over the mountains against a quartering wind. I would have taken off, then headed a little south, so I could cross flying directly against the wind. It would have been slower going, but a lot more comfortable for everybody aboard."

"Oh. I see what you mean," Maggie said. "So you think that's what Ted French did?"

"You said he was a very experienced pilot," Bud put in, "Connie and I figured that's what he probably did, and if he did, he would have flown way south of Asheville, made his turn to the northwest, then cut across the Great Smoky National Park at its most narrow part. That would have been smart flying, and that's where we ought to search. I think the State people and the Feds concentrated their search much further north of there."

And that was where they did look. Criss-crossing alternate grids of twenty miles wide, well into Tennessee and back.

For three days.

And found nothing.

With nearly numb fingers, Maggie wrote out a check for 900 dollars, handed it over with a wan smile to the apologetic brothers and left the office of Thompson Aviation, certain that the three-hundred dollar per-day quote she'd been given was maybe half, even a third, of their normal fee. She trudged to the parking lot, fighting back tears of disappointment. She unlocked the Honda, then sat behind the wheel for a few minutes regrouping. Talking to herself. "Okay, Maggie. You're a good anchor, and before that you were a damn good news reporter. The reason you were a good reporter was because you were patient. Also thorough. Never slopped over the details. The little things. Like a cop. All right, so the air search was a bust. That proves nothing. They're out there somewhere, and you know it. Face it. You're going to have to do this the hard way. Old fashioned leg work."

She stuck her chin out, reached forward to turn the starter switch, and patted the dashboard as if it were the neck of an old horse. "So be it. I hope you're up to this, old girl."

The Honda was up to it. Maggie paid no attention to the mileage the 'old girl' accumulated during the next week, carrying Maggie and Lena back to Hickory, then up 321 to Lenoir, past Grandfather Mountain and around Blowing Rock to Boone, then back south via 221 to Linville, down 19 to Spruce Pine, Burnsville, Mars Hill, Marshall, and every other town and village back toward Asheville, making inquiries and leaving flyers in store windows, service stations, cafes, even on telephone poles all along the way.

The printer had done a good job on the flyers. Good black-and-white likenesses of Robert and Bo Ellis smiled over the bold caption: HAVE YOU SEEN US? And, a plea to call the State Police.

Maggie was pleased— and not a little surprised— that Lena hadn't complained at all, not then, or when after a day's rest at the same motel in Asheville, they spent the following week visiting every town and crossroad hamlet between Chimney Rock and Sliding Rock. The beginning of the third week found them on narrow, winding roads that connected towns in the extreme western corner of the State, between old highway 64 and the Blue Ridge Parkway, south and east of the Great Smoky National

Park. Before the end of that third week, they had run out of flyers, and Lena was showing signs of running out of patience. "My back's bothering me, Margaret, and I don't have any feeling left in my backside."

Once more back at their Asheville motel "headquarters", Lena slept all day while Maggie went back to the printer's to order another thousand flyers, had the oil changed in the Honda, and checked in with the Highway Patrol. No phone calls had been reported. Both were too tired to eat that Monday night, and Maggie went into the bathroom and had her cry in the shower. When Lena, groaning from a stiff "everything", went in for her own bath, Maggie turned the TV volume down, leaned back on two propped-up pillows, reached for the phone, and dialed Sam's number. It rang only once.

"Maggie? For God's sake, honey, I've been worried sick. It's been over two weeks since you called."

"I know. I'm sorry."

Sam's tone softened. "How's it going?"

"I had to come back to Asheville. Ran out of flyers. How's everything there?"

"The same. You know how it is. Everyone misses you. I miss you."

"That's nice to hear, boss-man. I miss you, too."

"How's your mother holding up?"

"She's been a regular soldier so far, but we both need a couple days rest."

"Where have you been?"

"Where haven't I been! I've seen more towns in this state than Charles Kuralt. I think Lena's enjoyed it all so far, the scenery, I mean, but it's taking its toll."

"Honey, why don't you..."

"Go ahead and say it. Why don't I give up and come home? You know I can't do that, Sam. Not yet. There's one more place I have to go near here, then I'll start in Tennessee."

"Which place?"

"The reservation. The Cherokee Indian Reservation."

"Look, Maggie, I've got some time coming to me. You want me to—"

"No. No, Sam. This is something I have to do."

"Yeah. Yeah, I know. But please call me more often, okay? I worry about you."

"I know. I love you, Sam Abrahms."

"I love you, too, Maggie Ellis."

"Bye, Sam."

Lena came out of the bathroom, brushing her hair. "You should marry that man, Margaret. Should have married him already, in spite of how Bo felt— feels."

"You're right, Mama." Maggie, said with a sigh, closing her eyes. She was so tired.

Lena sat down on her bed, resumed her brushing and said, "All right, I'll change the subject. You remember the name of that pretty little town we were in yesterday?"

Maggie answered without opening her eyes. "Which one? They all look the same to me, now. You mean Carew?"

"No, the one before that. You know, the one down in that sweet little valley."

"Kaneville?"

"That's it. Kaneville."

"What about it?"

"That has to be the weirdest place I ever saw. I mean, it was real pretty, but it was...I don't know, funny."

"Funny." Maggie was so—oo tired.

"Well, peculiar. While you were talking to that man at the cafe, I walked down the street a few blocks. I didn't see one other man the whole time I was walking. Nothing but women. Women and kids. Where were all the men? If that wasn't strange enough, it looked to me like almost every one of those women I saw was young. Younger than you, and just about every one of them looked like they were pregnant. I never saw so many pregnant women on one street in my life. Weird."

"Uh-huh. Weird."

Lucifer's Children

"Then I noticed the church."

"Church."

"Pretty little white church, but that was weird, too. I mean, we were there on Sunday morning, but nobody was going in and out of it. Plus, every church I've ever seen has some kind of sign out front, like First Baptist Church, or First Methodist Church, or St. Paul's or whatever. This church didn't have any sign. Couldn't tell what kind it was. Might have even been a synagogue for all I know."

"Synagogue." Maggie's voice was a faint whisper.

"And I'll tell you what was more weird than that. All the time I was walking around and when we drove out of town, I looked, but I didn't see any cemetery. Every little town we've been to had a cemetery. No way anybody could miss seeing them. I notice things like that. But this Kaneville…I swear, I don't think they have one there."

"M-mm."

"There sure wasn't one behind that little church. You know something else, Margaret? One of those women I saw looked just like that blonde who was sitting next to Robert in that plane when it took off from Myrtle— Margaret?"

Lena put her brush down, got up and pulled the sheet over her sleeping daughter's body. "Stubborn thing. Didn't hear a word I said, did you?"

Lena turned Maggie's bedside light out, sat back down on her own bed and resumed brushing her long black hair.

ॐ

Chapter 9

Robert hadn't seen Beth climb the steps to the porch. When he turned to go back inside to see about his son, Beth blocked the door. "No, Robert, let me take care of Bo. You go on down. Abner's waiting for you."

Robert stared at Beth, whose face had compassion written all over it. In a croaking voice, he said, "Beth, for God's sake, tell me I didn't really see what I thought I saw down there."

Beth bit her lip, but didn't answer him. Her eyes said it all. Robert shook his head slowly. He felt weak in the knees. "It was Ted's body down there, wasn't it? Tell me you haven't been putting parts of him in that stew." He grabbed Beth's upper arms fiercely. Shook her. "Tell me, damn you!"

Beth's lower lip was trembling. Her eyes filled, but she remained silent. Robert felt another wave of nausea rising from deep in his gut. He thought he might faint. Struggling to fight off the enormous feeling of self loathing and disgust, his voice a mere whisper, he said, "Sweet Jesus, it's true, isn't it? We're all...we've become cannibals. But, why?" He shook Beth again, so hard her hair fell down across her face. "There's plenty of food... Meat, without eating..." He couldn't finish the sentence. Couldn't bring himself to say the words

Beth finally spoke, her own voice hoarse. "I couldn't help it, Robert. There was nothing I could... You'd better go down. Abner will explain everything. I'll look after Bo."

Robert released her, pulling his hands away from her arms as if he'd suddenly realized he had grabbed a leper. A ghoul. "Abner. Oh yeah. Abner will explain it all." Another emotion seized in Robert's chest. Anger. Unadulterated, white-hot anger. "You better fucking believe it."

Holding onto the rail because he didn't trust his legs not to collapse under him, he somehow made his way down the steps to the valley floor. Abner Highsmith, rifle casually slung over one broad shoulder, was waiting at the edge of the river. He lifted a hand in warning as Robert approached. One eye on the rifle, remembering that Abner had already shot both his earlobes off, Robert, who'd been ready to verbally explode, suddenly felt a cautionary pang of prudence, and waited for Abner to speak first.

"I am exceedingly sorry your son found my cold room before it was time for me to tell you of it. It appears I have underestimated both his progress and his curiosity. Well, what's done is done. Before you say anything, let's walk a ways. Exercise is a powerful cure for the poison of bad temper."

Without another word, Abner turned and started walking south. Robert had no choice but to follow. Seething, he caught up with the man and matched his stride. Highsmith kept his eyes forward, not even giving Robert the satisfaction of a side-glance. After maybe two hundred yards, Robert's impotent first question was, "Where are we going?"

They walked yet another ten paces before Abner answered. "To the other end of the valley. It is time you met my friend."

"Munoz?"

"Yes."

This unexpected turn of events caused Robert to clam up himself for another hundred yards or so. Then he couldn't resist asking, "Why did you shoot at me? I heard your voice loud and clear. If you'd told me to come down, I would have. I wasn't trying to get away."

"I know. You would never leave your son behind. But you were searching for a way out of the valley. I could not allow that."

"What if I had been willing to leave Bo. What if I really was trying to escape?"

Abruptly, Abner stopped. He looked at Robert with an indulgent smile. "I would have killed you. I could have put a bullet between your eyes as easily as I nicked your ears."

Robert shivered in spite of himself. "You're that good a shot?"

"Yes."

Robert had no trouble believing him. Anger welled up again. "And what would you have done then? Skin me and eat me? Cut me up in small pieces and cook me in that big pot?"

Abner sighed, looked down at the ground for a moment, and then looked back at Robert with a totally changed expression. The cold blue eyes seemed softer. "Robert, you are a man of considerable intelligence. It is only natural for you to doubt and perhaps deride what has happened to you, Miss Beth, and your fine young son, but you cannot deny the truth of it. You have already seen enough convincing proof. What I am going to tell you now is also the truth. Your ability to accept it, and live, depends on your ability to put aside your reactionary emotions and listen with an open mind. If you cannot, you will die. Here and now on this very spot.

"First, you cannot escape from this valley. None of you can. You must live here the rest of your lives, just as I must, albeit at an age you choose, young, middle-aged, or old. And yes, your new youth and health will be sustained by periodic consumption of human flesh, along with water from the river. At the moment, you may consider such a prospect revolting, but I assure you it is something you will soon become accustomed to, just as you once did the taste of fine spirits.

"Secondly, your crash was no accident. You were sent for. Brought here on purpose. You, Bo, and Beth each have unique gifts, which are needed here. That is why you are still alive. Mr. French, unfortunately, possessed no particular gift other than some skill as a pilot; a means of transporting you to this valley, yet his body and brain have also served an important purpose, which you unfortunately discovered before I had time to explain it to you, as I did with Miss Beth.

"I fully realize that what I am saying to you now is compounding the hundreds of questions you have already formulated, and which will eventually be answered to your satisfaction. Contrary to what you may have thought, I am not insane. As well, I could certainly give you answers to many of those questions. However, that is not my job. Others can and will."

"Others?"

"Yes. Beginning with Lieutenant Munoz. That is where I am taking you. To his home. His house, where he will open the doors to your future."

"What kind of future?"

"One quite beyond your wildest dreams. That is, if you desire it. Now. Do you want to live like a prince? Or die right here and now and, as you so graphically put it, be cut up in small pieces, so that others may live longer?"

"You'd actually do it? Butcher me like a hog, in cold blood?"

"I would indeed."

Robert's thoughts raced backwards. When Ted's plane had gone out of control and he'd known it was going to crash, he'd felt real, palpable fear for the first time in his life. Now, looking into those deadly blue eyes, he felt it again. Only worse. His choice was simple. "I want to live."

"Of course you do. Let's go, then. Senor Munoz is waiting."

They covered the remaining half-mile down the valley floor in silence. With each step, Robert's mind, so close to overload, began reducing his tacit thoughts to the smallest common denominator: He knew he was not dreaming. This nightmare was real. But he was alive, and very much wanted to stay that way. He remembered Bo's question. What if it's all true?

What if the unbelievable, the unthinkable, was true, and he could, if he chose to, live for hundreds of years, at say, age thirty or so. Would he really want to? One thing was certain:

Tom Lewis

The alternative was far, far less palatable. Highsmith's words— and his rifle— had convinced him of that. Still, even if it took a hundred years, two hundred, he'd find a way out of this place. Sure, he could, and would, play along with Highsmith, Munoz, and who or whatever else came along, but the bottom line was, he knew he was a captive. A prisoner. And he knew that someday, he would have to make a choice. A choice between literal slavery and freedom.

But Robert Ellis also knew himself. He wondered if when the time came, whether he would have the guts to make the right decision. And, there was also his son to consider. What would Bo— ?

"Here we are." Highsmith's voice broke Robert's chain of thought. He stopped, looked at Abner, then back at the wall of solid rock they stood facing. Abner smiled, then reached forward and gently pushed. As if it rested on unseen greased bearings, a portion of the granite silently opened into a passageway large enough to drive a truck through. As they stepped forward, into what seemed to be a long tunnel, the rock door closed behind them, and as the outside light disappeared, a new light, artificial of course, but with no apparent source, flooded the tunnel with the same kind of soft glow Robert had noticed in Abner's grisly cold-storage locker. Their moccasined feet made no sound as they walked down the tunnel for a distance Robert judged to be about a hundred yards, ending at a massive wooden door with no latch handle or doorknob. Robert glanced at Abner, to see if he would knock, but Abner simply stood still, smiling. Robert found that his heartbeat was surprisingly steady. He felt no new trepidation. Only a strange calm. The door opened inward, as quietly as had the outer rock-door.

Before them stood a slightly built man dressed in a flowing white robe that came down to his ankles. His small feet wore sandals. Robert looked back up into a dark face, made darker by the black beard and moustache of a Spanish Grandee; an ascetic face, with soft, deep-set brown eyes. The wide smile showed small, pearl-white teeth. From behind them came a voice of practiced authority, in English, and with an accent that sounded to Robert exactly like Ricardo Montalban. "Ah, yes. Mr. Ellis. Robert. Welcome to my house. We shall have a small luncheon, and then I have much to show you. Please, do come in. This way..."

Robert followed, not noticing that Abner Highsmith had not come through the door, which closed behind him without a sound.

⚘

Tom Lewis

CHAPTER 10

Cherry blossoms along the Potomac had long since disappeared, but the view, the warm weather, indeed the entire atmosphere at the river's edge was, to Ramon's way of thinking, far more pleasant than walking the banks of the filthy Tiber. Ramon was enjoying his visit to the American capitol. True to his promise, Cardinal Zimmer had not saddled him with any duties at all, not even taking notes of meetings they'd attended together, nor asking him to listen while he practiced his long-memorized speech, which was to be given the following evening. He'd also been pleased to discover that the Jesuits had not been at all hostile. On the contrary, they'd gone out of their way to make the visiting Cardinal and his secretary comfortable and welcome.

The guest house they'd been given for their stay was practically a mansion, and they'd been waited on hand and foot, belaying Zimmer's suspicions completely, and delighting Ramon, who had found several new friends with whom he'd already enjoyed lively, intellectual conversations, heavy meals, and altogether genial companionship. He picked up a small stone and skipped it across the slow moving river which seemed in such contrast to the helter-skelter traffic of downtown Washington. He felt light-hearted. Almost like a boy again. Four days with absolutely nothing to do! He looked up at the blue sky dotted with white cotton balls. "*Grazie, grazie. Mille grazie.*"

It was almost three in the afternoon when he found himself standing before the venerable university's library, his smile self-chiding. Trust his feet to carry him to yet another source of learning. Old habits are hard to break. He entered, walked around aimlessly, without any objective in mind at all. He smiled yet again, noticing the serious, concentrating students, oblivious to all around them, digging out answers to assignments. They reminded him of himself; at the Seminary in Mexico City, and later at Rome, where he'd done plenty of that. Plenty.

Without realizing why, he found himself picking up a thick volume someone had carelessly left lying on an empty table.

CATHOLIC CHURCHES OF NORTH AMERICA
A Pictorial

He sat down and began idly turning pages. All of a sudden, he knew he was looking for something. Not a cathedral. Not a colossal monument to God, but a particular church. A small, insignificant stone church set somewhere amongst a stand of pine trees. He found it fifteen minutes later, on page 489. St. Andrew's. In Chapel Hill, North Carolina. The black-and-white image was exactly the same as in his latest dreams. Brick for brick. Stone for stone. The same stained-glass windows. Ramon felt a trickle of sweat under his collar. His breathing became faster. For several minutes he silently studied the grainy photograph, turning the book so that the light didn't glare on the slick page. At last, he closed it, picked it up, carried it to the desk and quietly asked the reference librarian to show him everything they had on the State of North Carolina. There was quite a lot, and before he was finished, he had missed his dinner hour. Before he left the library, he consulted the map department, and was surprised to discover that he was no more than two hundred miles or so from Chapel Hill, home of the main campus of The University of North Carolina. Only a few miles from the state's capitol, Raleigh. He could be there within hours, even on a bus.

He left the library walking fast, paying no attention to the marvelous sunset, which had colored the Potomac blood-red.

Tom Lewis

"I'm Daniel O'Connor, Monsignor. I'm honored to meet you. How can I help you?"

Ramon smiled sheepishly at the sixty-ish, owl-faced Pastor of St. Andrews. He was at a complete loss as to give the bespectacled priest a real reason for his visit. Not without lying. This he was reluctant to do. He realized O'Connor was naturally suspicious, maybe even alarmed that a well-known officer of the Curia had showed up at his door like an inquisitor, totally unexpected and unannounced. His training and instincts told him the best way to allay the poor man's anxiety would be to get him talking about himself. "I'm sorry, Father, I certainly don't mean to cause you any concern. The truth is, I had a free day or two, and simply wanted to see your church. I've never been to this part of the country before, either. It's lovely here, and you have a beautiful church. Do you have a large flock?"

"No. A few hundred is all. Don't forget, you're in Bible Belt country down here. Lots of Baptists, Methodists, Pentecostal, and such. There are probably almost as many synagogues around here as catholic churches. Still, I keep busy. Especially since I lost my assistant a few months ago. So far, my Bishop hasn't replaced him. I hope he does before football season starts."

"Football season? I don't understand. What's that got to do with it?"

Father O'Connell grinned at him. "There are three major universities and several other, smaller, colleges within a short drive of here, Monsignor. All of them recruit athletes from all over the country, in every sport. You may not realize it, but collegiate athletics are a huge part of the big picture in this area. Many of those students are minorities, mostly blacks, often from some ghetto somewhere, and a good number of those are Catholic, sort of, anyway. I've been a big sports fan all my working life, most of which has been right here in this church. I do a lot of informal, unofficial counseling in addition my regular duties as Pastor. I guess you could say that over the years, I've developed a bit of a reputation. Student athletes often come to me for advice, and there's a new batch of them every fall."

"I see. You're like a father figure to them. No pun intended."

O'Connor laughed. "Your wit is as good as your English, Monsignor. Yes, I guess I'm kind of a southern Father Flanagan in a way. I enjoy it, though it's hard to keep some of these young men focused these days."

"I can imagine. I envy you."

"Really? Why?"

Ramon sighed. He hadn't meant to say the last part of that sentence. It had just come out. But he was glad he'd said it. It was something he'd thought a great deal about for many years, but had never allowed himself to express it. To anyone. "I've been a priest for a long time, Father, but I've never served as pastor in a diocese church. Not even as assistant. I've never brought one single soul to God."

O'Connor showed his own diplomatic skill. "The powers that be have obviously deemed it best to use your talents in other ways, Monsignor. From what I have heard and read about your work, Mother Church has been wise to do so. You should be proud that you have mended so many fences of the already converted."

"Pride can be a sin, Father."

"Not that kind of pride."

Ramon shifted gears. "Would you show me your church?"

"Certainly."

Ramon followed the fatherly father through the short tour. The church itself was truly pretty, inside and out. It was also warm. Comfortable. After making a call to Georgetown, he spent two days and nights there, as O'Connor's guest.

And slept like a baby.

Peter Rolf Zimmer rarely used the considerable power of a Cardinal for his own comfort, but when it came to flying, he bent his own rules ever so slightly. He always chose Lufthansa when he could; not because he was himself a German, but because he simply considered it the best airline. The one with the fewest problems. He was aware that creature comforts of all the major airlines had slipped in recent years, but not too much in First Class. Besides, one would have to be inhuman not to accept at least some of the extra attention and respect given to one dressed as he was. If only they would serve a decent wine now and then. Ah well. He'd soon be home. Home. He allowed himself a silent chuckle. It was funny how he no longer thought of Munich as home. Germany either. Home was now the walled City-state of the Holy Roman Church. His Spartan (as Peter Reilly termed it, though it boasted five rooms) apartment sequestered deep within those ancient and holy walls. It suited him, and he no longer liked to leave it for long periods of time. Thinking of it, he frowned. If the Holy Father took Ramon from him – and there was a better than good chance he would — more long-distance travelling would surely be in the offing. He knew he would never find anyone else like Ramon, and that fact bothered him, but if it was God's will—and John Paul's—that Ramon ply his craft at a higher level, he'd have to fly Lufthansa more often. Worse, some of the countries he'd have to visit might have no better means of transportation than bumpy trains or smelly buses. Ah well.

  He wondered how Ramon was faring back in coach. The boy had certainly looked better after his strange trip to North Carolina. A good deal better. He had to admit he'd been a tiny bit miffed when Ramon had called—less than an hour before his speech—asking if he could stay a day or two. No reason given for the request nor for the trip in the first place. No matter. The speech had gone well enough, and the Jesuits had treated him nicely, though he'd doubted their sincerity from beginning to end. Next time he saw Peter, they'd have some fun talking about—

  "Please excuse me, your Eminence."

Lucifer's Children

Zimmer looked up. The face of the ecclesiastically well-informed flight attendant was white as her starched blouse. She'd spoken to him quietly, in English, but with a certain tone. "You may speak *auf deutsch*, Fraulein, I am as German as you," he said with a smile.

The blond, blue-eyed girl couldn't have been more than nineteen or twenty, but the tastefully applied makeup she was wearing couldn't hide the anxiety behind her whisper, so much so that she continued right along in English, "There is a priest back in row fifteen-D. Do you know him?"

"Father Barillas? Yes, we are travelling together. Why?"

"He is—there is a problem. I don't want to disturb you, but—"

Cardinal Peter Zimmer was out of his comfortable chair in a flash, tearing aside the curtain that separated the two class sections, and hurrying down the aisle. He heard the screams even before he noticed the knot of people hovering over the passenger in 15-D. *Was ist denn los, hier?* Ramon's face was contorted in great pain. He was thrashing about, restrained only by his seatbelt, holding his head, screaming in agony with every breath. Zimmer ignored the horrified stares of those he passed and those clustered around his protégé. They made way for him, and he knelt down. 15-D was an aisle seat, *Gott sei dank*.

The frightened woman in the seat next to Ramon was leaning as far from him as she could, terror in her eyes. "He was just sleeping! Then, he started—"

"It's all right, my child," Zimmer said in his most calming voice. He grabbed Ramon's face with both hands. "Ramon. What is it, my son? What's the matter?"

"Head...Headache...Bad...So bad." Then he screamed again.

Zimmer, for the first time in his life, began to feel helpless. Totally useless. He was about to start praying, the only thing he knew to do, when a voice came from behind him. He turned to see a portly man dressed in an expensive suit.

"Excuse me, please. Let me through. I'm a doctor."

Tom Lewis

Zimmer, along with the others, including the three lip-biting attendants, made way for the chubby-faced physician, who looked down at Ramon, felt his forehead, pursed his lips, and said to Zimmer, "Migraine. I see this all the time. Some even worse." The doctor straightened, looked around, seeking out the most senior of the flight attendants, whose forefinger was clamped between perfect white teeth. "Come with me, please."

Zimmer watched the two of them retreat down the aisle all the way back to the station between the two toilets. He saw the attendant nod, seemingly suddenly relieved, then reach into one of the metal cabinets that were always so ingeniously built into the fuselage. She produced a white brief-case-like container with a red cross stenciled on the top. The doctor opened it, rummaged until he found what he wanted, then, like a sailor on the rolling deck of a ship, came waddling toward them, holding a hypodermic needle in one hand, a cotton swab in the other.

Without ceremony, or apparent respect for the rank of a Cardinal, he curtly commanded Zimmer to roll up Ramon's left sleeve. Zimmer did as he was told, and the doctor, who still hadn't mentioned his name, sought a vein, found one, and plunged the needle into it. Zimmer watched. The glass container had seemed full. He had no idea of how many CC's were squirted into Ramon's blood stream, nor what the substance was. As if reading his mind, the doctor said, "Demerol. He'll settle down in a minute or two." He eyed the senior attendant again. "We should move him back to the rear, where he'll be more comfortable, if someone will change seats with him. How long until we land?"

The flustered flight attendant, hearing a familiar question, instantly glanced at her watch and responded, a professional again. "Not for four more hours, sir."

The doctor nodded, as if he were talking to his nurse. "You have plenty of ice on board?"

"Yes, sir."

"Good. Then keep a very cold towel on his head until we land, just in case it isn't a migraine. It may be an aneurysm."

"Yes, sir. I understand."

Several people volunteered to assist with moving the already woozy patient back to the rear, and after Cardinal Zimmer calmly asked the concerned and the curious to retake their seats, assuring all that the young priest would certainly be all right, he turned to the physician and thanked him profusely.

"No problem, the fat man said. "It's what I do."

"And you apparently do it well. What is your name, my son?"

"Wittstein. Herbert Wittstein, and I'm not 'your son'. "

"Ah. God bless you, anyway, Dr. Herbert Wittstein," said the frail Prince of the Church, without missing a beat. "You are one of His, you know."

Before the blanket of darkness enveloped him completely, Ramon knew the pain was receding rapidly. So was the sea of faces in front of him.

All but one.

She had turned around in the hot tub to face him. His eyes had moved from the two full breasts to the neck, around which she wore a small gold chain with a tiny pendant in the shape of a footprint. A footprint with a black heel. Then his eyes had beheld the face, which had been kept from his view for thirty-five years. The headache had commenced the instant he realized that if he'd been a woman, he would have been looking at his own face. She was a mirror image of himself. Enough so to have been his identical twin. Hair was the same. Eyes the same. Nose the same. Mouth the same. Lips the same, and, they were moving, not smiling. They were forming silent words. "Help me. I need you. Help me, please."

༄

Tom Lewis

Chapter 11

Twice more on the drive from Asheville to Cherokee, Lena alluded to the unusual things she had noticed in the small town of Kaneville, and twice Maggie promised her mother they would go by there again before they ventured into Tennessee. Though she'd been exhausted the night before, and had heard less than half of what Lena had been saying about Kaneville, Maggie was nonetheless happy Lena had showed interest in something other than the local tourist-trap souvenir-shop spots they had encountered in practically every little town they'd stopped in. This thought was underscored when Lena didn't squawk once as they passed by Santa Land, the Cyclorama, and Frontierland as they made their approach to Cherokee on US 19.

They crossed the swift *Oconaluftie* just after noon, turned right on US 441 and cruised slowly past the "business" part of the village, following the signs to the parking area, which was already full. Maggie turned the Honda around, then stopped and pointed. "Look, Mama, there's a hot dog stand. Why don't you hop out and have a look around. I'll meet you back here in half an hour."

"Where are you going?"

"I noticed the police station back there just before we crossed the bridge. I think I'll start there."

"All right. Half an hour?"

"Shouldn't take more than that. I don't want to start tacking up these flyers without somebody's permission."

Lena nodded and got out, heading not toward the open-air food stand, but to the arts and crafts building, just as Maggie knew she would. Maggie backtracked through the heavy tourist traffic and pulled into the Police station parking lot, which also served as the lot for the bus station. Carrying a handful of the flyers, she walked inside. A burly, uniformed man, long hair braided in a pigtail and wearing sergeant stripes, looked up from the front desk. "Can I help you?"

"I hope so. I'm Margaret Ellis. Are you the officer in charge?"

"No, ma'am. Chief Hand is."

"Could I please speak to him a minute?" Maggie hoped her smile showed she was not having some kind of emergency. The smile worked. With one of his own, the desk sergeant punched an intercom button. "Chief, there's a lady out here needs to see you. You real busy?"

"No," the metallic voice answered, "Send her in."

The desk officer got up from his chair and opened the door for her.

Chief Thomas Hand was even bigger a man than his sergeant. He wore his thick, graying hair in a crew cut, and a warm smile cut across a broad face that would have been handsome if not for the deep pocks of old acne scars. He stood, resting knuckles on his polished desk. "I'm Tommy Hand, ma'am. Please have a seat."

Maggie sat on the front edge of one of the two comfortable armchairs, holding the flyers in her lap. Chief Hand moved from behind his desk and casually sat down in the other one, as if he had guessed Maggie wasn't there to talk about a stolen purse or lost dog. Maggie liked the man instantly.

"What can I do for you, Miss—"

"Ellis. Margaret Ellis, Chief Hand. "I'd like to ask your permission to distribute some of these." She handed him one of the flyers. It took her only ten of her self-allotted thirty minutes to explain her mission. In all the time she was talking, Chief Tommy Hand never lifted his eyes from the flyer. It was as if he was committing to memory every line and feature of Bo's and Robert's faces as well as the brief printed text. "My mother and I have placed these in practically every town in western North

Carolina. I would appreciate your allowing me to scatter some around Cherokee as well."

"I can't give you permission to do that," Hand said, then watching Maggie's face cloud with disappointment, added, "Don't get me wrong, I personally wouldn't mind, but the decision is not mine to make. Our Tribe Council will have to clear it. They usually frown on things like that, or anything else that might distract the tourists. We have a few small businesses going on the reservation, but our primary means of income is still tourism. But you may be in luck. Pure coincidence. The Council is meeting this afternoon at three o'clock. Open tribal meeting. I happen to be one of the seven Council members. Tell you what I can do. I could ask them to— No, wait a minute. Better still, why don't you let me introduce you and you can tell them what you just told me. With so many of our people out there in the audience who would most likely be sympathetic, I doubt if the Council would dare turn you down." Hand grinned at her. "Fair enough?"

"More than fair. I can't thank you enough."

"Don't thank me yet. Go have some lunch, then meet me at the Council House about ten till three. It's the big building just this side of the Museum and Culture Center." He held up the flyer he'd been studying. "And bring these with you. My guess is we'll have plenty of volunteers to pass them around."

Maggie hadn't been out of Hand's office two minutes before he reached for his phone and punched in the series of numbers of a private phone in the office of Sheriff Clay Yancey in Lee County.

"Yancey speaking."

"Sheriff, this is Tommy Hand, over in Cherokee."

"Yeah, Tommy?"

"She's here. Just left my office."

"We know. Everything's in place. Thanks for calling."

Chief Hand put the phone down with a smile. He glanced at his watch, and the smile became a frown. He'd known better than to ask what was "in place." Besides, he had more to worry about. He was already behind on his monthly reports, and today's meeting was sure to be another long one. For three years now, he and two other Council members had effectively sidetracked all discussion of bringing gambling onto the reservation. He knew it was inevitable. It would eventually happen. Tribes in other states were getting rich from it, but he hoped he and his cousins could keep it out for another five or ten years. After that, well, he'd be too old to worry about it, and he already had more money than he could ever spend. He glanced at his watch again. Just enough time to get home, have a bite to eat, and change clothes.

      Public speaking was not Maggie's forte. She was used to looking in the lens of a camera and reading from a TelePrompTer, not facing a live audience of two hundred strangers from a raised dais without a microphone. When she began talking, careful to project her voice and speak slower than she normally would, she couldn't tell whether the faces in the crowd were friendly or hostile, and she was nearly thrown off her rhythm when one woman who was sitting in the front row stood up, smiled at her, then silently moved up the carpeted aisle and left the room. But Maggie finished her plea with, she thought, just enough passionate tone as not to be melodramatic. There was a smattering of applause from the room. Chief Hand rose from his chair, shook her hand and said, "I'll show you out."

      He walked with Maggie and Lena to the parking lot. When they reached the car, he said. "I think you made a good impression. They'll discuss it for a few minutes, but I'm sure they'll vote yes. We're a fairly emotional people. Why don't you leave me a couple hundred of those flyers. I'll make sure they're placed in conspicuous places all over the reservation."

      Maggie handed him a stack and thanked him again.

      "No problem, Mrs. Ellis. I'm sorry I can't take the time to show you around the town, but before you leave, you might buy a souvenir trinket or two. Every little bit helps, you know." Turning to go, and with a twinkle in his dark brown eyes, he added, "Just make sure they don't have a tag on them that says Made in Taiwan."

An hour later, with two hand-made baskets resting on the back seat, They started back to Asheville. "We might as well, Mama. It's too late to try to drive to Kaneville. Come to think of it, I don't remember seeing a motel there anyway. Besides, I need to go over my map of eastern Tennessee again, and we both need one more good night's sleep."

Lena sighed loudly. "I think it's all a waste of time, Margaret. This whole fiasco. It's like looking for a needle in a haystack. We won't ever find them,"

Maggie set her jaw, determined not to respond to her mother's cliché, knowing it would start an argument that would last all the way back to Asheville. She'd been wondering when Lena's usual attitude would kick in.

She was about to pass a slow-moving car when she saw something out of the corner of her eye that caused her to ease her foot off the accelerator and fall back behind the car in front of her. It was a woman, holding a small child and hitch hiking. It took a moment or two before Maggie's mind, like a card-sorting machine, matched the face with that of the Indian woman who'd walked out of the council meeting while she had been talking. "Did you see that woman?"

"What woman?" Lena said.

Maggie glanced rapidly in the rear view mirror, then right, left, and forward to see where she might turn around. They were coming up to Santa Land. Maggie gave a left turn signal and slowed down. Three or four on-coming cars passed before she could turn. She wheeled into the gravel parking lot and did a one-eighty.

"What woman, Margaret? What are you stopping for?"

"It's the woman who got up and left the meeting right in the middle of my talk. She's out there hitch hiking. I'm going back."

"What for?"

"To give her a ride." Maggie pulled back onto the highway, heading west.

"Are you crazy? Nobody picks up hitch hikers these days."

"She was carrying a little child."

"I don't care if she was carrying the baby Jesus. Are you out of your mind?"

But Maggie was remembering the smile the woman had given her as she'd stood. There had been something behind that smile. Something enigmatic. Something—

"Margaret, we can't do this," Lena protested.

"Sure we can. She's probably not going more than a mile or so."

At that remark, Lena's mouth and the thoughts behind it got ugly. Maggie ignored her mother's tirade, concentrating on where to turn around again. Because of the traffic, she had to go all the way back to the police-bus station lot. She doubled back and pulled over to the shoulder, just past where the woman was standing. The woman hurried to the car, opened the back door and slid in. Maggie noticed the child she was holding was probably no more than a year old, obviously fast asleep, with a pacifier jammed in its mouth. Maggie couldn't tell whether it was a boy or girl. "How far are you going?"

"To the airport in Asheville. I missed the last bus. It's very kind of you to stop, Mrs. Ellis."

Maggie glanced sideways at Lena, who sat like a statue, arms crossed, staring straight ahead. "Well, you're in luck. We're staying at the Day's Inn. Not too far from the airport. I can run you by there. It's not much out of our way. Besides, It must have been my fault you missed your bus."

"It's all right. I wanted to hear your talk. I'm sorry about your son and your husband."

Maggie checked traffic again and pulled out onto the highway. "This is my mother, Lena." Lena never moved a muscle.

"Nice to meet you, ma'am. My name is Alice. Alice Crowfeather. I've been keeping my grandson for a few days while my daughter and her husband were in Washington. You've saved my life! I didn't think anyone was going to stop."

Maggie caught a glimpse of Alice Crowfeather's face in the rear view mirror. Her features were plain, but her face was unlined. Her coarse black hair was pulled back, held behind her head by a red band, but flowing down over her shoulders. She wore no makeup at all, and Maggie thought she couldn't be more than a few years younger than Lena. It suddenly struck her that the woman hadn't had the baby in her arms at the meeting. Maybe she'd left the child with her own husband while she'd gone to the Council meeting. She let the thought pass. "You live on the reservation?"

"Oh, yes. I'm the Tribe's historian."

"Really? Do you teach at the school I saw there?"

"No, not at the school."

Maggie decided to let that one also pass. "Well, I hope we can get you to the airport in time to meet your daughter's plane. Do she and her husband live on the reservation, too?"

"No. My daughter married outside the Tribe. So many of our people do nowadays. Soon, there won't be any full-blooded Cherokee left, I'm afraid."

"That's a shame." Maggie took another glance to her right. Lena hadn't budged, let alone open her mouth to speak. She and the Indian woman fell silent, too. Maggie concentrated on her driving, while Alice Crowfeather softly chanted bits and pieces of what Maggie guessed to be old Indian lullabies to the child, who never made a peep in all the time it took to reach the airport. She double-parked in front of the terminal entrance long enough for the woman to get out, once more expressing profound gratitude. Maggie said good-bye, then drove back to the highway. "Well, Mama, are you disappointed? Neither one of us got scalped."

Lena pouted through dinner and most of the night, while Maggie studied her map, penciling in the route they'd take the next morning. She was almost ready to ask Lena if she didn't want to take a bus back home when someone knocked on the door. Maggie and Lena looked at each other, and Maggie looked at her watch. It was nearly eleven.

"Who the devil could that be?" Lena wanted to know.

"No Idea," Maggie replied. She got up, cracked the door, then opened it wide. Alice Crowfeather was standing there, smiling.

Astonished, all Maggie could think of to say was, "Mrs. Crowfeather! How did you get here?"

"I walked."

For the first time, Lena, standing, piped up, "What are you doing here? What do you want from us?"

Alice Crowfeather never even looked at Lena. She kept her eyes locked with Maggie's. "I think I may be able to help you find your son and your husband, Mrs. Ellis. I believe I know where they are."

Maggie stared at the woman another full minute before finding her voice. "Please, come in."

၈

Chapter 12

Like an experienced tour guide, Robert's goateed, white-clad host led him through a series of Moorish arches connecting a suite of spacious rooms that might have seemed much larger if not for the massive furniture each room contained. ("It's old, but so am I," Munoz said.) Tall candle stands and real chandeliers supplied a shadowy light that totally subtracted gloominess from the dark atmosphere. Robert could well imagine he was walking through a section of a medieval castle. Rich floral tapestries hung on every wall; of such large dimensions it was impossible to tell if the walls themselves were painted, paneled, or plastered. Nor did Robert notice any hanging pictures, portraits, or any other sort of decoration. He half expected to spot a niche or two with a statuette of the Virgin Mary, or at least a crucifix, but there was none.

There were also no windows.

The low ceilings sported thick oak beams, but Robert couldn't tell whether they were structural or cosmetic. Floors were of polished hardwoods, though oriental-type rugs covered more than half their area. In four of the rooms— three of which were bedrooms and one a casual living room— fires burned in sizeable open fireplaces, but Robert could not feel any discernable change in temperature when they passed though them.

They continued through a formal dining room containing a long, sheeted table with chairs for maybe thirty people into an adjoining, intimate alcove with small table and only two chairs resting on a floor of brightly colored tiles. Munoz gestured for Robert to take one of the chairs. Robert did, and glanced down. Before him was a silver dish with a folded napkin of fine linen, a knife and fork, and a silver wine goblet. There was only one place setting. Robert looked up, eyebrows raised.

Munoz sat, chin resting on clasped hands. He smiled over them. "I have already eaten." He unfolded tapered fingers, picked up the tiny silver bell that was the only other article on the table top, and rang it. The echoes of its tinkling in the enclosed alcove were still sounding when a stunning brunette appeared. She looked to Robert to be about twenty, was also dressed in a white robe and was carrying a large wooden bowl of mixed fruit, which she placed on the table. She smiled at both men, then left silently as she'd come in.

"Do eat, Robert," Munoz said. "You must surely be hungry. "

Robert didn't want to admit how much. "I am. For anything but meat." He was reaching for an apple when the dark-haired girl came back, this time with a decanter and another goblet, which she sat before Munoz. Before Robert could object, she poured both goblets half full, and left again. Robert's eye's followed her this time, and noticed that when she moved between where they were sitting and the light coming through the arch, she was obviously wearing nothing beneath the sheer robe. He looked quickly back at the goblet in his hand, then at Munoz. "I don't know if I ought to— "

"Ah, yes. I understand. However, you need not worry. Your former sickness will not return. Our water has cured that forever. Besides, this is an excellent Madeira. One of my favorites." As if to prove his point, or to assure Robert the wine was not full of poison, he clinked Robert's goblet, then drank a couple of swallows, smacking his lips. "Delicious."

Robert sipped. The tart taste of the wine activated his taste buds instantly. He sat the goblet down and went to work on the bowl of fruit, not bothering to peel any of it. He'd already made a healthy dent in the supply when the girl made yet another entrance, this time setting a platter of mixed cheeses and bread on the table and refilling their goblets.

"Thank you, Isabella," Munoz said. "You may leave the bottle. We shall be talking for a while."

The dark-haired beauty nodded and left again. Robert sliced some of the cheese, wondering what kind of relationship the girl had to Munoz. Maid? Cook? Daughter? Wife? Between mouthfuls, he commented, "Isabella. Beautiful name for a beautiful girl. First woman I've seen here besides Beth. She's quite a lady."

"Yes. Named for a queen who was also quite a lady. And, I can see you are curious about her. Isabella is one of my granddaughters. Or perhaps a great-grand daughter. I cannot remember which. Robert, look at me. How old do I seem to be? Be honest, please."

"Well, you look like you might be, what, sixty or so?"

Munoz beamed. "Excellent guess. It is important for me to maintain an apparent age appropriate to my duties, which I shall explain to you shortly, after you have finished your meal. In truth, I am closer to six hundred years than I am to sixty. I was not a young man when I came to this valley."

Robert stopped eating.

"I am certain Abner told you were brought here for a reason. That is true. So was I, a long time ago, and was as bewildered as you are now, only in my case, there was no one else here to assist me, at least not at first. Now, fortunately for you, there are many."

Robert took another cautious sip of wine.

"How much of your history studies have you retained, Robert?"

"Not much."

"No matter. Do you remember reading about Ponce De Leon?"

Bells went off in Robert's head. The river water. Fountain of Youth. Ponce De Leon. Eighth grade history lessons. Legends. "Wait. You're not telling me you are—"

"That fool De Leon? Of course not. But I was with him in 1513. I was with Columbus, too, on that poor soul's last voyage. Allow me to explain. In each expedition the Crown sent forth, a secretary was dispatched with it. A scribe, whose duty it was to record everything in writing. I was such a scribe. Educated as a youth by Dominican monks, and later by Court scholars at Madrid.

"I was sent with De Leon on his first expedition, and was quite as fascinated with finding the legendary water as he was. But Juan was a proud man, and stubborn. Those traits would eventually cost him his life when he made a second voyage to the peninsula we had named Florida. In any event, I disagreed with him as to the exact whereabouts of the life-giving river. We argued constantly, and he accused me of insubordination. Threatened to send me back to New Spain in chains. At last, taking with me a common soldier who Juan had ordered to be flogged several times, three horses, and a Seminole guide, I deserted Juan's camp. I made my way northwest, eventually finding this valley, and the river. It was not an easy journey."

Robert sipped his wine, fully expecting to feel even more light-headed, but the Madeira had no effect at all, except to further increase his appetite. He reached for the bread, sliced a large piece, and waited for Munoz to continue his narrative.

"It is most unfortunate you and your son must absorb all this in such a short period of time. Both Abner and I would have preferred to bring you along slowly. You must forgive us both. Here, time, as you know it, has little meaning. Nonetheless, we depend on your wit to overcome your doubt, and as for your son, he will soon find interesting activities to occupy his curiosity."

Robert munched on the fresh bread, not knowing exactly how to respond.

"I also wish to replace the fear and self-loathing you felt following Abner's warning shots and the results of young Bo's untimely discovery by revealing to you your future, and his. I count on your keeping an open mind, and that you exercise a fair amount of patience, knowing full well that it will be difficult for you. When you have finished eating, I want to show you something which will automatically answer many of the questions I can see in your eyes."

"I'm finished, thank you. It was good, too."

"You are welcome. Come. I would like to show you my, ah, office."

Robert followed his host through yet another series of doors and hallways, wondering how big Munoz's "house" really was. At last they stood before a stout door similar to the one at the entrance. Munoz opened it and showed Robert in.

The room was an enormous cylinder. Robert gasped when he saw, from floor to ceiling, what he took to be hundreds of closed circuit television monitors, with one monster color monitor and desk-chair-console in the middle of it all. Not one screen was blacked out. Munoz sat down behind the immense console, smiled at Robert and said, "There is your future, my friend. Your son's as well."

"It looks like the master control rooms for NBC, ABC, And CBS combined. What is it? Who are all those people? There must be a thousand or—"

"Far more than a thousand. What you are looking at are some of our classrooms. All part of our school."

"School?"

"Yes. The most advanced University in the history of the world. Nothing is left out of the curriculum. Absolutely nothing. Not even sports knowledge. That is why you were brought here. You will be an instructor in our sports program. An important one, too. You see, we know everything about you, Robert. Everything. From the time you were born. You were blessed with what is called a photographic memory, and over the years, you have amassed considerable knowledge of most international sports; history, techniques, trivia, personalities, etcetera. This knowledge is valuable to us, and in return for sharing it, teaching and broadcasting it, you will be compensated beyond anything you can imagine, including eternal youth, health, and something which we know is important to you— respect."

"And Bo?"

Lucifer's Children

"Ah, yes. Robert Junior. Bo possesses near genius intelligence, plus keen imagination. He will eventually become a full professor of computer technology. You may have already noticed, before you came to us, that is, that there is a tremendous expansion taking place in computer technology. I submit to you that what you have seen, to date, is only the tip of an iceberg, so to speak. What is about to take place with computers is like a hydrogen bomb exploding from striking a single match, and your son will be at the cutting edge of it all. He shall have an extraordinary life and career."

"It's...it's staggering."

"Yes. Tomorrow, I will personally take you both on a tour. But for tonight, please consider yourself my honored guest. I am rather busy at the moment, but Isabella will show you to your rooms. You will find new clothes and shoes in the closets, and—"

"What about Bo?"

"Bo will spend one more night with Abner, who has a most effective way of explaining things to younger people. Perhaps it comes from the loss of his own two sons."

"He really was...is a Civil War deserter?"

"Oh, yes. Abner was General Lee's best sharpshooter. Unfortunately, he was given the unenviable task of sniping. Shooting Union officers from extremely long distances. He was quite good at it, but his successes gave him little satisfaction. One night, he simply climbed down from his spotting tree and walked away from it all. He eventually made his way back to his home in Atlanta, only to find his home burned to the ground and his wife and children dead. After that, with no more stomach for war and killing, he turned his back on the ashes of Atlanta and the Confederacy, and began wandering aimlessly, like the fugitive he had become. That is when we sent for him. We needed his unique talents here in the valley. In any event, don't concern yourself about Bo. He will join us early tomorrow for your first day of orientation."

Tom Lewis

Munoz pushed a button on the console. "Isabella will be here in a moment. One word of caution, Robert. Isabella will take care of your needs for tonight; bring you dinner, show you to your bath, and generally help make you quite comfortable, but it will do no good to attempt questioning her. She is a mute. It would be impolite to embarrass her. Ah. Here she is now. Get a good night's rest, my friend. Tomorrow will be a full day."

Isabella led Robert down a corridor he hadn't previously seen, to a separate apartment, which included a bedroom with mammoth, canopied bed, a dining room, a small living room with yet another fireplace, and a bathroom that featured a sunken tub large enough for a Roman orgy. He noticed it was full, and steaming. The idea of a hot bath, an all-over hot bath, instead of washing himself from a basin of heated water in Abner's primitive cabin was suddenly very appealing. He turned and glanced at the smiling Isabella, who nodded, then pinched her nose and pointed to his leather outfit, apparently agreeing with him. She gestured for him to follow her back into the bedroom, where she opened the twin doors of a large closet. Robert had time to notice more than a dozen suits and shirts hanging there before she extracted a white robe exactly like the one she was wearing. With yet another smile, she discreetly left the bedroom, and Robert wasted no time peeling off his clothes. He wrapped himself in the robe and padded to the bathroom.

He had no more than settled into the pool, which featured ribbed steps leading from shallow to deep, when Isabella reappeared, carrying a tray with sweet-smelling ointments and soaps. Robert watched as the lovely girl first pinned her hair up, then shed her robe and, carefully balancing the tray, moved into the bath as well. The tray actually floated. From it, with her left hand, she picked up a small bottle. Her right hand reached to Robert's face, and gently closed his eyes. The first thing she expertly washed was his thick new head of hair.

Chapter 13

Crossing her legs under her, Alice Crowfeather sat on the floor between Maggie's and Lena's beds. The only parts of her that moved were her lips. "Your son and his father are alive. I am sure of it."

Lena, barely disguising her scorn, said, "What makes you so sure?"

The Native American woman lifted her head and gave Lena a look of infinite patience. "When I was a small child, my grandfather, who was then our people's historian, recognized that I had a certain gift. I could sometimes 'see' things others could not. I knew where ripe berries could be found. I knew the exact day the corn should be planted. I could tell who was going to have a boy-child or a girl-child. I knew when the first snow would come. I knew who was going to die, and when. Things like that. Most of my people laughed at me, but not my grandfather."

"Sounds like your grandfather was quite a guy." Maggie said.

"Yes. He was very old even then. The reason he knew of my gift was because he had it, too. He knew I would continue his work after his death. He was well over a hundred years old when he died. As you may imagine, I loved him very much."

"And you can, um, 'see' Bo and Robert?" Maggie asked.

"Yes. I can see them both, but they are not as they were before."

"How so?"

"They have changed. One is older and one is younger. They were both badly hurt, but are well, now."

"Oh, for God's sake, Margaret," Lena said, "You're not going to sit here and listen to this—"

"Mama, please!" Maggie gave her mother a quick look of warning.

"I'm sorry, Mrs. Crowfeather. Go on."

"I saw them in my sleep before you came to the reservation, but it wasn't until you spoke to us that I realized who they were. When you were kind enough to pick me up today, I knew I had to help you find them."

"For how much?" Lena said, her voice dripping with sarcasm.

Maggie felt her face turning red and opened her mouth to chide her mother, but Alice raised a hand, then looked back at Lena with an indulgent smile. "I want no money from you, Mrs. DeVries. The Cherokee still believe in returning personal kindness. I ask no more than that you allow me to sleep here tonight."

"We can do better than that. Let us get you a separate room." Maggie offered.

"That won't be necessary. I can be quite comfortable right here on the floor."

Lena stood up in indignation. "This is too much. I'm going out for a walk." She grabbed her purse and left, slamming the door behind her.

"I apologize, Mrs. Crowfeather. Mama has the patience of a two-year old sometimes. Temper, too."

"Please call me Alice. It's—"

"And I'm Maggie, okay?"

A faint smile cornered Alice's mouth. "Fine. I started to say it's all right about your mother. I understand her nature. My father was like that, which was one more reason I spent so much time with my grandfather. He liked children, and tried to teach them the old ways."

"Your childhood must have been something else."

"It was. I would sit and listen to him for hours at the time. Days at the time. He had a way of making the past seem like the present. It was because of remembering some of his old stories that gave me the vision of where your son and your former husband are."

Instinctively, Maggie knew not to rush Alice. Push her. She leaned back on one of the pillows. She fluffed and pulled the other one close to her chest, wrapping her arms around it, the way she'd done when she herself was little, listening to her own father's biblical stories.

"Grandfather told me about a forbidden place his own grandfather had told him of. A certain valley. A valley no eyes could see. Not even those of the eagle. He called it the maw of the mountain."

"Maw of the mountain?"

Alice nodded. "Because it devoured all who went there."

"Sounds like a lovely place!"

Alice looked up at her sharply. "It is not a place to joke about, Maggie."

Maggie felt herself coloring again. "I'm sorry. Please go on."

"To this day not one of my people would dare go near it, even if they knew how to find it."

"I don't understand. This is a valley on the reservation?"

"No. Not on the reservation, but not far from it, either. It was part of our nation in the beginning, before the whites came."

"But you know where it is."

"Yes. My grandfather told me. His grandfather told him. There were ancient stories of brave warriors and hunters who went there and never came back. Of virgins who disappeared from their villages at night and were never seen again. The mouth of the mountain has an appetite for humans."

"Excuse me, Alice, but those are, as you say, ancient stories. Legends, surely you don't— "

"Don't say what you just started to. It's still happening."

"What?"

"The disappearances. Every now and then, since I was a child, hunters have occasionally gone out and never come home. In my own lifetime, several young girls, always the prettiest ones, have disappeared from their homes, never to be heard of again. It happened again to one only two years ago. The Tribe Council spreads the word that they have all run away from the reservation, to live among the whites, but my grandfather knew that was not so. I know it, too. They were swallowed by the maw of the mountain."

Her voice nearly a whisper, Maggie said, "Alice, this is 1986."

"Time means nothing, Maggie. It is a matter of—"

Maggie jumped at the ringing of the phone. "Hello?"

"Margaret, it's me. I've taken another room for tonight. You can sleep in the same room with that spooky woman if you want to, but I certainly don't have to. I'll see you at breakfast."

Tight lipped, Maggie said, "All right, Mama. That's fine."

Though her new friend said nothing, Maggie was certain Alice knew exactly who had called, and what her mother had just said. She hung up, started to apologize once more, but Alice shook her head. "It is late. You need as much rest as possible. I have made a list of all the things you should buy. I will be gone by the time you wake up. Pick me up at noon, two days from now, at the bus station in Cherokee, and I will guide you to the mountain. We can take your car part of the way, but it will take us three more days and nights, on foot."

Without another word, the Indian woman curled up on the floor and apparently went right to sleep. As if under some kind of spell, Maggie found herself yawning. She turned the light out, stretched out, and was also asleep in minutes, without even getting under the covers.

When she awakened the following morning, Alice Crowfeather had already left. Before she was fully awake, Maggie had the sudden thought that she'd dreamed the whole episode, but then her eyes focused on Lena's empty, un-mussed bed, and lying on top of it, the note, written in pencil and in a clear hand, which was a long list of items and where to find them. Maggie studied the list for several minutes, and then walked like a zombie to the bathroom.

After a wordless breakfast with her mother, Maggie went shopping. The first thing on Alice's list was wool socks. The second item, which took the longest time to find, was a pair of calf-length hiking boots that fitted snugly over the wool socks. Boots that didn't hurt her feet in spite of being brand new. Other items were easy to locate; tight-fitting Levi jeans, long underwear, and two flannel shirts. At a surplus store on the outskirts of town, she found a Coleman stove, flashlight, a lightweight two-man tent, two thermal sleeping bags, a quart canteen, and a cylindrical waterproof container for matches. The backpack, also of very lightweight material, she found at J.C. Penney's, along with a felt-lined hunting cap that had earflaps. Maggie wondered why rain gear, blankets, and insect repellant were not on the list, but she resisted the urge to buy them, trusting that Alice's list was complete.

The non-perishable foodstuffs on the list were a surprise, but Maggie quickly surmised how heavy canned food would be to carry. The sack of corn meal, dried fruits and beans would be easy to pack, and didn't weigh much. "Well," she said to herself, "This is not going to be a gourmet picnic in the city park, that's for sure. No Dinty Moore stew, no Hamburger Helper, not even salt and pepper!"

She was on her way back to the motel when the thought came to her that she should also have the Honda gassed up and serviced again. This she did, but had to wait nearly two hours for it, and it was already dinner-time when she pulled into the motel parking lot. It took two trips to bring all her purchases into the room, and only after dropping the second load on her bed did she notice all Lena's clothes were missing. She called the desk clerk and was told her mother was in 209, three doors down.

Maggie briefly debated whether to call the room, or simply march down the corridor, knock on the door of 209 and chew her mother out, then decided to let Lena stew in her own juices another half hour while she tried her new outfit on. Fifteen minutes later, she stood in front of the mirror, and almost didn't recognize herself, especially with the silly looking hunting cap on. She laughed at the image facing her, instantly aware of how warm her body had become. She hefted the backpack to which she had strapped one of the sleeping bags and the rolled-up tent, found that it was a load she should be able to manage, and spoke to her image in the mirror. "Okay, Wonderwoman, this ain't so bad. You ought to be able to keep up with a sixty-five year-old Indian gal for three days." She changed back into her street clothes, feeling a pervading sense of anticipation. New optimism.

"We're close, Mama," she said half way through the dinner. "I feel like we're closer than ever to finding them. I have a good feeling about it now."
"You're a fool, Margaret. It's absolute insanity to keep this up. I swear, I can't believe how you let that smelly Indian woman talk you into this. She'll probably get you lost deep in those woods, cut your naive throat, and steal your car."
"Mama—"
"All right, all right. I see you've got your mind made up and there's nothing I can say to change it. I won't say another word."
"That would be nice. What did you do all day?"
"Watched game shows and soaps. What else?"
"I thought you might have caught a movie over at the mall, or maybe gone shopping."
"Wasn't in the mood."
Maggie let it go at that. To her great surprise and relief, Lena was true to her word. They finished the meal, dessert, and coffee in silence, and Maggie decided to wait until bedtime to ask Lena if she wanted to wait for her at the motel for the week she

expected to be gone, or to take a bus home. She was not in the least unhappy that Lena had wanted to keep the separate room rather than move back into the one they'd shared.

When they reached room 203, Maggie told her mother she'd call her later, then slipped the key into the lock, turned and watched Lena stalk, stiff-backed and still silent, down to 209. Maggie opened her door, went immediately to the bathroom and drew a tub full of hot water. *You need this Maggie. No telling when you'll get the next one.* She walked back into the bedroom, stripped, put her hair up, walked back into the bathroom and stepped into the too-small tub, settling down an inch at the time. At least the water was hot. She had been soaking for maybe five minutes when she heard a soft knock on her door. "Come on in, Mama, I'm in the tub." she yelled.

But the knock came again. *Damn. She's forgotten she still has a room key, or she turned it in already.* "Okay, Okay, I'm coming. Just a minute."

The knocking persisted while she scrambled out of the tub, wrapped herself, more or less, with one of the thin bath towels which was almost too small to do the job, and went to the door. She opened it, and stared into the smiling face and gray eyes of—"Sam? Sam! What the hell are you doing here?" Between the time it took her to say that much and the time it took Sam Abrahms to ask if he might come in, Maggie realized he was there because Lena had called him, probably last night. No wonder she'd been so goddamn quiet. In the next instant, Sam was inside, closing the door, and Maggie's hastily-tied towel had dropped to her feet as she'd flung both arms around his neck. After the first fierce kiss, and the second, hungry one, Maggie leaned her head back and repeated her question.

"I've come to take you back home, honey."

And Sam Abrahms did have company on his return drive to Raleigh, but it was Lena, not Maggie...

Tom Lewis

The Brahms she'd been listening to finished, and Maggie turned the radio off. She allowed herself a crooked smile. The music hadn't calmed her much. The major movements of the symphony had seemed like her personal metaphor for the hours of the night before; first the hot, almost volcanic lovemaking, then the dreamy-quiet repose when she'd done all the talking—telling Sam of the futile search and of the hope Alice Crowfeather had brought, then a playful period of sensual contrapuntal touching; nibbling that had built into a passionate finale, but one that had turned discordant. They had argued with as much fever as their earlier passion. Unlike the Brahms, it had all ended in a sour, minor key, with the two of them sleeping what was left of the night in separate beds. And so, morning had come, with her driving west while an angry lover and a sulking mother had started back east.

Maggie turned it all over twice more in her mind, reached for the radio again, and fished with the selector button until she found a station with ear-splitting hard rock. She rolled the window down and yelled at the top of her voice, "I know you're out there, Bo. I know you're there, and I'm coming fast as I can. I won't let you get swallowed by the maw of the mountain. No way, do you hear? You hear that?" She wiped away hot tears with the knuckles of her left hand, checked her speed, and slowed down some. She'd been doing almost seventy.

Half an hour later, she felt that she had her emotions back under control, turned the radio off, and intermittently watched the odometer click off the remaining miles to Cherokee. Alice Crowfeather was standing by the door of the station, just as she'd promised, and Maggie unconsciously breathed a huge sigh of relief. She reached for the passenger's side door lock, failing to see the Indian woman glance at the rear window of the Police Station and swap small smiles with the dark face framed in the dirty glass.

She and Alice exchanged smiles of their own, but very few words. Alice grunted in near monosyllables, and Maggie followed her terse directions. After two dusty hours, they were on narrow roads Maggie was sure were not on any of her maps. The last town any sign had pointed to was Kaneville.

Chapter 14

From the closet, which was full of clothes and shoes, Robert chose gray slacks, a matching lightweight turtleneck sweater, a dark blue sports jacket and a pair of black loafers, somehow not in the least surprised that everything fit. He had slept soundly in the king-size bed, and while he was dressing, gave himself a mental pat on the back for not trying to make a move on the raven-haired beauty while they'd been naked together in the pool. Not that he hadn't wanted to. He had, in the worst way, but something in his brain had flashed a warning signal to the rest of his rejuvenated body that trying anything stupid with Manuel Munoz's granddaughter could very well be dangerous to his health. The bath Isabella had given him had certainly been sensual, but not overtly sexual, and Robert had instinctively, if reluctantly, felt the difference.

When she appeared again, this time wearing a pale blue robe, he thanked her again and followed her back to the dining room, where she served him a breakfast of hotcakes, eggs, and coffee. The minute he finished, Munoz appeared, this time in an obviously well-tailored three-piece suit. Right behind him was Bo, neatly dressed and looking for all the world like a college freshman. There was more than a hint of five o'clock shadow on his face. *My God, he needs a shave.*

Robert stood. Grinned. "Hey, pal. You look great. A grown man!"

Bo smiled back. "Morning, Dad. You look pretty good yourself."

Robert was sure Bo's voice was an octave lower. He glanced at Munoz who was beaming. "I trust you slept well?" he said.

"Like a rock."

"Excellent. Then let us go. You have much to see today."

With that, he turned on his heel and led the way through yet another arch and down a narrow corridor to a metal door. It automatically opened, and Munoz gestured for them to enter.

"An elevator?" Robert asked as the door silently closed.

Munoz nodded.

Robert and Bo looked around, then at each other. There were no buttons or controls, nor did they have any sense of rising or falling, as would have been normal in an ordinary elevator. Maybe half a minute passed before Bo asked, "Are we going up or down?"

"Down."

"I don't feel anything. Are we actually moving?"

"We are descending at a rate of perhaps five hundred meters per second."

"Outa sight!"

Munoz laughed at Bo's unintentional pun. "Quite out of sight, young man. Before I finish this sentence, we will have dropped nearly three miles."

"Wow."

"Why don't we feel, you know, pressure in our ears?" Robert wanted to know.

"Because of engineering far more advanced than anything you have ever experienced. Ah. Here we are."

Again there was no physical sense of the usual change of equilibrium as the door opened into a mammoth vault; bigger, Robert thought, than Grand Central Station in New York, and maybe a thousand feet high, lit by the same bright light he'd noticed before. It was like sunlight, yet not like sunlight, but it did not seem artificial. Nor was he aware of any change in temperature. The sheer size of the underground cavern took Robert's breath away. The next instant, he realized why he'd thought of Grand Central. They were standing on a kind of platform, but the tracks leading both ways from where they stood were not double tracks.

"Monorail?" Bo said.

"Four of them on this particular level." Munoz replied. "There is a great deal of traffic here."

Even as he spoke, a single streamlined car eased up to the platform and stopped. It was more or less the size of an average subway car, the lower half of which was of the same burnished-looking metal Robert had noticed in Munoz' house and in the elevator. The top half, from seat level up, was an arched dome, of either glass or clear plastic. As in the elevator, there were no apparent controls, nor could Robert tell what kind of energy powered the car. Glass doors slid back, and Munoz gestured for them both to take two of the four bucket-type seats. They did, and Munoz sat in one facing them. "Before we get underway, allow me to explain where we are going. What you are about to pass through is a series of connecting vaults, much like this one, only larger. We are several miles below the mountain ranges that extend from south of here through the Adirondacks, although this complex reaches only as far as just below the city of Pittsburgh. It will be your home, and your workplace. The reason this particular area was chosen was because it is not prone to earthquakes. There are several other complexes, other branches of the University, if you will, beneath mountain ranges located in other parts of the world, such as the Alps in Europe, the Himalayas, The Andes, and The Urals in Russia, among others. What you will see first are neighborhoods. Housing areas for our students and faculty.

"After that, we will pass through the University area proper. Finally, we will reach the area that contains our sports, shops, and entertainment centers. My plan is to take you from one end to the other, a distance of several hundred miles, then show you some of the things in detail on the way home. During the trip out and back, I shall attempt to explain some things to you, and answer some of your questions."

Lucifer's Children

Robert took a quick glance at his son. Bo's face showed absolutely no sign of fear or concern. On the contrary, he seemed eager to see what might come next. Robert couldn't tell when their car began moving, and had no idea how fast it was traveling as it passed from the first gargantuan cavern into what looked like a bedroom community; well-spaced houses, apartment buildings, and high-rise condos, all set on paved, tree-lined streets, but streets without cars or other vehicles. Or people. No one was in sight. Looking up, they saw blue sky and east-moving clouds "Have we come back to the surface?" Robert asked.

"No," replied their guide. We are still as deep underground as before. We use a technique that has been long used by your larger Planetariums, only far more developed. We can produce simulated day or night, complete with various weather conditions of all four seasons that is most convincing. The trees and grass you see are real enough, though it takes considerable work to maintain their growth and health. We actually grow a number of edible vegetables as well, but in another area."

"How fast are we going?" Bo wanted to know.

Munoz chuckled. "Not very fast at the moment, perhaps three hundred miles per hour. All the commuter trains, which run at levels below this one, are somewhat slower."

"Where is everybody?" Robert asked, remembering the bank of television monitors in Munoz' office.

"In class. You'll see them in a moment."

At that, the scenery on both sides of the car became a blur. At first, Robert thought they may have entered a tunnel, but then realized they had pickup so much speed, it was impossible to distinguish any detail of what they were passing.

Moments later, they emerged into an ocean of glass.

On both the left and right, geometric forms rose in planes, towers and spires that looked like a gigantic Feininger painting. It was breathtaking. Robert's first impression was, "It's a city of light!"

Munoz beamed. "An apt observation. The Headmaster would be pleased with your description, Robert. It is not glass, though it appears to be. The construction is of a material quite unknown in your world. At least, not yet. One can see into the various classrooms and laboratories, but those inside cannot see out of it. I shall slow us down, so that you can see a part of it." He pointed. "Bo, there, where you see those people working, is part of the Computer College. It is our hope you will quickly become a graduate student there, and eventually become a full professor of computer technology. The outside world, especially in the United States, stands today on the threshold of such an explosion in electronic advances, it will overshadow even the Renaissance. But more of this later. Robert, I want to take you to the place where you will work."

Again came the blur outside their bullet-like conveyance. Seconds later, they emerged into yet another area of stunning architectural beauty. Munoz pointed left. "The concert halls and opera house. Theaters for drama and movies. Parks." They passed a sizable blue lake, upon which were several small sailboats.

"Look over there." Munoz was indicating the opposite side. Robert turned his head, and then shook it in disbelief. They were passing a sports complex, which was bigger and more modern than anything he'd ever seen, including any of the Olympics. "Stadiums for football, baseball, soccer, basketball, track, field and ice hockey, all your competitive sports." Munoz was saying. "Over there are swimming pools, gymnasiums, training facilities, tennis courts, and three championship golf courses. Beyond that is the shopping area. Are you impressed?"

"Oh, yeah. I'm impressed," Robert whispered. He looked at Bo, whose mouth had fallen open. "It's pretty awesome, isn't it?"

Bo found his voice. "Dad's gonna work here?"

"He is indeed. You will also find time to enjoy much of it." Then, to Robert, he said, "I have arranged for someone to meet us. A man you will remember, who will show you around.

Lucifer's Children

I'm going to take Bo back to the University and show him the Computer center. I will be back for you shortly."

As Munoz spoke, the doors of the car opened. Robert and Bo realized they had stopped at another platform. There was a man in sweats standing there waiting. Robert stepped out and stared into the face he'd seen in thousands of photographs and on hundreds of baseball cards, but had only seen in person once. The tall man smiled at him and stretched out his hand. "Welcome to Paradise, Robert. Glad to make your acquaintance. They told us you were coming."

"Buck? Buck Mayhew?"

"Yep. It's me, all right."

Robert grasped the hand of the great Yankees pitcher, feeling as though he were shaking hands with a ghost. Rapid images of newspaper and television shots of a charred convertible and a burning gasoline truck flitted across his mind. "Holy—So you weren't killed in that car crash?"

"No. I wasn't even in the car. It was somebody else. It's all pretty complicated, but I was brought here, just as you were, about twenty-five years ago."

"I saw you pitch once, when I was just a kid. My Dad took me to an exhibition game between the Yanks and the Cards."

"That so? Was I any good? Never mind. That was a long time ago. Another life. Come on, I'll give you the fifty cent tour." With those words, Mayhew showed Robert how to step onto the broad sidewalk, which was like the conveyor belt walkways in some airport terminals, only faster. "No need for cars here. Good thing, too, if you ask me. They'd just mess up the good air we breathe down here. We got lots of bicycles, though. Anyway, all you have to do while you're on one of these gizmos is think about where you want to go, and it'll take you there."

Robert suddenly remembered how fast Munoz' elevator and the monorail car had moved, without apparent controls. "Are you saying these sidewalks operate by— telepathy?"

Tom Lewis

Buck Mayhew grinned. "That's right. Reminds me of when I used to stand out on the mound and look down at some poor slob standing in the box, and I'd try and pass my thoughts to him, like, 'here comes some heat, turkey, and you ain't even gonna see it.' Worked lotsa times. Anyway, where you want to go first? The ballpark?"

"Sure."

"I'm not the only one was brought here, you know."

"Really?"

"Nope. Not by a long shot. Remember that big-ass fullback named Jackson that played for the Bears?"

"You bet I do, but—"

"I got news for you. He didn't drown when that fishing boat of his went down in Lake Michigan. He's here. Runs the football program. Damn good one, too. Senor Munoz didn't tell you about him and the others?"

"No. How many others are there?"

"Come see for yourself."

Two hours passed before Robert stood once more on the platform waiting for Munoz' private car. Two hours that had seemed like only two minutes. His head was swimming with fresh thoughts of what and who he had seen: Sports facilities that gave the term 'state of the art' new meaning. Famous athletes of both sexes who hadn't died mysteriously in plane crashes, avalanches, and apartment building fires. An office of his own, complete with studio set, cameras, and monitors. And, a staff. Three bright eyed young men and a red-headed, mini-skirted secretary who looked as though she'd just stepped out of a centerfold.

"I can't believe it," he told Munoz when the bullet-car stopped to pick him up. "I just cannot believe it. And all I'm supposed to do is teach sportscasting? Do games? Spout off some trivia?"

"We thought you would be pleased. Your son was so excited with the Computer College, he begged to stay longer. I shall send for him later. In the meantime, I wish to begin answering your primary questions."

Robert mentally backtracked. "Okay. How many people are here altogether?"

"It varies, but at the moment, approximately ten thousand, ranging in age of from fourteen on. They graduate when they have finished their field of study, whether it takes four years or forty."

"But what's it all for? What's the purpose? Do they just stay here, then?"

"Only the permanent faculty members stay. The graduates are sent out into the world. Most of them will become prominent leaders in every active profession; politics, law, business, science, medicine, agriculture, academia, I could go on and on. The purpose, my friend, is that they, along with their colleagues from the schools in the geographic areas I mentioned to you earlier, will eventually control all that happens on the face of the earth."

"You're kidding, of course."

"No, Robert, I am not joking."

"But, you're talking about world domination."

"Precisely."

"To what end?"

"Enlightenment. Knowledge. The full realization of the potential of the human race. Much has already been accomplished. It will happen, as I said, eventually. We have plenty of time, and we are patient."

"How do you get them all out there?"

"They are funneled, a few at the time, through our town."

"Town? You own a town?"

"Oh, yes. A small place actually, but big enough for our needs, which also serves as a good pre-school through prep school environment for the children. We call it Kaneville. That is where your friend Beth is now."

The mention of Beth Oliver's name reminded Robert that Munoz had said something about her also having some kind of 'unique gift.' Munoz answered the next question before Robert could ask it.

"We judged Beth to be excellent mother material. She has been sent to Kaneville to bear her first child. She will eventually produce several more."

"Beth's pregnant?"

Munoz nodded, smiling.

"By Abner?"

"Of course by Abner. Abner Highsmith is one of our chosen fathers." Munoz' smile widened into a broad grin. He winked and said. "You have also been chosen to perform that pleasant task, in addition to your other duties."

"What?"

"You are to be one of our fathers, Robert."

Robert decided to let that one go by without comment. "You keep saying 'us'. "Who helps you run this school?"

Munoz laughed. "Oh, I have nothing to do with the administration of the University. My job is recruitment. I am charged with locating, ah, outside talent, so to speak."

"Like me."

"Like you and Bo. Yes."

"And then you kidnap them."

"That is a poor choice of words, Robert."

"Even if you have to kill people to do it."

"Sometimes it is difficult."

"Tell that to Ted French. By the way, you never did finish telling me your own story. What happened to the Indian guide, and the soldier you deserted with?"

"When we reached this general area, the Seminole hunter abandoned us, taking two of our horses with him. We were forced to slaughter the remaining horse for food. My companion and I were nearly starving before I located the valley, and the river."

"Before you located—Let me guess. You slaughtered him, too, didn't you?"

"It was necessary. I was commanded to."

"Oh yeah? By who?"

"By an angel. An archangel, to be more accurate, who also commanded me to begin work on all you have seen thus far. The Great One. The Headmaster of this University and all the others. The Prince of Light. None other than Lucifer himself."

"Lucifer? As in... As in Satan? The Devil?"

"He prefers to be called Lucifer. All the people you have seen here, including Abner and myself, are, in a manner of speaking, his children. And now so are you."

Robert's mouth went slack.

"Look at your watch, Robert. What is the date?"

Robert lifted his arm so that he would not have to remove his eyes from Manuel Munoz' face for more than a split second. He glanced down, then back up. "June fifth."

"Yes. And tomorrow is June sixth, 1986. The sixth day of the sixth month of the sixth year. Tomorrow the Master arrives. You may have the remainder of your questions answered by the highest authority, since he has informed me he wishes to see you."

Robert didn't respond to this. He was certain he had completely lost his own sense of reason.

His guide apparently sensed his feelings. "No need to be apprehensive, Robert. No need at all. Come, let me show you your quarters."

৵

Chapter 15

For the first three hours, with ten-minute breaks every hour, Maggie's adrenaline supplied enough energy for her to more or less keep up with her guide, mindful that she never took more than two or three consecutive steps on even terrain. One foot was always higher than the other. There was no discernable path, but Alice Crowfeather, surefooted as a deer, picked a way through the thick underbrush, pausing every hundred yards long enough to blaze their trail. She did this in two alternating ways; by tying six-inch-long strips of bright orange ribbon (she had apparently stuffed her pockets with) to bushes at eye level, and by chopping a gash into trees with the hatchet she carried. "Even the greenest tenderfoot can see these marks," she'd said. "And the ribbons are fluorescent. If we have to move back at night, our flashlights will spot them easily."

They had left the Honda at the edge of a narrow, sloped clearing, having long since run out of the logging path, which the dirt road had become. When Maggie noticed the temperature dropping and how fast the light was failing, she said, "Alice, how much further are we going today? It's going to be dark soon."

Alice stopped, turned around, and replied, "Not far, now. We need to find a place to make camp for tonight. Are you tired? Getting hungry?"

"I'm fine." Maggie gave Alice a confident grin and got a small one and a nod in return, whereupon Alice struck out again, but after a few steps, Maggie knew their pace had slowed somewhat. Another half hour went by before Alice abruptly stopped. "There." She pointed to a tiny plateau between two large trees that had fallen years before. They climbed up to it, and Alice looked around. "This will do fine for tonight. Almost level ground."

"Great." Maggie shrugged her backpack off, suddenly aware she was a little chafed under her armpits. "What next?"

Alice handed Maggie the hatchet. "The smaller limbs from those two dead trees will give us plenty of firewood. While you cut some, I'll set up camp. It won't rain tonight, so we won't need to pitch the tent. But be careful with that hatchet, it's very sharp."

"Okay. How far do you think we've come?"

A small frown appeared on Alice Crowfeather's broad face. "Maybe four miles as the crow flies."

Maggie's mouth dropped open. "Is that all?"

"The trouble with making distance in the mountains is you can't move in a straight line. Most of the time it's easier to walk around a mountain than it is to walk over it. We'll do much better tomorrow. Better start cutting. The light won't last much longer."

It didn't, and without lopping off her fingers, Maggie managed to cut enough firewood to suit Alice, who had dug a two-foot square pit, built a fire in it, and from her own backpack, produced a small frying pan and a matching saucepan, along with two plates, cups, and spoons. Reaching again into the pack, Alice brought forth an aluminum foil-wrapped package of frozen chicken legs that had finally thawed. "These will do fine for tonight. If we eat meat tomorrow and from now on, we will have to hunt for it."

Maggie didn't reply to this, wondering what on earth they were going to hunt with. The only "weapon" they were armed with was the small hand ax and Alice's hunting knife. She watched as Alice spooned into the pan some grease from a Mason jar she had also stashed in her pack. Next, she unceremoniously dunked the chicken legs into the open corn meal package, and dropped them into the grease-filled frying pan along with patties of the meal she mixed with water from her canteen. She poured more water into the small pot, dumped some of the dried beans and fruit in it together, clapped the lid on it, then leaned back, satisfied a good, solid meal would soon be ready. From somewhere inside her clothing, she extracted a cigar and promptly lit up. Maggie was surprised at the sight, but wasn't put off by the smell, since it did little to affect the pleasing aroma coming from the cooking food. Aroma which soon caused her stomach to growl, loud enough for them both to hear.

Alice grinned. "You should be hungry. How are you feeling?"

"I'm a little tired," Maggie admitted. "No, more than that. Like a lady Marine the first day of boot camp. Thank God I've never shirked those three-times-a-week aerobics classes."

"You did well, but tomorrow will be harder on you. Are you sore?"

"I probably am, but I won't feel it until tomorrow."

They ate their meal in silence, Alice cleaning both the pan and the pot by first wiping them with her fingers which she licked, then scouring both with pine cones she picked up from the ground. Maggie watched, fascinated, as the Indian woman then boiled some water in the saucepan, let it cool some, then washed both it and the frying pan, then their plates, and wiped them on the tail of her shirt. She poured more water into the pot, and when it boiled, she dumped three heaping tablespoons full of coffee into it, and popped its lid back on. After a minute or so, she took it off the fire, let it cool a little, and strained the coffee into their cups through some cheesecloth. The coffee tasted surprisingly good, and Maggie marveled again at the simplicity of Alice's culinary art. She smiled at her guide, who suddenly stood, spread her legs and emitted a long, loud fart. "Good for the body to do that. Belching, too."

Maggie laughed, wondering what Lena would have thought, and then watched Alice fish out yet another cigar, which she lit. She added a few more pieces of wood to the fire, leaned back against the stump of the dead tree, puffed contentedly a few times, then asked, "How did you meet your husband?"

Lucifer's Children

Maggie was surprised by the question, but could think of no reason not to tell Alice, "I was still a Junior in college at Chapel Hill, working on a degree in journalism. I got a summer internship at WRDU that turned into a part time job. Robert was the number two man in the sports department there. I was hooked on Television from the first day, and didn't mind being the most gullible 'gofer' they'd ever had. I did everything but clean the bathrooms. Anyway, Robert was already showing signs of brilliance as a sportscaster, and I was terribly attracted to him. He was really good-looking back then, and I didn't think he even knew I existed. But that Christmas, at the station party, he came over and sat down next to me. We got talking, and the next thing I knew, we were in his car, riding all over Raleigh. I was surprised he didn't try any funny business. We simply talked about careers, and I have to admit I was just a tad disappointed that he didn't even kiss me when he took me home. Just said he'd 'see me around' and drove off. I was sure he'd gone back to the party.

"But the next day he asked me for my phone number, and that night he called me. I think we talked three hours on the phone. We started dating, and that was that. I fell for him like, well, you know."

"He was your first man, then?"

Maggie felt herself blushing. "First and only. He gave me a ring the following Christmas, on my birthday, and we were married in Las Vegas three days after I graduated. I think I got pregnant with Bo that very weekend. Anyway, Robert's career took off, and for a while, we were happy as any couple could be. I was...I was naive. The marriage went south right after Bo was born. Booze, other women, you name it."

"You know what women of my people call men like him?"

"No, what?"

"Same as what your people call them. Assholes."

Maggie laughed again. "Not all of them. I finally found one who's a class act, in every way." She found herself telling Alice about Sam, and why she hadn't yet married him.

Alice puffed on her cigar, grunted, and finally said. "Your son is spoiled. You have not been strong enough with him. When you get him home again, you will have to correct it."

Maggie had no chance to respond to the truth of that, because Alice dropped the butt of the cigar in the fire, stood, pulled on her pack and said, "I'll be back in a few minutes." With that, she disappeared into the woods.

Maggie assumed Alice had gone to relieve herself, which she also had to do. She looked around, feeling slightly foolish, but managed, after moving a few yards away from the campsite. Alice returned ten minutes later, added more wood to the fire, and promptly crawled into her sleeping bag. without saying another word. Maggie took the hint and did the same. She shifted her body once or twice, and was asleep moments later.

The following day, Maggie discovered mountain hiking and "camping out" was a great deal more work than pleasure. The early morning stiffness she'd felt gave way to utter exhaustion when they stopped to make camp again, on the grassy bank of a small stream. Most of their walking had mercifully been downhill, zigzagging, and Maggie's legs felt like rubber. She was certain they had walked thirty miles in order to gain ten. She was astonished that Alice didn't seem to be the least bit tired, and while Maggie flopped flat of her back, Alice proceeded to collect two or three dozen small stones from the bottom of the fast flowing creek, setting them on the bank to dry. She dug another pit for a fire, which she lined with the smooth rocks. Maggie struggled to her wobbly feet and scoured for firewood. As soon as the fire was going, Alice smiled at her and shocked her when she said, "Take your clothes off."

"What?"

"Get out of those clothes. You need to rub your body down with this." She handed Maggie the jar of grease she'd used for cooking the night before.

"What is this stuff?"

"Bear grease. Trust me, it will take much of the soreness out of your muscles. Tomorrow's climb will be more difficult than today was. I know it will smell bad to you, but we are not going to a prom dance, are we? Besides, flies and mosquitoes don't like it either. Be real quiet now, too. I'm going to catch supper."

Maggie watched the woman move downstream while she stripped. There wasn't a place on her body that wasn't aching. As she rubbed the odorous goo into her naked limbs, she saw Alice slowly move into the shallow stream, having taken off her boots, socks, and jeans. Maggie thought Alice's legs looked like those of a weightlifter. The woman moved into an area where the stream widened into an eddying pool. Transfixed, Maggie watched her bend over, hands dropping down until they were up to her elbows in the cold water, then freeze into a motionless stance. Maggie continued to rub her body with the grease for maybe another ten minutes when Alice moved, faster than Maggie would have thought possible. Her arms flashed up and tossed a two-pound trout onto the bank, hurrying to capture it before the fish could flop back into the water. Grabbing the wriggling beauty by the gills, Alice held it up, grinned at Maggie, and said, "He'll fry up good, and there's enough of him for both of us." With that, she unsheathed her hunting knife and cleaned the trout right where she stood, allowing the entrails to fall back into the stream where they were quickly swept away. "This way, the smell of him will not attract raccoons." She brought the two halves of filleted fish back to the campsite, dropped them in the frying pan, then reached into her pack. It yielded, of all things, a comb, which she handed to Maggie. "You need to check all your body hair, too," she advised. "We've been moving through a lot of brush. Ticks can cause bad problems."

Maggie was suddenly more concerned about possible varmints on her skin than her modesty. After a thorough examination, she was relieved when none were found. She found herself enjoying the simple pleasure of combing her matted hair while she watched Alice make another trip to the edge of the stream, where she washed hers and Maggie's socks. When she came back, she asked, "Think you can cook this trout and some cornbread?"

"Sure."

"Good. While there is still a little daylight left, I want to go upstream a ways and set a snare. Might catch us a rabbit for tomorrow's dinner. Maybe even a small 'possum."

Maggie nodded. "You're really something, Alice. You seem more at home out here than I am in my own living room. Your grandfather teach you all this?"

"Most." She looked up. "We'd best pitch the tent, too. It will rain tonight. While I'm gone, go down to the creek and bring back at least fifty of those rocks on the bottom."

Maggie did as instructed, and when Alice returned to the campsite, Maggie watched her use them to build a cover over the fire, like a kind of oven, with an opening that faced downhill. "This way, we can keep the fire going all night. It also discourages any four-legged, unwanted guests. We can use the Coleman stove inside the tent for heat and to dry these socks."

The rain held off until they had eaten, and after cleaning up, they settled into the tent, wrapped snugly in their sleeping bags. Maggie fell asleep listening to Alice recount much of the sad history of the Cherokee and other Native American tribes. In her dreams, she imagined she was one of them, marching west in misery along the infamous Trail of Tears.

It was still raining at daybreak. Alice said. "Do you want to stay here until this stops, or push on?"

"How long do you think it will last?"

"All day, maybe tonight, too."

"Well, it isn't a cold rain. If it's all the same to you, I'd like to keep on going."

Alice merely nodded.

By the time they stopped for lunch, Maggie felt she had caught a kind of second wind. Her legs seemed stronger as they moved up, ignoring the cool, steady rain, which had soaked them both. Maggie guessed it was around five o'clock when they reached a ridge that was bare; practically solid rock. They followed it until they came to a spot that was more or less level, whereupon Alice stopped and said, "This is a good place for camp. It will be hard to sleep on, but the drainage is good."

The rain stopped as they were struggling with the tent. "Might as well just use the sleeping bags tonight," Alice said. "And the stove to cook some beans. No wood around here that isn't wet, so we'll have to wait till tomorrow to roast the rabbit I caught."

Maggie was too tired to do more than nod her agreement. She looked up in time to see the fading sun disappear over the blue-gray western horizon. But Alice was looking south, over yet another narrow valley, toward a mountain, already shadowed. She pointed toward it. "That mountain is your destination, Maggie. You will find what you are looking for on the other side of it."

Maggie was hardly conscious of going through the motions of making camp, putting on dry clothes and socks, or eating. All she felt was a new tingling inside her, a new feeling of anticipation mixed with a sense of tremendous pride in having already come so far. Accomplished so much of her mission. Only one more mountain to climb, and that one didn't look all that foreboding, either. With Alice Crowfeather humming the lullaby she'd sung in her car, Maggie, wrapped warm and dry in her sleeping bag, fell asleep gazing through tears at blurred stars. *I'm coming, Bo. I'll be there tomorrow, if it takes me right into the maw of the mountain.*

Tom Lewis

Chapter 16

"It's not quite a penthouse, but it'll do."

Robert's comment was a left-handed compliment which Munoz acknowledged as such. "We thought it would. As you can see, there are only the bare necessities here at the moment; a bed, a few chairs and dishes in the kitchen, but you will enjoy furnishing it, I'm sure. If you wish, you may employ one of the decorators to assist you."

"Decorators?"

"Interior decorators. There are ten of them here. Quite capable people, I assure you. Come, have a seat, Robert. Allow me to explain yet another few salient facts about our subterranean world." Munoz led Robert through the empty bedroom they'd been standing in to a smallish room Robert assumed would be a den, or maybe office. The apartment boasted six rooms altogether: Living room, kitchen/dining room, two bedrooms (one considerably larger than the other) and a large bath. Robert had seen no thermostat for heat or air conditioning, no any visible venting for it, which he'd mentioned to Munoz, who'd promptly informed him it would be regulated by Robert's mind. If he wished it to be warmer or cooler, it simply would be! The whole apartment— and the building containing it— was ultra-modern. Glass and chrome-like walls and hardwood floors throughout, although Munoz had told Robert he could have it changed to a more conventional appearance if he so chose.

They sat, facing each other, and Munoz continued. "You raised an eyebrow when I mentioned the decorator. You must understand, we are not training only people for high places. We also prepare many for less austere professions, such as accountants, barbers, clerks, mechanics, electricians, even landscapers and yes, decorators. Many of our people are, ah, out there in practically every job you can imagine. You will see practical evidence of this in our little town of Kaneville, which serves more than one purpose. We will arrange for you to visit there soon.

"Since this branch of the University is more or less inside the United States, so to speak, we use American currency. To begin with, you will be paid an annual salary of one hundred thousand dollars, paid in monthly installments."

"A hundred thou to start? Are you kidding?"

"No. Our faculty people are well paid. You can spend the money any way you choose. Through our shops and outlets here, you can buy practically anything you like, except firearms and motor vehicles of course, and it's all tax free."

"Oh, boy."

"Yes. Think of it Robert. All the money you will ever need, a larger place to live when it becomes necessary, a wonderful job to do, and for a long, long time, at whichever age you choose, whether thirty, forty, or even twenty. How do you like the apartment?"

"It's great, but..."

"But?"

"Isn't it going to be a little cramped for Bo and me? You know, only one bath—"

Munoz broke out in laughter. "Oh, my. Forgive me. I completely forgot to tell you. Bo will not be living with you. He shall have a place of his own."

"Oh. A dorm room."

"No. His apartment will be much the same as this one, although in a different building."

"I see. Senor Munoz, this is all too fantastic for words, but there is one thing that bothers me. About my job, I mean."

"And that is?"

"Well, you said there were about ten thousand people here. Those stadiums I saw would hold four, five times that many. Maybe more. I don't understand why—"

"Ah yes. I thought Mr. Mayhew would have explained. When you broadcast games and events, they will all be filled to capacity, every day and night you choose."

"But, how?"

"Holograms. A refined system of what soon will be known in the outside world as virtual reality. Mayhew and others will show you soon enough, but right now, we'd better start back. It's time to pick up your son."

While being whisked back to the commuting platform by the automatic sidewalk, Robert said, "It's going to take me a little time to get used to all this."

"Yes. We don't expect you to absorb everything immediately. Your new secretary will assist you in getting settled, show you where to shop, and guide you around. Someone will assist Bo similarly. You and he will be my houseguests until your own quarters are completed."

They moved for a while in silence. When they reached the platform where Munoz's car waited, Robert finally got up enough nerve to ask what had been on his mind for an hour. "How often do I have to eat...? You know."

Munoz turned to him and laid a gentle hand on his shoulder. "You will never know when or how much, my friend. It may be in your breakfast sausage, or mixed into some dish you order at one of our restaurants. After a short while, you will not even give it a second thought. I promise you."

Robert was doubtful, but decided not to pursue the matter further. Instead, he said, "You've showed me a lot of the good stuff. What about the flip side."

"Flip side?"

"Yeah. I mean, What if somebody breaks the rules? The law?"

"Oh. Well, there is no crime here. No one breaks the law. There is no police force. No fire department either. Nothing here will burn."

"Has nobody ever tried to, you know, escape?"

"Why would they?" Munoz studied Robert's face for a long moment, then added, "Listen to me, please, Robert. This is the only time you will hear it from anyone here. Our faculty, students, and graduates serve the will of the Master. That is all. Each has a job to do, each performs that duty, and there is total harmony within and without. Should anyone ever entertain any ideas of disobedience, or foolishly attempt even the slightest infraction of the Master's orders, their punishment would be immediate, and far, far worse than death. Worse than anything you could possibly imagine. I can tell you no more."

Without another word, Munoz opened the door to his car, and they took their seats. Within minutes, they stopped, Bo boarded, and immediately bombarded his father with gushing talk of microprocessors, gigabytes, mother boards, rem and ram, and a hundred other things which went into one of Robert's ears and out the other. All he'd seen so far had certainly lived up to Abner Highsmith's words. It was truly beyond wildest dreams. Mayhew had called it paradise. But Robert had not seen one single bird flying through the artificial air of this utopia, not one single dandelion growing in the too perfect grass, and Senor Manuel Munoz' last words were ringing in his ears as well. He and Bo were in a prison; beautiful and fantastic, sure enough, but a gilded prison nonetheless, and trying to get out of it would bring on horror quite beyond his wildest nightmare. Of that he was certain. And there was nothing, absolutely nothing he could do about—

"— surprise." Munoz was talking.

"What? I'm sorry. What were you saying?"

"I have a rather special treat for you, and Bo. Ah. Here's the elevator."

Munoz led them to his living room. In his current frame of mind, Robert could never have guessed what his host had in mind, nor was he in any way mentally or emotionally prepared for what he saw. Abner Highsmith rose from a couch, greeted Robert and Bo warmly, and said, "It is my great pleasure to present Miss April and Miss Marta. I believe you already know Miss Isabella."

Robert stared at the three young and gorgeous women, all three dressed in the flowing white robes, looked at Bo, Highsmith, and Munoz in turn, and stammered, "I, ah, hello. I'm afraid I don't— "

Munoz broke in. "Robert, these young ladies will join us for dinner tonight. After which, you will have the difficult task of choosing one to be your companion, although I daresay you already favor Isabella. Bo will have second choice, and Abner will, as usual, graciously accept the third."

"Bo?"

"Of course. This morning, you said yourself what a man he has become. Tonight, he will be relieved of the irksome and distracting burden of virginity. It is all based on need, Robert, yours and ours. Abner needs to replace Beth. You must begin your extra-curricular duties soon, too, and Bo needs a clear head for his studies. Here, have a glass of wine. This is truly a night for celebration."

৯

Lucifer's Children

Chapter 17

The climb was tortuous. Although they were not attempting to move straight up, Alice was changing the direction of their zigzagging more often than before. Maggie first thought Alice had shortened the angle of their ascent, left to right, because she assumed Maggie's legs were more conditioned than before, or perhaps to reduce the amount of time it would take them to reach the summit. Or, maybe Alice had sensed that Maggie's anticipation of finally reaching her goal had given her an extra boost of energy, like a long-distance runner's all-out closing sprint. Whatever Alice's reasoning was, Maggie soon found herself sweating profusely. Her own perspiration, intermingled with the bear grease, gave her even more incentive to keep up, thereby staying half a step ahead of the smell of her own body. The ordeal was not made any easier because the slope of the mountain they were climbing was much steeper than the others, and its vegetation more dense. Alice was vigorously hacking their way through, the higher they rose.

The sun was straight overhead when Alice halted for a lunch break. Maggie wasn't in the least hungry, only enormously grateful to fall flat of her back, breathing through her mouth, and feeling the muscles of her legs jumping involuntarily, like those of a bullfrog in a frying pan. Some three or four minutes passed before she realized she was lying on practically level ground. With effort, she pushed herself up on her elbows and looked around.

They had stopped at a spot that was a small indentation in the side of the mountain, as if some gigantic hand had scooped a part of the mountain out, leaving a natural, overhung shelf, free of small brush or young trees.

Maggie looked at Alice, who was sitting cross-legged, a few feet away, not even breathing hard. "You've been here before, haven't you?"

Alice shook her head. "No, but my grandfather must have. This little clearing is exactly as he described. He said there would be a series of false ridges further up, before you get to the top."

"You think we can make it to the top today?"

"The question is, can you?"

Maggie groaned. "My poor old body tells me it can't move one single step further, but my mind says I can. I have to."

"I believe you. You must eat something. Drink some water."

Maggie shook her head. "I'm not hungry. Speaking of water, I wish to God it would rain again. I'd strip and stand in it for an hour. I'm smelling so ripe I can't stand myself."

Alice chuckled softly, then looked up. "We have made good time. Why don't you sleep for half an hour. I'll wake you up."

"You serious?"

Alice nodded. "I promise."

"I think I love you, Alice Crowfeather."

Maggie struggled out of her backpack, stuffed it under her head and was asleep before she could think to say thank you.

It wasn't Alice's hand or voice that awakened her. It was the smell of smoke. Confused, Maggie sat up. Alice had already pitched the tent and set up camp. She was sitting a foot or so away from the fire, sharpening the hatchet with a whetstone. Maggie rubbed her eyes. "What's going on? There's plenty of daylight left."

"Yes. You should reach the summit before six o'clock."

"I should— What are you saying, Alice?"

Alice looked up. "I'm not going with you any further. You must go the rest of the way alone."

Maggie felt the bottom drop out of her stomach. "I don't understand. Why not?"

"I told you I would show you where the mountain was. I did that yesterday. I have already come too far, because I was not sure you could make it. Now I am. Just keep going up, the way we have been. I will wait here for you. For two days and nights. If you don't return by then, I will go home."

Maggie couldn't believe the words she'd just heard. Thinking back, it was true that Alice had not promised more than to 'show' her the mountain. Lead her there. Then, another thought came to her. "You're afraid, aren't you? You're afraid of being swallowed by the maw of the mountain."

Alice's answer was a simple shrug of her broad shoulders, not looking up from whetting the hatchet. Maggie was suddenly furious. She grabbed her pack, slung it on, shook her canteen to make sure it still had plenty of water, and took a few steps away from the fire before turning around. "Well, if you're thinking that by refusing to go any further with me you'll make me mad enough, just mad enough, to finish this climb, you're absolutely right. I'll make it, with or without you, goddammit." She started to move away.

"Wait."

Maggie turned back around. Had Alice changed her mind?

Alice stood, reached into her own pack, fishing out a plastic bag full of the orange ribbons. "You'd better take these. You still have quite a long climb before the brush thins out. Here, take the hatchet, too."

Maggie took the bag of ribbons, but shook her head. "I don't want the hatchet. It's too much extra weight. Besides, you may need it to protect yourself from the mountain bogeyman."

Alice ignored that, and said, "Go like we've been doing. Don't try to climb straight up. Pace yourself. I put some extra food in your pack. And don't forget to change socks tonight."

"You sound just like Lena."

Again, Alice ignored Maggie's sarcasm. "I'll wait here for two days."

"Fine."

The energy boost Maggie got from her vexation didn't last more than an hour. When she paused at the first deceiving ridge to have a drink of water, she realized how stupid and foolish it was to have lost her temper with the superstitious Indian woman, and resolved to apologize profusely when she saw Alice again. The next two hours were nothing short of hard labor. Although there was less low vegetation to scramble through, the angle of her climb was steeper. She began to doubt if she would reach the top by nightfall, and was grateful for the knowledge that the higher she climbed, the longer she'd have sunlight.

Going on sheer will power, Maggie doggedly kept climbing, gradually noticing that the sun, because of her change of direction, and its own movement west, was in front of her, not to her right. She stopped, talking to herself. "Christ, Maggie, are you lost? Aren't you supposed to be going south up this damn mountain rather than west? Is that next ridge up there the top? No it can't be, but it's blocking your view of the summit. Better turn left. Keep the sun on your right. That's another one of those false ridges Alice's grandfather was—"

"Stop, woman!"

The masculine sound of the command was so close, so loud, Maggie nearly slipped backwards. A shock ran from her boots to her scalp as she froze in place. When she looked up, what she saw nearly caused her to lose bladder control. Not more than fifty yards in front of her, standing on the ridge and highlighted by the westing sun, were three men. The one in the middle was carrying a rifle. He was the only one of the three who wasn't wearing a long robe. And it was the one in the middle who had spoken. No, not spoken; it had definitely been a command. Now he added a new one. "This is private property. You are trespassing. Turn around and go back."

Lucifer's Children

Maggie didn't budge. Several thoughts ran through her mind at lightning speed. Had Alice already seen the three men? Was that why she was afraid to come further? Had the men been watching them? Waiting for them? In any case, having come so far, she wasn't about to turn tail and give up now. She needed to buy a little time to sort all this out. "Trespassing? I'm sorry. My name is Margaret Ellis. I'm looking for—"

"Go back where you came from," the bearded man with the rifle said. "What you seek is not here."

"But you don't understand, I am only—"

"Go back, I said. I don't want to shoot you, but I will if you take one more step." With those words, the man raised the rifle and pointed it at her.

Maggie found herself shaking, but from anger, not fear. She didn't for a minute believe the strangers would shoot her down in cold blood for nothing more than simply stumbling onto private land. "Look, I'm sorry if I trespassed on your property, but I didn't—"

The rifle cracked. The bag of ribbons Maggie had been carrying in her left hand flew back behind her, taking two of her fingernails with it. Maggie yelped in pain as the echoes of the shot reverberated through the cascade of orange ribbons flying around her head, caught up in the swirling wind. Maggie stared at her bloody fingertips, then back at her tormentors. Before she could scream a protest, the rifle cracked again and she felt a searing pain on her left cheek. *He's shot me. The bastard actually shot me.*

"The next one goes through your heart. Go. Now."

Maggie needed no more urging. She went. Running, stumbling, falling, getting to her feet, stumbling again, rolling head over heels, she bounced off trees and the ground like a pebble in an avalanche, straight down the slope, losing her cap, brush tearing at her hands and face as she tripped, fell, rose again, and staggered on, helter-skelter, down the mountain she had worked so hard to climb. She paid no heed whatsoever to her direction. Only down. If she passed by a young tree or bush she'd fastened one of the orange ribbons to, she didn't see it. She only saw a blur of brown and green. She had no idea how much distance she'd covered in her descent when she finally collapsed, rolled over on her back and desperately tried to catch her breath.

Maggie closed her eyes, and then willed them to open. She no longer felt the cuts and scratches on her face, nor the crease the gunshot had made in her left cheek, nor her mangled fingernails. Her numb body was telling her it wanted to sleep. Rest. But her mind warned her that if she did, she might never wake up again. She looked around wildly. Where she lay, panting, was a kind of swale, and she could see the shadows of trees lengthening. There wasn't much daylight left, and she knew she was lost. She had no idea where she was. Where east was. Or south. She struggled back to her feet, not knowing where she got the energy to do so. She stood for a moment, thinking out loud. "Maggie, you have to beat this thing. You have to, or you're dead. Think. Think. How many of those false ridges had you climbed over before you met those men? Two? No, three. This must be the bottom of the second one. Alice has to be north, near the bottom of the third one. Which way is north? Look at the shadows, stupid. North is at the top of where a shadow falls. That way. You have to climb some, then go down again.. Always north. Always....north..."

It was dusk before she found the first orange ribbon. Thank God. Keeping north, she located a second one. Then a third. She smelled the smoke of the fire before she saw it, and crawled into the tiny clearing where she had left Alice as the last light disappeared. Alice was nowhere to be seen. The sleeping bags were both laid out by the fire, over which a rabbit was roasting, beginning to burn on its bottom side. Maggie automatically turned the spit. Where was Alice? There was a pile of firewood stacked neatly, between the sleeping bags. Maggie was far too tired to do more than lay a few more sticks on the fire before crawling into one of the sleeping bags. Wherever Alice was, she'd no doubt be back soon, and Maggie was too wiped out to care. She passed quickly into the oblivion of unconsciousness.

    When she woke up the next morning, feeling a few drops of rain on her face, Alice was still nowhere to be seen. The fire was no more than pale-glowing embers, the rabbit a charred, shrunken, probably inedible chunk of leather. No matter. Hunger was the last thing on Maggie's mind. She quickly rebuilt the fire, laying the grotesque corpse of the rabbit on the ground. Why had Alice left the camp? Why hadn't she returned? She's said she's wait for two days. The tent and Alice's pack were also missing. "She's already gone back, damn her," Maggie muttered aloud. "All right. Okay. I can find my way back by myself, if it takes me a week."
    She rolled up her sleeping bag, changed her socks, stuffed the blackened rabbit into her own backpack, and struggled to her feet. "I can do this."
    Tired as she was, Maggie found some grim satisfaction in being able to locate the ribbons and slash marks, concentrating on looking for them rather than allowing her mind to speculate on the three strangely dressed men, or of Alice Crowfeather's defection. She walked all day and into early evening through intermittent rain, back-tracking their trail, stopping only to rest and drink a little water. Darkness was closing in again when she found the earlier campsite by the small stream where Alice had caught the fish. Maggie was immensely proud of what she'd accomplished, but was too exhausted even to cry when she found a fire going, Alice's pack, and the tent, already pitched.
    "I take back everything I said, Alice, old girl. Out there hunting, are you? Well, when you get back, don't wake me up. I've had it." She found just enough strength to unroll her sleeping bag inside the tent and crawl inside. She never heard the sound of the rain that fell all night.
    Morning came, but Maggie had no idea what time it was. The rain was light, but steady, holding visibility to no more than thirty or forty feet. She remembered Alice had told her she'd

packed food in her backpack. Dining on two-day-old burned rabbit didn't seem very appetizing, even though she was hungry as hell, but the dried fruit wasn't much better. Maggie sat inside the tent, chewing and trying to figure out who those men were. Two of them in robes, yet. Some kind of mountain cult? Commune full of crazies? With paramilitary types? Maybe. But come to think of it, there had been no signs anywhere saying that land was posted. Would that good looking stud in the buckskin outfit really have shot me dead? Were they all bluffing? Lying? Why would they? And where the hell is Alice? Ten will get you twenty she knows a lot more about this than she's told me. But again, why?

With anger welling up inside her all over again, Maggie decided to go looking for her. For some answers. Ignoring the pain from her throbbing face and fingers, she started to the left of the camp, fanning in a semicircle on each side of their marked trail by no more than fifty yards at the time.

She hadn't made two trips back and forth across the radius of her search when she found Alice's clothes. Dumbfounded, Maggie stared at the boots resting on top of the neat pile for a full two minutes before she felt the first real stab of apprehension. She looked up, left, right, ahead. If Alice had gone to take a rain bath, she wouldn't have walked far from where she'd left her clothes, would she? Maggie walked another twenty paces north, and nearly stumbled over something else lying on the ground. When she stopped to see what it was, she caught her breath and nearly keeled over from shock. It was an arm. A brown, human arm. Severed at the biceps, stretched out straight, thumb and all but the forefinger curled, as if it were a grisly signpost, pointing— north. Maggie retched, then stumbled forward, only to find the other arm, fingers again pointing north. Maggie fell to her knees, throwing up everything she'd just eaten. She thought she was going to faint, but something inside her pulled her to her feet again, and pushed her further.

No more than a hundred yards up the slope, she found the left thigh and leg. The toes had been cut off and arranged in an arrow point. Wailing now like a wounded animal, Maggie thrashed up, north, following the trail of blood that she hadn't noticed before, now clearly indicating direction. Another hundred yards of stumbling into the trail revealed the other leg, toes arranged as before. Maggie, now dry-heaving, kept moving, knowing full well what she would find next. But there was nothing— absolutely nothing in all of Maggie Ellis' life experience that could have prepared her for what she saw. The bloody, naked torso of her guide was impaled, from vagina through the headless neck, on a young sapling. Both breasts had been hacked off.

Maggie knew she was trying to scream as she ran, but she also knew no sound was coming out, and her next thought was what a good thing that was, since who or whatever monster had done this to Alice might hear her, and, Oh God...Oh...my— - God. NO—

No longer capable of focusing, Maggie ran. She never saw the second stripped sapling, the one with Alice Crowfeather's head stuck on top, the hatchet protruding from between her wide-open, unseeing eyes, its bloody handle pointing north. Maggie ran.

Stumbled forward.
Crawled.
Fainted.

Came to, and ran again. Moved again. North. There was no day. No night. No knowledge of time. Or pain. Or distance. No awareness of thirst or hunger, or why she herself was alive when she fell the third time, the fourth time, the five thousandth time. Or when, knowing she was more dead than alive, reached a spot where it all had to end. Where she fell for the last time. And lost consciousness.

And dreamed she saw a face. A broad, frowning, pockmarked face with crew-cut hair. She dreamed strong arms and hands went under her. Lifting her. And all went white as milk.

֍

Chapter 18

The team of physicians at the small but very expensive private clinic located ten kilometers north of Rome were used to important and affluent patients— and guests. Even so, they were impressed that not one, but two high-ranking Cardinals of the church had not only guaranteed payment of the priest's bill, but had both visited him every single day for over a week, though they had politely but firmly been turned away each time. The bill was hefty enough, but Dr. Emile Sarasante, the neurologist who had been elected to speak to the two illustrious benefactors was, this time, reluctant to mention it. "We could find absolutely nothing physically wrong with him. We gave him every kind of scan and test known to medicine, and monitored him constantly. To be blunt, we think he is simply suffering from overwork. Stress. He gained five pounds while he was here, and slept around the clock twice."

The two high priests listened to his carefully delivered accounting of the patient's treatment and response without interrupting once. "In sum, there was no aneurysm, nor did we find any of the normal symptoms of typical migraine. In our opinion, and at the risk of seeming trite, Father Barillas' brain and body is close to overload. We recommend a long rest. Frankly, the longer the better."

Cardinal Reilly spoke for the two of them. "Thank you, doctor. So, we can take him home now?"

"Yes, your Eminence. He's waiting in his room. Right this way..."

Lucifer's Children

Neither man had ever been to the small *pensione* where Ramon lived, and both were aghast at the size of his third-floor room. It couldn't have been more than four meters square, yet it was spotless, and as orderly as Ramon was himself: A simple cot for a bed. One scarred table served as both eating area and desk, with a two-burner hot plate resting on it, along with Ramon's Bible. The table, with a single wooden chair tucked under it, sat directly beneath the only window, through which dangling laundry obscured the view of the courtyard below. A cloth-covered shelf hung over the sink, which held a few dishes and a mug, inside of which was an electric heating element for making one cup of either instant coffee or tea. To the left of it was an armchair that had certainly seen better days, beside which stood a reading lamp with a faded yellow shade. A battered wardrobe stood in one corner. One of its doors was missing, and Reilly and Zimmer, at the same time, saw that there were only two changes of clothes and an overcoat hanging there, and one pair of shoes rested on its floor, next to a battle-scarred soccer ball. Leaning in the opposite corner was Ramon's bicycle.

The wall to the right of the door was bare, except for a framed lithograph of the Virgin, at eye level above the chest of drawers. The opposite wall was covered with dozens of odd-sized pictures and snapshots of Ramon's family. Both Cardinals were surprised there were, with the exception of the Bible, no books there.

Cardinal Peter Reilly found his voice first. "I swear, Ramon, Trappist monks and Privates in the Italian Army live better than this. I had no idea you lived so... so frugally."

Ramon sat on the cot, hands between his knees. "I don't need much, your Eminence. There are five other priests living here. Some of their rooms are even smaller. It's quiet here most of the time, and I can be at Vatican City in ten minutes if I ride my bike. Please, won't you both sit down?"

Zimmer finally spoke. "No, my son, we can't stay. Are you sure you are feeling well?"

"Never better, Eminence. Really, I'm fine. Thank you both for everything."

Cardinal Zimmer cleared his voice, raised his chin, and spoke again, in his most stentorian style, "*Ja*. Well then, I have decided upon your next assignment." He reached into his inner pocket and produced a fat envelope which he handed to Ramon. "Inside you will find a first-class ticket to Guatemala City, and some extra money. The plane leaves Da Vinci at ten tomorrow morning. You are hereby ordered to fly home to rest and see your family. How long has it been, anyway?"

Ramon took the envelope and looked up. "Ten years. I went to my mother's funeral ten years ago."

"I thought as much," Zimmer said softly. "Now. You are also ordered to take thirty days leave. No more, no less." Zimmer looked across the room at his colleague. "Are you ready, Peter?"

"Ready."

"Yes. Then we must go. *Tschuss*, Ramon. Come back in a month, and when you come back to work, please be clean-shaven. That beard you are growing makes you look ten years older."

The two friends left the embarrassed priest and hurried down to the waiting Mercedes. "Can you believe that place?" Zimmer said.

"M-mm. You and I have both seen worse. How much was in that envelope?"

"Ten million Lira."

"There's hope for you yet, Peter the Kraut. Where do you want to go for lunch?"

Carrying a single light bag, Ramon waited his turn in line at the Alitalia check-in station. He hoped with all his heart the sin he was about to commit would eventually be forgivable. When he finally reached the counter he asked the smiling young female ticket agent if there would be any problem exchanging his ticket for one to a different destination.

Lucifer's Children

There wouldn't be a problem at all, he was told. "Where do you wish to go, Father?"

"The United States. Raleigh-Durham, North Carolina."

The clerk looked down and began clicking buttons on her console. After a minute she looked back at him, with even a wider smile. "If you don't mind a two-hour layover in Washington, I have a flight at Noon."

"That would be fine. Just fine. Now, can you show me where I can exchange money?"

Somewhere over the Atlantic, Ramon reached into his pocket and brought out a pen and the small notebook he always carried. Not being particularly gifted at drawing, it took him twelve pages before he was satisfied that the sketch of the foot, toes and blackened heel were close enough to the gold pendant that had danced before his tortured eyes for almost two weeks.

Father Daniel O'Connor looked at the sketch and chuckled. "Of course I have seen it before. Thousands of times. It's the tar heel. You can buy these pins and pendants in nearly every shop."

"Tar heel?"

"A symbol. Logo. It represents the nickname for people of this state, generally, but it's more commonly associated with sports teams from the University of North Carolina. Tell you what, let's take a little drive. As they say, a picture's worth a thousand words."

It took an hour. Only an hour for the Pastor of St. Andrews to give Ramon a quick tour that included peeks inside Kenan Stadium and the cavernous Dean Smith center along with the major sights of the UNC campus. During that hour, O'Connor explained as best he could several of the dubious legends behind the symbol of the Tar Heel state. Ramon listened politely, but seemed distracted, and finally asked if he could be dropped off at the library. "Would you mind leaving me here for a while? I won't be long."

Tom Lewis

"No problem, Ramon. I have a few errands to run anyway. Pick you up in what, an hour?"

"An hour should be enough. Yes, and many thanks."

Ramon needed only a few minutes to locate and carry half a dozen year-books called, appropriately enough, THE CAROLINIAN, to an empty table. While Father O'Connor had been driving, Ramon had already done a little mental calculation. If she was his age, she should have been a student here between 1968 and 1975, give or take. He found her picture in the both the '72 and '73 books, once more catching his breath at how much she looked like him. It was uncanny. He studied the name in both volumes for several minutes to make sure. DeVries. Margaret DeVries. From a place called Pella, in the State of Iowa, and was a Journalism major.

From that point, it was easy. With the transportation and local knowledge furnished by his new friend, Ramon visited the School of Journalism and was not at all surprised that two professors remembered Margaret DeVries, whom everyone had called Maggie, and one remembered that she had gone to work at WRDU. The kindly professor recalled that Maggie had gotten married, but didn't know her married name.

Nor was he surprised when the receptionist at WRDU told him Yes, Maggie Ellis—so, her married name was Ellis— was an anchor there, but was currently on a leave of absence. No, she was not allowed to give out personal phone numbers or addresses, but if it was an emergency, Maggie had left instructions to contact one Tammy Henderson, who lived at The Armistice Apartments in Raleigh. Yes, she had left a number for Miss Henderson.

Tammy Henderson was a very cooperative—almost too cooperative (or was the word talkative) neighbor who said, no, she didn't know where Maggie was exactly, but she thought Maggie had said Asheville. Yes, that's it. She'd phoned only once from some motel in Asheville. Wait a minute. The Days Inn. That was it. Poor Maggie'd had a really bad time lately, what with the loss of her son and former husband. No, it was no problem, Father. No problem at all. You're very welcome, I'm sure.

That night, Ramon told the entire story to an amazed Father Dan O'Connor, then made his confessional. The following morning, feeling better than he had in months, he caught a bus to Asheville. He took a room at the Days Inn, and was there only two days when he noticed the article on page three of the newspaper.

MYSTERY WOMAN IDENTIFIED
> The unconscious woman found yesterday in the mountains west of here has now been identified. Authorities now say the person found by Cherokee Chief of Police Thomas Hand is 35 year-old Margaret Ellis, of Raleigh. Ellis, who was taken to Asheville Memorial, is now listed in stable condition. Police say there is no evidence of foul play. It now appears that Ellis had simply become lost. Her car was found nearby. It was learned that Ellis is an anchorperson at WRDU-TV, on leave of absence. She had apparently been searching for evidence of the plane carrying her former husband and her son which went missing last January. No trace of the plane has ever been found—

Ramon didn't finish the article. He took a taxi to Asheville Memorial, and within the hour, sat at the bedside of the sleeping woman who looked like his twin sister. It was then, staring at the mirror image of his own face, that he realized the nightmares had not been random, purgative dreams. The headaches had been for a purpose. He'd been led to this woman. But why, dear God in heaven? Why?

Tom Lewis

Chapter 19

The trip in Munoz' private monorail car seemed short. Robert was aware they were travelling in the opposite direction than before, going south rather than north toward the University complex. Accompanied by Isabella and Susan, his new secretary, he had spent the entire day shopping for furniture and other household items, most of which Isabella, clapping her hands like a delighted new bride, had picked out and which Susan promised would be delivered and set into place the following day. From the combination of euphoria that had lingered from the night before, and the exertion of the shopping spree which Isabella and Susan had led him on— at a frantic pace— Robert was tired, and until now hadn't been thinking about tonight's dinner party. But when the thought occurred to him he was actually on his way to socialize with the Devil himself, he felt a sudden, gut-wrenching fear which he knew was patently obvious.

Munoz gave him a reassuring smile, patted him on the shoulder, and said, "Try to be at ease, Robert. You are in for a rare treat. There is nothing to be apprehensive about, I promise you."

Robert thought, This guy uses those two phrases a lot; 'I assure you' and 'I promise'. Still, Munoz hadn't lied to him about anything. Neither had Abner, for that matter. But there was no way he could control the trembling or the sweating, which was already beyond embarrassment. "Easy for you to say," he replied, with a forced grin. He wished to God Munoz had given him some kind of hint as to what to expect, or what was expected of him, but none had been offered.

Lucifer's Children

The car stopped at a short platform which led to an elevator door similar to the one that rose to Munoz' house. Robert felt as if his nerves were close to total breakdown, and when the elevator stopped and opened into a lovely garden, its view mostly blocked by the size of the man who stood there grinning, Robert thought he might pass out. The man was dressed in the now familiar white robe, but the garment did nothing to disguise the fact that he was the most powerfully built human being Robert had ever seen. Yet the man's size and physique was not what shook Robert to his toes; the huge, smiling creature was bald, had skin almost as light as his robe, and had pink eyes that bore into his own like twin lasers. Albino...An albino giant.

The pink-eyed monster spoke. "This way."

Munoz, with one last confidential nod, said, "I will return for you at midnight." The elevator door closed as soon as Robert stepped out. He followed the robed brute along a path through the most exotic, sweet smelling shrubs and flowers he'd ever seen, realizing at once they were outdoors—or at least what seemed to be outdoors—on a mountaintop! Overhead, stars twinkled in the clear, windless night sky. Millions of them, so close, he might reach up and grab a handful. He had no time to speculate as to which mountain they were on top of, or even which state he might be in; only that the cultured vegetation they were walking through bore no resemblance to anything he was familiar with, not that he'd ever paid much attention to North American flora.

He could hear his own heart pounding when they reached an ornate gazebo centered in a cleared area, where a small, white-covered table rested. In one of the matching two chairs sat a man of medium height and build, who rose as they approached. He was dressed casually but elegantly, in attire that might have been in vogue around 1920 or so, down to the two-tone shoes. His face was tanned, accenting brilliant white teeth which showed in a wide smile beneath a trimmed moustache. Soft, dark-brown and wavy hair was parted on the right side.

Tom Lewis

The hazel eyes were widely set, above an aristocratic nose. "Robert. Glad you could make it. Have a seat."

The voice was so...so ordinary, Robert shook the offered hand before he knew it was sheer reflex to do so. "You're him?"

The handsome head was thrown back in such genuine, unaffected laughter, Robert felt some of his tension vanish in spite of himself. "I mean—"

"Oh, I'm 'him' all right. Over time, I've accumulated lots of names: Old Scratch, Beelzebub, Mephistopheles, Satan, The Devil, but my favorite name is Lucifer. Has a nice ring to it, doesn't it? Also kind of dignified."

Robert could only say, "I just didn't—"

Lucifer chuckled again. "Hey, let me guess. You were expecting me to be some kind of leather-skinned, cloven-footed gargoyle that spoke breathing sulfur and brimstone, using a lot of thee's and thou's? Well, here I am, without all that comic book crap, although because I liked his looks, I am taking on the appearance of one of your fairly recent American writers. Pretty handsome guy named Fitzgerald, and, I liked the way men dressed a few years back more than I do today's styles. Last time I was here, I chose to look like Poe, who was also one of my favorites. Far as language is concerned, I speak every known tongue and dialect on earth, but I'll talk to you in your own vernacular, not like some stuffy, theatrical character straight out of a Hollywood melodrama. I don't mean to be glib or patronizing, I figure it'll help you relax faster."

"It does," Robert managed, meaning it.

"Great. How about some champagne? I've got some good stuff here."

Without being asked, the albino popped the cork and poured two flutes, handing one to Robert and the other to his master. Then he walked to one side of the clearing, remaining in earshot, like a well- trained houseboy.

Lucifer sipped, and gazed skyward. "Terrific night, isn't it?"

Lucifer's Children

Helpless but to take the cue, Robert said, "Beautiful. The stars seem so close."

His host pursed his lips, then said, "Closer than you think. They keep me pretty busy. Keeps the Boss busy, too, truth be told."

"I'm sorry, I don't understand. Are you talking about—God?"

Lucifer regarded his guest with a thoughtful smile. "Nowadays, I like to call Him 'The Boss'. It's His ballpark, you know, not mine. Let me put it this way. If you could imagine being able to actually count all the grains of sand on every beach on earth, then multiply that figure by the highest known mathematical power, you wouldn't even approach the smallest fraction of the number of stars in the universe, and, there are several planets swimming around each of them. Earth is one of the newer ones, and my work here has hardly begun. This particular branch of the University is the newest of the group, and the most important one at the moment. Because of all that, I manage to visit here, planet earth I mean, more often than others, say, once in every hundred years of your time. About once a day in mine."

Sipping the champagne, he waited for Robert to absorb what he'd just said, then asked, "What do you think of my school so far?"

"I don't have the words to describe it."

"Fair answer. I knew tonight was going to be fun. Usually, on my brief visits here, I like to amuse myself with other kinds of evening diversions, mostly with desirable women, but every now and then, I like to chat some with newcomers, especially doubters like you. You still have doubts about it all, Robert?"

"I don't know what I think any more, and that's the truth."

"Another good answer. Honest, too. Tell you what. You just sit right there and drink your champagne. Again at the risk of being cheap and theatrical, I'm going to give you a brief demonstration." With those words, He stood up and walked a few steps toward the edge of the clearing. As he walked, the clothes he was wearing simply dematerialized from his body. Naked, he turned around to face Robert.

"As you can plainly see, this is the body of a fairly well-developed male adult. Now watch." Robert nearly dropped his glass as the man turned around slowly, like a model on a runway. Now facing Robert was a totally nude woman of perfect proportions, but her voice was the same as the man's. "You got it. I'm totally amorphic. How about this?" Robert leaned back hard in his chair as the form ten feet away from him melted away, then reformed itself into a cud-chewing cow! Then, a sleepy looking alligator, which then became a strutting peacock. Robert was shaking his head, holding his breath when the magnificent bird disappeared, but the voice remained close. "Can you see me, Robert?"

Robert couldn't. The grinning albino walked a few steps toward him, and pointed down. Robert spotted a single tiny ant, hurrying along the ground. The albino spoke. "One word of caution, Mr. Ellis. My master is in a very good mood tonight, Almost nothing is out of bounds, but there is one subject he will not discuss."

"What?"

"His boss's son, or the son's mother."

Lucifer's voice came from a different direction. "Over here, Robert."

Robert turned his head toward the sound and instantly froze at the sound of the rattles of a six-foot diamondback. It moved its ugly, flat head to the right, and Robert found himself staring into the glinting eye. He shivered as the voice came again. "I've used this shape before." Laughter followed, but it was more like a mischievous child's giggle. "Or maybe you'd prefer something a little more traditional?" The snake's head became a horrible caricature of the horned, red-eyed, yellow-fanged image so familiar in pictures and books, but only for an instant, before F. Scott Fitzgerald re-formed, chuckling again.

"Hope I didn't mess up your appetite. Oh, don't worry. It's prime rib of beef tonight, not homo sapiens."

"I don't think I'm hungry."

"Really? Take another sip of that wine."

Robert complied, and was amazed that he was instantaneously ravenous. "Oh, boy."

"I thought so." Lucifer nodded to the albino. "We'll eat now. Bring some Cabernet for the beef."

The giant moved out of sight, and Robert, braver now, asked, "Who's the big guy?"

"His name is unpronounceable in English. You would know him as Cain. C-A-I-N. Been with me a long time."

"You mean the biblical Cain?"

"The very same. Very useful fellow. He keeps discipline intact in all my schools while I'm away, not that it's often needed. A kind of Sergeant-at-arms if you will. I set the rules and he makes sure nobody breaks them. He's sole Judge, jury, and, well, you know."

Robert shuddered. "Executioner."

"Yeah. Well, like I said, his talents—which include cooking—aren't needed often. Anyway, let's enjoy his nice dinner, without talking about unpleasant things. Okay?"

They ate without talking at all. Midway through the delicious meal, Robert was certain Lucifer was giving him ample time to digest more than food and drink. Whether it was the dinner, the wine, Lucifer's charming manner, or the combination of all of it, Robert found himself growing less and less fearful, almost to the point of physically relaxing. Emboldened, he finally said, "My son thought we might be dead and in hell. Are we?"

Lucifer laughed again. "That Bo's some young man. I'm expecting a lot from him soon, but no, you're not in hell, Robert, and you're certainly not dead. There is no such place as a literal fiery hell, although that smart-ass Dante made a good case for it in his book. It suits the Boss to let earth people think there's a hell, just as it suits me to allow silly myths and cults cloud my own existence. I get a real kick out of some of them. Devil-cults, Black Sabbaths, and all that other stuff. Cute."

When Robert didn't respond to this, Lucifer went on, in a more serious tone, "Tell you what. Let's walk some, work off some of this big dinner, and I'll try to clear up a few misconceptions for you. You know, fill in some of the gaps."

Robert pushed himself away from the table and walked alongside his host through the lush garden. He was feeling a little light-headed, weak in the knees, but he knew it was not from the champagne or the wine he'd drunk. They walked for several minutes before Lucifer stopped and pointed down. "That's the valley where your plane came down." Robert peered down, but could see nothing but black.

Lucifer took a few more steps, then pointed down the opposite side of the ridge. "See those lights down there? That's our little town of Kaneville. I named it after my faithful servant, but had it spelled with a "K", for obvious reasons. We'll show it to you soon, but tonight, I'd like to explain how all this has happened. First of all, Earth, as I said before, is only one of many planets where there is civilized state of being, although this is the only one with what you know as 'human' life. And, it is relatively new, in the overall scheme of things, so to speak. The Boss likes to think big."

"A long time ago, even in my time frame, the Boss used to listen to the ideas of his archangels. Most of us were what you might call 'yes men". None of us would ever pipe up with anything we thought He might disapprove of. When He got around to forming this planet, I realized He had become bored with the whole progression. He'd done one after the other, all in the same pattern, and with predicable results. When earth's turn came, I opened my big mouth and goaded Him into a kind of bet."

"You made a bet with God?"
"Let's call Him the Boss, okay?"
"Sorry. What kind of bet?"

Lucifer's Children

Lucifer stopped walking and sat down, leaning against a tree, arms behind his head, as if relishing the telling. Robert followed suit, wondering what he would hear next. As if reading his mind, Lucifer grinned, and said, "You remember your history books, Robert? Back a ways, some kings used to employ and tolerate people called jesters. Those clever entertainers often got away with figurative murder, good-naturedly tweaking their monarchs— so long as they didn't go too far. That's how it was with the Boss and me. I was a lot like His court clown, provoking Him, aggravating Him, teasing, all in good fun. An idea came to me one day, and I told Him He could spice up this earth thing by interrupting the slow evolutionary process by jumping way ahead in time, and creating a couple of already perfect human beings, with fully developed brains. What's more, I bet Him I could corrupt them with knowledge, and thereby make the whole creative process on this particular planet a lot more interesting. A diversion, if you will. Anyway, for some reason, He thought that was a novel idea, and agreed to do it. So, He created Adam and Eve, plopped them both down in a pretty little spot that looked a lot like where we're sitting now, and told me to take my best shot."

Robert stared at his smiling host. "Are you telling me Adam and Eve were created as, as a joke? A whimsical bet?"

"Right. The whole concept of Good and Evil, right and wrong, and what came out of original sin, as it came to be called, was no more than a kind of board game. It's still going on. Big time."

"And He— The Boss, I mean, lets you get away with it?"

"Sure. As long as it suits Him. He gets a kick out of it. Hey, don't misunderstand, my picayune powers are limited, to say the least. He could stop me anytime He wants to."

"If what you're saying is true, then there is no conflict between the biblical version of the creation, and the accepted Darwinian theory of evolution."

"Essentially, that's correct."

Robert puffed out his cheeks. "Man!"

Tom Lewis

"I gave mankind the ability to think and reason. He gave them religion. Right from the get-go. I think the only reason He lets me 'get away with it', as you aptly put it, is that in the end, He will win out, of course, but it sure is fun in the meantime. I have my schools and He has His churches and mosques. I have my writers, scientists, and philosophers. He has His priests and preachers. I win a few battles, but He'll win the war, eventually."

"Uh, huh. Speaking of the Bible, I remember enough of my Sunday School lessons to know that Cain was supposed to have been branded with a mark. I didn't see any marks on that big albino."

Lucifer laughed. "Ah, Robert, my friend. You still want to play the doubter. Don't you understand? Cain's being an albino is his mark. Why does everybody assume Adam and Eve were white? If the Boss hadn't sunk the original garden — and the smallish continent it was on— long before the geophysic separation of the other continents— and scattered those beautiful brown-skinned people all over the Pacific Ocean, well, all that's beside the point, anyway. The Boss allowed me to rescue Cain, who by the way, was about to do some nasty things with Luluwa and Aklemia."

"Who?"

"Luluwa and Aklemia. His sisters. Over the years, I've supplied him with plenty of women, which temporarily satisfies his, ah, other appetite. In return, he minds the store for me while I'm away."

Robert thought of something he'd been wondering about before. "But if you want perfect specimens of men, women, and brainy types, why go through the trouble of training them? Or kidnapping them? Why don't you simply clone them?

"Too easy, Robert. No fun at all. Besides, if I cloned my best people, they'd still be just as limited as the original, wouldn't they? No, better to selectively breed them. Takes more time, but produces better results in the long run. Plus, it gives me great personal pleasure to see how my children, as I call them, fight the good fight. I'm sorry, Robert, I'm forgetting my manners. Would you like some coffee?"

"Yes. Very much."

They walked back to the table, took seats again, and sipped the aromatic blend Cain had prepared. He was careful to pour his master's cup first. He then brought strawberries in cream, and before leaving, said, "Master, you won't forget my dessert tonight?"

"No, my son," Lucifer replied, I won't forget. Munoz will be bringing it when he comes for Robert."

Robert paid little attention to this exchange. While spooning the exquisite berries, he was trying hard to make sense of all he'd heard and seen. Lucifer seemed to again read his mind. "Have I been convincing enough, old buddy?"

"Yes, sir. I have no doubts about you now."

"Good. Glad to hear it. You know, your ex-wife had been looking for you. Well, looking for Bo, mostly, no offense."

This total change of conversation stunned Robert. He stared at Lucifer. "Maggie? Maggie's been what?"

"Smart girl. Pretty, too. She sensed you and Bo were not dead, and came looking for you."

A new apprehension invaded Robert's heart. "You haven't—"

Lucifer chuckled, raising a disquieting hand. "No, no. We simply discouraged her efforts. Not to worry, she's fine. I must say, though, I was tempted to have some personal fun with her. She's a feisty lady."

Robert left the remaining strawberries uneaten, suddenly feeling a little queasy.

"By the way," Lucifer said, changing the subject yet again, "How are you and the luscious Isabella getting along?"

Robert felt a new discomfort. Red-faced, he stammered, "Fine. I mean, she's, ah—"

"Well trained in the gentler arts? Damn right, she is. I expect you two to produce me another child soon, but take your time about it. Besides, you have to start work tomorrow. I'm betting you'll have yourself a ball."

Lucifer adroitly brought up the subject of sports and sportscasting, his knowledge of which astounded Robert, and caused him to practically shove everything else they'd talked about to the back of his mind. Before he knew it, Cain reappeared. "It's midnight, Master."

Lucifer stood. "Really? Too bad. I've enjoyed our chat, Robert. We'll have to get together again sometime soon." He reached out a soft hand which Robert shook, not knowing whether the emotion he was feeling was disappointment or relief. "Yes sir. Thanks for everything. "I'll do my best."

"I know you will," Lucifer said. "Very few of my children or my imports like you ever let me down. However, before you go, it's necessary for me to show you what happens to those who are foolish enough to try. Sorry to have to subject you to this Robert, but doubters like yourself sometimes need an extra ounce of, shall we say, motivational convincing?"

With those words, he snapped his fingers, and Cain, accompanied by an unsmiling Manuel Munoz, came into the clearing. Cain was carrying a large sack across his broad shoulders. Lucifer sat down, gestured for Robert to do the same, and nodded at his servant, who undid a drawstring and pulled the top of the sack down to the waist of a forty-ish, white faced man who was shaking so hard with fear, he was unable to emit more than little puppy whines. Cain held the poor fellow upright by the hair of his head.

Lucifer gave Robert a look of deep sadness. "This man has been with us eighty years, in the banking section of the business college. He was caught cheating on one of his final exams. Fortunately, his will not be a great loss. Dessert time, my son."

Robert had no time to turn away from watching Cain wrap one powerful arm around the man's head. With one quick jerk, which produced a loud snap, he broke the man's neck, and in one more motion, dropped the body back into the sack, pulling the drawstring tight. Hoisting the inert form back onto his shoulders, he grinned at Robert, whose mouth had dropped open, and said, "Also dessert for the swine herd."

Robert looked back into the expressionless face of Lucifer, who softly said, "His infraction was not terribly serious, Robert, therefore his punishment was a quick, nearly painless death. Cain, here invented torture. He can make a man suffer for a month, begging for such an end, depending on which of my rules was broken. You do catch my drift, don't you?" In all of Robert's life, he had never seen such a smile as the one Lucifer said this with. He could only nod and croak some kind of hoarse assent. Munoz gently took him by the elbow, whispering, "Time to go, Robert."

Robert stumbled after him back through the garden to the waiting elevator, scattering strawberries and cream on both sides of the path. The last thing he remembered hearing was the sound of laughter. Unrestrained laughter.

༄

Chapter 20

Dr. Ruth Weiner led Lena DeVries and Sam Abrahms down the first-floor corridor to the coffee shop where they found an out-of-traffic table. No one wanted anything to eat or drink, but Dr. Weiner thought the cheerful informality of the coffee shop was perhaps a better place to talk than her own cluttered office. The Abrahms guy seemed calm enough, but Mrs. DeVries had been distraught and uptight from the moment she'd marched through the front door of Asheville Memorial, loudly demanding to know which room her daughter was in.

Dr. Weiner leaned forward, her elbows resting on the freshly wiped Formica table-top. She smiled at the good-looking man first, then at the tight-lipped mother. "Margaret's going to be fine, Mrs. DeVries. We'll keep her here another day or two, under mild sedation, but I don't see any reason you can't take her home on Monday. A couple weeks of quiet rest, and she should be good as new."

"When's she going to start talking again?" Lena wanted to know. Dr. Weiner knew the type. Probably had a lifelong mistrust of physicians to begin with, and even less confidence in those who wore skirts. "I can't believe she hasn't spoken one single word to anybody," Lena continued. "She didn't seem to recognize me, either, or Sam, for that matter."

"That's because of the medication. We had to get her calmed down. She was thrashing around so much when she regained consciousness, it took two orderlies to hold her. Whatever it was that had frightened her so badly, plus the extreme laryngitis caused by hours of screaming, has resulted in a temporary catatonic state. A kind of block. I'm sure she will start talking, maybe by tonight or tomorrow for sure. When she starts talking about her ordeal may take longer; days, weeks, even months. That part of her mind, her selected memory, has simply shut down for a while, like a blown fuse. We've seen it before. Rest and relaxation and a good long dose of TLC usually takes care of the problem. I wouldn't worry too much about her. Physically, she's fine, except for a few scratches and bruises. She wasn't dehydrated or anything like that when she was brought in, but she was totally exhausted, and her heart rate was way up."

Sam spoke up. "Any idea of what happened, doctor?"

"None at all, except that she'd suffered some kind of traumatic experience. The Sheriff over in Lee County was the one who brought her in. From what I could gather, one of his deputies had found Margaret's car way out in the sticks at the end of an old logging road. It was unlocked with the keys still in it. Some phone calls were made, and they found out Margaret was out there searching for her son and former husband, apparently on foot. She must have simply gotten lost, and panicked. In her state of mind, obsessed with finding her son like that, plus being lost in the mountains for several days would produce trauma enough for anybody, in my opinion. Anyway, The Sheriff organized a search party, and several members of the Cherokee tribe helped out. I think it was their police chief, Tommy Hand, who actually found Margaret, unconscious, not more than a mile from where she'd left her car. Oh, by the way, they had the car brought here. You can pick it up at the City garage. The cops think Margaret simply suffered a kind of breakdown resulting from being lost and terrified for three or four days. That's what I think, too. Anyway, when she came to, here at the hospital, she was completely disoriented and understandably hysterical. She'd obviously screamed and cried so much, she'd lost her voice. Look, are you sure you wouldn't like to have a cup of coffee? Tea or something cold?"

Both Lena and Sam declined, which didn't surprise Ruth Weiner. Abrahms didn't look like the nervous, coffee-drinking type, and the Ellis woman's mother was already hyper enough, fidgeting in her chair and drumming her fingers on the table. "Well, I've been up most of the night. I think I need a cup. Be right back."

She stood and walked over to the edge of the snack bar counter, poured herself a cup from the half- full pot with the orange decaff handle, and took her time stirring a package of Equal into it, sighing. She'd been guilty of the professional white lie again. The often-used lie of emission. Margaret Ellis had raved like an agitated maniac when she'd come to in the emergency room, screaming until she was hoarse-croaking about a mountain guarded by crazed white extremists, or was it white-robed extremists? One of whom had shot her. But there was, of course, no gunshot wound anywhere on her body, which had been smeared all over with something that smelled like rancid Vaseline and looked worse. Before the drugs had straightened out every kinked up muscle in her body, she'd mumbled something about crowfeathers and arrowheads, over and over until the heavy sedative reduced her to a snoring lump, allowing them to clean her up and X-ray her from top to bottom.

They'd finished with her exam, gotten her to bed and an I.V. started, not that she'd needed one, and had monitored her closely for twenty hours, but when she'd awakened, she'd refused to say a word to anybody, doctor, nurse, or Sheriff Yancey, who'd shrugged his broad shoulders and left, saying her mother and boyfriend had arrived. Far as he was concerned, since there was no evidence any crime had been committed, he'd had more important business to take care of back home in Lee County.

She carried the cup of weak, lukewarm coffee back to the table, manufactured the smile again, glanced at her watch, and said, "She's sleeping right now, but they'll wake her up for dinner in about an hour. Why don't you two go somewhere and do the same. I'll bet neither of you have eaten all day."

"Good idea," Sam said. "I am hungry." It took Sam a few more minutes, but finally managed to convince Lena to leave, but not before Lena wanted to know, "Who was that priest coming out of her room when we got here? The hospital chaplain?"

Dr. Weiner shrugged. "I don't know. Wasn't paying any attention, I guess. I didn't particularly notice him. Probably was one of the chaplains. They change them around in this hospital more than they do the linen. Protestant, Catholic, Jewish, you name it, we've got 'em, always around but never underfoot. Look, have a nice dinner, and don't worry about Margaret. She'll be fine. I'll see you tomorrow morning."

Ruth Weiner watched them leave, then made her way back to her office and dialed a number.

"Yancey."

"Ruth Weiner."

"How's your patient?"

"Still under. I'm going to release her Monday."

"Uh huh. What about the memory thing?"

"Not to worry. We've got some good medicine here."

Yancey chuckled. "You sound like Tommy Hand. Speaking of Indians, did her folks say anything about the woman?"

"Not a peep. Either one of them."

"Not surprised, but if they do, you call me right away."

"Ten-four, good buddy."

Yancey hung up, laughing. Dr. Weiner's own grin changed to a frown as another thought came to her. She toyed for a moment with her pencil, then used it to punch another number.

"Administration. June speaking."

"June, this is Dr. Weiner. Do we have a new chaplain? Catholic priest, maybe forty, nice-looking, wears a moustache and full beard?"

"Not that I know of, unless a change was made while I was on lunch break. Why?"

"Oh, nothing. I was just wondering. Sorry to bother you."

"No problem, Doctor."

Ruth Weiner replaced the receiver and chewed her lip, but only for a moment. There were other patients besides the one in 526.

Maggie was floating again, drifting in a white sea, beneath a pale sky full of moving white clouds. She felt that she was asleep, and dreaming, but knew she wasn't. She knew she was awake, yet she had no control whatsoever over her body or her thoughts. Worse, she couldn't budge her memory, any more than she could move her limbs. She was too tired to ever *want* to move her arms and legs, ever again.

But she did want to remember.

She desperately wanted to remember. Why couldn't she? Why couldn't she put the fleeting images that punctured the white space around her into focus? What were the images? Faces? People's faces? She knew she was not dead. Dead people couldn't smell, could they?

But she could smell. Oh yes, she could smell the mixture of, what? Alcohol? Mixed with disinfectant? And, another one. She could smell the perfume on one of the clouds that had been constantly hovering above her, and she could also smell herself. She didn't smell bad any more. She smelled clean. Like soap-clean. Where was she? Wherever it was, if she wasn't dead, and didn't hurt, she must be safe. No reason to be afraid any longer. But, why had she been afraid? Why couldn't she *think*? Reason? Remember? She knew she was tired. Far beyond tired, but if she was awake, and safe, why couldn't she think? Or talk?

It was too hard to even try. Forget it. Better to sleep some more. Sleeping was easy. Warm, and dark. Sleeping took all the glaring white away.

Problem was, the white kept coming back, but gradually, like a picture being dipped in developer, then swishing in the stop wash, forms and faces began to take shape. She thought she could recognize some of them. Mama? Sam? Tough to tell. It was like sorting out anagrams swimming in rice soup. Who belonged to the face with the long hair? The one with the nice perfume? What were the others trying to do? They all keep talking to me, and some are feeding me, but I can't talk back. And where is the other face? The dark one with ugly holes in it. The man. The man with the strong arms?

Not hungry. Don't want any more to eat. Just want to sleep some more. Sleep is nice. So tired. Another face. Looks so familiar. Who? Not a white cloud like the others. Black cloud. Nice cloud. No not a cloud, a man. Black is not a cloud, it's a suit. Black face. No, the face isn't black. The beard is. White above and below. Parts of a little white cloud? No. No, not a cloud at all. Teeth. Smile. Good smile. What's that under the beard? Collar? White collar? Soft hand. Strong, but soft. Who? "Who are you? I know you, don't I" *Hey, wait a minute. That's me talking! I can talk.*

"No, but I'm your friend."

"Friend? Where am I?"

"Hospital. Asheville Memorial Hospital, but you're all right. You're going to be just fine."

"I think I know you, but I can't remember. Can't remember anything."

"You will, in time."

"How long have I been here?"

"Not long. You'll be going home soon. Your people are here."

"You're a priest, aren't you?"

"Yes. You should go back to sleep, now."

"Will you stay with me?"

"I will always be with you."

"That's nice. That's...I'm so... sleepy... so. . ."

The following Monday turned out to be a lot easier than Sam Abrahms had expected. He had anticipated having all kinds of hassles getting Maggie's car released from the City garage, but there had been nothing but smiles and total cooperation from the officials there. All he'd had to do was sign a few papers and pay a twenty-five dollar storage fee. He'd had to take care of that problem early, since all Maggie's clothes were in a suitcase which lay untouched on the back seat. Having taken a taxi to the garage, he drove Maggie's Honda back to the motel, after filling it up with gas. Leaving her car in the parking lot, he drove his own Buick back to the hospital, taking the suitcase with him, turning over in his mind several things he and Maggie's mother had talked about over dinner the night before. He hadn't been surprised when Lena had told him she didn't drive. Never had:

"My husband always drove, Sam. After he died, Margaret took me anywhere I needed to go. If she wasn't around, I simply took a taxi, or the bus. Besides, there weren't many places I needed to go anyway; the grocery store and my church were both within walking distance..."

Sam had asked the motel manager if they could leave Maggie's car there for a few days, until he could come back for it, or send someone for it. Again he'd met with a friendly attitude.

"No problem. No problem at all, Mr. Abrahms," the manager had said. "You folks take all the time you need."

"How are you going to do that?" Lena had wanted to know. "Can you afford to take more time off from the station?"

"Maggie's the most popular anchor we've ever had, Mrs. DeVries. People who work there would do anything for her. If I can't get away, there are at least a dozen guys, reporters, camera people, who would be glad to drive up here and take her car back, especially under these circumstances," he'd said.

But what had surprised Sam the most was Lena's reaction to his plan to take Maggie home with him, not back to her apartment. He'd thought she would vehemently object to that idea, which would be no less than 'living in sin', but Lena had nodded and said, "Best thing in the world for her, Sam. I've told her any number of times she ought to marry you. I know she loves you, and Bo's attitude toward you isn't an issue any more, is it? Maybe this whole crazy adventure will finally convince her that Bo, bless his poor heart, and that good-for-nothing Robert Ellis, are dead. Gone for good. She needs to get on with her life. Her life with you."

"I'm glad you feel that way, Mrs. DeVries."

Lucifer's Children

"Stop calling me 'Mrs., DeVries,' Sam. Lena's fine. What do think happened out there?"

"I don't know, but whatever it was scared her pretty damn bad."

"I'm sure that ugly old Indian woman just took her out there in those mountains, got her good and lost, stole all that expensive stuff she told Margaret to buy, and left her to die. I wish I could get my hands on her."

"I guess Maggie's the only one who can tell us, eventually. Doctor Weiner said she'd get unblocked about it someday when she least expects it. Main thing is she's okay, now. I'll make sure she stays that way, too."

The germ of the idea of how to do just that had come to him the night before. He knew just the kind of therapy Maggie would need. Work. Get her back in the saddle. And being News Director of a substantial television station gave him enough clout to pull it off. Oh yeah. He'd use the time during the long drive back to Raleigh to mentally work out the details, but basically, he knew his scheme would work, and, he made a bet with himself that before the cruise was over, Maggie would marry him—aboard ship!

∽

Tom Lewis

CHAPTER 21

Ramon felt like a private detective, spying on the wife of a jealous husband; not that he knew much about either private detectives or jealous husbands. But he had to make sure. He needed to convince himself that Margaret DeVries-Ellis would be all right.

He had followed them back to Raleigh, and from the relative safety of civilian clothes and the rental car. From a discreet distance he had watched the tall man named Abrahms take her home, but only long enough to collect some of her clothes, which the Henderson woman, clucking like a hen, helped load into Abrahms' car, then to an apartment near the television station.

Every night for the first week, he'd gone back to the library where he'd studied old newspaper clippings of the unsuccessful search for the missing plane. He now knew why she had done what she did. His heart ached for her loss, but ached worse because he'd been too late to help her.

He'd watched them for ten days; following them to the Triangle Health Club, golf courses, tennis courts, restaurants, bars, and movies. He'd seen her color improve. Seen her laughing. Walking with her head up. She seemed fine, now. Healthy again. She was going to be just fine.

And now, he was going to be, too. He was sure of it.

He turned in the rental car, bought a ticket to Guatemala City, via Dallas and Mexico City, and telephoned St. Andrew's.

"This is Father O'Connor."

"Dan, this is Ramon Barillas. I'm waiting for a plane at the airport and wanted to call before leaving. I'm sorry I didn't have a chance to see you personally."

"That's okay. You found her, I take it."

"Yes. I think she will be alright, now. She seems to be in good hands."

"I'm glad. Are you going back to Rome?"

"No, not directly. I'm going home for a week or two. Guatemala City, but I couldn't leave without thanking you for all your help."

"I didn't do much. Do you think you will be alright as well?"

"I think so, Father. I didn't reach her in time, but she survived everything and seems to be recuperating in fine fashion. She seems very happy, and so am I."

"Good. I hope you have a nice long visit with your family."

"Thank you, and I hope your Bishop will soon send you a new assistant."

"So do I, Ramon. Spring training is long over. The football season won't be far away."

"Good luck, Dan. You are a good friend, and I won't forget you."

"Nor I you. *Vaya con Dios*, Ramon."

By day he'd ridden around all over Guatemala City with his father, who, in his eighties, nevertheless still drove his taxi with long-practiced skill. *Why not, my son? It's all I know how to do anyway.* By night he'd rollicked with his nieces and nephews. There were twenty-two more of them than there had been the last time he'd been home. And, on them and their parents, he'd spent most of the remaining money Cardinal Zimmer had given him, guessing that his crusty superior had expected him to do just that!

His tearful father had given him a lift to the airport, kissed him on both cheeks, and watched him board the jet which would carry him back to Rome. Ramon had also cried like a baby, but by the time he landed at Leonardo Da Vinci, he was composed, beardless, and ready to go back to work. Anxious, even.

One month to the day after he'd gone, he reported to Cardinal Zimmer's office, briefcase in hand, and well-rested. He'd slept thirty consecutive nights without dreaming even once.

ഗ

Lucifer's Children

Chapter 22

Within the span of a few weeks, Robert had managed to push the mountaintop meeting with Lucifer into a distant cubbyhole of his memory. The reason was simple; he was too busy to think of anything beyond his new life, which was nothing short of incredible. With the help of his new secretary and his eager-beaver staff, he had settled into the daily schedule of a workaholic; teaching sports broadcasting three mornings a week at the University, endless hours of film study in his sunny, spacious office, and preparing for his own actual broadcasts, which at this time of year included select Major League Baseball games, golf tournaments, and preparing for the upcoming NFL season. He was looking forward to the World Series games, which he'd be "covering" with Buck Mayhew acting as color man. Even more satisfying was the fact that he knew his work, now totally rescued from the chains of alcohol, was rapidly approaching the level of such respected sportscasters as Dick Enberg, Al Michaels and Brent Mussberger.

His time off was equally enjoyable, whether he spent it quietly at home with the adoring Isabella, or 'out on the town' with various new friends, like Buck and Buck's latest 'wife', Annette, a tall, busty blonde who reminded him a little of Beth.

On the Friday morning of his fourth week, he was informed he had a personal call. He clicked off the VCR, picked up the phone and leaned back. "Robert Ellis."

"Hello, Dad?"

"Bo! How's it going, Champ?"

"Great. You wouldn't believe. Say, Dad, you got any plans for tonight?"

"Nothing that can't be changed. Why?"

"They gave me a night off. Wonder if we could have dinner together somewhere?"

"You bet. You mean the four of us or just the two of us?"

"Just you and me."

"Sure. You know the Piccadilly? Over on LL Street?"

"No, but I can find it. What, about eight?"

"Eight's fine. I'll call for a reservation, and my treat, okay?"

"Super. Gotta run, now. They're cracking the whip again. See you at eight."

Robert hung up, smiling. Bo's voice was that of a man, for sure, but his language usage was still pretty much that of his fourteen-year-old kid. His smile turned into a frown of guilt. Damn. I should have called him long before now. Well, I'll buy him the best dinner in the house. Wonder if he's drinking yet...?

"This is some joint, Dad. Sure you can afford it?"

Robert looked across the table at his son. The money Bo had told him was included in his "scholarship" was evidently sufficient for him to dress well, but not so much he could splurge on dinners at four-star restaurants. "Sure I can. Isabella and I come here often. You want a beer or something?"

"A beer would be fine. They have Heineken here?"

"They have anything you want here. Don't ask me how they do it, though. Food's a little pricey, but very good. Crab legs especially. You like seafood?"

"I like just about everything. You order. I'll just have what you have."

Robert smiled, and motioned for the waiter. He couldn't get over the feeling, like he was a proud Papa taking his Harvard freshman son out to dinner at the best restaurant in Boston. He felt tremendous pride in the way Bo looked and acted. Self assured, somewhat polished, and good-looking as hell. He gave the middle-aged waiter their order, got a "Very good, sir" in return, and leaned forward. "You look great, son. How're you getting along with Marta?"

"Fine. She doesn't know an electron from an election, but she's a big help to me in, ah, other ways."

"I'll bet." Robert's smile broadened into a locker-room grin. "Sex wipes out problems faster than anything I know of."

Watching Bo's face turn beet-red, he was instantly sorry he'd said that, and changed the subject, asking Bo how his studies were going. Throughout their meal, which Bo ate with surprisingly good table manners, Robert listened to his son talk about his sophisticated course of study, equipment, devices, and computer language, which was far beyond his own comprehension. In turn, he told Bo about the amazing way he could sit in his broadcast booth, push a few buttons, and fill a fifty-thousand-seat stadium with screaming fans, then do the play-by-play, commercials and all, or sit the next day in a simulated tower and follow the shots of Nicklaus, Watson, and Greg Norman from tee to green. Three hours had passed before they knew it.

Their waiter had poured a third cup of coffee when a voice interrupted the flow of their conversation, which had turned nostalgic, with Bo saying how much he still missed his mother. "I sure wish she was here, Dad. If only you two—"

"Well, if it isn't Messrs. Ellis, Junior and Senior. Good Evening."

Robert and Bo looked up into the smiling face of Manuel Munoz, dressed in elegant formals, escorting a forty-ish, olive-skinned brunette who could most charitably be described as buxom. She seemed stuffed into her black taffeta gown. For once, Robert engaged his brain before he did his mouth, remembering that a few centuries ago, men liked their women to have figures that were...substantial. "Senor Munoz," Robert said, rising. Bo followed suit.

"Permit me to introduce Miss Inez Conti." Miss Conti's smile exaggerated the upper of her two chins, but she didn't open her cupie-doll mouth to say one word. Munoz pronounced the heavy lady's first name 'Ee-ness'. "We have been to the opera. Excellent performance of 'Fidelio'. Have you enjoyed a good dinner together?"

"Yes, sir," Bo replied. This is an awesome restaurant."

"True, but don't you have a midnight curfew, young man?"

A stricken look instantly came over Bo's face. "Ohmygod, I forgot what time it was. Dad, I gotta run. I can just make it. Thanks for the dinner."

"No problem, Champ. Enjoyed it. We'll get together again soon. Promise."

When Bo rushed out, Robert said, "Would you like to join me?"

"Thank you, Robert," Munoz said, "But I have a table reserved across the room, in the area where I can enjoy my cigar. But I am happy to see you. I was going to give you a call anyway. Tomorrow is Saturday. Can you take the day off and come to my house at say, nine o'clock? I'd like to take you on a tour of Kaneville. I'm sure you will find it interesting."

"Sure. I'd enjoy that."

"Good. Until tomorrow then. Oh, by the way, I'm told Robert Junior is making great strides in his studies. You should be quite proud of him."

"I am, believe you me. See you tomorrow at nine."

"Nine sharp, please." It was a military order.

"Nine sharp. You got it."

Robert shook the offered hand, then remained standing for a moment as Munoz led his lady through the maze of tables. Watching them, Robert suppressed the urge to giggle: Ricardo Montalban, for sure, pulling a shiny Steinway baby grand behind him. He sat down for a few more minutes to finish his coffee, utterly satisfied with the evening so far, and thinking about how lovely it was going to be in the hot-tub with Isabella for an hour before bedtime when he got home. He gave no thought at all to dropping two hundred bucks on the table when he left, which barely covered the bill, plus a twenty percent tip.

Lucifer's Children

Appropriately, it was named Kane Street instead of Main Street, and was split into two halves by a shallow, south-flowing stream that wasn't quite wide enough to be called a river. Shops, stores and other small businesses rested on the lowest tier, on both sides of the stream, while the major residential areas and the schools nestled high on its western bank, where they would be protected from the winter northwesterlies. From the center of the town, West Kane ran for maybe a quarter mile south before it petered out into no more than a dirt cart path. North, it became State Road 89, which Munoz told Robert it eventually led to a main east-west highway, Kaneville's only link to the rest of the world. From north to south, East Kane and West Kane were linked by only two bridges; the Fourth Street bridge and the Eighth Street bridge. None of the narrow, bisecting streets were called Avenues, Munoz explained, "When we designed the town, we knew it would grow, but we wanted it to always seem as though it was laid out with no idea it would ever become more than a small village, which of course it was, originally. As you can see, we have been very careful to keep the town looking rather ordinary. Typical of any small mountain town one might encounter."

Robert stopped walking and took a second look around. Nothing stood out. The buildings were a mixture of old brick and timber, stucco, concrete, and wood plank; some old, some new, just as they might have been anywhere in rural North Carolina. Probably the most modern looking edifice was the Federal Post Office building, which Munoz informed him was only twenty years old. "Before it was built, the post office was located at Tyson's General Store, two blocks south. It doesn't look like it, but Kaneville is a fully incorporated, quite legitimate town of approximately ten thousand souls. We are in Lee County, and have our own "city council", Town Hall, a mayor, a volunteer Fire Department, even a Police Chief and one Police car. All the trappings of a regular, thriving small town."

Robert nodded. Looking left from where they stood, he could see a sizable supermarket, a gas station/Quick Mart, and two blocks down, the familiar golden arch of a McDonald's. To his right, he spotted a number of other small business storefronts, a café, bank, and sidewalk arts and crafts type shops that featured baskets of apples along with an assortment of handmade furniture and whatnots. Munoz caught his glance and said, "We don't get too many tourists, but those who wander into our valley find the inevitable doo-dads and mountain grown apples. There's a fifties style soda fountain in the drug store, and we even have an old fashioned blacksmith shop, but no motel as such. The tiny old hotel you see up there is much too quaint for the few visitors who may be thinking of spending a night."

He pointed east. Part way up the steep slope was a collection of low buildings. "Up there is our 'industrial area' so to speak. The cap making factory, the rendering plant where we make and package the popular Kaneville Sausage and canned ham, and further up, that's the new bottled water plant. We're soon going to be shipping a lot out, taking advantage of the new craze for spring water."

"Amazing," Robert said. "I see you even have a church."

Munoz chuckled. "Yes, well, that is a necessary prop. Would you care to have a cup of coffee, Robert?"

"Sure. Why not." Robert got the clear impression that Munoz didn't want to offer any further comment about the forlorn little church. As they walked up West Kane to the café, Robert noticed there was Saturday morning traffic, both vehicular and pedestrian, that would have been normal in any town, but was completely surprised that several people spoke to him in passing, calling him by name and smiling, as if they'd known him for years. Some even asked about Isabella and Bo. So did the aproned waiter at the café who brought their coffee in white mugs. "Been enjoying your games, Mr. Ellis. You do a helluva job. Who you think's gonna win the Series?"

Flattered, Robert said, "Well thanks. I don't know, the Braves seem pretty strong. Got good pitching."

"That's what I think, too," the man said, moving back behind his counter. "Ya'll need more coffee, just sing out."

Munoz' smile was smug. "It appears you already have a following. And, I hear good things about your classes. You will go far, Robert."

The two of them made more small talk until the door opened and Robert's spine stiffened as Cain came through the door. Ignoring him completely, the albino spoke to Munoz. "The bus is in."

Munoz gave Robert a pat on the arm. "Excuse me, please. I may be an hour. Meantime, make yourself comfortable. Look around all you like. Nothing in town is out of bounds for you." With those words, he followed the giant out. Robert stood, walked to the window, sipped his coffee, and watched them walk down to the gas station that apparently also was the bus station. A Trailways bus was sitting there idling, and at least a dozen well-dressed people of various ages and both sexes got off and waited for the bus driver to fish their luggage from the side panel bins. Munoz and Cain greeted the new arrivals warmly, and Robert watched as several cars materialized from nowhere, and within minutes, the parking lot was deserted. The bus driver went inside the station, leaving the luggage bins open. An idea suddenly erupted in Robert's mind. If somebody sneaked inside one of those luggage bins unseen, maybe at night—

The fleeting thought of escaping was interrupted by someone walking right past him. A pregnant woman with blond hair. *Beth?* He put the coffee mug on the windowsill and ran out. "Beth? Beth, wait up."

Hearing her name, Beth turned around, recognized Robert, turned back and started walking away from him, fast. Robert caught up with her, grabbed her arm and stopped her. "Beth? Don't you recognize me? What's the matter?"

"I shouldn't be talking to you, Robert. Let go of my arm."

"Sorry. Why the hell not? Can't you have a cup of coffee with me?"

Beth shifted the sack she was carrying to her other arm. "I just shouldn't, that's all."

"Who says? Look, where were you going? Maybe I could walk you home."

"No. You can't. I mean, I'm not going home. I'm on my lunch break from the cap factory."

"What? You're pregnant and working? On Saturday yet?"

"We don't normally work on Saturdays. There's a special order that has to be filled. We make all kinds of billed caps there; baseball caps, seed caps, whatever. Most of the women who work there are pregnant. The work isn't hard."

"Can't you take five minutes to sit down, for Christsakes? What about that bench over there?"

"Well, just for a minute, maybe."

They walked to one of the empty green-painted wooden benches that graced nearly every storefront. Beth sat down heavily. "I get pooped out so easily these days." She turned to Robert, her face softening. "You look good, Robert. Prosperous. How's Bo? Have you seen him?"

"Just last night. We're both fine. You're looking great yourself."

"I don't feel all that great. At least I won't have to carry this kid around but nine months. Some of the women aren't so lucky."

"Sorry, I don't understand."

"Those fathered by that monster take a whole year to get born."

"Are you talking about Cain?"

"Who else? He rapes at least one girl per night."

"Rape?"

Beth gave him a sharp look. "Of course rape. You don't think any woman in her right mind would want to go to bed with him, do you?"

Robert nodded. "I guess not." He decided not to mention the evening in Lucifer's garden.

"What's worse is, the poor girl he 'chooses' for the night doesn't have a damn thing to say about it. They say he's potent as hell. Like a stud horse. And, all his kids are twins. I hope he never gets a yen for me."

"Speaking of studs, have you seen Abner lately?"

Beth's face contorted into something ugly. "Abner! Are you kidding? Not since they brought me here. He probably doesn't even remember my name."

"Jesus, Beth, you make this place sound like a baby factory rather than a cap—"

"That's exactly what it is." Beth's eyes narrowed. "Have you done your first share of Daddy-duty yet?"

Robert's face suddenly felt warm. "For God's *sake*, Beth."

"Don't you mean for Satan's sake? Where are they keeping you, Coach, locked up in some ivory tower? Don't you have a clue as to what's really going on here? Don't you understand that we're nothing more than slaves? Especially the women, unless they're practically Einsteins. They use you up, and when they've squeezed all they want out of you they feed you to the fucking hogs."

"What the hell are you talking about, Beth?

"Oh, I know all about your new job and the fancy apartment. Your new lady who can't talk. You fool, don't you understand that when one of those bright-eyed kids you're teaching gets to be good as you, you're history. They will—Oh *shit*."

Beth's eyes had looked past him, widening with fear. Robert turned to see what had stopped her tirade in mid-sentence. Cain was walking toward them, a sickening smile on his pale face. "You, there," he said, "You're supposed to be at work. What are you two talking about?"

"We were talking about my son, that's all," Robert lied.

It was obvious the albino wasn't buying a word of it. "Senor Munoz is looking for you," he said to Robert. To Beth, he sneered, "You would do well to gossip only with the other women, Miss Oliver."

Beth stood, grabbed her sack, and stammered, "I—I'm sorry, I didn't realize what time it was. I'm on my way. Good to see you again, Robert."

She waddled down the sidewalk fast as her overloaded legs could carry her.

Robert could have sworn he heard a low chuckle coming from the Albino's throat. He turned back to Robert and said, "Attractive woman, but talks too much. She will learn. Senor Munoz is waiting for you at the café. How do you like my town?"

"What? Oh. Terrific, Mr. Cain. Just terrific. Beats anything I've ever seen. If you'll excuse me..."

Robert left the giant standing there smiling, and hurried back to the café, wrinkling his nose. As he opened the door of the café, he remembered where he'd encountered that smell. Long ago, when he was a kid with his father at the circus. They'd passed by the straw and shit-filled elephant cages, and he'd had to hold his nose. The odor was exactly—

"—a good visit with Miss Beth?" Munoz was talking to him.

"Yes. It was nice to see her again. She looks fine."

"Of course. Most pregnant women look radiant."

Robert tried to change the subject. "Who were all those people getting off the bus?"

"Ah, yes. You noticed them. They are former graduates. Alumni who have done particularly well on the outside. They've been invited back for the Headmaster's cabal, which is coming soon. Between now and then, we will be welcoming over fifty thousand of them. It will be what you might call, in sports language, homecoming."

"Really."

"Yes. But now we'd best be going back. I have a rather busy evening of entertaining to do, and I'm sure your lovely Isabella is missing you. Have you enjoyed your tour?"

"I sure have. Will I have a chance to come back here sometime?"

Munoz pursed his thin lips, seemingly thinking the question over. Then he smiled again. "Perhaps. Perhaps you will, Robert. Someday."

༄

Chapter 23

"How did you manage to pull it off?" Maggie asked. They were walking out of the station manager's office. "I don't believe what I just heard old Scrooge say."

Sam grinned at her like a kid who'd just found a ten-dollar bill on the street. "Let's run over to the Ratskeller. I'll tell you over a celebration drink."

The Ratskeller, only a few minutes' drive from the station, had been their favorite watering hole ever since they'd started dating. It featured old-fashioned high-backed booths that offered a modicum of privacy, and during the afternoon hours, the owners didn't care whether or not their customers ordered anything to eat, so long as they kept buying their overpriced drinks. Sam gave the *dirndl*-clad waitress his order; Vodka on the rocks for himself, and a glass of Chablis for Maggie. Maggie never drank much of anything alcoholic, partly because liquor, any kind of liquor, went to her head instantly, and partly because of her past life with Robert. The more Robert had drunk, the less she had, but she still liked to sip an occasional glass of light wine.

"Okay, Mr. Smug. "she said when the waitress had brought their drinks and left them alone, "How did you do it? Three and a half *weeks?* And the station's picking up the tab for *both* of us?"

"Yep." Sam was enjoying this. "Charm, Maggie. Pure charm"

Maggie's eyes narrowed. "Chutzpah, you mean. You've got your share, that's for sure. I'm a living testament to that, but nobody's got charm enough to talk that bean-counter into shelling out money enough for a long Caribbean cruise for two, first class no less, and call it an assignment. Are you blackmailing him?"

"I'll never tell."

"Come on, Sam. Everybody knows our illustrious leader's so tight with a nickel he'd recycle the toilet paper if he could get away with it. What's the catch?"

"Okay. The catch is, you'll come back full-time after we get back. Chief anchor, Monday through Friday. No more reporting and no more weekends. Big raise, too."

"Sam!"

"Walsh thinks our ratings will start climbing back up if you anchor the six and the eleven. I think so too. That's why he's so generous. He'd sacrifice his wife and kids for better ratings."

Maggie stared at her lover while he explained it all to her. She knew he was telling the truth. Emmitt Walsh was able to put furs on his wife, plant his children in posh private schools, and drive around in a big Mercedes because WRDU had stayed on top of the market since he'd been station manager. He could be downright niggardly with budgets and staff, but not where ratings were concerned. Maggie's prolonged absence had caused enough of a dip for him to be alarmed, and he was determined to bring her back, with raise, promotion, bribes— anything to re-establish his spot on top of the fickle market share.

"So," Maggie said, "Walsh is dangling a big carrot instead of wielding his usual stick. I feel like a piece of meat."

"Prime choice."

"Uh-huh, and you had nothing whatsoever to do with it."

"Well, I did sort of point out to him that doing a major piece on the new cruise ship mania was something he'd already tentatively approved. When I mentioned it might be a nice way to kill two birds with one stone; one being to finish up your home-therapy, and the other to do a socko story while getting you back to work, he put two and two together— "

"And came up with two? You and me?"

Sam grinned again, waving at the waitress for a refill, "Hey, you have to have a cameraman, don't you? Besides, Walsh is no fool, he knew neither of us could turn it down if we could go together."

"He was right. So when do we leave?"

"Next Monday. He wants the whole package done up before Christmas. It's already December third. We'd better go bikini shopping for you."

"You've got a one-track mind, Abrahms. "A new bikini's way down on the list of things I'll need to get for such a trip, not to mention all the packing, and, *I'll* do the shopping, thank you very much. If you were with me, we'd never get past Frederick's." She looked at her watch. "Might as well get started on it, too. Come on, finish your drink and drop me off at my apartment. I'll need to call Mama, and I ought to talk to Tammy, too. Tell her I'll be gone for a while again."

They both stood, and Sam dropped a ten and a five on the table. He caught Maggie's questioning look and chuckled. "Last of the big spenders."

Smiling, Maggie shook her head, then in an afterthought, said, "Speaking of spending, don't you have some things to shop for yourself?"

Sam put his arm around her waist as they walked to the door. "Already did." His left hand dug down into his pants pocket, his fingers enclosing the small, velvet-covered box. "Got everything I need for the trip."

Tammy Henderson, Maggie's across-the-hall neighbor, lived alone. Well, not quite alone, if you counted the Cocker Spaniel whose disposition toward anyone (with the singular exception of Bo Ellis) was as surly as Tammy's was bubbly. Earlier in her tenancy in 4C, Tammy had also had, from time to time, at least a dozen cats, but her dog had hated them, too, plus the cats had been far too independent for Tammy anyway. They were loving when *they* wanted to be, not when she wanted them to be. So, Cleo (short for Cleopatra) slept on her bed every night,

Lucifer's Children

which was no mean trick, since Tammy slept on a single bed, and her own body took up most of it. She had acquired the dog from the pound while it was still a puppy, and promptly named it before she'd known its sex. Cleo, of course, didn't mind having a famous feminine name, as long as the bowl of Alpo was filled every morning, and he was taken out religiously every night, which had often been Bo's task; a kind of reciprocation for the many nights Tammy had baby-sat him when he'd been younger.

Tammy had been truly fond of Bo, just as she was of Maggie. She had been especially sympathetic— and actually helpful— during Maggie's bad period after Bo's plane had disappeared, mainly because she was always at home. Tammy Henderson hadn't worked for several years; collecting a hefty disability check every month, although she never mentioned to anyone what had caused her disability, which was a 'bad back.' Maggie had never asked, either, and Tammy had often wondered if it was because of good manners or whether Maggie could care less. It was hard for Tammy not to envy Maggie's life style— professional and personal, but she was always careful not to pump Maggie too much about the glamorous world of television, or to ask too many of the wrong questions about her private life, especially about Sam Abrahms, and especially now that Maggie was back on her feet again after her terrible ordeal of being lost in the mountains for several days. But she was curious as hell about the priest. Only thing was, since Maggie'd been back home, there had been no opportune time to bring the subject up. Maybe this time, she thought, settling down onto Maggie's bedroom couch. She'd brought a Whitman's Sampler across the hall with her, as a sort of welcome-home-again present, knowing full well Maggie wouldn't eat more than one. She sampled a couple herself while Maggie told her of the cruise, all the while emptying closets and drawers and frowning at everything she dumped on her bed.

"...and after you guys get back, you're gonna start working full time again?"

"Yep," Maggie replied, holding up a short summer dress and wrinkling her nose. "I guess it's about time. Sam was right to start with. I need to get on with my life."

Tammy sighed, shifted her bulk on the sofa so she could reach her plump fingers into the Whitman's box she'd placed on the end table, and said. "God, he's a gorgeous man. You're one lucky lady, Maggie Ellis."

"Don't I know it. Only thing I don't know is how he was able to take so much time off to take care of me. Our boss usually frowns on people taking time off, unless they're in the hospital with quadruple pneumonia or something. But Sam got away with it somehow. Talk about a physical therapist! Since I've been back, he's kept me busy as the devil; swimming every day, plus the workouts three days a week, tennis, handball, you name it. I'm in better shape than I've ever been."

"It shows, honey. You look terrific. I bet the nights haven't been half bad, either."

Maggie gave her friend a knowing, indulgent smile. "Let's just say I've been able to sleep well." She held up a year-old red party dress. "Jesus, I can't go to the Captain's table wearing this old thing."

"I've missed you. Your Mom comes around faithfully every other day. After she told me about your being in the hospital, she doesn't say more than hello and good-bye to me, but this apartment looks spotless."

Maggie looked around. "Ain't it the truth. It's almost embarrassing. I'll tell you something, Tammy, I thought she'd pitch a fit when Sam took me to his place, but she didn't make a peep. So unlike her."

"Maybe she thinks you two will make it, you know, permanent."

"Not without a wedding ring. But I think she really likes Sam."

"What about the head part?"

"I give up. I swear, I don't think there's one thing here I can— What about what? Oh. Well, I guess I've finally begun to accept the fact that Bo's gone."

"And you don't remember anything at all about what happened in the mountains?"

"No. It's like *nothing* happened. I mean, there's just a void there. Just a white blur. I can't remember anything at all before I woke up in Sam's car, coming home. Sam and Mama told me that doctor said I might remember someday, and then again, I might not. But I've decided not to worry about it anymore."

Watching Maggie discard item after item of her wardrobe, skirts, blouses, and dresses she herself would kill to have a figure small enough to wear, Tammy chewed two more chocolates while she turned over in her mind how to bring up the subject she really wanted to talk about. Was it better not to mention it at all? If Maggie couldn't remember anything, she most likely wouldn't remember him either, even if she'd seen him. At last, she couldn't hold back. "Maggie, a priest came here looking for you. A Catholic priest."

"A priest? I don't know any priests. When?"

"While you were gone. Funny, he sure acted like he knew *you*. I told him you were in that motel up in Asheville. You didn't see him? Monsignor Barrias, or something like that."

Maggie flopped down on the bed, exasperated. "Who knows? I don't even remember what my *doctor* looked like. What did he want?"

"Beats me. He just wanted to know where he could find you. Are you sure you don't know a priest? Maybe your age, good looking as he could be, had a beard, and the softest eyes I've ever seen on anybody, man or woman. Talked with an accent, maybe European. I couldn't tell for sure, but he certainly wasn't American."

"I'm Lutheran, Tammy, or was, I guess. I don't even have any Catholic friends, let alone any priests."

Tammy decided not to push it. "Well, I guess it's not important. What's next?"

"I'm going shopping for the cruise, that's what. Not that I have all that much money left to shop with, now that Robert's checks..."

"Want some company?"

"Why not? Sure. Maybe you can help me find a place that sells summer things in December. Just let me call Mama first."

But Lena DeVries was not at home. She was sitting in Sam Abrahms' office. "That's the most beautiful ring I ever saw, Sam. When are you going to give it to her?"

Sam closed the box and pocketed the ring. "I don't know. Haven't planned that far ahead, but I'm sure I'll know the right moment when it comes. I asked you to come by for a reason, Lena, besides telling you about the cruise, I mean. In some ways, I'm a little old-fashioned. I plan to speak to the Captain the first chance I get, hoping we can get married on board ship, but before we sail, I'd like to know I have your blessings. I don't have any folks of my own, so it's kind of important to me that—"

"Oh, for heaven's sake. Of course you do, Sam. Don't you worry about that. You just worry about when that 'right moment' comes. I just wish Margaret had met you... Well, that's all water under the bridge now. But I'll kill you both if you don't get that wedding on video tape."

"Full color and stereo. I promise."

Maggie and Sam, struggling mightily to keep focused on their primary mission, got enough tape and interviews during the first week of the cruise to fill a dozen packages. They were somewhat surprised that not all the passengers were members of the rich and famous, though there were plenty of them, along with the pairs of blue-haired, sharp-eyed women looking to erase their widowhood, several obvious fortune hunters, and a number of young middle class honeymooners.

The remaining two weeks plus was a fairytale honeymoon of their own. By day, they sunned and swam, shopped like every other tourist at the quaint shops on every island, enjoyed several fabulous dinners at the Captain's table, and made love every night.

While Maggie slept in one morning, Sam managed to talk to the Captain about the possibility of the on-board wedding, and was assured by the genial officer that there would be no problem at all, and who even suggested a date— at the turn around point of the cruise, when there was to be a lavish costume ball. Sam thought about that, and decided that night would be the right time to give Maggie the ring that was burning a hole in his pocket, and asked if the Captain could perform a quiet, simple ceremony the following day. Captain Lars Jensen affably agreed.

For her part, Maggie also liked the charming Scandinavian Captain of the *Blue Princess,* and joked to him at dinner one night that since he seemed to be everywhere, all over the ship, always dressed in his immaculate whites, he might not really be the chief sailor of the boat at all, but an actor hired to play the part of a Captain, like the toothy character on the old Love Boat series, while the real Captain was busy navigating to, from, and between the islands. Captain Jensen guffawed, then seriously assured Maggie that he actually worked up to fourteen hours per day, and was always on the bridge during the critical times of docking, anchoring, and leaving port, and always kept one watchful eye on the weather, just in case.

The night of the party was upon them before they knew it. The assistant purser had patiently helped them with appropriate costumes; Sam as a dashing, black-clad Zorro, and Maggie as a vampish, provocatively-dressed Mata Hari. On their way to the main salon, Maggie wryly commented, "Jesus, Sam, I've got enough makeup caked on to paint the whole ship. You sure you want to go in there with me?"

"You look sexy as hell, madam spy. Just don't dip your eyelashes into your champagne glass. I guess I look pretty ridiculous too, don't I?"

They were both still a trifle self conscious about their garb until the noticed how outlandishly some of the other passengers were dressed. The orchestra was in full swing when Sam pointed at a couple on the dance floor; the man, dressed as Sir Walter Raleigh, trying to get a little closer to his Queen Elizabeth, but failing miserably because of her dress. Their chuckles became louder when they spotted an elderly couple; he dressed as a medieval knight in cardboard armor trying desperately to keep his sword out of the way of his animated partner who was dressed as a twenties flapper, expertly executing the steps of the Charleston. Other couples were equally hilarious, but Sam pointed to a pair who were the most mismatched of all. "Look at those two, honey. That John Smith can't be more than five feet tall, and how about his Pocahontas. She's got to be seventy if she's a day, and what, two hundred pounds maybe? The Purser must be laughing his head off."

Also laughing uncontrollably, Maggie watched the sweating, triple-chinned woman for a moment, whose enormous bosom threatened to bounce out of her too-tight, fringed buckskin dress at any moment. "God, Sam, she looks about as much like as Indian woman as—"

Sam glanced at Maggie, instantly sober. Beneath the garish makeup, her face had gone pale.

"Maggie? Maggie, what is it?"

Maggie stood abruptly and rushed out the nearest door to the rail. Sam caught up with her. "What's the matter, honey?" He grabbed her and turned her around to face him. Her eyes had gone blank, her mouth open, lips moving, but making no sound. "For God's sake, Maggie, What's happening?"

Maggie's body had gone stiff as the stanchion she was leaning against. Then she was shivering. Shaking. Sam searched her eyes, which gradually focused on his own. When her voice came, it was no more than a wheezing whisper. "I remember. I'm remembering it, Sam. All of it."

Sam stared at her for another minute, holding her vibrating body up. He had no idea what to say.

He watched her Mata Hari face contort into obvious pain. Maggie's fingers suddenly gripped his arms like twin vises. "What's the next stop, Sam?"

"Tomorrow. Antigua. Why?"

"I've got to get off this ship."

"But why?"

"I have to go back, that's why."

༄

Chapter 24

On December 15th, Robert went to work as usual, but for some reason, found his mind was wandering. He couldn't concentrate on the game films he'd planned to study— his early preparation for the Super Bowl was a little over a month away. All the players' numbers he was trying to memorize seemed to jam together in his head. He couldn't even distinguish the color of their jerseys. He caught himself mispronouncing many of their names.

Disgusted with his state of confusion, he decided to take a walk. Fifteen minutes later, he found himself meandering through the rows of empty seats in the football stadium, which as yet hadn't been cleaned up from last Sunday's game. He kicked aimlessly at empty cups and soiled hot dog wrappers. Finally he sat down in one of the pastel-painted seats, staring out onto the carpeted, striped field, now quiet as a cemetery.

He crossed his arms, allowing his thoughts to come and go, willy-nilly, without trying at all to channel them in any one direction. The first one that bounced in and out was that he'd seen Bo only once since their dinner at the Piccadilly. The cookout in the east park had been a somewhat stilted outing. Isabella couldn't make conversation, of course, and Bo's Marta had spent most of the afternoon and early evening complaining about Bo's at-home hours, so crammed with intense study, he had precious little time for her. The steaks had tasted bland. Artificial.

Robert rolled the word around in his mouth, and then spoke it aloud. "Artificial." Other words— synonyms, like a string of boxcars in a train, rolled past his closed eyelids: Manufactured. Constructed. Simulated. Pretended. False. Phony. He frowned. It was easy to live and work in this artificial, phony world. Too easy. Why wasn't he happy? What was bugging him? Like Buck Mayhew had recently reminded him, "Man, have we got it made. Heaven on earth. Everything we want. Everything we need. All the money we could ever spend. Great house. Women. Respect. We've got it all, Robert."

Yeah, right.

All but one thing. Freedom. We can come and go as we choose, but only inside this glass cage. Huge as it is, it's still a cage. A prison. It isn't real. This life isn't real. Beth was right. Cut it any way you want to, we're still slaves. Lucifer's robots. Robert slowly began to realize what Lucifer's secret was. What Munoz and Abner Highsmith and all the others knew but didn't talk about. Given enough time, he would, like Buck Mayhew and the others, forget it was phony. He'd start to believe, actually *believe* it was all real. Once that happened, he'd be lost forever. *And I mean fucking forever, man.* This place isn't heaven on earth. It's hell on earth. A hell as tangible as the rock it was carved out of. But there never was any prison built that somebody didn't escape from, was there? What was it Beth had said? They use you up and then feed you to the—

Robert suddenly thought about something else he'd seen in Kaneville. Without another thought, he jumped up, made his way to the monorail station, and twenty minutes later, was leaning across the desk of the male secretary of the Computer College. "I need to see my son, Robert Ellis, Junior. It's rather important."

Bo came through the door wearing a spotless white smock. "Hi, Dad. What brings you down here? Anything wrong?"

Robert gave the secretary-receptionist a quick side-glance and a smile. He put his arm around Bo's shoulders. "No. No, nothing's wrong. I was just in the neighborhood, and, hey, can you take a break for a few minutes? I had an idea I wanted to talk to you about."

Bo looked at the receptionist as if to ask for permission. A slight nod was given, and Bo said, "I guess so, my lab doesn't start for another twenty minutes or so. Want to walk outside for a few minutes?"

Outside, they both sat down on the grass. The 'sun' was warm. "Must be seventy-five out here," Bo said, grinning. "Some winter, huh?"

"Yeah. Like December in San Diego."

"Okay, what's on your mind, Dad?"

For the first time in a long while, Robert wished he had a cigarette. He took a deep breath, looked around to see if anyone might be within earshot, then leaned forward. "Bo, I think I've found a way out of here."

Bo's brow knitted. "Out of where, Dad? What are you talking about?"

"I'm talking about escaping. Getting out of this nightmare."

Bo's voice matched the incredulous look on his face. "Escape?"

Realizing he didn't have much time, Robert, keeping his voice low as possible, told Bo of his trip into Kaneville and his talk with Beth Oliver.

"...There are two buses a day. One at noon, one at night. I think we could sneak on board, hiding in the luggage compartment. The buses are always parked with one side hidden from the street. I think we could sneak on board. Crawl back into the luggage bin. If we're careful, the drivers won't see us. They always go in the bus station for a coffee, or maybe to go to the bathroom. It gets dark in Kaneville by five o'clock this time of year. We'd have to wear heavy coats and gloves because it'll probably be cold in those compartments, but it would only be for twenty, thirty miles before the bus stops somewhere else. Then we could—"

"Whoa, Dad. That's crazy. You can't be serious about this."

"I am, son. Dead serious. We've got to get out of here, and those buses may be our only chance."

Bo shook his head from side to side, as if he thought his father had totally flipped out. "I can't believe this. Even if such a hair-brain thing is possible, I want no part of it."

"What are you saying, Bo?"

"I'm saying I won't try it with you. Don't you understand? I don't *want* to leave here. They've just put me to work on a computer that's bigger than anything IBM ever built. It's absolutely fantastic. It'll do things you wouldn't *believe*, Dad. It takes up less space than..."

Listening to his son gush about his latest toy, Robert felt sick to his stomach. Bo was lost. Brainwashed. He'd already forgotten. Forgotten how he'd almost died. Oblivious to how his life depended on eating parts of other human beings. How utterly and unwittingly he'd come under the manipulative power of the Devil himself. Forgotten how much he'd loved and missed his own mother. *Maggie... Oh, Maggie, I'm sorry. I'm so goddamn sorry...*

In a near stupor, he made his way back to his office. If Bo refused to go with him, could he make it alone? Was it worth it to try? Would he have the guts to try? What if he didn't make it? What if they caught—?

"Mr. Ellis, a Mr. Highsmith called."

Robert stared at his secretary, not really hearing what she'd said.

"Mr. Ellis? Are you all right?"

"What? No, I'm fine. What was it?"

"Mr. Highsmith called. You're to go home right away. I... I didn't know where you were. I'm sorry. Is there anything you want me to—?"

Robert was on his feet and out the door before she finished her sentence.

He burst through his own front door to see Abner Highsmith, now dressed in a Brooks Brothers suit, sitting on his living room sofa. Even as Highsmith rose to greet him, hand outstretched, Robert saw Isabella coming from the bedroom, a suitcase in her hand. She had a smile on her face, and there was a light, a new light, in her dark eyes. Robert, in that very instant, was struck by what he'd failed to see before. Isabella's hair, her eyes, her figure, were so much like...*like Maggie's*. "What's going on, honey?" He turned to face Highsmith. "What's the matter? Why are you here, Abner?"

Highsmith said, "How do, Robert. I hope I haven't caused you undue alarm. Munoz sent me. He is mighty busy just now with all the people who are arriving. Nothing is the matter. You are to be congratulated. Miss Isabella, here, is expecting. I'm here to take her to Kaneville."

Robert stared at him, then looked at his mistress, who smiled sweetly at him, dropped the suitcase, and held her arms up as if rocking a baby in them. Then she ran to him and threw her arms around his neck. In the confusion of the moment, Robert was unable to tell whether her gesture was one of joy or desperation.

"Why don't you come with us?" Highsmith was saying. "You will need to choose another young lady, and it will save me from having to make another trip. Senor Munoz is keeping me uncommonly busy these days."

Robert blanched at Highsmith's words. He didn't dare look at Isabella, whose mortification at Highsmith's talk of his choosing another woman had to certainly exceed his own embarrassment. Yet, he couldn't help but think there might be one more chance to case the bus station, and like a seed pearl, the grain of a plan was rapidly taking shape in his mind. "Sure. I'd like to. Last time I was there, I noticed an old-fashioned barbershop on East Kane. I could use a haircut."

Highsmith nodded approvingly, then laughed. "Yessir, you do. That head of yours looks thick as a blackberry patch!"

Lucifer's Children

Keeping his face and demeanor neutral as he could, Robert paid more attention to the details of his second trip into Kaneville, noting, for instance, how cleverly the tunnel passageway from the university was connected to the town— through the back wall of an old barn located at the extreme southern edge of the town. The biggest difference in how the town looked now as compared to before was there were fewer people out and about, no doubt because of the weather. It was freezing. Robert was glad he'd followed Highsmith's advice to wear an overcoat, hat, and gloves.

At the corner of 8th street, Highsmith, carrying Isabella's suitcase, paused and said, "Why don't you go ahead and get your haircut now. I'll take Isabella to her new quarters, and meet you in an hour at the town hall. We have arranged to have a number of young ladies there. I am sure you will find one to your liking."

Robert nodded, feeling a gut-wrenching sadness as he looked into the soft brown eyes of the woman who had shared so much of his life lately, and would soon bear his child. He silently reminded himself to play the game out, and didn't ask whether he'd ever see Isabella again, or whether he'd ever see his new son or daughter. Instead, he leaned forward, kissed her softly on her forehead, whispered, "Goodbye, Isabella. I was very, very happy with you." Then he turned on his heel and began walking north, without looking back...

The barber, who said his name was Ed Conway, snipped away, chattered about the upcoming Super Bowl game, and charged Robert five dollars. Robert gave him a ten, told him to keep the change, and strode back out into the icy air on West Kane. The whole time he'd sat in the barber chair, he'd watched the bus unload yet another group of Lucifer's children, saw them climb into the waiting cars and leave, obviously heading, one at a time, south— toward the barn.

Robert tried his best to look casual as he walked by the bus. Then he ducked quickly around to the side that was hidden from street view and from those who might be peering out the windows. He scanned the lower portion of the bus body, eyeing the still open luggage compartments. It would work. He knew it would, if only he could sneak on the six o'clock bus, after dark. He knelt down so he could have a better peek into the mostly empty bin. Then he heard the crunch of heavy footsteps behind him. He turned and stood in the same motion, staring into the grinning face of the huge albino, who was dressed in what looked to be a Navy pea-jacket and watch-cap.

"Thinking of leaving us, Mr. Ellis?"

"No, I—"

Cain gave him no chance to say more. He grabbed Robert by the arm and began literally dragging him down the street. In the four or five blocks before turning off East Kane, Robert suffered the mute, pitying stares of shopkeepers, shoppers, even the barber who'd just cut his hair. Cain's massive hand held his upper arm in a steel grip. He dragged Robert into the blacksmith's shop. There were two men standing there, waiting. One wore a blood-stained apron and a white cardboard cap. In his hand was a large meat cleaver. *Butcher?*

The other figure, dressed in the garb of a Victorian country squire, frowned and slowly shook his head. Then Lucifer sighed heavily. "Ah, Robert. I'm so disappointed."

Before Robert could respond in any way, Cain snatched the cleaver from the butcher, forced Robert to his knees, and laid his already numb left arm over a wooden block. Robert had time only to see Cain's look of satisfaction and Lucifer's slight nod. Cain's own hairless arm rose and fell, and Robert saw his left hand drop to the sawdust floor, severed at the wrist. The pain didn't begin until Cain dragged him to the open fire and plunged the bloody stump into the blue, cauterizing flames, holding it there until Robert, screaming at the top of his lungs until he lost consciousness, sagged against his knees.

"Nicely done," Lucifer said to his servant. "Very neat." He took the cleaver from Cain's hand, handed it back to the butcher, and said, "Thank you, son. You may go back to your work, now."

Lucifer's Children

The butcher, having said not a single word, wiped the cleaver on his apron and left the shop. When he had gone, Lucifer turned back to Cain. "Let him suffer the pain for one night, then dip his arm in some of the water." He wrinkled his nose. "He's messed himself, too. Get him cleaned up and bring him to me tomorrow, after dinner. I've changed my mind about his wife."

෯

Chapter 25

They ganged up on Maggie in her living room.

Sam argued.

Lena begged.

Emmitt Walsh pleaded, but Maggie refused to listen to any of them. "No, Mr. Walsh, I'm sorry I messed up the story and made Sam cut the cruise short, and I appreciate your patience, but I have to go back. A woman died a horrible death up there in those mountains. I can't have that hanging over my head, even if I don't find my son. If you feel you have to hire somebody else, I'll understand. I can't blame you. Thanks again for everything."

She didn't give Sam or Lena a chance to explain why neither of them had said a word about Alice Crowfeather after she'd been released from the hospital in Asheville. She really didn't care. All she could think of was that a kind woman had been viciously murdered and it was her fault. For all she knew, the hacked pieces of poor Alice's body were rotting up there, or were frozen under recent snowfalls, and there was no one but herself to blame, or for that matter, to grieve. It was wrong. It was unfair. And, it was probably against the law. She stood. "Look, I'm sorry, but I need to be by myself a little while to think all this out. I'll call all of you later."

But Maggie had already thought it all out. She'd thought of nothing else since the night of the costume party on board. When they'd gone, she sat down on her couch and went over all of it again. Then, on impulse, she walked across the hall and knocked on Tammy Henderson's door. From the other side, she heard Cleo's instantaneous, hostile barking, then Tammy's voice.

"Just a minute." Maggie knew Tammy was shutting the dog in her bedroom. She came to the door wearing a bright orange *muumuu* that reminded Maggie of the tent she'd shared with Alice, and was nearly the same size. Tammy's hair was a frizzy mess. Obviously, she hadn't been expecting company. "Maggie? Come on in. Is anything the matter?"

Maggie knew for a fact that her neighbor, like always, had probably been glued to her window and had seen everyone coming and going. Maggie walked into Tammy's cluttered living room. "No, nothing's the matter. I need your help with something. A favor."

"Sure, honey, have a seat."

Maggie looked around. She removed half a dozen soap opera magazines from the nearest armchair and sat down. "Tammy, does your brother still work at Clemmon's Ford?"

"Larry? Sure does. Been their top salesman two years in a row, now. Why?"

"Could you maybe call him? I want to trade cars, but I need to do it today."

Larry Henderson was not Clemmon's Ford top salesman for nothing. By turn, he could be shrewd, merciless, solicitous, and could lie through his teeth when necessary, affecting his good-old-boy manner with guys, and be snake oil charming with gals. He loved 'ups' when they were women, who usually were mostly concerned about the color of a vehicle, not its power train. When he eyeballed the Honda Civic his sister's buddy drove up in, his hopes rose higher, and when she told him what she wanted, he saw the chance to unload a unit they'd had in inventory far too long. No one had been able to sell the two-year old green Bronco, because it had been owned by a hog farmer, and no matter how many times they'd cleaned and fumigated the damn thing, it still smelled like shit inside. He explained this to Maggie in more civilized language, of course. "But it's just what you'll need for driving in the mountains, Miz Ellis. Plenty of power, and you can go to four-wheel drive with just a flick of the wrist. This baby will go-through-the-snow-like- a -lo-co-mo!"

"It smells awful."

"That's 'cause it's wintertime. We haven't had a chance to keep the windows rolled down. Come spring, it'll air out just fine, trust me. Besides, it's got real low mileage, and, well, because you're my sister's friend, I'll give you absolutely top dollar for your Honda." This part of his spiel was the truth. He'd be able to turn the Honda at a neat profit, making good money on both vehicles. Not bad for an hour's work, and he didn't have to spend a lot of time out on the freezing lot. When he promised to finish all the paperwork, licensing, and insurance transfer before the day was over, plus fill the green monster up with gas, Maggie made the deal, and wrote out a check for fifty-eight hundred dollars.

Larry promised he'd have the Bronco ready for her by four o'clock, watched her drive away, and went back to his glassed-in cubicle. His fellow salesmen were waiting for him, all four with admiring grins on their faces. But Larry Henderson's grin was wider. He'd just cinched another eighty bucks from the private bets he'd made with each of them that he'd move that shit-dipped Bronco before Christmas. Sitting down to start the paperwork, he resisted the urge to gloat. Instead, he chuckled and said, "Beer's on me tonight, guys. One pitcher apiece."

One of his colleagues spoke for the others. "You're one fat-ass, lying fucker, Larry, but you got style."

Larry didn't look up to retort. He was scribbling a note remind himself to buy his sister a big box of candy.

Surprised at how easily the foul-smelling beast handled, Maggie drove home, parked, checked her purse again to make sure the cash and traveler's checks were still there, and sighed. She'd taken the last penny out of both her savings and checking accounts. She got out of the Bronco and walked to her apartment door, where she got another surprise. Lena De Vries was sitting there, on top of her huge suitcase, her fur coat draped across her lap. "Sam dropped me off, Margaret. I know what you're up to, and I'm going with you. But this time, I'm not going to let you out of my sight. Not for one second."

Maggie hugged her mother, fought tears back, and fished out her key. "All right, Mama. Come on in. Let's make a bowl of hot soup."

They left Raleigh on the 22nd, early in the morning, making good time until they ran into some light sleet just past Greensboro. When Maggie slowed down, Lena said, "I don't like the looks of this weather."

"The salesman told me this Bronco would handle anything that came along, including a blizzard. We'll be okay."

"Maybe, but somebody sure forgot to hold this bronco's tail down. It smells like ca-ca in here."

"I know," Maggie said, laughing, "But the heater works fine."

"Just makes it worse."

"Try to ignore it, Mama. It's going to be a while before we get to Asheville, especially at this speed. Want to sing Ninety-Nine Bottles of Beer on the Wall?"

"No, I don't want to sing Ninety-Nine Bottles of Beer on the Wall, what I want you to do is tell me what really happened up there."

Maggie frowned, but kept her eyes on the road, which seemingly was not getting any worse, due to the heavy traffic. At least not yet. "I told you. I told all of you."

"You were holding back, Margaret DeVries. I know you. What was it you left out?"

"Nothing, only..."

"Only what?"

"Okay. You remember those three men I saw? The ones who warned me about trespassing? I wasn't lying, Mama, one of them did shoot at me. Twice, and hit me, too. One shot took the bag out of my hand and tore off two of my fingernails. The other shot grazed my cheek, yet you and Sam said that Doctor— what was her name?"

"Weiner. Ruth Weiner."

"Right. She told you when they examined me, I didn't have any marks on me. Nothing. *Nada*. Somebody's been lying. First thing I'm going to do when we get to Asheville is go back to that hospital and ask Dr. Ruth Weiner some very pointed questions. Another thing, too. Day before yesterday, I did a little research. The ridge I was climbing couldn't have been private property. That mountain and at least fifty more, in every direction, is part of the National Forest. It's owned by the Federal Government. Those guys were phony as the language that one guy spoke: 'What you seek is not here.' "

"That's what he said?"

"That's what he said, alright, just before he shot me, the bastard. How the hell did *he* know what I was looking for? I think they're the ones who killed Alice, too."

A sudden gust of wind rocked the top-heavy Bronco. Maggie caught her breath and regained control, thankful she'd had the foresight to examine the big, wide tires before she'd made the deal. All four had plenty of deep tread, and the spare had never been on the road.

"It's getting worse out there," Lena said. "I hope we're not running into a major storm, ca-ca Bronco or not."

Maggie shot a quick glance at her mother, glared back through the windshield again, and picked up the rhythm of the wiper blades. "Ninety-nine Bottles of Beer on the wall, ninety-nine bottles of beer. If one of those bottles of beer should fall, ninety-eight bottles of beer on the wall..."

She was quite aware she hadn't told Lena— or any of the others— about also remembering the Priest with the soft hands and eyes...

"I'm sorry," the hospital receptionist said, "Dr. Weiner is on vacation. She won't be back till after New Year's. Is there anyone else who can help you?"

"No. Do you have a number where I can reach her?" Maggie asked. "I really do have to talk to her. It's very important."

"I'm afraid not. We're not allowed to give out private phone numbers. Besides, I'm pretty sure she isn't at home. I think Dr. Weiner has gone out west somewhere. I heard somebody say she was going on a skiing trip. If you'll leave your number with me, I'll ask her to call you if she calls in for her messages."

Maggie gave the woman the number of the Day's Inn, and she and Lena left. "Might as well go somewhere and eat, Mama, and turn in. I want to get an early start tomorrow morning. Looks like this weather isn't going to let up, and it's probably going to be slow going to Cherokee."

It was slow going, but the green beast performed steadily as a dray horse. They arrived at the Police station shortly before noon, in a light snow. Maggie parked the Bronco and looked at Lena. "You want to stay here or come in with me?"

"I'll come with you. I need a breath of fresh air."

The same broad-shouldered Sergeant with the long braids was sitting at the front desk, but he didn't seem to remember Maggie at all. Worse, he told her that Chief Thomas Hand was no longer there. "He resigned last month, ma'am. Went out to Oklahoma to retire."

"So who's the new Chief?"

"Don't have one yet. I'm sort of acting as Chief until the Tribe chooses a new one. This time of year is pretty quiet, thank God. How can I help you?"

"I want to report a murder."

"A murder? Who?"

"One of your own people. Alice Crowfeather. I believe she was your historian, and taught somewhere on the reservation."

"Alice Crowfeather? I don't know the name. Maybe you'd best have a seat there and tell me what this is all about."

Maggie sat down and took a deep breath. As if she was delivering a newscast, not wasting a word, she gave her own personal background story, then recounted, in fine detail, every minute from the time she'd picked Alice up hitchhiking until the moment she'd passed out on the mountainside.

The Sergeant listened to the entire report without opening his mouth. His response, after hearing the full account, was the beginning of surprise that quickly built to frustration, then anger and disbelief in Maggie's chest. He said he knew practically everyone on the reservation personally, but knew no one named Alice Crowfeather. There was no such person. Never had been any such person. The Tribe historian was a man named John Starling. And even if some mysterious woman had been murdered, it hadn't happened on the reservation, and therefore was out of his jurisdiction. "Sounds like Lee County to me. That'd be Sheriff Yancey. I'd check in with him if I was you, at Carew. That's the county seat, 'bout fifty miles from here. And, I'd do it fast. Looks to me like a bad storm's coming in."

Maggie stood. "Just one other question, Sergeant. Were you a member of Chief Hand's search party when they found me up on that mountain?"

The stolid face didn't change a whit. "Search party, ma'am? I don't know anything about any search party. No offense, but I think you must be confused about all this. I can't remember ever seeing you before in my life."

In a white-hot fury, Maggie dragged Lena out of the office to the Bronco, which she drove straight into town. With her mother in tow, she spent the next two hours stopping in every building that was open, accosting every person she passed on the street, but no one had ever heard of a woman named Crowfeather.

Too bewildered and upset to even think about having some lunch, she guided the Bronco out of town.

"Where to now?" Lena wanted to know. "Carew?"

"Right, but first, we're going to make a stop in that little town of Kaneville. There's something wrong here, Mama. Something terribly wrong."

"For sure. Hey, I just thought of something else. That Indian man said the Lee County Sheriff's name was Yancey. Wasn't that the name of that fat police chief down in Myrtle Beach?"

"That's true, come to think of it."

"Coincidence?"

"I don't know, Mama. I don't know what to think about anything anymore, but somebody's going to have to talk to us, and soon. It's starting to snow again, and it'll be dark before you know it."

"I'm not worried. We've got a good old warm ca-ca-mobile." With a giggle, Lena began singing. "Ninety-nine Indian cops on the wall, ninety-nine. . ."

༄

Chapter 26

Robert had only part of one day to brood over the loss of his left hand. He'd gotten through a night of excruciating pain, although he didn't know how. He was vaguely aware he'd passed out several times during that endless night, and each time he'd come to, he'd seen a different face; first the hated, laughing Cain, then a more sympathetic-looking but silent Abner Highsmith, and finally, Manuel Munoz, whose countenance was as impassive as ever, but who had brought with him a pail of the curative water, into which he helped Robert dunk the throbbing, beet-red stump of his forearm, and had then left, saying he'd be back after dinner time, and for Robert to be ready.

Robert could guess why.

He stumbled around his condo, trying to avoid the shock of staring at his new deformity. The physical pain was gone, but his mental anguish had quadrupled. He wanted desperately to talk to Bo, but the phone wasn't working. He dared not try to leave his apartment, either. Where would he go anyway? To his office, and bear the additional pain of humiliation? Out on the conveyor-belt sidewalk, his stump stuck in his pocket, and suffer the knowing stares of everyone he saw?

He had seen Cain execute a man for committing a 'minor infraction'. A mere trifle, and he'd been caught thinking, no, actually *planning* an escape, which was certainly more than a trifle. Caught red-handed. *Damn!* The choice of those particular thought-words caused him to kick out at the first thing he saw, the table with the useless telephone. The thought came to him that he'd like nothing more than to sit down with a bottle in his remaining hand and drink himself into an anesthetizing stupor. But the strongest thing in the house was a few bottles of the Kaneville Mountain-Spring Water, which as yet hadn't been marketed on the outside. In frustration, disgust, self-pity, and fear, Robert let fly a steady stream of profanity. This vocal venting died out within minutes. There was no one to hear it.

    Robert went into the bedroom he'd shared with Isabella. He sat, then stretched out on the bed he'd shared with her. Made a baby with her. Within a few more minutes, he became conscious of not thinking of her. He was thinking of himself. Only himself. His self-loathing pushed everything and everyone from his mind. He started to bring his left arm up to glance at his watch, stopped it in mid-motion, and cursed again. His new Rolex had been on the part of his wrist that was now missing. Lying motionless, helpless, he squeezed his eyes shut, willing the time to go by. Minutes became hours, hours became lifetimes. He was almost grateful when Munoz knocked once, let himself in, and said, "Get dressed, Robert. It's time to go."

    Robert heard music before they were half way down the long corridor. With a finger to his lips, Munoz led him into a large, high-ceilinged room that looked like a Star-Trek set, except that the furniture seemed borrowed from the nineteenth century. For all Robert knew, it probably was. The room was cool, maybe in the mid-sixties, but he was sweating profusely. Lucifer had his back turned to them; sitting at an ornately carved grand piano, vigorously pounding out some piece of classical music Robert didn't recognize. It took another two or three minutes before Lucifer finished, with a theatrical flourish, and stood, amidst dying echoes of the loud *opus*. He was dressed in a beautifully tailored tuxedo. "Come in, please, Robert. I was just playing some Liszt. Did you recognize it?"

    Robert shook his head, unable to verbally respond.

    "Mephisto Waltz," Lucifer told him. "Liszt was one of my favorites, until he went off the deep end and joined the, ah, other side." He dismissed Munoz with a wave of his hand. The Spaniard gave a slight bow and withdrew. Robert stood rooted in the same spot. He hadn't recognized one note of the music, but he'd grasped its title easily enough, and hadn't been in the least surprised that Lucifer played the piano expertly.

His host pointed at an old-fashioned love seat which looked about as comfortable as an apple crate. "Sit down, Robert, before you fall down. And try to relax. This isn't your day to die."

Hearing those words, Robert felt little relief, but did as he was told, keeping the mangled stump of his forearm jammed into his trouser pocket. He looked quickly around the ultra-modern room, but not at the furnishings. Then he allowed himself to breathe. They were alone. Cain was nowhere to be seen.

As if reading his mind yet again, Lucifer smiled. "He's not here, my friend. You will come to no harm tonight. Here, let me show you something." Lucifer picked up a device that looked like a television remote switch, pointed at the far wall, and said, "Cain is taking care of last minute details for my guests."

Robert's mouth fell open as the entire wall transformed itself into an enormous screen. He instantly recognized the football stadium, which was rapidly filling up. Lucifer bounced on his heels, turned back to Robert and said, "My children. Well, a few of them anyway. I'm going up there in about an hour to talk to them. Looks kind of like an Amway convention, doesn't it?"

When Robert failed to grasp his humor, Lucifer looked down at the floor for a moment, shaking his head, then looked Robert in the eye. "But I wanted to talk to you a few minutes before I go up there and give them my pep-talk. How's your arm feeling?"

Robert dropped his head. He couldn't bring himself to look up. "It's okay," he whispered.

"Mm. A hand is one of those things one takes for granted, until it's missing. How'd you like to have it back?"

This brought Robert's head up sharply. "What?"

Lucifer's Children

Lucifer chuckled, then his face took on a serious look. "You know what symbolism is, Robert?"

"Symbolism? I— I think so."

"My taking your hand was symbolic. I'm sure you're wondering why I didn't allow Cain to inflict more, um, substantial punishment for your transgression. Actually, I blame myself for what you were trying to do."

"I don't understand."

"What I mean is, in your case, I made a mistake. Oh, yes, I make mistakes now and then. Bringing you here was a basic error in judgment on my part. I should have left you to wallow in your own stink until you bottomed out completely, or killed yourself. I could always find another kid as bright as young Bo, but I thought I could do something with the two of you. Anyway, that's neither here nor there. Let me ask you something. Have you ever said to yourself, 'if only I could start over, knowing what I do now'?

"Sure, I have."

"Most people have, especially those whose lives have been a series of failures. Would you like to start over, Robert? Knowing what you do now? Knowing you're free of my little demon of alcoholism, and knowing you have the natural talent, and now that you have your looks, youth, and health back, would you like another shot at being the best sports broadcaster in the whole United States, working for the network of your choice? Top of the heap? King of the hill?" *Crème de la crème?"*

Robert stared at his tormentor. "Who wouldn't?'

Lucifer rose, began slowly pacing the floor, and speaking as if to an audience. Robert suddenly wondered if the lecture he was getting was being televised and shown to fifty thousand laughing people sitting in the stadium.

"Right," Lucifer said, more than a hint of sarcasm in his voice. "Who wouldn't, indeed. Even if it meant giving up a life of total pleasure; infinite security, living in a place that's crime-free, germ-free, with plenty of money and deluxe creature comforts, friends who like and respect you, women who love you— " He stopped, turned to look Robert in the face, and continued. "Speaking of love, who and what do you love, Robert Ellis? Aside from yourself, I mean."

"I love my son."

"Bo. Of course you do. What about your former wife?"

"Maggie?"

Lucifer sat down on the edge of the piano bench, casually crossing his legs. "Yes, Maggie. Isn't it true that in spite of all the times you cheated on her with bimbos and available women like Beth Oliver, in spite of all the excremental grief you caused her while you were married, you still love her more than any other woman, don't you? Even the lovely Isabella?"

Robert hung his head again. He was ready to admit the truth of everything Lucifer was saying. Deep down, he knew he still loved Maggie. He'd never stopped loving her. Every time he'd awakened next to some other woman, he'd felt sick with guilt, but he'd never been strong enough to resist—

"Answer me, please."

"Yes. It's true. I do love Maggie. I love her very much."

"How much? How much do you love her and Bo?"

"What are you getting at?"

Lucifer stood again. He walked over to where Robert sat and looked down at him, contempt showing like the paint on a clown's face. "What I'm 'getting at' as you put it, is your price."

"My price?"

"Pardon my use of an old cliché, but yes, everybody has his price. What's yours, Robert, old boy? What price would you be willing to pay for such a second chance, another chance to make it to the big time on the outside, the so called freedom you were willing to risk more than your left hand for? Look carefully inside yourself, man. I want an honest answer."

Robert's mental misery became also physical. He didn't know what he needed to do worse; throw up or relieve his bursting bladder. He was afraid if he moved at all, he'd do both. "I—I don't know."

"Oh yes you do. So do I. You'd be willing to let me sleep with Maggie, wouldn't you? You'd stand by and watch while I screwed her brains out, and never raise your voice, wouldn't you? You'd be willing to leave your son here, too, wouldn't you? Never set eyes on him again. You'd be willing to do anything. Anything at all, wouldn't you?"

Robert was choking on his own disgust.

"Like many another man has done, you'd sell me your very soul, wouldn't you?" Lucifer bent down, took Robert's face in his own hands, lifted it up so that Robert's was an inch away from his own. In a tone that was gentle as a caress, he whispered, "Wouldn't you, my son?"

Hot tears of shame and humiliation leaked from Robert's eyes onto the fingers that held his nodding head.

Lucifer stood abruptly. "I thought so." He removed the handkerchief from his breast pocket and began wiping his fingers. He inclined his head in the direction over Robert's left shoulder. "A bathroom is just through that door."

When Robert returned from his much-needed trip to the toilet, his relief was short lived. Munoz had reappeared, and was helping his master into a light overcoat. Robert went weak in the knees when Lucifer said, "We will put this theoretical problem to a practical test tomorrow night, Robert. I've decided to bring Maggie here for a little family reunion. Munoz here can vouch for the fact that in spite of what people think, I am big on families."

"Maggie's coming *here?*"

"She's on her way as we speak. I have to go to the stadium now. Lieutenant Munoz will take you back to your apartment. I'll send for you tomorrow evening, after I've put the finishing touches on a little plan I've worked out; one with a couple of pleasant surprises for you. I expect your full cooperation, too. Remember what I said about symbolism?"

Robert nodded.

"Good. If you do as I ask, you may get that second chance we were talking about after all." He reached the door, turned and warned, "On the other hand, if you get any more stupid ideas of defying me, tomorrow will surely be your day to die. Believe me, I never make the same mistake twice. Goodnight, Coach."

Munoz touched Robert's arm. "Shall we go?"

"Can I use the bathroom again first?"

CHaptER 27

The falling snow was thicker when they rolled into Kaneville. Like millions of miniature, bleached doilies, wet, heavy flakes kept the Bronco's windshield wipers busy, on high speed. Maggie pulled into the first available parking spot, left the engine running and the wipers going while she and Lena surveyed the picture-postcard scene. Both sides of the main street were decked out in Christmas finery. Red decorations, strings of colored lights, and green garlands stretched between the lamp poles and across the narrow river, which, in stark contrast to the virgin snow, looked like a thin black ribbon cutting through the middle of it all. Cheery carols blared from unseen loudspeakers. No cars and trucks were moving, but there were scattered families, a few single men, and several women and children hurrying between doors to do last minute shopping.

"Pretty. Reminds me of Pella," Lena said.

But Maggie was in no mood to get caught up in holiday festivities. She was already reaching for a stack of flyers resting on the rear seat. "Why don't you take this side of the street, Mama. I'll take the other side."

"No way. I told you before I'm not going to let you out of my sight, and I meant it. It may take us twice as long, but we're going together."

"All right, have it your way. Where do you think we ought to start, the police station?"

"No. Seems like we get nowhere when we talk to officials. You want to get some answers, go where the people are." Lena pointed down East Kane. "There. That's a supermarket. People will always talk to you in a grocery store."

Maggie nodded at the logic of her mother's words, shut off the Bronco's engine and turned off the wipers and lights. "Good idea. Let's go, then."

They emerged from the warmth of the snow-caked vehicle and started down the sidewalk. Several people smiled at them, wishing them a Merry Christmas, as did a Salvation Army Santa whose bell ringing was luring more snowflakes than coins into his black pot. Carrying a bundle of flyers each, they entered the IGA supermarket, walked past the produce department, turned into the first aisle, and ran smack into a very pregnant Beth Oliver. They recognized each other simultaneously, but Beth reacted faster. Her eyes opened wide, and she abandoned the half-full grocery cart she'd been pushing, turned, and fled.

Maggie caught up with her before she reached the door, Lena a step behind. Maggie grabbed the trembling woman by her coat sleeve. "Beth? Beth Oliver? It's me, Maggie Ellis. Don't you—"

Beth tore away from Maggie's grasp and ran, as best she could, through the door to the street, but Maggie caught her before she could get ten steps further. "Beth, it *is* you. You have to talk to me."

Beth's face had turned the color of the snow falling on her long, blond hair. She shook her head violently, and tried to get away. Maggie dropped the flyers on the sidewalk and seized the spooked woman by both arms, ignoring the obvious terror showing in her eyes as well as the stares of the female traffic going in and out of the store. "You *are* going to talk to me, goddamn you, if I have to deck you, baby and all. You're alive, and here. Where's Bo? He's alive too, isn't he?" Maggie shook the woman like a rag doll. "*Talk* to me, damn you."

Freezing tears sprang from Beth's eyes and ran down her tortured face. She opened her mouth, but only a couple of coarse, guttural sounds came forth.

"Margaret," Lena had caught up with them. "Margaret, for God's sake, *look!* She *can't* talk. She— her tongue is gone."

Maggie peered closer, and as she did, Beth collapsed onto the snow-trampled sidewalk, making little whining yelps. Maggie knelt down. "Good Lord. What's happened, Beth?"

Lena squatted down next to them. "Let me handle this." She grabbed Beth's contorted face between her hands, looked her in the eye, and said, "Just nod your head for 'yes' and shake it for 'no'. First, is Bo alive?"

Beth nodded once.

"Robert, too?"

A second nod.

"Are they here? In Kaneville?"

Negative shake.

This stumped Lena, but only for a second. "Do you know where they are?"

A nod. Yes. Beth pointed toward the east.

Maggie took over. "They're on the mountain?"

Beth emitted another pitiful sound and shook her head. With a gloved finger she traced the words IN IT in the fresh snow.

"*In* the mountain? You mean in*side* the mountain?"

Beth nodded, and traced some more words in the snow. PLEASE LET ME GO.

Maggie tenderly wiped the tears from the poor woman's eyes. It was clear she was frightened to death of something. Or someone. In a much gentler tone, she said, "I'm sorry, Beth. Are you in some kind of danger from talking to us?"

Vigorous nod.

"Christ. What kind of place *is* this?"

Beth reached down again. With a shaking finger, she scribbled, HELL. GET HELP. With that, she struggled to her feet, looked around wildly, and began running. Maggie and Lena watched her stumble and slip until she was out of sight.

Lena said. "You believe her?"

"Yes. I believe her." Maggie started back toward the Bronco. Lena had to hustle to catch up with her. "What now?"

"Just what she said we should do. Go for some help. Carew's the county seat of Lee County. Thirty miles from here. With the Bronco, we can make it in an hour if we start now, and that's where we'll find Sheriff Yancey. He ought to remember me..."

"Sure, I remember you, Miz Ellis. Never forget what a state you were in when Tommy Hand brought you out of those woods. Please have a seat. What can I do for you on this fine Christmas Eve?"

The man's smile and words shocked Maggie into two realizations at once: Yancey had to be the twin of the Myrtle Beach Police Chief. His body was solid where his brother's was fat, and he was an inch or so taller, but his face was nearly identical. Too, Maggie had lost all track of time. Which day was which. Tomorrow was her birthday! She quickly pushed both thoughts to the side of her mind. Like beads falling from a broken strand, her words spilled out, "I've just found out my son and his father are alive. So is the woman who was on that plane with them. We saw her over at Kaneville, and she's in grave danger, and—"

"Whoa. Slow down some. You're overwrought. Take a deep breath and tell me one thing at the time. Best start at the beginning, too. Tell you what, let me get you both a cup of coffee. I've always found it's easier talking with some kind of drink in your hand."

Maggie found that Sheriff Yancey's psychology of the drink-in-hand to be true. After a sip or two, she was able, just as with the Indian Sergeant at Cherokee, to clearly and slowly relate to the man everything that had happened, from her unsuccessful helicopter flight to the moment she and Lena walked into his office in the town hall of Carew. She was especially careful to describe Alice Crowfeather, and the grisly way she'd died.

To his credit, the gray-eyed law enforcement officer didn't interrupt her one time. Neither, thank God, did her mother. "...And we believe Bo and Robert are being held prisoners by somebody in Kaneville. Poor Beth Oliver's tongue has been cut out, and she was petrified someone would see her talking— I mean communicating with us. You've got to go back there with us, Sheriff. Please. I know it's a lot to ask during the holiday, but I—"

"That don't bother me none, ma'am," Yancey broke in. "It's the weather. Looks like we're in for a good old-time blizzard. I bet the wind's picked up ten more miles per hour since you started talking. What are you ladies driving, anyway?"

As if to answer his own question, Yancey got up from behind his desk and walked over to the window, separating the blinds. "That your Bronco out there?"

When Maggie nodded, Yancey glanced at his watch, studied the tips of his boots for a long moment, then asked, "You sure you ladies don't want to spend the night here at the motel and take care of this business tomorrow? It'll be after ten before we can get there in this mess."

Maggie stood. Put the half-empty coffee mug on the desk. "Sheriff, if you don't go back there with us, we're going back anyway, and knock on every door until we get some answers."

Yancey grinned and threw his hands up in mock surrender. "Okay, okay. Just let me get my coat and hat."

Those items were hanging on a coat rack next to the front door. Yancey pulled them on, and said to the lone deputy who sat behind the reception desk, "I'll take the Land Rover, Kenny. Look for me when you see me, but keep an ear to that radio. All right, ladies, you ready?"

The return trip to Kaneville took nearly an agonizing hour longer than the trip from there to Carew. There was no doubt a major storm was swinging in full force, but Maggie paid it no more mind than a spring rain. The Bronco held up to all Larry Henderson's promises, following in the tracks of the high-slung Land Rover like a faithful St. Bernard. It was nearly ten o'clock when they passed the sign marking the Kaneville city limit, but the sign was the only thing that was normal.

The town was deserted. Not one soul was in sight.

Not one building was open.

Not a single shop light or street lamp shone through the ghostly curtain of snow.

The bright Christmas decorations had disappeared, as had every car and truck that had been parked there earlier. There was no sound except the purring of the Bronco's big engine, and, as they slowed to a crawl down East Kane, the scrunching sound of wide tires on new snow.

They followed the Land Rover into the Quick Mart-bus station lot, and stopped. Both women were holding their breath as Yancey got out of his vehicle and walked to the pay phone booth. When he opened the door, no light came on. Maggie and Lena both knew the phone wouldn't be working either, even before Yancey tramped over tell them so.

"Goddamndest thing I ever saw. You two stay put. I'm gonna have me a look around."

Through the twin semicircles made by the wipers, Maggie and Lena watched as the Sheriff climbed back into the Land Rover, turned his searchlight on, and began a slow, methodical cruise of every street in the town. He was back less than half an hour later, this time with a big-time scowl on his red face. "Something bad's going down here, folks. You got chains for the tires on this Bronco?"

"No," Maggie said, cursing herself— and Larry Henderson— for not having thought of that beforehand. "No chains. Why?"

" 'Cause my radio ain't working all of a sudden, and this storm's getting worse. Look, I don't know what's happened here, but whatever it was, I need some backup. A lot of backup. Nothing to do but go get some. Best for you two to just lock your doors and stay put. I'm going for the State Police."

"How— how long will you be gone?"

"Hour, maybe two, I reckon. Don't worry, though. Don't seem to be anybody here who'd cause you any trouble. I'll be back soon as possible. No panicking, now, you hear? Stay right here in this parking lot till I get back, and make sure you keep your windows cracked open a little."

He searched their eyes, and seeing their terror, tried to lighten things up a little. "Hey, maybe I'll bring us a bucket of the Colonel's chicken back, too. You like regular or extra crispy?"

Maggie rewarded his gallantry with the best smile she could manage. "We'll be all right. Just— just hurry, okay?"

She rolled up her window to within an inch and watched him slog back to his own vehicle, gun it a few times, then ease it back onto the road which no longer showed its perimeters. The red tail-lights passed from view in seconds. Maggie turned to face her mother. "Lock your door, Mama."

Lena complied, asking, "Why'd he tell us to keep the windows cracked open?"

Maggie tried to keep her voice calm as possible. "Carbon monoxide."

Lena stared through the twin arcs again, catching the beat. Her reed-thin voice piped up, "Ninety-nine bottles of beer on the wall, Ninety-nine bottles of beer, if one of those bottles of beer should fall..."

Lena had counted nearly four hundred bottles of beer when she was rudely interrupted by Maggie's profanity. "Shit. *Oh shit.*"

"What?"

"Look at that." She was pointing to the fuel gauge. "We're out of gas. We completely forgot to fill up..."

Her words trailed off under Lena's wail, "Out of *gas*? How could you let that happen?"

"I didn't think of it, Mama." She immediately turned the lights off and cut the engine.

"What did you do that for?"

"We've got to save what's left. No telling how long it'll take for Yancey to get back." She glanced at the luminous dashboard clock. "He's already been gone an hour."

"For God's sake, Margaret, we'll freeze to death!"

"No we won't. I'll start it up again when we get real cold. Where's your fur coat?"

They felt the drop in temperature even before they both got into their heavy coats. Twenty minutes later, they were frantically digging into their suitcases for more clothing. The windows were quickly caked with swirling snow, coming from every direction. They rolled the windows all the way up to keep the snow— and the icy wind driving it— out of their faces. Maggie, praying the battery wouldn't give out, started the engine every fifteen minutes, but it took longer and longer for the heater to come close to putting out warm air.

They rummaged into the suitcases again for anything to wrap their heads, hands and feet in. They couldn't see a thing outside. Maggie knew it was useless to run the wipers, so she didn't bother. After the next hour, Lena began to cry. Maggie didn't try to stop her. It was all she could do not to cry, too. Under her breath, she began cursing herself again, this time for not insisting that Yancey take them with him. Come to think of it, why hadn't he offered to?

She started the Bronco's engine again. It took a good ten minutes and precious fuel before the air between their feet to feel slightly warmer. Their breath was coming in gray clouds. Maggie began to worry that Yancey *wasn't coming back*. Maybe he'd gone off the road somewhere. Maybe the highway had become impassable. Where had he gone anyway? Back to Carew? No, he'd said he was going to try to get help from the State Police. Where would he have to go to find them? Find anybody?

She started the engine again. It ran for about five minutes, coughed, and died. Maggie tried the starter again, pumping the accelerator. The idiot light on the panel came on, glowing red. She tried again. And again. It was useless. She knew it was useless. The Bronco's tank was bone dry. She glanced at her mother's tear-streaked face. There was nothing she could say. She reached over and pulled Lena into her arms. They huddled together as close as they could get. Maggie was conscious that her feet had gone numb. She looked at the dash clock again. Yancey had been gone almost three hours. Was this it? Had they come this far only to freeze to death in a truck that smelled like shit, stranded in a ghost town?

She desperately began rubbing her mother's small feet and hands until she was too tired to move. Lena was praying, and Maggie gradually realized she was, too. They huddled together even closer, sharing their waning body heat. Maggie lost track of time. Didn't care anymore. The cold was a sneaky thief, robbing them even of the will to fight. With the last of her mental reserve, Maggie thought of Bo. "We were so close, Bo. So close. I'm so sorry. So—"

"Maggie!" Lena's croaking voice in her ear stopped her in mid-thought. She nearly laughed, numbly realizing her mother had not called her Margaret. "Yes, Mama. It's all right, honey. I love you."

"Maggie, there's light out there!"

Maggie opened her eyes. Looked around. The left side of the Bronco *did* seem lighter somehow. And the light was—was *moving*.

Maggie shook her head to clear it. There was a sound. A scraping sound. She turned to her left. A gloved hand was scraping the snow away from her window. She saw an arm attached to the hand, a body. A face. A man's face.

She tried to roll the window down. It was stuck. Summoning the last ounce of strength in her own body, she banged on the window. She heard the ice crack. She tried the handle again. The window came down a few inches.

A voice came through it. "Ladies, you look as though you could use some assistance. May I help you? I have a warm car. Here, let me help you out."

Maggie didn't have sufficient energy left to cry, let alone speak, but she found enough strength to unlock the Bronco's door.

∽

Lucifer's Children

Chapter 28

Maggie felt that if her lips weren't frozen, she'd have kissed both the handsome good Samaritan *and* his huge chauffeur, who was holding the door of the black limousine open for them. Looking like two rag-picking refugees from Siberia, she and Lena stumped through the snow that had drifted two feet deep against the side of the Bronco, which was now white, not green. They practically crawled over each other to the far side of the limo's rear-facing seat, as far away from the howling weather as they could get. Still clinging to each other, they were both far too numb to feel anything other than the sudden, blessed warmth enveloping them the moment the door closed.

Maggie had no idea how many minutes passed before she was able to control her shivering enough to accept the glass their rescuer held out to her. "Drink this."

Maggie didn't question his suggestion. She lifted the glass to her lips and poured some of its contents over her chattering teeth. It was like liquid fire going down her throat. After taking a second swallow, she thought to hand the glass to her mother, but Lena was draining a glass of her own.

In fact, it was the resilient Lena who recovered enough to talk first. "Thank God. Thank the Good Lord you came by. I was sure we were going to die."

Maggie felt like saying something similar, but when she opened her mouth to do so, she felt a lurch. The big car was moving. She nearly splashed the brandy on her chest. The first thing she managed to say was, "You saved our lives. If you hadn't come by, we..." She interrupted herself to take another sip of the liquor which was spreading heat throughout her entire being, and much too fast. She felt befuddled. Confused. Thick tongued. The smiling man dressed in formal clothes sitting across from her said, "It's quite all right. Glad I could help. It's a terrible night to run out of fuel."

Maggie's mind was not yet so frozen she couldn't wonder how he *knew* they'd run out of gas. She decided to repress the thought. "All the same, it's a miracle you were driving by, Mr.— ?

"Beliar."

"Mr. Beliar. Mama's right. We would have frozen to death."

The good-looking man with the hazel eyes lifted a hand in modest acknowledgement. With his other one, he held up the cut glass decanter. "Would you care for some more brandy?"

Maggie shook her head. "No, I'm fine, now. Liquor doesn't agree with me, but thanks. Thanks for everything."

Mr. Beliar offered Lena more, and to Maggie's surprise, her mother eagerly held out her glass. While he carefully poured, Maggie noticed his cuff links and shirt studs. She knew diamonds when she saw them. This Mr. Beliar was certainly no pauper. She glanced around the opulent interior of the limo. Beliar had thoughtfully left the ceiling lights on, but she couldn't have seen out anyway. The car's windows were tinted. This mattered little to Maggie. She had no desire to be reminded of the blizzard raging outside their mobile sanctuary, which was having no trouble at all moving through the storm.

Lena was apparently having similar thoughts. "Some car you've got here, Mr. Beliar. I guess when you've got one of these, you don't worry about driving around in a blizzard."

Their host laughed lightly. "It's useful, that's true, plus I have an excellent driver. I was on my way home from a— a kind of company party."

"You live here in Kaneville?" Maggie asked.

"Occasionally. I have a house nearby, and insist you be my guest tonight, Margaret. You and Mrs. DeVries."

Maggie instantly felt ice-cold all over again.

And again, it was her mother who reacted first. "How did you know our names? Did you see Sheriff Yancey? Did he send you?"

The man sitting across from them ignored Lena's questions, locking eyes with Maggie, which only increased her new apprehension. Warning signals, hotter than the brandy, flashed through her body.

"I know all about you, Margaret. Who you are and why you are here. Allow me to show you something." He reached into his inside pocket and handed Maggie two photographs. As Maggie accepted them, with a shaking hand, he turned the ceiling light up brighter. Maggie broke eye contact with him and stared at the two pictures in her hand. The first showed a very handsome young man in a white smock. The second one was— *Robert*, as he'd looked the first day she'd ever seen him. A tiny cry started to form in her burning throat, as she quickly focused once more on the first photo. As recognition washed over her brain, Alice Crowfeather's words pounded against her temples. *'They have changed. One is older and one is younger...'* She unconsciously handed the pictures to her mother, looked back at the smiling Beliar and croaked. "That's my son, isn't it? And?"

"Your former husband, Robert. Yes. Those photographs were taken earlier today. They are well, as you can see, and are also my house guests. You will see them both soon, provided you—"

The limo jerked slightly. They had stopped. From the driver's seat came a deep voice. "We are here, Master."

Beliar reached into a side pocket and extracted a small box with buttons on it, one of which he touched, and a moment later, the big car moved forward a few feet, then stopped again. In another second, both doors were opened. Beliar was out in a flash, and offered a hand to assist Maggie. She and Lena slid out, and found themselves standing not inside a carport or garage, but a— a *barn?*

Maggie was suddenly aware of several other incongruities; the black limo they had been riding in didn't have one speck of snow on it. Not one flake. The barn, complete with dirt floor, stacked up bales of hay, animal stalls, tools, and a loft, was dry as a desert, clean as her own kitchen, and warm. Toasty warm, but it didn't *smell* like a barn. And Beliar's chauffeur, whose face she hadn't noticed before now, was like none she'd ever seen before. The brute's eyes were actually *pink*.

Maggie felt weak in the knees. When she realized she was still clutching the two photos, she glanced at them and as calm as she could, said, "Are Bo and Robert here? On this— this farm?"

The man who called himself Mr. Beliar laughed. So did the pink-eyed monster, who was leaning against the limousine. "No," Beliar said, "They are in my house, as I told you."

Maggie shook her head. She wished she had someplace to sit down. "I don't understand. This looks like a barn."

"It is, for all practical purposes. It is also the entrance to my home. My front door, so to speak." With those words, he raised the hand that still held the remote switch, pressed another button, and turned to the back wall, upon which hung old horse collars and sundry other tackle. It opened inward to reveal a wide tunnel; a straight, carpeted passageway big enough to drive the car through.

Maggie could not see to the end of it, though it was lit by some kind of hidden light source, as was the inside of the barn. She heard the sharp intake of her mother's breath, and what she thought might be a curse, then looked back at Beliar. "Who are you, really," she whispered.

"I told you. My oldest name is Beliar. Or Belial, Mastema, Asmodeus, among others. You may know me as Satan. However, I much prefer Lucifer."

Lena moved to Maggie's side as he spoke. She grabbed Maggie's arm and whispered, "These people are crazy, Margaret. We've been rescued by a pair of lunatics." She summoned courage, looked Lucifer in the eye and demanded, "What have you done with my grandson? Why have you brought us to this— this horse barn?"

Lucifer's Children

"Your gratitude is overwhelming, Madame."

"*Damn* you!" Lena retorted.

Lucifer chuckled. "I've been damned for a very long time, Mrs. DeVries, and I caution you to hold your tongue." He looked at Maggie and said, "I presume you'd like to see your son now."

Maggie felt herself slipping into some kind of shock. She could only nod.

"Good." Lucifer held out his hand to his giant chauffeur, who reached into the still open door of the car and brought him two garments. White robes. Lucifer took them, held them out and told them, "The clothes you are wearing are unsuitable for entrance into my house. Take them off."

"What?" Maggie said.

"Take those clothes off. These robes will fit, I promise."

"You mean strip right here? In front of you?" Lena's voice was shrill.

"Every stitch, please."

"Like hell I will. Margaret, they're going to *rape* us!"

Lucifer glowered at Lena. "You are beginning to irritate me, woman. I wouldn't soil my fingers or any other part of my anatomy on your old bag of bones." To Maggie, in a calm voice he said, "If you want to see your son, do as I say. Now."

As if drugged, Maggie swayed on her feet, and started removing her coat.

"Don't *listen* to him," Lena shrieked." She started toward Lucifer, her hands balled up into small fists. "You perverted bastard, I'll kill—"

The huge albino grabbed Lena around the waist, lifting her off the ground, one of his gigantic hands over her mouth. Lena's furious struggling was useless.

To her, Lucifer said, "I'm warning you for the last time, old woman. If you don't do as I say, you will spend a long and very cold night here."

Muffled defiance was his answer. He crossed his arms and watched as Maggie peeled off all her clothes. When she stood before him, humiliated and naked, Lucifer smiled. "You are indeed a lovely and desirable woman, Margaret. It is a shame to cover such beauty. Never mind. Here, put this on."

Trance-like, Maggie took the robe from him, slipped it over her head, and let it fall over her trembling body. Lucifer turned, gestured down the corridor, and said, "Shall we?"

Maggie watched what happened next as if seeing a slow motion, surreal scene from a sepia-tinted movie. Whether the albino had become distracted by watching her disrobe, or whether her mother had found superhuman strength from some hidden, kinetic reservoir, Lena wriggled free of the giant's grasp and flew at Lucifer in a rage, screaming. But Cain reacted fast, caught her by the hem of her fur coat, and flung her aside as he might have tossed a helpless baby. Lena crashed against one of the stalls, scrabbled to her feet again, and launched herself toward Lucifer again. Cain reached for a pitchfork lying against a hay bale, took one quick step, and skewered Lena through the middle of her body. He held the small form up in the air, laughing. A frothy bubble appeared at Lena's mouth. Her eyes bugged out, and her body, pierced through by three of the four tines of the pitchfork, wriggled momentarily like a fishing worm on a hook, then collapsed, folded over, her hair falling far enough forward to hide most of the blood seeping into the dirt floor. Cain tossed her body, pitchfork and all, in a heap, back against the horse stall. "For the swine, Master?"

Lucifer, holding the nearly comatose Maggie up by her arms, answered, "They are not *that* hungry. No, my son, I have a better idea. Let us go. The others are waiting."

Maggie felt herself being carried along down the corridor by some force she couldn't understand or fight against, even if she'd had the strength. She wanted to deny what she had just seen, but couldn't. She wanted to resist the idea of a sadistic, insane murderer who arrogantly called himself Satan, but she couldn't. She wanted to scream, cry out at the horror of it all, call out her dead mother's name, but couldn't even open her mouth to do that. All she could do was be carried, without taking a single voluntary step, along what seemed to be the passageway to hell.

  She was not aware of how long it took to reach the arched, iron-strapped wooden door, which opened into the most beautiful room she'd ever seen. A room that smelled like the perfume only the world's most exotic flowers could exude. A room where two men stood as she was pushed inside. One of the men, the one who looked slightly younger than the other, raised his arms, took a step toward her, and said words she thought she would never hear again. "Hi, Mom."

Chapter 29

Robert watched his son fly into his mother's arms. It struck him that while Bo now looked like a twenty-one year-old man, he was still a fourteen year-old kid. No, fifteen, now. It had been almost a full year... Tears filled his own eyes as Bo and Maggie both collapsed onto the sofa, clinging to each other, too overcome by emotion to do anything but claw and blubber. He glanced at Lucifer, who crooked his finger. Robert obeyed.

"Touching, isn't it?" Lucifer said. "Rather a nice birthday present for her, don't you think?"

Not knowing how he was supposed to respond, Robert said nothing. Lucifer said, "I'll leave the three of you for a while. I need to change clothes anyway. Do you think an hour of privacy will be sufficient?"

"It'll have to be, I guess," Robert replied.

Lucifer gave him a malevolent wink. "You're learning, Robert. You're learning. Use this hour well." With those words, he turned on his heel and left the room.

Robert turned back to his son and ex-wife, wondering how he could explain to Maggie in only one hour the unbelievable events of nearly a full year: The crash. The time spent in Abner's cabin. The discoveries of both the miraculous water and the horror of their cannibalism. His own transmutation. Bo's. The work they'd been doing. Munoz. Cain. Lucifer himself. Could he bring himself to tell her of Bo's girlfriend, Marta? Could he look her in the eye and tell her about Isabella? That he'd fathered another child? How in the world could he explain— to an already overwhelmed mother— truths about himself and their son that couldn't possibly be believed? All in the space of a single hour?

Feeling the weight of the entire universe on his shoulders, Robert trudged over to the sofa and knelt down. He waited until Maggie finally noticed him. "Mag, I need to—"

"Robert," Maggie wailed, "Mama's dead. They— they slaughtered her like an animal."

"Lena? Oh, Maggie, I'm so sorry. So sorry. It's all my fault, too." Fresh tears came to his eyes. He shook his head. "It would have been better if we'd all died in that plane crash. You would have gotten over it someday. It's my fault. I never should have—"

Maggie interrupted him by releasing her hold around Bo's neck and grabbing his own face between her hands. "You and Bo— Bobby, what in God's name is *happening* here?"

Robert looked into the anguished, tear-streaked face, immediately aware that his own looks had caused her some kind of mental slip backwards in time. She hadn't called him Bobby since before Bo was born. He took a deep breath. "Maggie, we don't have much time. Please listen to me. Everything I'm about to tell you is true. I swear to God it is. We were flying over the mountains in Ted's plane. One minute we were fine, the next, he lost control, and we went down..."

The door opened as Robert was relating how he'd lost his hand. Lucifer strode in, Cain hard on his heels. Lucifer walked to the middle of the room, raised his arms and pirouetted. "How do you like my outfit?" He was dressed in a full length, beautifully embroidered Arabian garment. "Gift from one of my children who lives in Libya. Talented fellow named Quadaffi. Well, Robert. I'm sure you've done a good job of filling Margaret in, and I forgive you for being a tiny bit biased. Mind if I join you?"

Robert stood. Stiffly, because he'd been on his knees for an hour. He watched as Cain placed an armchair in front of the sofa, upon which Lucifer sat, crossing his legs. It didn't escape Robert's notice that Cain had placed the chair so that the fire roaring in the room's large, open fireplace was directly behind his master, highlighting his head and shoulders with the effect of a mirage, like water's reflection shimmering on an asphalt highway.

"Now then. Robert, if you would be so kind as to take a seat there with your son, I have a few things I wish to say to all of you, and each of you."

Robert complied. Bo shifted slightly to make room on the sofa for him, but didn't relinquish his protective clasp around his mother's body. All three stared at their tormentors with undisguised fear.

Lucifer pursed his lips, and turned to Cain. "You may be excused, my son. Your presence here is making my guests feel uncomfortable." Without a word, Cain left, and Lucifer continued. "For pity's sake, do try to relax, all of you. This is your lucky day. No harm will come to you. On the contrary, I feel in such a generous mood, I'm prepared to see this heartwarming reunion become permanent. What do you think of that?"

He smiled at the suspicion showing all over their faces. "I have a proposition for you, but first, Margaret, I hope you will believe me when I tell you I am sincerely sorry for what happened to your mother. She wouldn't listen, and I lost my temper. So much for that. Now. Before I get to my surprise, let me recite a few facts: It's human nature for everyone to want something. Often, most often, I daresay, they invariably want more than they have, no matter what their circumstances are. You three are no different. Take Bo, here, for instance. What does Bo want? Not a lot, to be honest. He'd like to become a computer expert, but he wants his family back together again more. He wants his mother and father— under the same roof.

"And Robert? What does Robert want? He wants, more than anything, the chance to prove that he's the best sportscaster in the world. And you, Margaret? What is it you want? Well, I think that is crystal clear. You have already gone through many hardships in proving how much you desire to have your only son back, alive and well."

He paused, searching their faces for any change of expression. There was none. All three sat like time-frozen images in a photograph. "So. What would you collectively think if I were to tell you each of you could have your wish? Never mind, don't try to answer. I know it already. But there are a few small problems, aren't there? Let me explain. First, Bo probably wouldn't like reverting back to his former appearance. Those ugly braces, thick glasses, skinny physique, and all that. Rather unattractive, weren't you, Bo? But my guess is you wouldn't want him back any other way would you, Margaret?"

Maggie managed to shake her head.

"I thought not. Nevertheless, old Bo here would be willing to go back to his former self if necessary. Am I right, Bo?"

"Yes, sir." Bo croaked.

"And Robert would— well, the fact is that each of you would do anything to get what you want. Isn't that so? Let me see if I can sum up: As I said, Bo wouldn't want to look like he did before, but he'd do anything to get what he really wants, which is a permanent mother and father; a harmonious family.

"Robert, bless him, would also be willing to make enormous sacrifices in order to fulfill his desires. In fact, he would be willing to leave Bo here with me and never see him again. He'd even be willing to leave you in my clutches, Margaret. He'd do it in a heartbeat. And you. In order never to lose your beloved son again, you'd be willing to give up your career, your lover, even become my own mistress, and live here as my slave, my personal play-toy forever, wouldn't you?"

Lucifer paused again. The three statues sitting in front of him could not even glance at the guilt on one another's faces. They were hardly breathing. Lucifer stood, walked around the armchair and placed his hands on the top of it. "It might be fun to keep all three of you here, but I think it would be much more interesting to watch each of you realize your dreams. Therefore, I'm willing to set you free, on one condition."

This statement got a response from each member of his small audience. There was a faint glimmer of hope in three pairs of eyes. "The condition is this: Margaret, you and Robert must remarry. After a quiet, dignified wedding ceremony, which must be performed tonight, I will do the following: Bo, where I will send your family to live, you will eventually have access to what will become the top of the hill regarding the computer industry, and I will not remove from your brain any of what you have learned here. Robert, you will, with the help of my children, get that second chance you so selfishly desire, *with* your youthful looks and both hands, too. All you have to do is be a good father and husband this time around. And Margaret, you will have your son back, plus enough money to guarantee you shall never want for anything. You may even go back to work in television if you wish. The choice is yours."

Maggie somehow summoned to strength to say, "Robert Ellis is the last man on earth I want to be married to. What if I refuse?"

"Then Robert and Bo will continue their work here as before, and after I've tired of you, which I'll admit might take a few days, you will spend the rest of eternity as one of my mothers, raising my children." He smiled at the stunned looks on their faces, walked to the door, and said, "I'll give you half an hour to decide."

When Lucifer was gone, ten minutes passed before anyone said a word. Each was examining their own thoughts. At last, with new tears streaming, Bo looked at his mother and father in turn, and begged, "Mom? Dad? I love you both so much. Can't you try to make it work? We'd never get another chance."

Robert added, "What about it, Mag? You were crazy about me once. Can we start over again? From scratch?"

Maggie pushed the indelible image of her mother's horrendous murder aside, and looked at the two men who were practically strangers to her. One looked like the man she'd fallen in love with so many years ago. The other seemed to be the promise of what her son would grow into. The past and the future, both begging her to put the present humpty-dumpty wreckage of their family back together again. She got to her feet, walked over to the fireplace and stared into the fire. She was still standing there when Lucifer came back into the room. She looked up at him and whispered, "What time is the wedding? Can I take a bath first?"

"Of course. Everything has been prepared." He snapped his fingers and three young women, all dressed in the same style white robe Maggie wore, came into the room. "These girls will assist you. Take as much time as you wish."

One of the girls stretched out her hand and smiled. "This way, please." She took Maggie's hand in a completely unthreatening way, and led her through the door. As she left, she glanced back at Robert and Bo. "I'll do my best to make it work."

The scented, circulating water in the huge sunken tub was almost too hot, but Maggie soon found she was enjoying it in spite of herself, and the attention she was being given by Lucifer's three handmaidens, which amounted to outright pampering. No more inhibited than innocent children, they shed their own robes, and joined her in the tub, washing her hair, her face, her body, clucking over how beautiful she was, how wonderful it was that she was getting married, and how they envied her. Sinatra, Maggie's favorite, backed up by lush orchestrations, sang from somewhere in the atmosphere. When she said she was ready, they helped her out of the tub and into the largest, softest towels she'd ever seen or felt. She allowed herself to sit at the dressing table while the women did her nails, her hair, and produced her favorite makeup and perfumes. Eventually, all was done, and the three girls clapped their hands in delight at the result. Maggie, when clad in a fresh white robe, had to admit to herself she felt a thousand times better, and asked, "What now?"

"Oh," said the one who called herself Anya. "Master has prepared a little treat for you. Come along."

Maggie allowed herself to be led down yet another carpeted hallway, to yet another massive wooden door. It opened as she stood there, and Lucifer's voice came from within. "Come in, come in."

Maggie walked into the room which she immediately saw was a small, private dining room. Lucifer had changed clothes again, too. He was now wearing a pale pink Nehru jacket, which, on him, didn't at all look silly. The door closed behind her, and she realized they were alone. He came around the table to politely hold her chair. "Please have a seat. You must be terribly hungry. My chef has prepared something for you."

Maggie wasn't the least bit hungry, but felt as if she had no choice but to comply. She sat, not daring to ask where Robert and Bo were. The table was set for only two. "I'm afraid I don't have much appetite," she stammered.

Lucifer reached into the ice bucket beside the table. He held up a wrapped bottle of chilled wine. "This will take care of that little problem." He poured two glasses, and handed Maggie one of them, while raising his own in a toast. "You look radiant. Quite beautiful in fact. I salute the bride-to-be."

Maggie took a sip of the delicious wine and was instantly hungry. Lucifer chuckled, as if knowing ahead of time what effect the rosy wine would have. "I thought so. This is a relatively young wine. Too young for my taste, but it does the job it's supposed to." He rang a small golden bell that was in the shape of a snorting bull, and a dark-complexioned, bearded man of around sixty came in, smiling. Lucifer said, "This is my faithful Manuel, who will be serving us this evening."

Maggie nodded at the slightly built man who somehow looked familiar. She looked back across the table and said, "What about—?"

"Cain? Busy in the kitchen." From his pocket he removed a red silk handkerchief, which he unwrapped slowly, revealing, in its middle fold, a golden chain with a ruby pendant the size of a Malaga grape. Maggie couldn't keep her mouth from falling open as Lucifer said, "Small wedding present. I think it suits the color of your eyes and hair, Margaret. Manuel, will you?" He handed the jewel to the dark man who took it and from the back of her chair, hung it around her neck.

Beaming as Maggie blushed, Lucifer said, "You may bring the first course now, my son." As the servant hurried out, he looked across at Maggie, leaned forward with his forearms on the table as if to affect an air of informality, and said, "Though you may not think so, Cain has any number of unique talents. One of those is cooking. This evening, he has prepared a special dish in your honor. A tasty main course, which he calls Brisket DeVries. Here, let me pour you another glass of wine."

Chapter 30

The wedding was held in the tiny Kaneville church. Maggie knew where she was, but had no idea how she got there, having been carried along like a flimsy wisp of smoke blown before the wind. In such a state of unfeeling shock, she was aware of sensations, but none of them seemed physical. It was as if her eyes and her mind had detached themselves from the shell of her body, registering everything; all the five senses, yet from some distance away from the white-robed figure, which stood by the red-covered altar. Her separated self noticed that red and white were two of only three colors inside the chapel. Black was the other one. Red and black flowers. Red and black candles, altar cloths, aisle carpeting.

She smelled something she thought might be incense. Tasted the brass of her own bile. She heard choral music, but there was no choir or organ visible, not even a piano. Must be a recording, piped in from some unseen source. Though its volume was suppressed, she recognized the jagged measures of Orff's *Carmina Burana*. She wanted to laugh at the choice of such profane tonality and rhythms, but her out-of-body brain had no control over the reactions of the pale manikin with the large jewel hanging around her neck, standing stock still next to Lucifer, who wore a blood-red robe with a black sash, and whose face was showing a look which could only be described as gleeful.

And, there were other white-robed figures, all standing like carved ivory pieces on a chessboard: Her Maid—No, Matron-of-Honor. None other than Alice Crowfeather. Either a reconstructed Alice Crowfeather, or an identical twin. From

Lucifer's Children

descriptions she'd been given earlier by Bo and Robert, she recognized the other two as Bo's recent companion, Marta, and an obviously pregnant Isabella. But Robert's latest mistress was not nearly as pregnant as the third bridesmaid, Beth Oliver, who was spilling genuine tears onto her enormous belly.

Robert, standing close to her, white and immobile as a glacier, was flanked by his best man, Bo, and three men— the same three men she'd seen on the mountain, except the middle one was armed this time with a grin, not a rifle. There couldn't be more than two-dozen pews in the small sanctuary, but all of them were full. Full of smiling, ordinary looking people. Most of the women were also in various stages of pregnancy.

And in came the minister. A tall, wide-shouldered man who looked far too much like her long-dead father to be coincidental. And it was Joseph DeVries' voice that began intoning the service. Maggie heard the familiar words come from her father's mouth. Heard Lucifer himself say he'd give the bride away. Heard herself and Robert whisper the same promises they'd made once before. Saw Robert Ellis place a gold ring on her finger for the second time. Saw herself slipping an identical ring on his finger. Heard her father make the ultimate pronouncement, and advise Robert he could kiss the bride. There was no veil for Robert to lift, and Maggie felt his breath as he leaned toward her. The instant his lips touched hers, all her senses vanished. All her awareness disappeared. All became as black as Lucifer's eyes.

Robert had reacted fast when Maggie had collapsed, but Lucifer was faster. He'd caught Maggie by the waist, picked her up with no more effort than lifting a toy doll. "Nothing to worry about," he told Robert, "Poor thing's overcome with emotion. She'll be fine in a few minutes." With those encouraging words, Lucifer, carrying the inert form in his arms, had turned and walked through the single rear door, which opened into a small room with steps that led to the passageway connecting the church to the barn. Once there, Robert realized only he and Cain had followed Lucifer. The others, including Bo, must have left through the front door of the church. "Excuse me," Robert said. "Where's my son?"

Lucifer handed his still unconscious burden over to the albino, turned to Robert, and answered, "He's gone with Abner and Manuel. His re-transformation must be done right away. Don't worry, Robert, it's a painless procedure, but it does take a little time. Until tomorrow morning, in fact." They passed through yet another of the huge wooden doors into Lucifer's house. "Ah, here we are," he said. "And don't concern yourself about your bride. She likes my wine." He winked. "With another glass or two, she will be just fine, and ready for your wedding night." He turned to the giant. "Just lie her there on the sofa. I'll take care of her revival. You take Robert up to his surprise." He glanced at Robert. "Little wedding present for you, too,"

Cain nodded to his master, gently laid Maggie on the sofa, and motioned for Robert to follow him. He led the way through a series of connecting rooms and hallways until they reached another of the strange elevators. Cain never said a word as he ushered Robert inside. It seemed the door opened again in only a second, and Robert was astonished to find himself standing on a transparent, glass-like floor, through which he could see down to the apartment he'd just left.

"This way," the albino said, and Robert followed him down a mirrored corridor, which led to another closed door. Robert looked into the pink eyes as Cain opened it. "What surprise was he talking about?"

There was a hint of a smile on the brute's face. "Go right in. You'll see soon enough."

But Robert couldn't see anything at all. The room he'd entered was dark, and after Cain closed the door, pitch-black. Nor could he see anything below him anymore. He felt a sudden mixture of foreboding mixed with a tinge of vertigo as he sensed he was alone. Cain had not entered with him. Not wishing to stumble over anything, he simply sat down. The room—or whatever place he was in—was cool, but not uncomfortable. He felt a slight breeze on his cheek, whether from some unseen opening or an air-conditioning vent, he couldn't tell. It occurred to him to stand up, turn around and try the door he'd just come through, to let in some light. But when he stood and turned, he couldn't find any handle or seam. The wall surface he touched was smooth. Thinking he'd become disoriented, turned around more times than he thought, Robert sat down again. Nothing to do but wait to see what kind of macabre 'surprise' Lucifer had in store for him, not that the wedding ceremony wasn't weird enough, what with all those ugly flowers and music, plus the guy Lucifer had found to play the part of the preacher, who'd looked enough like Maggie's father to be his twin.

To occupy his mind, he began mentally calculating time, by counting seconds. One thousand one. One thousand two... When he reached what he thought was about ten minutes, he noticed light coming from between his legs. He stopped counting and peered down. More light was coming now, revealing a room beneath him. A bedroom. Robert scrambled to his knees. Leaned over on all fours, like an animal. Fascination rapidly overtook curiosity as more light reaching up to his glass cell revealed the standard furnishings of not just a bedroom, a *hotel* room. No, it was more than that. Down to the last detail, which included flowers and a magnum of champagne, already opened, it was a replica of their honeymoon suite at the Sands in Las Vegas!

Robert stared down. Maggie, wearing the same lace button-down-the-front nightgown she'd worn on their wedding night, was lying on top of the king-size bed. Her own eyes, which Robert could see clearly, seemed to be glazed over, as if she was more than a little drunk. Robert's mind began racing. Sweat broke out on his forehead. He stood quickly and looked around. The light coming from below was enough to show him he *was* in a small cell. Worse, he couldn't see the frame of the door he'd come through. There was no way out.

He yelled, at the top of his voice. But Maggie, lying no more than twelve or fifteen feet below him, heard nothing. Robert didn't yell again. He knew no one would hear him, and he gradually began to understand what Lucifer's surprise was. He was certain of it when he saw a man come from the bathroom and sit on the edge of the bed. Robert gaped. The man, dressed in the new dressing gown he'd bought just for the occasion years ago, was reaching for the bottle and glasses. Robert watched in silent fury as the man poured two and handed one of them to Maggie, who sat up against the pillows. The moment she took the glass and raised it to her lips, the man looked up at Robert and smiled. Robert's mouth fell open. "My God. It's *me!*" A millisecond later, he understood it all.

It wasn't him down there.

It was Lucifer.

Lucifer, who could turn himself into any kind of form, had taken over Robert's being, looking exactly the same as Robert had the night of his wedding, and was preparing to go to bed *with his wife.*

"You bastard!" Robert yelled uselessly again. "You miserable *bastard.*" With his one good hand, Robert banged on the transparent floor. All he could hear from his efforts was a dull thud, which also produced pain. The glass, or whatever the damned floor was made out of, must be a foot thick. There was, of course, no response from below, which further infuriated Robert. He went into a raging fit. Cursing. Screaming. Stomping his feet. Banging his body against the solid walls of his tiny prison until he was completely exhausted.

When his futile exertions reduced him to a whining lump, he lay on his stomach and cried. He cried tears of torture, anger, and pity. After a while, he glanced down. Helpless, he watched as Lucifer stroked Maggie's hair. Her arm. They were apparently talking. It took what Robert guessed to be an hour before Lucifer gathered Maggie in his arms. Robert could hear no sound, but knew Lucifer was saying all the soothing, comforting, loving words, and when he bent to kiss her, Maggie didn't resist. Didn't turn away. Didn't fight.

As he watched them, Robert, with bottomless shame, became aware that Lucifer was slower, gentler, more caring, more considerate of his bride than he'd been that night, or for that matter, any other night. As Lucifer slowly unfastened the topmost of Maggie's nightgown buttons, Robert cursed himself for the memory of practically ripping it from her body, anxious as he'd been.

He watched.

He wasn't sure when his fury turned to admiration. It took a long time. He saw Maggie begin to respond to Lucifer's expert lovemaking. Robert guessed their foreplay lasted at least another hour. His wife was more than responding now. She was actively participating. Giving back as much as she was getting—touch for touch, kiss for kiss. Robert could see the fever mount in her face. He saw her body, now writhing in raw hunger for the body of her expert lover. He saw her reach for him. Ask for him. Practically beg for him, twisting and jerking in heat for him. Still Lucifer waited, until Maggie was clawing at him. Heaving up and down on the bed. Robert suddenly felt gross embarrassment at the awareness of his own tumescence.

He wanted to squeeze his eyes shut when Lucifer finally rolled on top of her, his back full of marks from her fingernails, but he could not. He was fully cognizant he was viewing not a disgusting, pornographic exhibition, but the unfolding of human union in its most perfect, beautiful form. New tears sprang to his eyes as he stared at their passion. Their oneness. Physical joy in its purest state. He couldn't hear a thing, but he knew full well what kind of sounds were emanating from the nuptial bed. Knew the crescendo that would already be coming from Maggie's throat, in rhythm punctuated by the counterpoint of her lover's voice. He hated himself for not being able to take his eyes from their climb to the top of the mountain.

Nor was he able to shut out the sight of what happened next. At the peak of their imaginary summit, Robert saw Lucifer inexplicably roll off Maggie. He saw that Maggie couldn't understand it either. Robert saw the bewilderment, the hurt in her wide eyes, but it only lasted a moment, because another form had entered the room.

A very large form.

Who removed his robe and pinioned the sexually suspended body of the bride back onto the bed in one motion. He then began other motions. Robert caught the eye of Lucifer looking up at him. He saw the broad smile on Satan's face and thought he heard laughter as he broke eye contact and was instantly hypnotized by the sight of Cain viciously, brutally ripping into Maggie's body. Mercifully, the rape didn't last more than a minute or two, and as mercifully, the now quite audible sounds of Lucifer's laughter and Maggie's screams began to fade, as Robert knew he was going to pass out. His last conscious thought was a prayer. A prayer that Maggie had fainted, too.

Robert awakened lying next to Maggie in the big bed. Naked, he turned to his wife, who was not asleep, but staring vacantly at the ceiling. He turned on his side, reached a hand over to touch her, realizing at once it was his *left* hand, which had been fully restored. Good as new. But the moment he touched her side, she withdrew, moving as far away from him on the bed as she could. Her voice was a hoarse whisper. "Don't you dare touch me, Robert. Don't you ever touch me again."

"Mag, I'm so sorry. It wasn't really me. It was—"

"I know who it was."

"Please, Maggie, I couldn't help it. There was nothing I could—"

The interruption was the unannounced entrance of Manuel Munoz, who ignored their nakedness. Robert scurried to cover himself but Maggie didn't move. Munoz politely diverted his eyes and said, "It's almost time to leave. You'll find proper clothing in the chest drawers and closets." Having said no more than that, he turned on his heel and left as quietly as he'd entered.

Robert thought to employ a little discretion of his own. Wrapping one of the bed sheets around his body, he climbed off the bed, careful to keep his eyes away from Maggie. "I'll wait in the bathroom till you're dressed. Just holler when you're finished, okay?"

Maggie didn't respond at all, and Robert made his way into the bathroom where he found a razor, shaving cream, and the other usual bathroom articles, both his and hers. He took a long shower, taking also plenty of time to towel his body, grateful he could once more use both hands. He wrapped a fresh towel around his waist leaned close to the door and called, "Maggie? Okay to come out now?"

There was no answer.

Robert opened the door. Peered inside. Maggie was already fully dressed and sitting on the edge of the bed. Her hair was a tangled mess, but she either was oblivious to that fact, or didn't care. Robert headed to the closet. Over his shoulder, he said, "There's a hairbrush in the bathroom, Mag. You don't want Bo to see you looking like— well, you know."

Again Maggie didn't respond, except to move like an automaton to the bathroom. She didn't bother to close the door. Robert sat down on one of the armchairs and peeked through the door at her. She was standing in front of the mirror, methodically wielding the brush, her face blank as a fresh sheet of typing paper, and almost as white. Robert suddenly guessed she hadn't slept at all. She stood there, robot-like, until a knock came at the outer door. Maggie put the brush down and walked back into the bedroom only when Munoz reappeared, nodded his approval, and said, "It's time. Follow me, please."

The passageway led back to the barn. Lucifer was waiting, arms folded, standing beside the green Bronco, which was now turned around to face the barn doors. Lucifer stood, rocking back and forth, with the usual smile on his face. Cain was nowhere to be seen. Lucifer glanced at Robert's left hand. "You see how I keep my word? That's part of what you wanted, Robert, old buddy. Here's the rest." He opened the driver's side door of the Bronco and lifted something from the seat. Robert's eyes grew wide when he recognized what it was. "Right," Lucifer said, "It's a money belt. Stuffed inside, you'll find two million dollars in cash, along with the names, addresses and phone numbers of some of my children. Should get you jump-started in your new career." He handed the belt to Robert, then looked at Maggie, who was staring at the spot where her mother had so recently been murdered, "Margaret, my precious, I believe this is what you wanted?" He turned back toward the opening to the corridor at the same moment Cain came through it, one step behind Bo.

Robert caught his breath. Bo was fourteen again. Mop of hair. Skinny as ever beneath the sweat-shirt jeans he was wearing. The braces on his teeth glinted as he hurried to hug his mother, his voice cracking, "Hi, Mom. Happy Birthday." Robert watched in abject pain and utter loneliness as Maggie fiercely clutched her son to her breast, dry-heaving because she had no more tears to cry with. Bo, on the other hand, had plenty for both of them.

After a few minutes, Lucifer nudged him. "Bo, I'm going to miss you. We all will, but now you have your family back. What you wanted more than anything. It pleases me no end to see this happy reunion." To Robert he said, "This vehicle smells a bit like Cain's hog pens, but it has a full tank of fuel, and should get you safely to the airport at Knoxville. There are three tickets in the glove compartment."

"We're— free to go?" Robert couldn't quite believe it was actually happening. As if to answer him, Lucifer reached into a pocket of his suit, extracted the remote device, and touched a button. The barns doors swung open, and brilliant, snow-reflected sunlight flooded the entire area.

"Anytime you're ready. When you get to the airport, just leave the Bronco in the parking lot with the keys still in the ignition. It will be taken care of. Good-bye and good luck."

Robert hustled his family inside, started the Bronco, which to him smelled like a rose garden, dropped it into 'drive' and eased forward. He, of course, couldn't hear the comments that were made as he drove out, toward Kaneville.

Munoz, watching the Bronco become smaller in the distance, said, "I can't believe you let them go, Master."

Lucifer's smile never wavered. "They think they've escaped hell. Now they are going to find out what hell really is." He clapped his servant on the shoulder. "Besides, Manuel, my son, they'll be back. Come, we have things to do. You know, it really is cold out there."

It was also bitter cold in Northern Ireland. In a damp hotel room in Belfast, Ramon Barillas was too tired to have celebrated his birthday, even if he'd thought about it, which he hadn't. He hadn't even had time go to confession. He went to sleep, only to wake up in the middle of the night screaming. Paralyzed with another headache. Several other guests heard the screams, but no one looked in on him for three days.

᧖

Tom Lewis

Chapter 31

Cardinal Peter Reilly forced himself to smile rather than frown. He knew Ramon's mental condition was so precarious, even the hint of chastisement could very well send his former protégé into another period of deep depression. He shifted his girth in Ramon's lumpy old armchair, and in as soft a voice as he could manage, he said, "I wish you had come to me to begin with, lad. I'm not so busy I can't take time to help the best man I've ever known. Can you tell me what Father Kennagin's conclusions were?"

Reilly knew he was treading on eggshells here. Kennagin was the senior priest who was, unofficially, sanctioned by the Pope to perform the ancient and controversial rite of exorcism. In 1972, John Paul's predecessor, Paul VI, had eliminated the minor order of those mysterious, highly secretive priests, but like all high-ranking men of the church, Reilly knew the practice had not altogether been stopped, since Paul had shrewdly left a loophole: A Bishop still could, under certain conditions, appoint a qualified, experienced priest to perform the ancient rite, and after all, John Paul was the Bishop of Rome, and Kennagin was the most experienced exorcist in all of Catholicism.

Ramon sighed. "He saw me twice, Eminence. The first time, he spent an hour listening to me, and then sent me to a whole army of psychiatrists. Well, five of them anyway, and all five had a different diagnosis. Most of their mumbo jumbo went right over my head. When I went back to Father Kennagin the second time, he read all their reports, then threw them all in the wastebasket."

"That sounds like Patrick Kennagin, sure enough."

"Do you know him?"

"I've met him a few times. Go on, my son."

Ramon sat on the edge of his cot, fidgeting with a frayed coat sleeve, staring at some imaginary object on the floor. In nearly a whisper, he said, "He looked me in the eye and told me he'd seen Satan several times, in various forms. Either Satan or one of his 'soldiers' as he called them. He told me Satan was a very real, palpable force, and had been since the beginning of time. Then, he did a strange thing. He got up, washed his hands, dipped them in some oil, then came back to where I was sitting and grabbed my head. He must have held me like that for fifteen minutes. I don't know whether he was praying or not. He made no sound, and I had my eyes closed. Anyway, he sat back down, facing me, and told me he didn't think I was possessed at all, at least not by the Devil."

"Really?"

"No. He said my visions were probably caused by an Angel."

"What?"

"Actually an Archangel. Probably Michael."

"Um. Over the centuries, Michael is the Archangel who has had the most battles with Satan. But I don't understand, laddie, why would Michael torment you so? A good priest?"

"Father Kennagin said, not to put too fine a point on it, that Michael was trying to 'get my attention.' Those were his exact words, your Eminence."

"Well, if that's so, he has certainly succeeded. But why?"

"Father Kennagin just shook his head. He didn't know." Ramon lifted his head and looked deep into his former mentor's eyes. "But I do. At least I do now."

Cardinal Peter Reilly saw something in the young man's eyes that caused him not to respond. Something like light. He kept silent. Waiting.

When Ramon spoke, it was in a voice so clear, so convincing, Reilly knew he was hearing a profound truth. "I can't explain why it is that she is my sister, even my twin, but this much I do know. Margaret Ellis is one of God's children, and is close to death and eternal damnation. And I am the only one who can help her. I have to return to the United States and become a priest in the truest, simplest way. A practical, working priest, if not to save her life, to save her immortal soul, and perhaps my own as well."

Ten minutes passed before either man spoke again. With tears in the clear eyes, Ramon said, "Will you help me, your Eminence?"

Reilly cleared his throat. "Of course I will, my son. So will Cardinal Zimmer. The Germans and the Poles have never had much love for each other, but Peter Zimmer is closer to John Paul than any of us. A word from him, and the Holy Father will surely grant your petition." Reilly came out of the armchair and got down on his knees. "Pray with me Ramon, and for me. And pray for God's church and all His children"

Unmindful of the falling rain, Father Daniel O'Connor stood impatiently outside the dingy Amtrak station in Raleigh. The train from Washington was late, but that was not what was bothering him. What was making him so nervous was how in the name of God he was going to cope with having a new assistant pastor who outranked him! Whoever heard of a parish priest having a bishop for an assistant? A *bishop?*

He'd read the letter from his own Diocese bishop a hundred times if he'd read it once. Along with the copy of the letter that had come to the Diocese office from the office of the Pope. From The Holy Father himself! God does indeed move in mysterious ways. It was certainly true he needed help, and help in the form of Ramon Barillas was a welcome miracle in and of itself, but the letter—both letters—had been specific. Clear as a bell. Bishop Ramon Barillas' duties at St. Andrews were to be those of an assistant pastor. Nothing more, nothing less. It was weird. Unprecedented, as far as he knew. Unheard of!

O'Connor, being, in his own mind at least, a simple priest, had hardly ever given much thought to the difference between diocesan and titular bishops, but he knew full well the church considered a bishop not a vicar of the Holy Father, the Bishop of Rome, but a vicar of Jesus Christ himself, and that Ramon's period of consecration would surely take no more than the minimum three months. At least, that was what his own bishop had thought, having immediately made some discreet inquiries to his personal contacts in Rome. Apparently, Ramon Barillas had friends in high places, especially in the Curia, and was favored by John Paul, who had maybe ordained him as a reward for 'exemplary service' to the Holy See. Why on earth had he really been sent to St. Andrews? Well, his was not to question his superiors, especially *those* superiors. There were reasons for everything.

The train pulled in and Ramon Barillas got off, wearing a purple *biretta* but still carrying the same battered old suitcase. Father Daniel O'Connor embraced the young new bishop warmly. "I'm so glad to see you again, Ramon. Here to save a few souls, are you?"

Ramon smiled and bear-hugged his friend. "At least one, I hope. How are you, Dan?"

Chapter 32

Bo Ellis was not a happy camper. He didn't like his room, or rather his three rooms, in the new house. He didn't like San Francisco. He didn't like the Bay City Academy, or any other private school for that matter. But Bay City was worse than the others had been. It had no girls. Not that it mattered all that much. There had been girls at the two schools in Seattle, but they had all been too young, too gawky and silly acting, and none of them had given him the time of day anyway, because of his looks. They didn't give a damn about how bright he was. They could care less that he knew more about computers than any kid in Seattle, and that several of the computer companies were interested in him. They didn't even care that he had plenty of money in his jeans pockets. He didn't yet have a car, did he? Not yet. Didn't even have a learner's permit, and he doubted his Dad would let him do much learning in his new Beamer. That is, if his Dad would ever take time off from work to spend a lousy hour with him in the first place.

And Mom was no help, either. She was either sitting in her bedroom all day long or walking all over every neighborhood she could get to. Mealtime was a drag, too. The new cook couldn't even fry up a decent hamburger, and there wasn't even a frozen pizza in the fridge. And that wasn't all. The maid kept messing his room up once a day; putting books he was reading back on the shelf before he was done with them, picking things up and putting them where *she* thought they should go, not where he wanted them to stay. Stuff like that. She really pissed him off.

Matter of fact, everything pissed him off. He couldn't even go into a nice bar or restaurant and get a beer, for Christsakes. This whole deal wasn't working out the way he'd thought it would. Not even close. He swore, and turned the computer off. That was another thing. His Dad had bought him the latest Apple to be had, but it was so junky, so juvenile, so fucking *retarded*, man. Wasn't even worth kicking. Face it. He was missing the university. He was missing Marta. Dumb-ass Marta, but she had done, every night, what he had to do for himself now. It wasn't fair. It just wasn't fair, man. He'd kept his part of the deal, for sure, but Mom and Dad seemed further apart now than they'd ever been. No, this whole thing isn't working. Any damn fool could see that.

He heard a door slam somewhere downstairs. *Dad home?* He looked at his new sports watch. Not even five yet. He heard voices. Are they at it again? He left his room and started down the stairs. They were talking so loud they didn't hear him. Halfway down, he sat down and listened.

"You've been drinking again."

"I had a few at the club. Celebrating."

"You smell like it was more than a few."

"Get off my back, Maggie. Where's Bo?"

"What do you care where he is. You don't give him the time of day anyway."

"That's a buncha bullshit. I offer to take him to the games. Play golf."

"Why don't you take him double dating. I'm sure your latest bimbo has girls she can fix him up with."

"Jesus, Maggie."

"Why not? He's got his braces off now. Shouldn't be too tough. The way you throw money around, my guess is any number of those whores of yours would be glad to give him a tumble or two."

"You been bird dogging me, Maggie?"

"Not since Seattle. I saw enough there to convince me you were well on your way to the gutter again. Leopards can't change their spots. Look at you. I'll bet you've gained thirty pounds. Love handles for your ladies."

"Well, if I've been seeing other women, whose fault is that? From day one, you're the one who insisted on separate beds and separate fucking bedrooms to boot. What the hell did you expect? I buy you a new house in Seattle, you hated it. When I get the Giants job here and buy you this house, you hate it, too, not to mention the servants."

"I've never had servants in my life, Robert Ellis. I don't need to keep up with any Joneses. I didn't ask you to join those country clubs, either. How much of that money is left, by the way?"

"What do you care? I'm making good money now. Why don't you maybe think about going back to work? My contacts can help—"

"I don't feel like going back to work. Truth is, I don't feel very good at all anyway. Haven't for some time, now."

"You don't look so hot, either."

"What did you want to see Bo about?"

"I wanted to tell him the news. You, too, if you gave a shit."

"What news?"

"I'm going to New York. ABC Sports."

"So, you finally got it."

"Yeah, I finally got it."

"What about your contract with the Giants?"

"They're buying it out. Listen, Mag, we've beat the Devil at his own game. We can get to the top. The very top. You can have anything you want. We can make a fresh start. All of us, you, Bo, and me. We can—"

"You're drunk, Robert."

"I'm not drunk. I told you, I only had a few with the guys at the club. Look, why don't you get dressed, and we can stop all this arguing and all go out somewhere and celebrate. Just like old times. Hey, Bo? Bo, you home, son?"

Lucifer's Children

Responding to his Dad's yell, Bo got up from where he'd been sitting and slowly walked down the stairs. His mother passed him, going up.

Maggie sat on the edge of her bed. Her eyes were dry. Had been dry for two months. Two short months. That was all it had taken for Robert to revert to his past lifestyle, and for Bo to become a surly, ungrateful, walking, talking stranger. Maggie reached for the telephone, dialed a long-memorized number, and this time, didn't hang up before he answered. "Hello?"

"Hello, Sam?"

"Maggie? Maggie, is it really you?"

"Yes. It's really me. I found Robert and Bo. Sam, I have an awful lot of explaining to do, but first, I need to ask you a couple of questions."

"I can't believe it's really you. Where are you, Maggie? I'm sorry. Ask away."

"Sam, do you suppose there's a chance I might get my old job back? I want to come home."

"We have a new weekday anchor, Maggie, but I'm sure you could have your old weekend job back. Matter of fact, I can guarantee it. I'm the station manager, now."

"You are? Congratulations."

"Thanks. Next question."

"Do you still love me, Sam? As much as I still love you?"

"I never stopped loving you, and never will. Come home, Maggie, and marry me. Please."

"Sam, I'm pregnant."

The pause was only a short one.

"Like I said, come home, Maggie, and marry me. Please."

❦

Tom Lewis

Chapter 33

The Universities of North Carolina, Duke, N.C. State, and most of the other area colleges were on Christmas break, giving Father Daniel O'Connor a break of sorts as well, not that he'd been particularly swamped during the past ten months. Having Ramon Barillas, bishop or not, performing weddings and funerals, saying most of the masses, doing the majority of hospital and home visitations, and generally taking upon himself most of the day to day parish duties had freed O'Connor to do what he loved most— counseling his student athletes. He allowed himself a satisfied sigh. Things couldn't be better. Too, in what little spare time he could manage, Ramon also liked to visit the campuses now and then. He especially enjoyed the open practices of the UNC women's soccer team, which was nationally respected.

Dan O'Connor heaved another sigh of contentment. Ramon himself had been in the best of spirits as well, but his tenure at St. Andrews hadn't begun that way. O'Connor had been more than a little concerned at Ramon's earlier depression and off-his-feed disposition. But that had suddenly turned completely around. O'Connor could trace the exact date of the young bishop's mental and physical change for the better. He'd come into O'Connor's office one morning with a clipping from the *News and Observer*, and with a broad smile on his face, had showed him the photo and mention of the marriage of Margaret DeVries to Samuel Abrahms. Ramon had actually produced a bottle of Sherry, and they'd both had a snoot full. From that day to this, Ramon had been the happiest of men, and a parish plow-horse.

Lucifer's Children

Knowing how much Ramon loved soccer and liked all the American sports in general (with the singular exception of boxing) he'd invited Ramon to come over to watch a specific Christmas Day sports program that lately had been promoted to the hilt by ABC. When he glanced at his watch and heard the doorbell ring at almost the same instant, he grinned yet again. The man was *never* late.

O'Connor got up from his E-Z Boy to let his young friend in. "Come in, come in, Ramon. How is Mrs. Kearns?"

"She seemed better today. The people at Duke are taking great care of her."

"I'm sure. That's one fine institution, that hospital. Sit down, please. The program is just beginning. Would you care for something hot to drink? It's raw out there today."

"No, thank you. I had some coffee at the hospital." He took a seat on the sofa. "What is this program you're so anxious for me to see?"

O'Connor reached to turn the TV set on.

"It's a sports first. Three-part-series. Today's show will have the commissioners and player-reps of Major League Baseball, the NFL, the NBA, and the NHL all together in a kind of open forum to discuss the future of professional sports in America. Ought to be really interesting. Tomorrow, they're going to have the Olympic—"

The announcer was saying, "From our studios in New York City, the following program is a special presentation of ABC sports. And now, here is your moderator, Bob Ellis. Bob, take it away."

The stocky, tanned host took his place on a high stool and began by introducing his guests, working without a script...

Bo had ordered a pizza with pepperoni and green olives. There was already plenty of Heineken in the fridge. It was a nasty day outside and he'd told his Dad he'd just stay home and watch the program on TV instead of going with him to the studio. He didn't have much interest in watching the show, but he knew his Dad would quiz him on it when he got home. That is, *if* he came home.

Some home. He hated the upper west-side apartment he had to share with a father who came home loaded most of the time these days, and often with some high-priced call girl on his arm. Bo sneered at the television screen. ABC had told his Dad they would use the shortened version of his name. 'Robert' was too formal for a national sports figure, they'd said. Typical New York bullshit. Bo hated New York even more than he had Seattle or San Francisco, and for pretty much the same reasons. The school he was going to was only fit for Neanderthals, man. And, he'd mastered all the current computer games when he'd been a kid. It was boring. New York was boring. His whole damn life was boring. Besides, there was no sex. His dad never once thought to bring one of those girls home for *him*. Probably just as well. With his looks, they'd probably only do it with their eyes squeezed shut, holding their noses. The main thing that had caused him to decide to come here in the first place was the Mustang. That, plus when his Mom and Dad had that last big fight in San Francisco, his Mom had made it pretty damn clear that if Bo wanted to go back with her to Raleigh, he'd have to do some big-time shaping up. Hell, she didn't even love him anymore. He was sure of it. All she could think about was that geek, Sam Abrahms. On the other hand, Dad had promised him the new Mustang on his sixteenth birthday. Once he got behind the wheel of that red Mustang, things would be different, man. Oh yeah.

He went for a beer, tore into the already cold pizza, and stared at the TV screen. His Dad sure wasn't the flat-belly he'd been at Kaneville. Bo munched and watched. He didn't know any of those guys his Dad was talking to, or even what they were talking about. Could care less. He was thinking of turning the thing off when something caused him to freeze in mid-bite. Right there, on national television, before millions of people, a large clump of his Dad's hair fell right out onto his lap! When his

Lucifer's Children

Dad reached up to his head, still talking like nothing had happened, his hand was shriveled up like a gross-out claw!

Bo stopped eating...

The director cursed into his headset, then wrapped a hand around its mike. He looked wildly around at his producer, who was smiling. *Smiling?* "Go to commercial, quick!" he yelled, but the producer clamped a hand on his shoulder. "NO. No commercial. Let it run."

"What? Are you crazy? His hair's falling out all over the place. *Look.* What the hell's wrong with his face?" You gotta go to commercial. NOW."

"You heard me," the producer said, his voice calm and with that huge grin still on his face. "Hold your shot."

"Joe, we'll both be fired if we do this. Look at that hand. Jesus Christ."

"You'll be fired if you *don't* hold that shot. Do as I say."

The director, cameramen, and the entire tech staff behind the glass couldn't turn away from the pathetic sight of the man who was literally falling apart before their very eyes. Within the space of less than a minute, Bob Ellis, sweating like a fat man in a sauna, had aged twenty years. Hell, *thirty* years. He'd stopped talking. Was staring at the withered thing that had been his left hand, shaking his head, which was now bald as a cue ball. Another whole minute went by before he realized the cameras were still on him, and before he could climb off the stool and stumble out of the studio, heard, just as all the others in the studio did, the sound of laughter coming from somewhere out of sight.

Only then did the producer lean over and whisper to the director, "Okay, now you can cut. Go to commercial. We've got the backup guy ready."

Before he could cough up the pizza still in his mouth, Bo heard the phone ring. "Hello?"

"Bo it's me. I—"

"Dad? Dad, what's *happening?*"

"Shut up, Bo, and listen. Listen carefully. Go look in my closet. There's five shoe boxes stacked on the bottom shelf. There's some money in the third one. The middle one. Get it, all of it, and take a cab to the studio. I'll be waiting out front."

"Okay, but Dad, you—"

"DO it, Bo. Right now. We don't have a minute to lose."

Bo dropped the phone without hanging up. He ran to the closet, found the shoe box, stared for a few moments, then jammed at least ten thousand dollars into his pockets, grabbed the first coat he could find, and ran out of the apartment. He covered the three blocks to the Ansonia Station at 72nd in less than five minutes, running faster than he'd ever run in his life. The ninth taxi he signaled for actually stopped...

The moment the commercial hit the screen, Father Dan O'Connor looked at his guest. "My God. Can you believe what we just—Ramon? Ramon, what is it? What's the matter?"

Ramon stood, holding his head, trying not to cry out from the pain. "I...I'll be alright. Headache coming on. That was Margaret's husband, Dan."

"It was? Are you sure? I thought he—"

"I'll explain it to you later. Right now I have to ask a favor. May I borrow your car? It's very important."

"Of course you can." O'Connor reached into his pocket. Handed Ramon the keys. "Just pump the gas twice very lightly. It should start all right."

The old Chevy did start, and when Ramon drove away, fast, Dan looked from the window to the coat rack. Ramon had run out without his overcoat.

They were not at home. His head was pounding now. Where were they? Fifteen minutes later he felt real panic. They were not at WRDU either. Then he remembered the woman. *The former neighbor.* What was her name? Anderson? No.

Henderson. That was it. Tammy Henderson. Armistice apartments.

It took him another agonizing twenty minutes to drive to the apartment building. When he knocked on the door, the barking of the dog on the other side of it only increased the torment between his ears. The woman cracked the door, peering over the chain, frowning. "Can I help you?"

"Miss Henderson, please, I need your help. I'm looking for Margaret El—I mean Margaret Abrahms. It's terribly important."

In the few seconds it took to say this, Ramon watched as the woman's eyes grew wide with recognition. It had taken a moment, because he'd had a beard before. "Be quiet, Cleo! Oh, my Lord! You—you're her brother, aren't you? Her twin *brother?*"

"I'm sorry. There isn't much time. Can you tell me where she is?"

"She's at the hospital."

"Hospital? Which hospital?"

"Duke. She's about to have her babies."

Ramon felt suddenly very dizzy. "Would you please let me come in? I need to sit down for a moment."

"Sure. Just a minute. Let me put the dog up. Come on, Cleo."

Ramon leaned against the door-jamb. The pain was nearly unbearable now. Then she was back, removing the chain, leading him into her living room, offering a glass of water. He drank it gratefully, and listened as she told him Maggie was expecting twins. Maybe it was the twins that had caused her to be so long overdue. "Least that's what her doctors are saying. She's been carrying those two kids for eleven months, Father. Eleven whole months. Can you believe? Last time I saw her she couldn't even walk. I never saw anybody that—that big in my life. I call her all the time, you know. She went into labor last night, and Sam took her—"

Tom Lewis

"Thank you, Miss Henderson. Thank you very much. Ramon hurried out before she could get around to asking questions. Questions he couldn't answer. Not yet. The car had warmed up some, and he drove it hard to Duke University Hospital...

The team of doctors and nurses in delivery room number two were as talkative as ever. More so, because they were collectively cognizant they were about to add a new chapter to the book of baby birthing. Not even at Duke had any of them seen anything like it. None could ever remember a woman carrying a baby more than a month past normal delivery time, but this woman, a well-known local television personality no less, had obviously carried not one but two for an entire year! It would certainly be a birth worth writing a decent paper about. Historical.

But when the first fourteen-pound boy was extracted from the mountain that was Maggie Abrahms' belly, was spanked once and cleaned up, his bellowing became the only sound in the room. The chief gynecologist had to steady his nerves as he bent to complete his task. Even as the second one emerged from the cavernous C-sectioned womb, every member of the team had to concentrate on keeping control. Sweat showed on every forehead. None was willing to speak, though each was highly aware of the one sudden thought which was thundering in every brain; the specter of malpractice, although both babies were perfectly formed. Each weighed exactly fourteen pounds. But both had no hair at all, a full set of teeth, and pink eyes. *Albinos. Industrial size albinos.*

Two of the experienced nurses, wide-eyed and silent, took the twin monsters out while the team hurried to close up, hands shaking. Not one of them said a word. As soon as he was convinced the closing-up would be finished properly, Dr. Henry Villem, Jr. rushed out of the room and out of the hospital, tearing off gloves and mask as he went. Still in his scrubs, he got to his car, opened the dash pocket, and removed a brown paper sack with a bottle inside. He took two quick, long swallows of the odorless vodka, which set his throat on fire, but calmed him enough to try to think through what he was going to have to do next. How in the name of God Almighty was he going to be able to face Mr. Abrahms? What could he possibly say to the man? An idea came to him as he ran back into the hospital, nearly bowling over a priest who was also apparently in a hurry to get in. He'd call his Dad for advice. Right. Old Henry the First, as he liked to call his father, had seen it all in his time. Thank God he was miraculously still alive, still mentally sharp, and able to talk. He'd know what to tell the man...

It had been five hours, but Bo Ellis could still taste the foul staleness of pepperoni and green olives as he helped his Dad into the taxi outside the airport in Knoxville. It had been a wild five hours, too. And lucky. And expensive. His Dad had known there wouldn't have been, on Christmas Day, a seat on any commercial airline out of New York— to anywhere— so he'd paid a small fortune to the Manhattan cabbie to drive them to Newark, breaking every speed limit on the way. Bo had then found out how money talks. Five grand. Five large. Five thousand dollars was what they'd had to pay the pilot of Air-Exec to fly them to Knoxville. The Lockheed Jetstar had made the flight in under two hours, once his Dad and the pilot had stopped haggling and they'd finally gotten off the ground.

But the flight had been anything but enjoyable. He could hardly bring himself to look at his Dad's face. Or his broken-up body. The black guy with the gold tooth outside the terminal at Knoxville who owned his own cab–the only one left–had told them there was no way in hell he was gonna drive them all the way to Kaneville, North Carolina on Christmas Day. "I got a *family*, mister." But twenty-five one hundred dollar bills in cold, non-reportable cash convinced him his family could wait. Most of the night, if necessary. Twenty-five hundred tax-free bucks would fill a whole buncha stockings, man.

The weather and the roads were clear, and the back seat of the Pontiac was reasonably clean. Not a word was spoken by any of them until the red-striped taxi pulled into the parking lot at Kaneville. Bo helped his Dad out, and breathed a sigh of relief as he recognized the two men emerging from the bus station door...

Dr. Villem, Jr. found Sam Abrahms standing in front of the maternity gallery, his hands on the glass and a huge smile on his face. He was staring with unmistakable pride at the twins who dwarfed the half dozen other babies. Somebody had already told him they were there. Villem could hear their bleating right through the half-inch thick window. "Mr. Abrahms, would you, ah, please come down to my office? I'd like to talk to you."

"Oh." Abrahms' eyes never moved. "If it's all the same to you, I'd rather stay right here."

Villem looked around. They were alone. "All right. Look, I don't really know what to say, but—"

"They're beautiful, aren't they. Look at them. Wow."

Villem looked through the glass again, and stole a side glance at the elated man standing next to him. Poor guy. Didn't he realize they were not *his?* No way could he be the father of those two... those two creatures. He *had* to know, didn't he? "We, that is, I'm sure you can see that the boys have, well, certain characteristics, certain—"

"They're perfect. Both of them. Perfect. You and your team did a helluva job, Doctor. I'm tickled to death."

Is this man crazy or what? "Their eyes are...very unusual, Mr. Abrahms, they are pink."

"Yes."

"And they were born with a full set of teeth."

"I see that."

"Uh, huh. And do you notice anything else?"

Now the man finally turned to look at him. "That they are albino? That they are huge? That I'm obviously not their father? That what you're trying to get at, Doctor?"

"Well, I—"

"Hey, Doc, where I come from, you make a commitment to a woman you love, you keep it. No questions asked."

"I see. Where would that be?"

"Oh, some little mountain town you never heard of. Besides, I'm a twin myself." He turned back to stare through the glass. "Those little guys are going to be a blast to raise."

Villem sucked in a deep breath. This guy was insane. And insensitive as hell to boot. He hasn't even asked how the mother is. "Well, we did our best. Your wife is fine. I want to wish you both all the luck in the world and, um, congratulations."

Neither man had noticed the priest come in and was also staring through the glass...

Ramon couldn't help but overhear the last part of the subdued conversation between the two men standing ten feet away from him. His head was throbbing so hard he didn't know if he'd heard accurately, but the evidence was there, in plain sight on the other side of the glass partition. He turned and hurried down to Margaret's room. Peeked inside. They had left her there alone, and she was sleeping. Good. She seemed to have come through her terrible ordeal alright. He backtracked and took the elevator down to the first floor, turned right, and entered the small ecumenical chapel, knelt and genuflected, then began praying as he'd never prayed before. After perhaps fifteen minutes, his headache went away, replaced by a clear vision of what to do. A mission. A duty. He stood, took a deep breath, and went outside to Dan's car, unmindful of the cold.

He knew where he was going, though he'd never been there before. He also knew he was being led there, and why. And by whom. He pulled into the parking lot of TRIANGLE SPA EMPORIUM with the certain knowledge that the owner and one of his truck drivers were there, working on Christmas Day. As he stopped and got out of Dan's Chevy, he also now knew why he'd withdrawn all his money from the bank earlier. In his pocket was more than four thousand dollars...

Father Dan O'Connor had, by now, seen Ramon Barillas at his best and at his worst, but when he put the phone down, he shook his head in total bewilderment. He had never heard Ramon—or anyone else in his life for that matter—sound so... so desperate. But he'd been wise enough not to ask questions. Ramon must have a good reason for the unusual request, which had sounded awfully close to an outright order. O'Connor put on his overcoat, overshoes, hat and gloves and went to the back of the church where the storage shed was. Muttering to himself, he found the two water hoses which, thank the Lord, were not frozen stiff. He joined them together, connected them to the outside spigot, and began spraying water around the church, starting at the rear. By the time he had worked his way to the front, his fingers nearly freezing, he was astonished to see a delivery truck pull right up over the curb, Ramon, in his own car, right behind them.

When the two men got out of the truck and unloaded a hot tub *Hot tub?* and placed it directly in front of the front door of the church, he finally found his voice. "Ramon? What in the world is going on here? Why are these people— ?"

Bishop Ramon Barillas interrupted him, and in a tone that seemed colder than the water from the hose which was still in his hands, spraying the ground in front of him, said, "Dan, I don't have time to explain this. You have to trust me and do as I ask. A life depends on it. When you have finished spraying all around the church, fill this tub with water, then bless it."

"Bless it?"

"Yes. Bless it with all the faith you have. We need holy water. A lot of holy water."

"But Ramon, I—"

"DO IT, Father O'Connor. I'll be back soon."

Lucifer's Children

O'Connor heard more than Ramon's voice in those words. The command. He turned the hose into the tub as the young bishop got back into the Chevy and drove away. Then he turned back to his task. He squeezed his eyes shut, and began intoning the ancient Latin phrases. He hadn't noticed that he wasn't cold anymore...

Abner Highsmith hugged Bo warmly. "So you came back to us. "I am powerful glad to see you. Master will be pleased, don't you think, Manuel?"

Munoz's face also sported a big smile. "Indeed he will."

"Will he let me come back to school?" Bo wanted to know. "Please?"

"I have no doubt of it," Munoz said. "We've been expecting you. But who is this you've brought with you? Robert? Is that you?"

"You look like one of last year's cornstalks, Robert," Highsmith added. "Things out there been a trifle unsatisfactory, have they?"

"I want to come back, too," Robert croaked. "I want to be like I was before. Please, I'll do anything. I'm begging you."

Munoz and Highsmith exchanged frowns. Munoz stroked his chin whiskers, and softly said, "Abner, Bo looks like he's starving to death. I'll wager he could eat two or three Big Macs. Why don't you take him down to McDonald's while I take care of poor Robert, here."

Robert watched Abner nod, put his arm around Bo's shoulder and lead him away, down West Kane. He turned to look at Munoz. "Please, Senor Munoz. I made a mistake. A bad mistake, but it won't ever happen again. I swear it won't."

Munoz's frown deepened. "Ah, Robert, my friend. I'm afraid it will be impossible for you to go back to your old job. One of the young men you trained so well has been doing very adequate work since you left. However..."

"What? Like I said, I'll do anything. I'll sweep the floors. Wash windows. Anything."

"Well, actually there *is* something useful you can do for us. Come, I have an idea."

Robert, too feeble to resist, allowed Munoz to guide him to the waiting green Bronco. The engine was running and it was warm inside. Close. And smelled just as bad as it had before. "Where are we going?"

"You'll see."

Robert's hopes began to rise as they drove through the town, up the street that led to the industrial area. He didn't begin to worry until they had already passed the cap factory and the bottled water plant. Well, if he had to work in the sausage plant, that would do. But they passed the sausage plant as well, and the rendering plant. He glanced sideways at Munoz, but the Spaniard, eyes forward, kept right on going to the end of the road— where the hog pens were.

Munoz stopped the Bronco, but before Robert could say a word, his door was jerked open and he was bodily yanked out. Whatever cry had started to form in his throat when he looked into the pink eyes was stifled as Cain carried him like a puppy down the ramp between two enormous pens. The smell of the Bronco was perfume compared to the stench permeating the windless air. Below the ramp, two thousand dark shapes began grunting.

Robert's scream, as he finally understood what was happening, could be heard over the entire valley. He didn't lose consciousness until he saw his right arm, wrenched off at the socket, fall into the stinking slop below. The last thing he saw was Lucifer's face. Lucifer's smiling face.

༄

Lucifer's Children

Chapter 34

It took Ramon ten extra minutes to find the deliveries entrance. He parked Dan O'Connor's Chevy in the alley where the garbage bins and dumpsters were located, hoping a security guard wouldn't notice it before he could return, and grimacing that leaving the car there illegally for maybe ten or fifteen minutes would be the least of several crimes he was about to commit. This time, he left the motor running. It was vital the car would be warm inside.

Ignoring the surprised staff, he made his way through the kitchen back to the chapel. When he'd left there before, he'd noticed that someone had left his "Chaplain" badge in a small basket next to the letterbox. Thank God it was still there. He pinned it on his breast pocket and headed for the service elevator. Another five minutes went by before he found the next thing he was looking for, a spare gurney. He pushed it into the elevator and went up to the third floor. Checking to see if anyone was in Maggie's room and finding no one, luckily, he pushed the gurney into her room. He took a moment to gaze at her sleeping face, then he went back out.

He knew, from his earlier survey, that all the fire alarm boxes on floors two through seven were located in the exact same spot; no more than a few steps from the service elevator. He took it down to the second floor. While it was going down, he removed his right shoe. When the door opened, he placed the shoe so that it would jam the door. Keep it from closing, and automatically heading to the next floor. He hurried to the fire alarm box, glanced around casually, but needn't have worried.

Tom Lewis

There was considerable hallway traffic, going both ways, but no one paid him the slightest bit of attention. He broke the glass, pulled the handle down and was back in the elevator just as the first bell shrilled.

The shoe trick worked on floors three and four, and by the time he pulled the alarm handle on the fifth floor, people were no longer walking. As he'd hoped, chaos and panic was beginning. People were running every which way, yelling and shouting orders. He took the elevator back down to floor three, looked both ways, and ran to Maggie's room. She was still asleep. He lifted her, top sheet, pillow, and all, onto the gurney and wheeled her out into the corridor, weaving his way through the mass of confusion to the elevator. He pushed the button for the ground floor, praying no one in between would think to use this particular elevator.

Again he was lucky. He slipped his shoe back on before he reached the ground floor and joined the rush of employees hurrying to escape via the same door he'd come in through. It was every man for himself. Ramon had counted on that. No one gave a second look at the Catholic Chaplain who was doing his bit to get patients out of the hospital which must surely be burning fiercely by now, from the racket the alarms were making. Nor did anyone notice him lie the kidnapped patient in the back seat of the '57 Chevy which then snaked its way through the crowd to the street before the fire trucks appeared...

Night was swallowing the pines around St. Andrews when Father O'Connor finished filling the tub. Not knowing what else to do, he simply dropped the still running water hose on the ground, which was already saturated. He was cold, and his fingers were numb, but his mind was not. He had long wondered why Ramon had been sent to him, and knew he was about to find out. He stood there by the hot tub for a moment, debating whether to continue blessing the water in the tub or run inside and get a swallow of brandy, when he noticed headlights approaching. Turning toward them, he saw it was a taxi. The thought flashing through his mind of what the poor driver must have wondered at the scene in front of a Catholic church vanished as he noticed the man emerging from the back seat. A Cleric, like himself.

The coatless priest was tall. Very tall, and skinny as a vaulter's pole. His eyes were so deep set, O'Connor couldn't tell what color they were. The man paid the taxi driver, who turned his vehicle around in the cul-de-sac and sped away as the strange priest stalked toward him, hand outstretched, his sunken eyes taking in everything at once. "Father, I am Patrick Kennagin." He shook O'Connor's frozen hand and said, "You and the boy have done well. Good. There isn't a moment to lose." Pointing a bony finger at the tub, he asked, "Have you blessed this water?"

"Yes, Father."

"What about the rest?" He was indicating the water soaking the ground around the church.

O'Connor was stunned. "Why, no, I haven't. Ramon didn't tell me—"

"Quick, man. You take this side, I'll take the other. Pray, Father. Pray like you never have before."

"Why are we doing this? Why are you here?"

"I'm needed. Stop asking questions. We must *hurry*."

O'Connor jumped to it. He was halfway around the left side of the church when another pair of headlights illuminated his work. Ramon hopped out of the Chevy, opened the back door, and gently gathered his unconscious passenger in his arms. Recognition of who she was registered immediately when O'Connor saw the face. He froze in mid gesture. *God in heaven. She must be his twin!*

O'Connor saw Ramon's face light up with a brief smile of recognition when Kennagin hurried to assist him. His mouth fell open when they removed the woman's hospital gown and unceremoniously placed her, stark naked, with the fading light reflecting off the long row of metal stitches in her belly, into the tub of freezing water, immersing her totally, head, hair and all. He heard Father Kennagin begin the Latin rite of Baptism just as he heard the sirens. He turned to the right. Flashing blue lights and squealing brakes of the police car arrived at the same moment of the first thunderclap. Surprised more by the sound above his head than the arrival of the police, O'Connor automatically looked up. There was not a single cloud in the sky above the pines. The beginning of real fear then seized his heart. It was only increased tenfold when the two men got out of the car. One was the largest human being O'Connor had ever seen. The other spoke, in a military-type voice. "You are all under arrest. Stand where you are!" To the giant cop, he said, "Get the woman out of there."

Some inner, defensive mechanism took hold of Father Daniel O'Connor's body, moving it forward, toward the tub. Kennagin was faster. He took a step in the direction of the big man, ripped the crucifix from around his neck, and held it up. "Get back!"

The huge man in uniform stopped. Looked back at the other one.

"Do as I told you!" the handsome officer commanded.

The brute took another step forward, onto the watered lawn. The moment his foot touched the wet ground, he yelped in pain, and jumped back. O'Connor felt Ramon's wet hand on his arm. "Dan, listen to me. Here, you take hold of her. Hold her head above the water. Yes that's it. Don't let go of her, whatever you do."

"I have her. Ramon, who are they? They aren't policemen, are they?"

"No, Dan. You are looking at Satan himself, and his dog."

As Ramon said these words, another thunderclap came. Deafening. But not as loud as what O'Connor heard next. Ramon was striding forward, speaking, only it wasn't Ramon's voice saying the words. It was the voice of the thunder itself.

"Go back to your hole, Satan, and take your hound with you."

The young officer crossed his arms. "Aha. Is that you, Michael? I was wondering if you would show up."

Lucifer's Children

O'Connor was suddenly aware that Kennagin had moved to the tub beside him, but he couldn't take his eyes from the incredible sight before him. Ramon was enveloped in a sphere of brilliant light. A living torch. The words coming out of his mouth were not of this world. "You are too late this time. Go back where you came from."

The uniformed man didn't budge, nor raise his voice. "I want the woman."

"No."

"She's mine."

"Not any longer, she isn't. She's in safe hands now."

Lucifer pointed. Laughed. "Those two? I eat little priests like them for breakfast. Get out of my way, Michael. She's not worth your bother."

"That is not for you to say. Begone!"

"I see I've upset you, old friend, you're beginning to revert to last year's language. Who are you trying to impress?"

"I am warning you."

Lucifer took a step forward. "And I'm warning you. The woman is not worth your interference. If you don't hand her over, I'll burn all of them to a crisp. This stupid little church, too." With that, he raised an arm, and fire immediately enveloped the shrubs, trees, grass, everything around St. Andrews that had not been watered. Standing behind the flames, Lucifer chuckled. He shifted his gaze to O'Connor and Kennagin. "Clever little fellows, aren't you?" He looked back again through the white aura surrounding the rigid body of Ramon Barillas. "But not quite clever enough, Michael. Let's see how long it takes for your holy water to evaporate." He raised his other arm, and the heat increased to unbearable. O'Connor felt his eyebrows being singed. Then, Kennagin was whispering. "Listen to me. When I give you the signal, take her inside and lie her down on the altar."

O'Connor nodded. He wanted to hold a hand up to protect his face from the searing heat, but he dared not release his hold on the still unconscious woman. He looked back as

Satan spoke again. "Well, my old and honored adversary, what's it going to be? The woman, or three of your best men and one church?"

Another thunderclap, louder than all those before, sounded in answer, and then it began to rain. O'Connor saw Lucifer lift his head to it, and then laugh. It was laughter like nothing he'd ever heard. "So be it. Fried priests will be on your head, my old friend." He raised both hands, balled them up to fists, and uttered the most hideous ear- splitting shriek that shattered every window in the church, as well as those of the two cars. The heat became hell itself.

"NOW," Kennagin yelled. Take her in right now."

O'Connor lifted the woman from the tub. Kennagin held the door open and he carried her inside, but not before seeing an unbelievable sight. Ramon Barillas ran out of the white frame, through the wall of fire, straight at Lucifer. He got through the flames, only to run straight into the arms of the giant who had stepped in front of Satan. Cain grabbed Ramon, jerked him off the ground, and with no more effort than with a chicken, tore the head from his body, and held it up like a trophy, distracting Satan long enough for Kennagin to slam the church door behind him.

With shaking hands, O'Connor laid Maggie on the altar, wrapping her nakedness with the altar cloth, then turned and stared through the open window in time to see a gigantic lightning bolt strike and vaporize the albino creature, leaving only a dark spot where he'd been standing. Ramon's body lay on the grass, his head dropped in the gutter by the curb.

Holding his breath, he dared to look at Lucifer. But all he saw was the form of a small black cat, who cried out once, then fled through the burning trees. For a moment, there was total silence. Then the rain came down in a torrent. O'Connor barely noticed there was glass again in the church windows. He opened the front door and walked outside. The rain was not cold, but it was like a waterfall. Father Kennagin was standing by the hot tub, arms raised, praying in Latin. O'Connor was

Lucifer's Children

astonished to see the fire all around the church disappear as rapidly as it had begun. The police car had also vanished, but there were the sounds of other sirens in the air, coming closer.

Kennagin was grabbing his arm. "Quickly, Father, help me with this." O'Connor didn't have time to wonder why the plastic hot tub was now empty, and not very heavy. It took the two of them only a few minutes to move it around to the shed in back, and return to the front of the church. All was as it had been before, except the body of the young bishop, lying in a heap on the lawn. His head, eyes still open, lay in the gutter. The rain was washing all the blood away.

Kennagin's voice was calm. "Those fire trucks will be here soon, but they won't find anything out of the ordinary. Don't concern yourself about that." The tall priest fished two brown envelopes from his pocket and handed them to his fellow priest. "These are your instructions. For now, I will need your car to take care of Bishop Barillas. Take the girl to your house for the time being. She is still drugged, but her body needs time to heal. I will be back in time to assist you with midnight mass."

O'Connor took the two envelopes and shook his head even as the rain stopped. "Christmas mass?"

"Of course." He placed a hand on O'Connor's shoulder. "I'm sure no one ever told you the priesthood would be easy."

O'Connor watched the thin priest lovingly place the body of Ramon Barillas in the trunk of the Chevy, then the handsome head, carrying it as though it was a valuable relic. Perhaps it was. He watched until the tail-lights of his car had faded away, went back inside, and carried Maggie DeVries Ellis Abrahms to his house. He gently laid her on his own bed, read the two letters, and was back inside his beloved stone church when the three fire trucks arrived. On Christmas day, the assistant Chief was careful not to curse and blame a frail Catholic priest for setting what must have been a false alarm.

It was only after their tail-lights had also disappeared that Father Daniel O'Connor looked up at the stars, bowed his head, and wept for his friend. What he had seen and experienced

that night would take him a long time to absorb, live with, and ultimately put behind him.
    Twelve years, in fact.

Lucifer's Children

EPILOGUE

July fourth was unusually hot in 1999, even for New Mexico. But at the end of the day, the temperature outside the thick walls of the Convent on the outskirts of Taos dropped rapidly. Monsignor Daniel O'Connor noticed this and remarked to his hostess, the Mother Superior, "It's cooling off fast, Sister Alicia."

"Yes. I love to sit like this on the patio of an early evening and watch the sunsets. They are truly magnificent out here. I often think this is the way it all looked at the beginning of time."

O'Connor nodded in agreement. "I look forward to every one of them. To me, they're like God's reward for a lifetime of faithful service. The sunrises, too." He forced a wan smile. There was no need to tell the good sister he doubted he'd get to see more than a dozen of them. The cancer rampaging through his stomach like a forest fire would guarantee it. Still, this was a lovely place to spend his last days on earth; this small adobe sanctuary with its cloister of silent nuns. And, if he felt up to talking, Sister Alicia would be glad to furnish the company.

She hadn't changed at all in the twelve years since he was here last. She looked exactly the same; unlined face, eyes that needed no glasses, teeth that were all her own, though she must be close to his own age. "You must have near zero humidity here, Sister. It's really dry. I wonder if I might trouble you for a glass of water."

"Of course, but for our new Chaplain, something special."

Tom Lewis

She got up and floated on sandaled feet from the tiled patio. O'Connor smiled and looked westward again. The view was impressive, sure enough. Reminded him of the mountains of Guatemala. Every four years of the past dozen, he'd made a pilgrimage of sorts to that desperate country, to visit Ramon's grave. Twice, he'd been surprised to see two frail Cardinals there as well, holding each other up, as unashamed of their tears as he was of his.

And now, Mother Church had sent him here. Just as he had been instructed to bring Maggie here twelve years ago. Where had those years gone? It was as though he'd been here only yesterday.

His stomach was hurting bad now. He'd actually asked for the water to wash down two of the pills that nowadays gave him less and less relief. When he looked back, Sister Alicia was returning, accompanied by another nun who carried a tray with a small bottle and a glass, which she set before him. He looked into her face and his heart nearly stopped. It was his face. Ramon's face, and twelve years hadn't aged it one iota.

She smiled at him, turned and left. With a shaking hand, he poured the bottled water into the glass, used it to swallow the pills he'd already popped into his mouth, and looked at Sister Alicia. "She seems as young and beautiful as when I brought her here."

"Do you think so? It must our climate. Sister Claire took her final vows ten years ago, Monsignor. And like the others, she hasn't spoken a word since. I never have seen a harder working, more devout sister in my life than she is. Such a joy to all of us. How do you like the water?"

"What? Oh. The water's fine."

"Remarkable thing about that water. One day, about a year after Sister Claire came to us, a nice young man—a salesman I think--came by here and left a complimentary case of it with us. I thought it was such a nice gesture, I wrote a thank-you letter to his company, and would you know, three free cases of it have been delivered to us like clockwork on the first day of every month. It's so much better than the water from our well. The Lord will provide. Isn't that so, Father?"

O'Connor nodded again, reading the bottle's label. It was a brand he didn't know. But beyond that, he paid no attention to it. His mind was on Sister Claire's face. The thought came to him that as long as she lived, Ramon would also be alive. He was enormously grateful he'd had a chance to see that before he died.

Except right this minute, he didn't feel the reaper's long shadow creeping up on him. With every swallow of the water, which really *was* delicious, the flame in his gut receded. Almost bearable.

The Mother Superior was talking. He brought his head up. She was looking out north and west again, saying, "You know Monsignor, God did a beautiful thing when He created mountains, don't you think?"

O'Connor allowed his own eyes to follow her gaze. The sun was falling fast, melding mountains and sky into a palette of colors no artist could ever copy. For the first time in years, he felt at ease. An inner peace. Perhaps God would grant him a few more such sights. Thinking that thought, he felt better physically, too. A good deal better. "True, Sister. Absolutely true. Say, do you suppose I might have another bottle of this? You were right. It's like none I've ever tasted."

"Certainly. I'll fetch it myself."

Dan O'Connor watched her rise and leave, as quietly as before. He smiled, turned back to the sunset and sighed. If he had a few more of these days, that would be good. The remainder of his life would be wonderful, in fact. But if not, this place was indeed a fine place to die.

A very fine place.

Tom Lewis

ABOUT THE AUTHOR

A native Tarheel and son of amateur musicians and writers, Tom Lewis was born in Rocky Mount, NC, graduated from New Bern High School, and was further educated in the US and Europe. Before retiring to seriously write for publication, Tom spent 38 years as a symphony orchestra conductor in Europe as well as Charlotte, NC, Roswell, NM, Rochester, MN, Tulsa, OK, and Sioux City, IA.

In addition to his trilogy, PEA ISLAND GOLD, he has written five other novels, a collection of short stories, and one book of non-fiction. Tom currently resides in New Bern, NC.

Lucifer's Children

1) What was the significance of Two stillborn children at beginning of book?

2) Ideas — where do they come from?

3) You, Mr. Louis are such a peaceful laid back individual --- the voice of this book and others --- is somewhat surprising.

4) The battle of good vs evil --- I don't believe that I have read anything so far that illustrates this so clearly \ vividly.

5)

Tom Lewis

₮ TEASE PUBLISHING LLC
Quality Women's Fiction and Literature
www.teasepublishingllc.com

With something for everyone, Tease Publishing is a publisher committed to bringing readers quality works of both fiction and literature sure to keep you coming back for more!

Tease Publishing is a GREEN company, utilizing POD (print-on-demand) printing and E books so there is no waste and no unneeded stress on the environment.

Shop Tease books online at All Romance E books and Amazon.com and in print at bookstores around the world.

Lucifer's Children